Family Matters
Harborview Immortals #1
By
C.L. Ingro

Table of Contents

CHAPTER 1

2014

JACOB FELT LIKE A STALKER. He glanced at the dashboard clock as his fingers tapped against the steering wheel to the tune of Freddie Mercury's powerful voice. It was just past two in the morning and although it felt like longer, he had only been sitting there, two houses down from Xan's new place, for about ten minutes. Surely it would take another twenty or more to achieve official stalker status.

It was time to get on with what he had arrived unannounced to do before the good citizens of that quaint Harborview, Pennsylvania neighborhood—the ones who were still awake at that hour—questioned why some random man was sitting in some random car in the middle of the night. That the car was a sleek black Audi instead of some souped-up monstrosity was likely the only reason he had not yet been accosted by nosy folks and cops alike.

Jacob removed the key from the ignition and flipped down the sun visor, examining his reflection in the lighted mirror. He smiled as he thought about one of the many myths that pertained to those like him. Outrageous theories derived from fiction, as Dominic often said. The face that stared back at him wasn't half bad for someone with over two centuries under his belt. He still looked every bit the twenty-five-year-old man he was back in 1804.

He ran his fingers through the chocolate brown locks that ended at his shoulders and were always on the verge of haphazardness, not quite wild but far from tame. Unlike his hair, his eyes and skin were lighter shades of brown. Being biracial wasn't as big a deal in 2014 as it was during his early years, back when there was a fine line between master and slave, and crossing that line brought about serious consequences. His father had crossed that line. For that, he died before Jacob was born, though his body was never found. Not all of it.

Confirming that everything was in order—or as much as could be in the case of his hair—Jacob got out of the vehicle and pocketed his key, then retrieved something else for later. He looked up at a full moon suspended in a starless sky and lamented the absence of the specks of dancing, twinkling light he had relished since he was a child. When he got home, he would curl up on one of the rear deck chairs and spend the rest of the night gazing at all the vast blackness. He hadn't done that in a while, but tonight it seemed like a marvelous idea.

First, he had to see Xan. He *needed* to see Xan. Four days without seeing the young man's face was three days more than he could stand, and he refused to wait any longer.

There were no signs of movement in the first house he passed, a white two-story with a matching mailbox. But Jacob's hearing was sharp, and while he didn't care to know that the inhabitants of that abode were going at it like dogs in heat, it was hard for him not to hear the ruckus. The second house was more obvious about its inner activities. Even if not for the five cars crammed into the driveway, the low thump of bass, sounding more like the erratic heartbeat of a giant than anything remotely pertaining to music, was enough to indicate to anyone within earshot that a good time was being had by all.

Jacob headed up the walkway that led to Xan's front door. His house was one of the few single-story homes on Norman Street, beige in color and modest in style. Given the needs of the previous owner, an older Irish gentleman with a severe aversion to sunlight, simplicity was essential. It would not do for an outsider to discover what was in the basement and, more importantly, why it was there. That Xan had wanted the house specifically to have such a thing readily available when he entertained guests with the same aversion was not something Jacob cared to contemplate.

He could hear him griping about what should go where and punctuating his statements with creative profanity. Jacob rang the bell and soon sensed Xan staring at him through the peephole. He waved at the tiny lens, feeling stupid and elated, and seconds later, the door opened to reveal the one human being whom Jacob loved more than any other.

"Hello there, stranger," he said.

A flash of guilt passed over Xan's face but was instantly replaced by the smile that Jacob knew well. It was the same one Xan used when he needed to crank up the charm and talk his way out of a sticky situation. Or into someone's pants. Jacob chose not to think about that, either.

Xan smoothed a hand over his spiked golden blond hair in an effort to subdue it. It didn't work. He was wearing a plain white T-shirt that showed off the intricate network of tribal tattoos that covered both of his arms. Jacob didn't like them or all the piercings at first, but over time they grew on him.

"Hey. What are you doing here?" Xan took a step back, granting him entrance. "Not that I'm not happy to see you."

Jacob teasingly ruffled Xan's hair as he stepped past him. "I thought I would stop by and say hi, make sure you weren't dead, that kind of thing."

"You haven't been to the club this week," Xan responded, closing the door.

"Neither have you, from what I hear."

"I was there Monday. And part of Tuesday."

"And what about Wednesday and Thursday?"

Another do-no-wrong smile. Xan was laying it on thick tonight. "I needed a couple of nights off."

"Funny how that happens every week. Lucky for you the owners like you."

"I don't think they have much of a choice."

Jacob smirked as he surveyed the living room. It was as unremarkable as the house's exterior with its off-white walls and tan carpet. Numerous boxes were strewn about, each of them labeled with black marker in Xan's jittery handwriting. Many of them were filled with books, both regular and comic. One of the boxes marked as manga was currently being used as a makeshift desk and temporary home to a laptop. There were also video game consoles with their respective games, tons of Blu-rays, and other forms of recreation treasured by most men in their early twenties. The high definition television with a screen large enough to rival some movie theaters was overkill, but it was necessary for optimal gaming. Or so Xan claimed.

"I'm going to do some remodeling later," Xan said, noticing Jacob's silent appraisal. "I want to put in a new carpet and slap some color on the walls. I guess interior decorating wasn't the Old Man's thing."

Jacob cleared his throat.

"Mr. O'Malley," Xan amended.

"That's better."

"Dominic gets to call him Old Man. Even though he's like, what? Two hundred years older?"

"Closer to three. Two... eighty... something. It's all a blur after a while." Jacob took a step closer to Xan. "I've missed you," he said, cupping his left cheek.

Xan turned away, but not before Jacob spotted another flash of a shame-filled countenance. "It's only been a few days."

"*Four* days. That's a long time when I'm used to seeing you almost every single day." Jacob's fingers danced over the platinum hoops and cuffs that lined Xan's ear. Feigning astonishment, he pulled his hand back and presented a shiny quarter lodged between his thumb and forefinger, the same quarter he snagged from his pocket when he put away his key. "Well, well, well. Look what I found. What else are you hiding in there?"

With a groan and an eye roll, Xan dutifully offered his upturned hand and accepted the coin that Jacob dropped onto his palm. His expression softened, and he stared thoughtfully at the vampire. "I'm not a kid anymore, Dad. If you're going to keep pulling this old trick, start using paper money."

"Twenty-five cents was a king's ransom when you were little."

"Yeah, well, inflation's a bitch." Xan shoved the quarter into his pocket. "Sit down and stay awhile."

"Don't mind if I do." Jacob pushed a big brown box labeled *PORN* out of the way—the boy had no shame—and sat down on a plush hunter green sofa. "Four days," he reiterated while looking fixedly at his son. "Care to explain?"

ALEXANDER DAWSON, KNOWN to most as Xan (or Xanadu because his best friend loved to torment him), took a seat in the chair next to the sofa where his father sat. He was surprised that the vampire hadn't contacted him sooner. This was doubtless his other father's doing, as Dominic wasn't *quite* as overprotective as Jacob.

He knew that he wasn't in any real trouble, but Jacob sometimes had a knack for making him feel bad. Like right now. "I lost track of time," he began, trying not to squirm. "I've been really busy between working and trying to get everything unpacked."

And that was the truth... for the most part. But when Jacob saw the item that was tucked between the cushions beside him, Xan knew that his excuse wasn't going to sound nearly as sincere.

"Among other things, I see." Jacob blinked at Xan over the red boxer briefs that were pinched gingerly between his fingers. "What is this? A housewarming gift?"

Xan was tempted to tell him that the underwear was a leftover of the *real* housewarming gift, and what a gift it had been. The owner of the briefs—Danny or Denny or Donnie or some other D name—had a mouth so talented that it should have been against the law. The experience was one of Xan's more memorable hook-ups as of late. If only every trip to the grocery store ended with orgasms.

He snatched the briefs from Jacob and tossed them into a nearby open box of comics. "Sorry about that," he said, biting his lip and trying not to laugh.

Jacob didn't fare so well. "I don't know which I find more disturbing," he said, unable to stop himself from grinning. "The fact that I'm sitting on a sofa where you exchanged bodily fluids with someone else, or that you sent some poor bastard home without any drawers."

"Well, he was in a hurry so..." Xan shrugged off the rest of the sentence, to which Jacob could only shake his head in response. "He wasn't a vampire, if that's any consolation."

"It is."

Jacob loathed the idea of Xan being intimate with vampires. Living in a world where one was viewed chiefly as a food source was not without risks, and Xan knew how much his parents had worried about him over the years because of it. But he was twenty-two now. His own man. One who enjoyed sex very much, even if it happened to be with someone who wanted his blood as much as his body. Fortunately, Jacob respected Xan enough to keep his opinions to himself. Usually.

"Do you want a drink?" Xan asked. "Or some blood?"

"No, thank you. Please tell me you don't keep that stuff in plain view for your human guests to find."

"There's an old blood bank fridge down in the basement," Xan explained. "Old Man—I mean Mr. O'Malley had it installed for me before he moved out."

"A refrigerator *and* a coffin? You're all set for your vampire booty calls."

"Dad..."

"I'm kidding." Jacob rose to his feet. "Let's have the grand tour."

"It won't be all that grand since there are boxes all over the damn place," Xan warned. "I never realized how much crap I owned."

"Dominic did spoil you rotten."

Xan quirked a brow at the statement. "Really?"

"I didn't say that I didn't contribute. Now hush and show me around."

Xan smiled warmly at his father, who was a good three inches shorter. The young man wasn't as tall as Dominic, who was an imposing six feet four inches, but he was close. Sometimes he couldn't believe that the day had ever come when he was no longer craning his neck to look at both of them. Jacob and Dominic had once been as big as the world to the boy they had taken in to raise as their own. While they were still formidable in many ways, stature was no longer primary among them in Xan's adult eyes.

They started in the kitchen. Xan could tell that Jacob was struggling to hold his tongue when he spotted the stockpile of ramen noodles in a cupboard next to the fridge, eager to reprimand him for not eating properly. It was a good thing that he had taken out the garbage bag stuffed with pizza boxes and other carryout containers earlier that evening. Just past the kitchen door was the garage that also doubled as a laundry room where Xan's grey '77 BMW, a hand-me-down from Dominic, was parked next to his crotch rocket, another on the list of Jacob's not-so-favorite things when it came to Xan's safety.

After that, they moved down the hallway, past the guest bathroom and into a spare bedroom where most of Xan's video game consoles would go, along with all of his books and figures once the shelving was in place. From there they went into the master bedroom. Matching black dressers lined one of the walls and another flat screen television sat on a black stand in the corner. Xan had only used his new king-size bed for sleeping so far, and he was anxious to test it out in other ways. In his mad rush to get down Danny-Denny-Donnie's pants, they never made it past the living room.

"Very nice," Jacob said.

"Thanks."

Xan took a seat on the edge of the bed as Jacob checked out the connecting bathroom.

"I've always been amazed by the amount of product required to make it look like you crawled out of bed without any concern whatsoever for your hair."

"Not all of us are blessed with naturally sexy bedhead." Xan tugged at a lock of hair. "Some of us have to work for it."

"I had no idea that unkempt hair was so desirable." Jacob stepped around a box of extra bedding and stood at the foot of the bed. "Are you saying that I'm sexy?" he asked cheekily.

"Don't be gross."

"Why is it gross for me to be sexy?"

"Because you're my dad and... just... *ew*." Xan shuddered. Like most people's children, he had zero desire to think of his father as a sexual being. "And how do you even know what 'booty call' means? Update your files, by the way, because no one says that anymore."

"Really? But I like saying it. Booty call."

"Dad."

"Booty call, booty call, booty call."

"Oh, my God."

"Okay, I'm done," Jacob said with a devilish grin. "Anyway, I may be old but I know things. You wouldn't *believe* some of the things I know."

"Let's just leave it at that. Come on, before you scar me for life."

They returned to the living room. Xan guessed that Jacob wouldn't care to see the basement given its purpose. When the vampire made no mention of it, he knew that he had presumed correctly.

"So what do you think?" he wanted to know.

"It's a good house, son," Jacob replied with an affirming nod.

Xan released the breath that he had been holding. Although he wasn't the type to base any of his decisions on either parent's approval, having it still made him feel better.

"I'll have a housewarming party once I get everything sorted. It'll be small. Just you and Dominic, Becky, Luca, and Uncle Demetrio." He noticed the uncertainty on Jacob's face after mentioning his uncle's name. "Do they still hate each other?"

"Who knows? One day they do, the next day they don't. When it comes to your father and your uncle, I've learned to stay as far away from the blast radius as possible." Jacob fished his key out of his pocket. "Okay, I'll leave you to it. Are you coming over for dinner? You may not live with us anymore but it's still tradition."

"Like you'd ever let me hear the end of it if I didn't."

"You know me well."

The vampire patted Xan on the cheek and left. Xan locked the door and went to the jumble of boxes. He stared at the boxer briefs that had clung to their owner in all the right places. With an impish gleam in his baby blue eyes, he pulled out his phone and scrolled through the contact list until he found the name he was looking for. The initial, rather. He was still unsure of the name.

I'm pretty sure it was Danny, he thought as he pressed *D?* and called the number attached to it. *Definitely maybe.*

"Hey, guess what I found... No, it's not too late. Come on over."

Unpacking could wait.

It wasn't until Xan was bent over the back of the sofa that he learned his guest's name was David. Once again, they didn't make it past the living room, but at least this time David remembered to take his underwear with him.

AFTER JACOB ARRIVED home, he went into the kitchen. On the black marble countertop sat an assortment of pots and pans and other items Dominic used to prepare a variety of Italian dishes. The Friday night dinners had started when Xan was a child because Jacob and Dominic both felt it was important to embrace the ritual of a family meal. Even though they were unable to eat the food themselves, they wanted Xan to have fond memories of their times together.

He set out all of the makings for coffee for Luca, the muscular mountain of a man who kept an eye on the house while Jacob and Dominic slept. He began working for them when they brought Xan home and realized soon after that babies did not strictly adhere to a vampire's up all night/sleep all day schedule. Luca was now pushing forty, but he was the only human the couple would ever trust for daytime protection.

With the coffee ready to go, Jacob flipped off the lights and left the kitchen, then walked through the dining room and entered the living room, all of which were modernly decorated in black and white. The house, in all of its architectural glory, was a far cry from the dilapidated shack in which Jacob had spent the first fourteen years of his human life. If the decision had been solely up to him, he would have gone with something a little less... *much*. But Dominic loved the house and Jacob loved him, therefore it was home.

He moved past the staircase which ascended to an upper level that was no longer in use now that Xan was gone, through the exit that led to an expansive rear deck that overlooked Lake Erie. The moon hung over the water, breathtaking and picturesque, a lone sphere of brilliance amidst the nothing. Even without the stars, Jacob was transfixed. No matter how much the world changed, and it had changed plenty over the years, he would never tire of witnessing the beauty of nighttime.

"There you are."

Dominic's voice was quiet but crystal clear in the wind that emanated from the lake, as smooth and deep now as it was the night when their paths aligned, though bearing no trace of the thick Italian accent that had taken him decades to eliminate. He was sitting on a loveseat that was flanked by two chairs and staring out at the lake as if it held the answers to all of life's secrets, his long black hair flowing over his shoulders save for the strands that had fallen victim to the breeze.

Jacob took a seat beside him. He didn't bother asking how the vampire knew that this was what he had planned to do. They didn't have the telepathic bond that some vampires shared, but after more than two centuries together, sometimes one just knew what the other needed without having to say anything.

With fingers intertwined, the lovers sat in silence and watched the moon's reflection waver hypnotically on the surface of the water. Jacob followed the light to its source and beheld the moon in all its splendor, thinking back to the times when he would sneak out to a ramshackle porch to stare at a starry Georgia sky and try to forget that he was a slave child of taboo destined to live a life of servitude. At the time, he thought it was as close to freedom as he was ever going to get.

"How is Alexander doing at his new house?" Dominic asked after a while.

"He's got a lot of work ahead of him. Of course that hasn't stopped him from 'breaking in' his new furniture."

"That child..."

"He's *your* son."

Dominic turned his piercing green eyes on his partner. "Why is he *my* son when he does something that displeases you?"

"Because I said so."

"I can't argue with that."

"You could try but it won't do you any good."

Dominic's smile was a beautiful thing. Very few outside of his family ever had the privilege of seeing it.

"I know he's a grown man now, but I'm still worried," Jacob continued. "How are we going to watch over him if he's not living at home anymore?"

"We'll do what we can." Dominic brought Jacob's hand onto his lap and covered it with his own, his fingers absentmindedly toying with the ring he had given Jacob shortly after they met. "He's made it this far without incident. Most vampires aren't senseless enough to think of hurting him... and *I'm* not the reason for that."

"I'm not that bad," Jacob insisted.

"You're even worse."

Jacob considered defending himself until he remembered the many instances that supported Dominic's claim. "I can't help it. He's our boy."

Dominic squeezed his hand. "That he is."

"Twenty-two years..."

It seemed like just yesterday when they first heard the heartbreaking cry of an abandoned infant left to die. Had it been any other person under any other circumstance, they would have kept on moving, maintaining their distance from all things human. But forever was far too long for Jacob to live with the remorse of ignoring that desperate plea for help, especially since he knew all about maternal rejection himself. When he picked up that emaciated body for the first time, he knew in an instant that he never wanted to let him go.

Dominic's arm moved around him, coaxing him closer. "He has many years left, Jacob."

"I know that. I'm still going to worry."

"And I know *that*."

Leaning into Dominic's side, Jacob sighed contentedly. They had about an hour to go before the sun made its unwelcome appearance. Until then, he just wanted to sit there in the waning darkness and lose himself to the tranquil serenade of the wind and water, side by side with the one he loved.

AT 5:30 A.M., THE VAMPIRES went inside. After a daycap of warm brandy and blood, they retired to the lowest level of the house, a windowless basement-turned-bedroom designed specifically for the daylight-challenged. There was a four poster canopy bed against the wall farthest from the basement entrance, one that was far more comfortable than any coffin they had ever used. Jacob sat down on it and kicked off his shoes.

"How did your meeting go last night?"

"Frustratingly unproductive," Dominic answered, sitting down beside him. "Tomah and CCL have their hands out for even more blood than we're currently providing them. I never thought I would say this but I miss the days of Prohibition. Alcohol was so much easier than this."

"They're just trying to save lives, Dominic."

"So am I."

Jacob knew that Dominic was justified in his frustration. More vampires placated by a ready supply of blood meant fewer people being injured or killed for it. But unlike alcohol, which they had been able to obtain and move with ease during the 1920s, the trafficking of blood had special limitations—*human* limitations—that resulted in the demand being greater than the supply.

"We'll figure it out," Jacob reassured him. "Or run it by Elliot and let him work his magic."

With an outstretched hand, he swept back Dominic's hair and moved down along his cheek, gliding over alabaster skin. Dominic closed his eyes and angled his head, seeking more of his touch. Jacob kissed him tenderly, and that alone ignited a desire within him that hadn't diminished in the slightest during their time together. He pushed through with his tongue, delving into the wetness of Dominic's mouth and tasting brandy and blood as his fingers slid through the vampire's hair, mussing it in his grasp.

"You're eager today," Dominic murmured.

Jacob felt his way along his partner's shoulders and over the chest that looked entirely too appealing beneath a form-fitting black shirt. "It's been too long since we've done this."

"It's been a week, Jacob."

"Almost a lifetime."

Dominic chuckled and wrapped his arms around Jacob. His hands trailed up his lover's back and over the outline of scars from the past, a permanent reminder of the cruelness inflicted upon Jacob's once human body. He rid Jacob of his shirt and pushed him down to the bed, then crawled on top of him, pressing their bodies together and gazing at him with eyes like emeralds.

Jacob trembled as Dominic unfastened his belt... moaned while he unzipped his pants... and cursed when his phone started ringing.

Since Dominic was already in the vicinity, he reached into Jacob's pocket and grabbed the phone. After checking the display, he swiped the screen to accept the call. He raised the phone to his ear with one hand while playfully tugging at the waistband of Jacob's underwear with the other.

"Good morning, Alexander."

Jacob could tell by the sound of Xan's voice that he wasn't in the throes of a crisis. Knowing this, he was able to relax while Dominic talked to him.

"Yes, Luca is staying for dinner... I think he would like that very much... Jacob couldn't answer because I'm on top of him... Why is that gross?"

Jacob snickered as he listened to them debate the alleged grossness of the couple's sex life.

"Stop being so dramatic, Alexander," Dominic continued. "I highly doubt that your brain is broken. Now get some sleep while I make love to your father." He ended the call, abruptly cutting off Xan's anguished wail.

"That was so mean," Jacob said between bursts of laughter. "But after all the years we had to hear what was going on in his bedroom, I don't feel nearly as bad as I should."

"Neither do I." Dominic placed the phone on the nightstand and returned his attention to Jacob, his hand sliding over the vampire's flat stomach and lower. "Where were we?"

IT WAS A GOOD THING that David had already come (two times) and gone before Xan called to ask about bringing over the imported beer for Luca. Had he called before the festivities, there wouldn't have been any because of Dominic's mind-rupturing admission. Nothing ruined a hard-on faster than learning that your dads were about to get it on, too.

"So gross."

Xan covered his head with a pillow while trying to unthink the unthinkable. He loved his parents, but there were some things about them that he didn't need to know.

AFTER THEY WERE FINISHED doing all of the things that Xan didn't need to know, Dominic fell asleep, his arms curled around Jacob and his face hidden away in a nest of hair. Jacob was still awake, and he peered into the darkness while mulling over the upcoming gathering and the family and friends who would be attending.

Luca was moving quietly around the kitchen, or as much as he could due to his size. It was sweet of Xan to bring over something special just for him. Then again, Luca was basically a godfather to him so the gesture was understandable.

And then there was Becky. The British vampire was like an annoying little sister to Jacob and Dominic and an annoying big sister to Xan. The dinners never lacked for entertainment when she was there being her usual boisterous self.

Speaking of boisterous, Jacob hoped that Dominic's brother would do his part to keep the peace for one night. Demetrio was often turbulent where Dominic was serene, and he tended to act on impulse while Dominic exercised restraint. Their opposing natures were even evident in their outward appearances, with Demetrio's short hair and laid-back dress versus Dominic's long hair and tailored clothing. With all of their differences, it was hard for most, even Jacob, to believe that they were only separated by ten minutes as opposed to ten years. There was no way to predict what might happen when the siblings were in the same room together.

As Jacob's eyelids grew heavier, his thoughts returned to the hard-fought journey between back then and right now. With a tired smile, he closed his eyes, thankful for his family and basking in the perfection of a life that was once unimaginable.

A perfection that would begin to unravel later that night.

FAMILY MATTERS

CHAPTER 2

"XANADU!"

Xan barely managed to get one foot through the door before being crushed in a bear hug by Rebecca Hardwick, his dearest friend and occasional worst enemy.

"Jeez, Becky," he grunted. "Let me get inside the house before you attack me." He tried to pull away from the two humongous breasts pressed against him and added, "I see that your cups runneth over as usual."

"What can I say? They have a mind of their own." Becky released him and adjusted her assets before they spilled out of her blue low-cut dress. "Most men wouldn't mind having my tits shoved in their faces. Neither would most women."

"Then go suffocate one of them," Xan responded while closing the door. "Just keep those things away from me. Or grow a dick and then we'll talk."

"I can't grow one but I have some toys that might suffice."

"And there goes my appetite."

"Don't be a shit," Becky said, her English accent jokingly stern. "Never be a shit to someone who used to change your nappy."

"Can we not do this, please? I've already been traumatized enough for one day."

"So I heard."

Becky recounted Jacob's version of Xan's early morning conversation with Dominic. She took much joy in the young man's shock over learning that not only did his fathers have penises but actually used them from time to time.

"Shut up," Xan grouched as they walked through the foyer toward the living room. "I know what they do. I just don't need to know when it's happening."

"Isn't that a bit hypocritical?" she asked, linking their arms. "Remind me again how much sex you've had in this house?"

"That's different."

"Why?"

"Because I'm young and I'm supposed to fuck anything that moves. But my parents—"

"Should act old and decrepit and have nonworking genitalia." Jacob looked up from his book as they entered the room. "Does that sound about right?"

"It does if you care about my sanity."

"I *do* care about your sanity," Jacob said. "I care about it so much that I won't even go into explicit detail about everything I'm going to let Dominic do to me tomorrow morning."

Becky sat down beside Jacob and cackled at Xan's horrified expression. Xan glared at the two vampires, his poor mind once again trying to vanquish the mental image of his fathers doing the nasty.

"That's not nice, Dad."

"But it's funny."

"Leave him alone, Jacob." Luca Melani came into the living room with a tray of bruschetta with assorted toppings. "He doesn't want to know what you and Dominic do in bed."

"I want to know," Becky said.

"Pervert," Xan mumbled.

"Slag," Becky shot back.

"Play nicely," Jacob ordered them both.

"That'll be the day." Luca went to Xan, eclipsing him with his massive frame. "How's the house? Have you turned it into a proper bachelor pad yet?"

"I'm working on it. It might take some time."

"If it's anything like I remember on the inside, good luck."

Jacob once told Xan that Luca had lived with Mr. O'Malley for a brief period before he started working for them. Xan had never inquired about the living arrangement, but he determined that nothing untoward was afoot since the old vampire remained a close family friend throughout the years. If his parents knew the secrets that lurked within that wall of muscle and how they pertained to an Irish vampire hundreds of years Luca's senior, they never spoke of it in Xan's presence.

"This is for you." He gave Luca a bottle of dark lager made by an Italian brewery that catered to an exclusive—and mostly undead—clientele. Luckily, it was unharmed during Becky's attempted murder by mammaries. "I'll go put the rest in the fridge."

Luca smiled gratefully. "You're too good to me."

Xan was swept into another heartfelt and oxygen-depriving hug. The smell of Luca's cologne filled his nostrils and brought to mind numerous occasions from his youth when the two of them would venture out into the sunlight. Trips to the park, the mall, the movies, and the lake, where Luca once screamed like a girl when a walleye bumped into his leg and Xan laughed so hard that he cried.

Becky pouted as the two men embraced. "Why is he allowed to smother you but I'm not?"

"Because Luca doesn't have boobs," Jacob replied as he turned a page and continued reading.

After prying loose from Luca's beefy arms, Xan helped himself to an appetizer, smacked Becky on the head, and darted into the kitchen, ignoring all accusations of being a wanker.

"You missed your calling, Dominic," he said while munching away on a piece of bruschetta topped with tomatoes and basil. "Screw the underworld stuff. You should've been a chef."

"I can't imagine people lining up to eat food prepared by a corpse." Dominic stirred a pot of bubbling sauce with a wooden spoon. His hair was pulled back into a ponytail, same as always when he was at the stove. The gaudy floral print apron was new.

"What the hell are you wearing?"

"A gift from Jacob." Dominic added a pinch of chopped garlic to the pot, thus disproving another vampire myth. "It pleases him when I look like a fool."

Xan placed the beer in the refrigerator. "The things you do for love."

"You never know, Alexander. Perhaps the day will come when you meet someone who inspires you to don frighteningly patterned attire."

"I doubt it."

Dominic took a tray of prosciutto-wrapped asparagus from the oven and instructed Xan to transfer them to a platter. The young man did as he was told, devouring a number of the spears in the process. "I refuse to take sides when Luca fights you for the rest of those," the vampire warned him.

"I gave him beer so he won't complain too much." Xan claimed another spear for himself but decided to share the rest.

Dominic placed a lid on the pot. He went to the counter and started carving into a freshly baked loaf of Italian bread. "Are you working tonight or will you be doing more... unpacking?"

Xan knew exactly what the vampire was getting at. "I can only do so much unpacking at one time."

"True. I would hate to see you wear yourself out."

"It's all about pacing." Xan grinned and rinsed off his hands. "I'll be at work," he promised. "Are you guys going to stop by the bar and see me?"

"I think we'll stay in the office," Dominic answered. "We wouldn't dream of interrupting you while you service the patrons."

"It sounds dirty the way you say it."

"Isn't it?"

"Sometimes," Xan admitted.

"I trust you still use protection?"

Protection in this case meaning the foot-long solid silver stake that Xan kept with him at all times while tending bar at his fathers' club, the Rising Sun. Dominic was never fully convinced of his ability to use it should the need arise as panic had a way of overshadowing reason in life-threatening situations, but it was Jacob's one stipulation when he realized that he was unable to talk his son out of seeking employment at the club.

"Dad would kill me himself if I didn't."

"He probably would."

Dominic selected a thick slice of bread. He slathered one side with butter and handed it to Xan.

"Thank you, Domi."

Green eyes narrowed suspiciously. "You said you were too old to call me that."

"I am, but I guess it wouldn't be the end of the world if it slips out every now and then."

"No, I guess not."

Xan shoved the bread between his lips, then grabbed the platter and rejoined the others in the living room. He didn't see Dominic return to the stove and continue stirring the sauce or the look of affection on his face while doing so.

WHEN DINNER WAS READY, everyone took a seat at the dining room table. The fine china was laid out for Xan and Luca, and the fine goblets were reserved for those lacking a pulse.

The seat across from Jacob was empty. "Are we going to wait for Demetrio?" he asked.

"No," Dominic stated firmly. "I refuse to accommodate his lack of regard for punctuality."

Jacob said no more. Long gone were the days when he attempted to be the voice of reason between the brothers.

The food was served and the blood and wine were poured. Talk was simple and pleasant, most of it revolving around Xan's new house and the raven tattoo he planned to get.

"Where?" Becky wanted to know.

"Somewhere you'll never see."

"You're acting like I've never seen you naked before."

"I was a baby," Xan pointed out.

"I bet you still are in some places."

"*Children*." Jacob refilled his goblet. "Can we get through one dinner without the two of you bad-mouthing each other?"

"No," Dominic and Luca answered.

Becky relented and changed the subject, which was the least she could do after implying that Xan had the penis of an infant. "Guess what I found out?"

"That it spits when you pet it?" Xan suggested through a mouthful of spaghetti.

Unfazed, the vampire twirled a brunette lock around her fingers. "You would know."

"You're just jealous because I get more dick than you."

"Alexander, please." Dominic turned to Becky. "What did you find out, Rebecca?"

"Niccolo Alessandrini is going to tour the States. I've never had the chance to see him in person."

"I'll bet he's no Freddie Mercury," Jacob huffed.

Dominic smirked into his wine glass. "You are aware that music existed long before Queen, aren't you?"

"Even you would like Alessandrini, Jacob," Becky said.

"Oh, I *love* Niccolo Alessandrini!"

All eyes looked to the dining room doorway. There was Demetrio Castigliane, beaming at his family and friends.

"I saw him perform a few times in the 1600s, back when it was still socially acceptable to sever a boy's bits and pieces for the sake of song." After pausing to kiss Xan's cheek, Demetrio took a seat and poured himself a generous serving of blood. "He was such a pretty thing, and he had the loveliest voice. Heavenly, it was. I always wondered what he looked like *down there* but sadly I never had a chance to see for myself."

Xan frowned. "Wait. You're saying that this guy doesn't have any balls?"

"Or a cock," Demetrio said. "Possibly. That's what I was dying to find out."

"He's a castrato, Xan," Becky explained.

"What's that?" Xan asked.

"A singing eunuch," Luca clarified.

Demetrio nodded. "He has the face of a goddess, the voice of an angel... and most likely the crotch of a doll."

"Here we go," Jacob muttered.

"What? It's true. I think."

"Man, forever's a long time to live without your junk," Xan said.

"Yes, it is," Luca agreed, grating a block of Parmesan cheese over his pasta. "I sure as hell couldn't do it."

"From what I understand, he volunteered to be cut when he was a child," Becky informed them.

"He did," Demetrio confirmed. "Isn't that *nuts*?"

The bad joke prompted a chorus of groans. When the noise died down, Dominic spoke up, his voice as cold as ice.

"Thank you, Demetrio. I'm so glad that I can count on you to bring just the right amount of tastelessness to the dinner table." The vampire excused himself and went into the kitchen, leaving the others to silently watch his retreat.

"I'm sorry," Becky whispered. "I shouldn't have brought him up in the first place."

Jacob pressed his fingers against his temples. "There's no reason for you to apologize. You didn't do anything wrong."

He glanced at the one who *did* do something wrong.

"Fine," Demetrio sighed, rising to his feet.

DOMINIC WAS SLICING more bread when his brother stepped into the kitchen.

"Are you going to use that on me?" Demetrio asked, pointing at the knife in Dominic's grip.

"I don't know. I haven't decided yet."

Demetrio smiled at the petulant demeanor of a little brother scorned. This was a side of Dominic that no one else knew, not even his own partner.

"Okay, Domenico. Let me have it."

"All right." Dominic set down the knife with more force than necessary and pushed the cutting board aside. "One thing, Demetrio. All I have ever asked of you is *one thing*. Come over for dinner once a week. That's it. I'm not even asking for myself. I'm asking for my son because he happens to love you."

"I love him, too. You know I do."

"Then stop treating him like an afterthought and be here. We may have all the time in the world, but Alexander doesn't. I want these dinners to be special to him, even if all we ever talk about are eunuchs you want to fuck."

Demetrio was taken aback by Dominic's bluntness. He hadn't heard his brother curse in years. Rarer still was the mention of Xan's limited lifespan. Demetrio knew that it pained his twin to even think about the young man's inevitable demise. It wouldn't be the first time that Dominic lost a loved one to the affliction known as humanity.

"You're right. I'm sorry."

Their eyes met across the counter. Dominic's hard gaze eventually softened.

"You are insufferable."

"I do my best."

Dominic's lips twitched, revealing his reluctant amusement. He grabbed a metal bread basket from one of the cupboards and started filling it with the newly sliced loaf. "What's your excuse today? Some woman? Some man? One of each?"

"I was talking to Father."

Dominic paused, his hand hovering over the basket. After a moment, he continued neatly arranging the bread. "Being our maker doesn't make him our father, Demetrio. How many times have I told you that?"

"As many times as I've told you that I disagree."

"That's why you're his favorite."

"I'm his favorite because I don't shun him." Demetrio sniffed a piece of bread, having long since forgotten the taste. "And I don't deny his name."

Dominic snatched the bread from him and returned it to the basket. "The Castigliane name means nothing to me."

"Yet you wouldn't be where you are without it. You can refuse to use it or hide behind all the aliases you want, *Dominic*. That doesn't change who you are."

As the sound of laughter wafted in from the dining room, Demetrio fiddled with the edge of the basket. There was so much more that he wanted to say about the rift between his father and brother, but he knew Dominic would refuse to listen.

"He called just as I was leaving to come here," the vampire continued. "That's why I was late. I wanted to wait until after dinner to tell you this, but your theatrical exit forced my hand."

"What did he want?"

"The same thing he always wants. To see you. And this time he's not going to take no for an answer."

28

CHAPTER 3

MICHAEL FUKUHARA WAS hungry. It wasn't the kind of hunger that would be satisfied by food of dubious origin and minimal nutritional content, like the fast food and ten-cent packs of ramen noodles he once considered a feast. This was a deeper, dire hunger, one that was so intense that he thought he might go insane from it, and no amount of cheap fare would help. His days of eating food of any sort were gone. Had anyone told him a month ago that he would have a thirst for blood so strong that he was going to do something heinous to the stray dog that refused to leave him alone, he would have claimed that vampires didn't exist and to believe otherwise was pure nonsense brought on by one too many scary movies.

He was wrong.

After taking refuge behind a Quick Fill convenience store, he looked around to confirm that he hadn't been spotted. The rear of the building was secluded and dark, but thanks to Michael's new and improved eyesight, he was able to determine that he was in the clear. That was one of the advantages of being undead; his vision had never been better. But the books and movies never went into detail about the *disadvantages* of the vampire condition. None of the stories he knew of talked about how you pissed and shat yourself during the process of becoming immortal. There was a morbid beauty in most depictions that conveniently failed to mention those things. A little heads up would have been nice.

Falling back against the graffiti-covered brick wall, Michael closed his eyes and evaluated his situation. He had no money, no shelter, and he was technically dead. In about eight hours, the sun would rise. What would happen to him when the rays of morning light hit his unprotected skin? Would he burn? Would he blow up? Would he be reduced to a bloody and gelatinous splotch on the ground like days old roadkill? Whatever the case, it was sure to be nasty. He knew that he should have had a game plan before taking off the way he did, but the idea of being a maniac's plaything one more night was unbearable. Anything, even death, was better than that.

Michael slid down the wall until he was seated, then drew his knees up to his chest and wrapped his arms around his legs. He could hear people entering and exiting the store, all of them going about their merry lives and unaware of his existence. The shaggy brown mongrel that had followed him faithfully for almost a mile nudged at his hand with a wet nose, seeking acknowledgment. Michael could smell the dog's blood beneath her dirty and matted fur, and he hated himself for wondering how it tasted. It wasn't like he wanted to rip out the poor thing's throat and drain her dry, but he was *so hungry*.

"You're a good girl, aren't you?" He scratched the pup between the ears. A wagging tail confirmed that she was most certainly a good girl. "Why are you out here all on your own? Are you a runaway like me?"

The dog sat down beside Michael and blinked at him with big brown eyes that made him ache with guilt. She had no collar or tags, and chances were strong that she wouldn't be missed if anything happened to her. Better to put her out of her misery now than leave her to wander the streets and get hit by a car or abused by some asshole kids. If she was impounded then the odds were high that she would be euthanized anyway. In a way, he would be doing her a favor by killing her now.

He wondered how many times he would have to tell himself that before he believed it.

Strong fingers seized the animal's soiled fur. Michael's upper cuspids extended in anticipation of feeding.

"I'm sorry, girl," he whispered sadly. "I really am."

WHILE A NEW VAMPIRE was dealing with a most difficult decision, Xan swerved into the parking lot of the Rising Sun, narrowly avoiding a group of bloodsucking loiterers. After stopping in the space reserved just for him, he inspected his reflection in the rearview mirror and combed through his hair with ringed fingers. A quick breath check confirmed no traces of garlic from dinner, and the stake was safely concealed beneath the long sleeve of his black turtleneck. Everything was good to go.

He got out of the BMW and made his way toward the entrance, all too aware of the hungry stares of those he passed. It was nothing new and it didn't bother him in the least. Who wouldn't want their ego—and other things—stroked like that?

"Hey, Xan."

Xan sought out the voice and found his favorite cop sitting in a squad car a couple of rows over from where he had parked. Officer Brian Goodridge was one of the many public servants on vampire payroll, handsomely compensated to keep human stragglers from wandering onto the property. He was also kind enough to engage in some after-hours role-play whenever Xan was in the mood to be handcuffed and fucked over the hood of a government-issued vehicle. What a nice guy.

"Hey." Xan wisely kept his distance from the car. Dominic and Jacob had yet to arrive and the last thing they needed to see was their son getting plowed in the backseat. "How bad is it?" he asked, nodding at the building.

"Vampires as far as the eye can see. Your folks should really consider relocating to a bigger place." Noticing the intentional space between them, Brian smiled knowingly. "Another time?"

"Yeah," Xan answered. "*Soon.*"

The officer was disappointed, but he was also smart enough to know that no good could come from getting caught with his dick in the bosses' son. "Deal. See you."

"Later."

Xan forced himself to keep moving before he caved to the other man. With his hazel eyes and chestnut hair and athletic body, Brian was one of Xan's favorite ways to pass the time at work. If given enough opportunity, he would have opted to spend a chunk of his shift diverting the cop's attention from more important—though far less pleasurable—matters of security.

Two male vampires were guarding the main door. They weren't quite the size of Luca but still very intimidating. "Evening, boys," Xan said.

"Good evening, Mr. Dawson," they replied in unison.

Xan knew there was no point in telling them for the thousandth time not to call him that. It was better than the names that some vampires called him; not everyone took too kindly to treating a mere human as an equal because his parents said so. To those vampires, he would never be anything other than food. Or a privileged meatbag, as he once overheard.

He stepped inside and was greeted by a haunting and sensual darkwave tune—fuck-music, according to Jacob. The boarded windows of the main level were concealed by crimson velvet curtains, and there were matching chairs and loveseats strategically arranged around a large dance floor where dozens upon dozens of vampires writhed to the beat. Black walls and dim lighting added to the eerie and erotic atmosphere, giving the room all the ambiance of a macabre whorehouse. For a place that managed to stay under the radar from humans, the Rising Sun was one of the most popular gathering spots of its kind in the Northeast. It served as a haven for vampires to bare their fangs *and* their skin if the mood came upon them, safe from prying eyes.

Xan worked his way through the enormous crowd. He passed by the elevator that led to an underground level that was frequented by older vampires who had no urge to wallow in debauchery. The club office was also located there, where his fathers' trusted assistant, Elliot Ledford, was tucked away and overseeing things from below. The inexplicably bespectacled vampire was another one of Xan's favorite workplace distractions. He had yet to penetrate Elliot's somber exterior, or Elliot in general, but he always had fun trying.

As he approached the bar, he saw an exceptionally attractive vampire checking him out and reciprocated with a roguish smile.

"Don't even think about it." Xan's red-haired co-worker, aptly named Ginger, gave him a dirty look through her long bangs.

"You're right," Xan agreed solemnly. "I should get to work."

"Thank you."

But instead of taking his place behind the bar, Xan made a beeline for his admirer. "Would you like a drink?"

"For fuck's sake," Ginger grumbled as she resumed mixing drinks.

The stranger was humored by Xan's blatant disregard for his fellow bartenders. "Keep that up and you're going to get in trouble."

"Offering you a drink is well within the limits of my job description." Xan took a moment to appreciate the vampire's ebony hair and eyes and his firm, muscular body. He decided that he wanted to offer him a lot more than a drink, but since spreading himself over the bar for the taking wasn't the wisest idea, a handshake would have to do for now. "Xan Dawson," he said, extending his hand.

"I know who you are. I'm Paul Marin."

"I don't know who you are, but I'd like to change that. What can I get for you, Paul Marin?"

Paul pulled him close and whispered something astoundingly lewd in his ear.

"That's not on the menu, but I'll see what I can do." Xan looked at Ginger, who was serving a blood-laced drink to a leather-clad lady vampire. "Hey, Red. I'm taking a break."

"Damn it, Xan. You just got here!"

"Don't give me any shit and I'll set you up with Becky."

That did the trick. Ginger loved women almost as much as Xan loved men, and she had been smitten with the chesty vampire since Xan introduced them months ago. Becky didn't visit the club often, but Ginger had hoped that they would meet again.

"Fine. Hurry up."

"You're an angel."

"Bite me."

Xan turned back to Paul, anxious to get him naked. "Follow me."

SHORTLY AFTER DEMETRIO and Becky left, Jacob effortlessly lifted an incoherent Luca over his right shoulder. The beer got the best of him as it usually did, and since there was no way that he would have made it back to his own place without causing a major traffic accident, he would sleep in Xan's old bed tonight.

"Come on, lightweight," Jacob said while carrying the big man up the stairs.

"Thangujagob," Luca slurred into his back.

"You're welcome."

While Luca drunkenly professed his love for Jacob and Xan and Dominic (hilariously mispronounced as Nominic), Dominic sat on the sofa and studied the slip of paper in his hand. On it was written a phone number he didn't want to call. Life was so much easier before the telephone came along. Dominic was once able to avoid his maker with ease, but now he was just a handful of digits away.

"Is he tucked in?" he asked when Jacob returned to the living room.

"Tucked in and passed out." Jacob plopped down beside him. "I'm kind of disappointed that there was no naked serenade this time. You really haven't lived until you've heard all of Frank Sinatra's hits with a monstrously proportionate penis dangling in your face."

Dominic smiled faintly, prompting Jacob to address the subject he knew his partner was not eager to discuss. "Vincenzo?"

"Yes, Vincenzo."

"When is he coming?"

"I don't know." Dominic frowned and crumpled the paper in his fist. "I have to call him and arrange a meeting."

"Tell him 'the slave' says hello."

The vampire's frown deepened. While most of the issues he had with Vincenzo existed long before Jacob was born, the decision to take a mixed-race slave as a lover was the biggest offense of all to the one who turned him. And he never let Dominic forget it.

"Why is he demanding to see you now?" Jacob asked.

"Because he wants to, and he always gets what he wants."

"Not always," Jacob said, running his knuckles over Dominic's cheek.

Dominic kissed Jacob's fingers and let out a heavy sigh. "I'm sure he will explain at great length why I'm such a thoughtless son. He will also remind me that everything I am and ever will be is because of him."

"That's not true."

"But it is, though. No matter what name I choose or how much distance I put between us, I'm still Domenico Castigliane. And I always will be." Dominic sighed again. "I'm going to the club now. Stay here and keep an eye on Luca. See that he doesn't mistake Alexander's closet for a toilet like he did the last time he got drunk."

"Are you sure?" Jacob asked. "I don't mind going."

Dominic got up and pulled Jacob to his feet. "I have to go over the numbers with Elliot anyway thanks to our greedy medical friends."

"Oh, yeah. Better you than me."

"Be nice or I won't do that thing you like when I get home," Dominic warned, wrapping his arms around Jacob's waist.

"The finger thing?"

"The *tongue* thing."

"I like that thing."

"I know." Dominic's kiss was brief but passionate. "I love you."

"I love you, too."

As soon as Dominic left, Luca started singing at the top of his lungs. This time it was Dean Martin.

"Luca!" Jacob yelled as he stormed up the stairs. "So help me God, you better not be naked!"

MICHAEL FUKUHARA WAS still hungry. But the dog was alive.

He regarded the mutt on his lap. The smell of her blood was still maddening, but as much as he had visualized biting his way through fur and drinking every drop from her body, he just couldn't do it.

"I suck at being a vampire."

Realizing his unintentional pun, Michael laughed wildly. When he couldn't stop, it occurred to him that he might be going crazy.

"Fuck me." He ran a shaky hand over his face. It smelled like dog.

So what was he going to do now? Sit there and wait to die? He had taken the first step toward freedom by getting away from his demented captor, but why had he even bothered if he wasn't willing to do whatever it took to survive on his own? He didn't want to hurt people (or dogs), but he was also partial to living. To live, he needed blood. But it wasn't like he could just walk into Quick Fill and buy some.

Michael sat up with a jolt. There *was* a place where he could buy some blood. Steven had told one of his equally deranged friends about it. Michael had been nearly unconscious from being repeatedly flayed and dosed with corpse blood, but he was fairly confident about what he had overheard.

"A vampire club," he said, trying to remember the details while forgetting the pain. "Just outside of the city. The Rising Sun."

That's right. A vampire club called the Rising Sun. The name had brought a hint of a smile to Michael's face at the time, even in his mutilated state.

With a goal in mind, he moved the dog aside and hopped to his feet. Even if he did find this magical place where blood flowed like water, there was a chance that he would see his tormentor there. Hopefully he would be safe in full view of others. If not, he would run.

Michael was still very much flat broke, but he would worry about that when he got there. He thought he could find at least one vampire with a taste for pretty Japanese guys who would be willing to buy him a drink. As for what he might be asked to do for it... never mind that right now.

He rounded the corner of the Quick Fill and took to the road beyond, keeping his eyes forward and ignoring the mouth-watering smell of blood from people who were gassing up their cars. When he heard the click of nails on concrete behind him, he turned around and discovered his new friend once again following him faithfully.

"Go on, girl. I can't take you with me."

The dog tilted her head.

"I almost killed you."

A wagging tail was her only reply.

Michael surrendered. "Whatever. Come on, then." He started walking again. The mongrel fell in line beside him.

They made their way through the streets of Harborview, just a couple of runaways in the night. For someone who had no clue what the next few hours would bring, Michael felt cautiously optimistic.

He quickened his pace, each step taking him closer to his destination and, unbeknownst to him, the human who would change his life.

FAMILY MATTERS

CHAPTER 4

BACK IN THE 1980S WHEN Dominic and Jacob first decided to turn an old single-story textile mill into a vampires-only nightspot, they saw no need for the bathrooms within and had them all removed during an extensive interior renovation. That changed last year when their human son decided to utilize his Economics degree by working as a bartender in the establishment. As a result, Xan now had his own private restroom at the Rising Sun, located at the back of the building between a supply closet and an electrical room. It was a place he used frequently while he worked, although hardly ever in the manner for which it was intended.

"Fuck!"

Xan grabbed the head between his legs. That David guy had been something else, but even his oral prowess couldn't compete with the way that Paul was damn near swallowing him whole. Perhaps it was because vampires spent so much time sucking blood that they were so good at sucking on other things as well. There was also the twisted thrill of knowing that the blissful lap of a skilled tongue could just as easily turn into vicious fangs sinking into the femoral artery just beneath his thigh. The thought of it, the *chance* of it, was enough to excite Xan beyond measure.

"Paul," he whispered, his hips moving faster and his cock driving deeper into the vampire's willing mouth. When someone you just met was nice enough to go down on you, giving them an early warning was the polite thing to do.

When Paul showed no signs of stopping, Xan cast aside what self-control he had left and placed his hands along the sides of Paul's head, forcing his way between tightly pursed lips. He came hard into Paul's mouth and didn't even try to silence the sounds that escaped him. If anyone happened to hear what Dominic once described as Xan's coital caterwauling, then tough shit.

He let go of Paul's head and steadied himself against the counter while nails lightly raked along his inked abdomen and the tribal sun that was tattooed around his navel. "Fuck," he said again, trying to catch his breath.

Paul stood up and smirked at him with slick lips. Xan grabbed him by the shirt and kissed him. When someone you just met was nice enough to swallow your load, this was also the polite thing to do.

After they parted, Xan took a tube of lubricant from a basket of toiletries on the counter. There was no need for the condoms since vampires were disease-free, but he kept them on hand anyway for Brian. Paul peeled off his shirt, exposing a flawless, hairless chest, and then he unzipped his pants. He was about to pull down the black briefs that concealed what looked to be an impressive erection when Ginger called out to Xan from the other side of the door.

"I'm not done yet!" Xan yelled, his fingers tracing the outline of Paul's cock. He didn't mean to put his co-workers in a bind by ditching them, but there was nothing Ginger could say that would get him out of that bathroom before some thorough fucking took place.

"So if Dominic asks, I should just tell him that you're too busy getting laid to do your job?"

Except for that.

"Shit. I'll be out in a minute." Xan let out a disappointed sigh and placed the lube back in the basket. "Sorry."

Paul shrugged. "I'm just glad it's not Jacob."

Xan understood the sentiment. Dominic never actively encouraged Xan's special brand of generosity, but unlike Jacob, he also never threatened—or in a few cases, flat out attempted—to kill anyone over it.

"If you're still around in a few hours, find me," Xan said as he zipped up. He wasn't done with Paul and had every intention of introducing him to his new bed later.

"I will," Paul promised.

Xan took one last look at what he was abandoning and swore under his breath. They stepped out of the bathroom and found Ginger waiting with a mile-wide smile.

"Sorry for interrupting."

"I can tell," Xan mumbled. To Paul, he added, "I'll see you later." He helped himself to an eyeful of ass as the vampire walked away, a vision so engrossing that it took Ginger three tries to get his attention. "What'd you say?"

"I was going to ask if he was any good, but you've pretty much answered that."

"His mouth was good. I don't know about the rest of him yet."

"Don't you ever get tired of fucking around with random guys?"

"Don't you ever get tired of fucking around with random girls?"

Ginger looked away. "Never mind."

"Exactly. Now if you'll excuse me, I have to be a good son."

"Don't forget about Becky."

"I won't."

Xan disappeared through a door that led down to the floor below. As he descended the steps, he wondered how he was going to inform his best friend that he just pimped her for some bathroom nookie and wished that she were there now so he could break the news to her in public. No matter how mad she got, her British conditioning would never allow her to lash out at him with others watching. Since she usually spent her nights sitting at home with a cup of tea and *Doctor Who* or *Sherlock* or *Downton Abbey*, Xan had no choice but to wait until they were alone to tell her.

Some might have called the atmosphere on the basement level conservative. Xan called it boring. The walls and furniture were dull, mediocre shades of brown, and the only music to be found was in the gentle murmur of conversation. Even so, he didn't mind the occasional shift spent serving the much older clientele and listening to tales of events described (sometimes inaccurately) in history books. The patrons on this level had been around long enough to have very little interest in catering to their carnal whims every waking moment. Xan respected that, even if he personally never wanted to reach an age when he didn't want to have sex all hours of the day and night.

He went into the office where Elliot was sitting at his desk and furiously calculating something. Elliot was *always* furiously calculating something, whether it was money or blood or club-goers. If it had to be counted, he was on top of it. To Xan, the vampire had a way with numbers that was uncanny. And kind of sexy.

"Hello, Ellie."

Elliot stopped assaulting the calculator and blinked at Xan through thick, black-framed glasses. "Dominic is in the vault. And please stop calling me that."

"Give me a kiss and I'll think about it."

Elliot rolled his eyes and continued working. Xan went behind the desk and peered over his shoulder at the vast rows of handwritten figures on sheets of paper spread out across the desktop. Like some vampires, Elliot was slow to embrace certain technological advantages and preferred endless piles of black and white documentation to the computer software that would make his job a lot easier.

After some speedy mental calculating of his own, Xan asked, "Are we short on blood?"

"A little bit. Don't pet me."

Xan stopped caressing Elliot's honey blond hair. "I can't help it."

"Try." Elliot wasn't swayed when Xan's hand slid down his chest. "Try harder."

"Alexander."

By the time Xan stopped groping Elliot and glanced at the open vault door, Dominic was already standing beside him. "Hey. I was just looking for you."

"Did you expect to find me in Elliot's crotch?"

"Apparently," Elliot said.

Xan gave up his attempted molestation and moved away from the desk. "Why didn't Dad come?"

"Thanks to that beer you brought over, he's now babysitting Luca."

"Oh, yeah?" Xan scowled when he recalled the last time that Luca got wasted during a family dinner. "He better not piss in my closet again."

AFTER ENDURING A LENGTHY discussion about Elliot's sexiness, Dominic ordered Xan to get to work. "Let's see if you make it *behind* the bar this time."

"A happy customer is a repeat customer. I intend to make that one very happy. Repeatedly."

"Get out." Dominic closed the door, shutting out his son's laughter. "If I were human, he would be the death of me."

"He knows what he likes," Elliot said.

"And he likes it very much."

"So it would seem. You know he caught this discrepancy in about five seconds. Give him an office job. At least then you wouldn't have to worry about him... doing what he does."

"I don't want him any more involved with this place than he is already." Dominic took a seat on the edge of Elliot's desk and pointed at a piece of paper covered with numerical scribbles. "How bad is it?"

"Five to six pints every week for God knows how long. Maybe for years, but I haven't gone that far back yet." Elliot took off the glasses that did nothing to enhance his vision and tossed them on top of the desk. "Since we anticipate a weekly loss due to comps and such, I would have never noticed that something was off until I cross-referenced the usage with how many drinks were served. If you hadn't asked me to determine how much we could spare, there's no telling how long it might have continued."

"One of the bartenders?" Dominic asked grimly.

"They're the only ones with access to storage besides me, you, and Jacob. I'll check the camera footage, but that will take a while."

If it had been anything other than blood, Dominic might have been tempted to let it go with just a warning. But blood was his business. Anyone who had the nerve to steal it had to be dealt with.

He placed a spare chair beside Elliot and sat down. It was shaping up to be a very long night.

THE RISING SUN WAS located almost five miles past the Harborview city limits on a semi-desolate stretch of Erie County road. Michael could hear the muted pulse of music from the edge of the parking lot. Even better, he could smell the blood. At first, he wondered why the owners hadn't bothered to make the place more presentable on the outside, but after giving it some thought he believed he understood their reasoning. Clubs that looked like clubs drew attention. Clubs that looked like deserted factories did not.

It had taken him almost an hour to get there. He could have made it sooner had he really wanted; another vampire perk he recently discovered was the ability to move *very* quickly. Instead, he decided to take his time since the stray that accompanied him wouldn't have been able to keep up. The dog had grown on Michael during their short time together, and he even stopped at a dumpster along the way to root out some discarded food for her to eat. It was the least he could do since she insisted on tagging along.

"Here we are, girl." Michael rubbed the mongrel's head. She was such a darling and raggedy thing. "Stay here, okay?"

To his astonishment, the dog sat down. Michael bent over and offered his hand. "Shake?"

A calloused paw landed on his open palm.

"Huh." Michael let go of her and scratched her neck. "Wish me luck."

There wasn't much he could do about his clothes. With his black boots, blue jeans, and black shirt, he wasn't nearly as dressed up as some of the vampires he passed in the parking lot, plus he smelled like a dog and a dumpster. But he was too hungry to turn back now.

He pressed forward with his head high. The closer he got, the stronger the smell of blood, and he immediately saw part of the reason. He had no idea why the club would employ a human police officer. Even in his own steadily wasting state, Michael was sure that he could still overpower him if he wanted. Maybe the cop wasn't there so much to keep the vampires in line but to keep other humans out. He must have been getting some major hazard pay for that.

There were two gigantic vampires guarding the door. Michael was glad that he no longer had a functioning bladder because they were the most intimidating guys he had ever seen. When he reached the door, he was positive that they would stop him. He was so preoccupied with anticipating that reaction that he was well inside the club before he realized that it never happened.

"I'll be damned," he whispered, gawking at the extravagant interior that resembled something right out of a macabre whorehouse. Michael had never felt so out of his element.

"You're backing up traffic, sweetie."

The vampire was skeevy. And old—physically speaking, anyway. Figuring out vampire ages was another thing Michael had to get used to. Steven was in his fifties but hadn't looked much older than a teenager. This guy looked like he was in his seventies but could have been hundreds of years old. It was confusing as hell.

"I'm sorry," Michael said. He was about to move aside when a hand seized his arm.

"I haven't seen you around before."

Michael tried not to cringe as fingers started kneading his skin. Was this really going to be his one decent chance to get some blood tonight? "I'm new. Here and... in general, I guess."

"Oh? Who's your maker? Anyone I know?"

"Probably not. He doesn't get out much." *Since he's too busy gutting people for fun,* Michael thought.

"And he just let a pretty little thing like you wander off on your own?" The elderly vampire hooked his arm through Michael's and led him into the heart of the club. "Well, his loss is my gain. For tonight, anyway. May I buy you a drink?"

Michael's lips did something that he hoped resembled a smile. "Sure."

The vampire directed him to the bar. A hand slid down Michael's back and cupped his ass. He wanted to push it away, but his hunger currently outweighed his self-respect.

"Have a seat right there," the vampire said, ushering him to a dark red padded stool.

Michael sat down, grateful that he was given a reprieve from the fondling... until that same wandering hand came to rest on his upper thigh. All the dumpsters and stray dogs in the world couldn't make him feel as dirty as the grubby hand rubbing on his leg.

While he fumed about his predicament, the vampire beckoned for a bartender. Michael kept right on fuming until one arrived, at which point he forgot why he was even angry in the first place.

The bartender was human. And *gorgeous*.

"Hi, I'm Xan. What can I get for you?"

C.L. INGRO

CHAPTER 5

XAN RECOGNIZED THE older vampire right off the bat. He was a regular at the Rising Sun who hit on anyone that stood still long enough for him to try. The younger one was new. And *cute*. He had a distinctive deer-in-the-headlights thing going on, plus the unmistakable look of revulsion over being felt up by a pervert. And was it just his imagination or did one of them smell like dog?

"Hi, I'm Xan. What can I get for you?"

"I'll take a bloody Bloody Mary," the older vampire said. "And whatever my friend wants."

Xan waited for the young vampire to speak and wondered why he would let that creepy prick touch him in a way that was obviously displeasing.

"May I have some blood?"

"Just blood?"

"Please."

"Coming right up." Xan flashed his best bartender's smile, to which the young vampire responded with a shy twitch of the lips. The cuteness increased significantly.

After elbowing Ginger out of the way, he grabbed a couple of glasses and went to work. As he measured and poured and mixed, he mulled over the cutie's request. It wasn't all that unusual; some vampires didn't care for combining blood with liquor or any other beverage. However, there was an urgency beneath the vampire's polite tone that implied hunger. Xan could think of no other reason that he would purposely subject himself to the old guy's nauseating antics.

His fathers had repeatedly urged him not to interfere when it came to the patrons. They had also advised him not to fuck any of them, but that didn't seem to be working out so well. The more Xan thought about whatever might be going on between those two vampires, the more it bothered him. And the more it bothered him, the more inclined he felt to do something.

When he finished preparing the drinks, he brought them over to the duo. "Here you go."

The geezer removed his hand from the young vampire's crotch and reached into his pocket. "What do I owe you?"

"No charge."

"Really? Thank you."

"You're welcome. Now *go away*."

MICHAEL WAS STUNNED and awed by Xan's daring. It was pure insanity for any human to surround himself with beings capable of ripping him to shreds in the first place, let alone to basically invite one of them to fuck off. And even more amazing than Xan's bold demand was that the vampire obeyed. He snatched up his drink and vanished into a sea of bodies without protest, looking for someone else upon whom he could lavish his unwanted attention. When Michael could no longer spot him in the crowd, he turned around and found blue eyes staring attentively at him.

Who *was* this guy?

"I know it's none of my business, but you can do a lot better than that."

"Oh, he wasn't... I mean we weren't..." Michael let out an exasperated sigh. He didn't want Xan to think that he had actually wanted anything to do with that vampire, nor was he in a hurry to admit that the only reason he was with him in the first place was because he was attempting to whore himself for a drink. That was not the sort of first impression he wanted to make. "He's not my type. Not at all."

"That's good to know." Bobbing his head to the music, Xan propped his elbows on the bar top. "What's your name?"

"Michael."

"Hello, Michael." Xan pushed the glass of blood his way. "Drink up before it gets cold."

"I don't have any money," Michael said skittishly, waiting for the bartender to summon those two behemoths at the door to kick him out.

"I told you it's on the house."

"Why?"

"Because." Xan winked and moved on, leaving the vampire to stare after him.

After three weeks of hell, Michael had almost forgotten what kindness felt like. It felt good. He tried to appear civilized while raising the glass to his lips. He even managed to keep his fangs hidden, which was easier said than done when he was so ravenous. As much as he wanted to drink it all in one gulp, he forced himself to go slowly. There was no telling when he would have an opportunity like this again so he needed to make it last.

He studied his environment while he sipped. It was like a scene straight out of a movie except the atmosphere was far more ominous than anything he had ever witnessed on-screen. All around him were nocturnal creatures that feasted on human blood. So was he, but he hardly felt like he belonged.

His focus returned to the human smack dab in the middle of it all. Xan was at the far end of the bar, serving a drink to a vampire who looked like he belonged on a runway. How could he work in a place like this without any apparent fear of being harmed and send a vampire scurrying away with a simple command? His eyes trailed down Xan's body, or as much of it as he could see from where he sat. The human was tall and had a lovely physique, and Michael felt a stirring that he would have never thought his body was capable of so soon after everything Steven did to him. He didn't want to assume that Xan was gay, but the vibe he got from him and the dark-haired vampire didn't leave much room for doubt. Not that he would ever have a chance with a guy that hot, but it was nice to know.

Michael almost died when Xan caught him looking, and he whipped his head around so fast that it was a miracle he didn't give himself whiplash.

XAN WAS SURPRISED THAT Michael didn't give himself whiplash as quickly as he turned his head.

He stepped away from Paul and approached the embarrassed vampire. "Ready for another one?"

Michael shook his head, causing some of his hair to fall forward and conceal his eyes. Xan had a sudden urge to sweep it back, which was not unusual as he often had sudden urges to touch strangers. Only this time it wasn't a sexual urge. Well, it wasn't a *completely* sexual urge. For one whose life hinged on all things sexual, Xan didn't have a clue what to make of it.

"I told you I don't have any money," Michael replied.

"I heard you the first time. Don't worry about it." Xan poured another glass of blood for Michael and a shot of Jim Beam for himself. When Ginger yelled at him to get back to work, he told her to keep her panties on.

"I'm not wearing any," she informed him.

"TMI, Red." Xan looked at Michael and felt that odd, touchy-feely urge again. "So what's your story?" he asked before downing his shot in one stomach-burning chug. "You're not from around here, are you?"

"I was born in Japan. My father brought me here when I was a baby."

Xan chuckled. "I wasn't questioning your citizenship, you goober. I meant here as in Harborview."

"Oh." Michael rubbed nervously at the back of his neck. "I'm—I used to be a student over at Mercymore College. Now I'm... this."

"You make it sound like you didn't have a choice."

"I didn't."

Xan observed Michael's despondent face and wanted to hurt someone. Over the years, he had heard of people being turned against their will, but to his knowledge he had only personally known of one. Even that was one too many. Though Jacob never said much to Xan about his years as a slave or the one who forcibly turned him, he always stressed that he was happy things worked out the way they did. Still, it wasn't right to steal someone's life, and the very thought of it sickened Xan.

"That's terrible."

"Yeah, but what can I do?" Michael polished off the blood and stood up. "Thank you, Xan. Goodnight."

He disappeared into the crowd. Xan knew that he should have left it at that and gone about his business. Of course he didn't.

"Ginger, I'm taking another break."

"You suck, Xan."

"Very well, from what I'm told."

He took off in search of Michael, hoping like hell that he would be able to catch up with him.

MICHAEL WALKED OUT of the club feeling better than he had walking in. Now that he was no longer hungry, there was just the small matter of shelter to worry about. The sun would be up in a few hours, and he had nowhere to go to escape it. He could have stowed away in his dorm closet until the sun went down, but after being gone for so long, he wasn't certain that the room was even his anymore.

Home was out, too. The idea of facing his father on a good day was daunting enough, let alone after three weeks of being murdered and maimed by a sick fuck. No one inside the club had even given him a second look, which meant that Hideaki probably hadn't even bothered to report him missing for fear of the dishonor a runaway son would bring. Either that or vampires didn't pay attention to the news. At any rate, home was a no-go.

He knew that he could have asked Xan for help, but he didn't want to seem desperate and homeless (even though he *was* desperate and homeless). It was bad enough that the bartender had taken pity on him by serving him for free, and Michael wanted to save what face he could. Besides, a guy like that had better things to do than waste his time finding a home for a vampire he didn't know.

Michael didn't acknowledge the cries of "Hey!" that he heard since he had no reason to think they were meant for him. In addition, he was too busy trying to decide if a dumpster would provide adequate protection from sunlight. He guessed it might work as long as no one disposed of any trash until sundown. If he could just secure the lid from the inside—

"Michael!"

The vampire spun around and gasped when he saw Xan coming after him.

"Do you have somewhere to go?" the young man asked after catching up with him.

"No, but I'll think of something," Michael responded, clinging to his useless pride.

"I have a coffin in my basement."

The statement was so odd and unexpected that Michael didn't realize he was being offered a place to stay.

"You're welcome to sleep there for the day," Xan clarified. "If you want."

Michael was so touched that he could have kissed him. Only as a show of gratitude. Nothing more than that. "Does that line work on all the vampires?" he asked.

"I don't know. You're the first one I've tried it on."

"I've never slept in a coffin."

"I did every now and then when I was a kid. It's not so bad." Xan folded his arms. If he happened to notice the way that Michael was eyeing his chest, he didn't mention it. "I also have an air bed if you prefer that. Whichever one you want, the basement's lightproof so you'll be okay."

"Why are you being nice to me?"

"Because I want to. And you smell like dog."

Michael groaned. "You noticed?"

"Hard not to. So how about it?"

The vampire knew that he should not immediately trust this man, but the fact that Xan was human tipped the scale in Michael's favor. Now he was the one with superhuman strength, and there was no way that Xan could hurt him if he tried. Michael didn't suspect that he would; there was a blunt sincerity about Xan that left little room for the possibility of deceit. He was also dying to know why this intriguing stranger was a person of importance among vampires.

"Just one day."

"Just one day," Xan agreed. "After that... I'm sure we can work something out."

"Okay, but there's just one thing. A small thing, really. Sort of."

"What?"

Michael stared at Xan, who stood about four inches taller (and smelled much better) than him. "Can I bring a friend?"

DOMINIC RAISED A BROW at Elliot's monitor, which showed the various displays from the cameras scattered around the club. On the dance floor, a couple was gyrating so provocatively to the music that he wasn't entirely convinced they weren't having sex. Near the DJ's booth, the vampire Xan had chased away was at it again, this time sniffing after another pretty young thing and once again failing miserably. Right outside of the office, a group of vampires old enough to think of Dominic as an adolescent were engrossed in what appeared to be a heated debate given the way that heads were shaking and hands were waving. But the view that interested Dominic the most was of the parking lot, where his son was presently getting to know a vampire. And a dog.

He watched in fascination as Xan played with the scraggly mutt. Growing up, the boy had claimed that he never wanted a pet, but the look on his face right now suggested otherwise. Dominic would have given him ten dogs if he had known it would make him happy, whereupon Jacob would have complained about spoiling him before buying him ten more.

The thought occurred to him again. In truth, it was never far from his mind. *Twenty-two years gone by already. How many more to go?*

"Dominic?"

Dominic turned to Elliot. "Yes?"

"I think I have a solution."

"You usually do."

He sat back as Elliot launched into a presentation about how to keep the blood and money flowing for everyone. Out of the corner of his eye, he saw Xan exchange words with the human officer who enjoyed screwing him before leading the vampire and pup to his car and letting them in. Dominic wondered what prompted the change of heart since the young man had insisted on further befriending the vampire he met earlier that night, the one who looked like he belonged on a runway. Who knew? There was never any sort of rhyme or reason when it came to his son's quest to have sex with everyone in the world.

This new vampire was just another notch in the very long belt of Xan's conquests. Nothing more.

⁙

THE VAMPIRE WITH THE mismatched eyes finished his drink and signaled for another. The bartender who served him was cute. She had red hair and a nice rack. A dimple formed on her right cheek when she laughed. She said her name was Ginger.

The club wasn't so bad. It was a lot raunchier than he guessed it would be based on the rumors he had heard, as evidenced by the two vampires on the dance floor who were practically fucking. He wasn't there to get laid himself, but it was good to know that he had that option should he ever have the urge to do it right out in the open.

Beside him sat a vampire with jet-black hair and eyes. He looked like a model. "How are you?" he asked.

"Other than being ditched, I'm good." The vampire scooted closer. "What about you? What brings you out tonight?"

Steven offered him a smile that in no way betrayed the rampant madness beneath. "Me? Oh, I'm just... looking for something I lost."

FAMILY MATTERS

CHAPTER 6

ANY RESERVATIONS MICHAEL had about going to Xan's house vanished when he spotted an old Nintendo 64 console on the floor next to an oversized television. He recalled the many hours spent playing video games on that very same system back when he was a kid, before his father decided that doing so was a waste of time.

Michael gazed at the unit like it was a long lost artifact. "Whoa."

"Do you play?" Xan asked.

"I used to. Seeing it brings back a lot of memories."

"Good ones?"

"Mostly."

Xan stepped around the dog that had been sitting patiently by his feet since they first entered the house. "What's your favorite game?"

"*GoldenEye 007.*"

"You can stay." Xan smiled at Michael in a way that would have made the vampire's heart beat faster if only it could beat at all. "Come with me and I'll show you the basement."

Michael whistled to the dog, and the two of them followed Xan down to a basement that had everything a vampire needed to pass the time. There was a standard definition television and a VCR which, as Xan explained, was about as high tech as the previous owner had ever gotten, a bookshelf filled with an admirable selection of books, a fully stocked blood bank refrigerator, and a microwave for heating blood. There was also a bathroom just beyond the door next to the bookshelf. The toilet wouldn't serve any purpose for Michael, but the shower and bathtub would come in handy.

In the center of the room was a large oak coffin. Although Michael was recently deceased, the sight of it still unnerved him. "I can't believe you slept in one of these when you were little," he said, running his hand along the coffin lid. "How did that not freak you out?"

"My dads are vampires. I guess it takes a lot to freak me out."

Michael had been given the short version of Xan's life story during the ride to his house. A discarded human baby found and raised by vampires was easily the strangest spin on the concept of family that Michael had ever heard. But unlike his own miserable upbringing with a father who had often acted anything but human, Xan's brief rundown of his childhood sounded warm and loving.

"I'll go dig up the air bed and find something for you to change into." Xan looked at the dog. "Will she eat ramen? I know it's not the best thing for her, but that's all I've got for food right now."

"I don't think she's all that picky."

"I'll be back in a bit."

After Xan left, Michael went into the bathroom and stripped off his clothes, anxious to rid himself of the smell of mutt and muck. He filled the tub and climbed in, groaning loudly at the pleasure of submerging his body in warm water. He then drew up his knees and slid all the way down until his head was underwater. Since there was no risk of drowning, he decided to stay that way for a while.

He was in a safe place now, but there was still the uncertainty and ever-present worry of what the future would bring. Michael feared that it was only a matter of time before his maker tracked him down and attempted to resume their grisly affair. He'd seen enough movies to know that Steven could probably locate him if he really wanted. But what if he decided to move on? Michael was horrified to think that someone else might be subjected to his fate, but what could he do? A three-week-old vampire didn't stand a chance against someone far older and much more powerful. And for all he knew, Steven's behavior was perfectly acceptable among vampires, even though the impression he got after hearing Xan speak so highly of his fathers seemed quite the opposite. Maybe they were the exception to the rule.

After a few more minutes of soaking, Michael drained the tub and turned on the shower. On the pole caddy was a vast selection of soaps and shampoos and conditioners. He chose a bottle of shampoo that listed all sorts of fancy extracts and essences as ingredients and costed more than what he spent on all of his toiletries in a year. As he massaged the thick liquid into his hair, he reflected on his kind host. Michael liked Xan. For the obvious physical reasons, but also because he seemed like a genuinely likable kind of guy. What might have happened if it had been Xan in the pub the night he died instead of Steven? Would Xan have even given him the time of day? Whatever the answer—which in Michael's mind was a resounding no—Xan's decision to take in a stinky vampire was almost worth the torment that Michael had suffered. Or so he thought now that his body had healed from the trauma caused by Steven's knife and fangs. He really didn't want to leave, despite his "just one day" stipulation. But if Xan asked him to stay...

After working the shampoo into a lathery mess, he grabbed a bottle of body soap and a poofy, spongy thing (whatever they were called—he had only ever used bars himself) and went to work on the rest of his body. He continued thinking about Xan while scrubbing along his neck and shoulders, over his chest, and down his stomach until he reached—

"Seriously?"

Michael looked down at himself. After almost a month without indulging, he had some catching up to do. But could he really jerk off right there in the shower? It seemed like such an ill-mannered thing to do.

The vampire wrapped his hand around his cock. That alone was enough to make him shiver. And it wasn't like Xan would know what he was doing.

"Fuck it," he muttered before hastily proceeding.

MICHAEL WAS STILL IN the shower when Xan returned to the basement with the air bed, bedding, some clothes for his smaller guest, and a bowl of microwaved ramen noodles. He sat down on the floor and called the mongrel over, then offered her a bite which she greedily devoured.

"I gave up sex for this," he said with a wry smile.

The dog sniffed and licked his hand.

"You're welcome."

Xan scratched her head and continued feeding her until Michael came out of the bathroom with a towel around his waist. The first thing that caught his eye was the colorful dragon tattoo that covered Michael's left shoulder and upper arm. As a tattoo enthusiast, Xan thought it was a thing of beauty.

"Very nice." When Michael pressed a hand to his mouth to hide his smile, Xan corrected himself by babbling. "I meant your tattoo. Your tattoo is very nice. Not that the rest of you isn't very nice either, because it is. It's quite nice. But I was talking about your tattoo. I'm going to shut up now."

What the hell was that? Mentally scolding himself for coming across like a flustered idiot, Xan set down the bowl for the dog and gave Michael the clothes he had gathered from his bedroom. "Here you go. I'll wash your stuff later today."

"Thanks."

Xan was suddenly very much aware of Michael's closeness. He scolded himself some more for his inability to refrain from imagining what the vampire looked like underneath the towel. Couldn't he just be a good Samaritan without wanting to turn the situation into a bad porn movie?

"I found the bed," he continued, moving away from Michael while he still had the chance. "I couldn't find the pump for it, though. Do you want me to blow it with my mouth or can you do it yourself?"

"Um..."

"*Up,*" Xan quickly clarified. "Do you want me to blow it *up*... with my mouth?"

"I think I can do it myself," Michael replied, his lips pursed to keep from laughing in Xan's face. "With my mouth."

"Then I'm going to leave before I put my other foot... in my mouth. Holler if you need anything."

Xan picked up the bowl that the dog had licked clean while he was busy making an ass of himself and left the basement. After shutting the door, he closed his eyes, cringing at his uncharacteristic lack of couth. It wasn't like he had never been around half-naked guys before. He was constantly surrounding himself with men in various stages of nudity. Why was this one making him act like such a moron?

When no answer came to mind, Xan took the bowl into the kitchen and escaped to his bedroom. He undressed and got into the shower, washing himself from head to toe and then beating off because his dick was right there and it seemed like the logical thing to do. Afterwards, he slipped into a pair of shorts and climbed into bed with an exhausted sigh, his thoughts lingering far too long on the vampire in the basement.

AFTER MAKING THE PHONE call he had been dreading all night, and a second phone call to inform Demetrio it was done so the vampire would stop pestering him about it, Dominic went down to the basement and found Jacob reading in bed. Jacob was almost always reading or watching television and movies or listening to music; Dominic had never seen someone so devoted to absorbing all forms of entertainment as his partner. The only good thing that Jacob's maker had ever done was unlock his desire for intellectual stimulation, an act committed in brazen defiance of the laws that prohibited educating slaves.

As was the case every so often when he stepped into a room and laid eyes on his lover, the memory of their first meeting on a star-filled night 210 years ago surfaced in his mind. But this Jacob was nothing like the Jacob from that night, a physically and emotionally brutalized vampire slave who would have rather ended his own life—and almost did—than face a ceaseless existence in captivity. From the very start, Dominic had felt an almost obsessive urge to protect him. It was little wonder he was experiencing the same urge right now after talking to Vincenzo.

"Hey." Jacob closed his book—*Bertram Cope's Year*, one of his favorites. "Is Luca awake?"

"Not yet." Dominic fell on top of the comforter and rested his head on Jacob's lap. "I doubt he'll be very productive today."

"As long as he wakes us up if the house is on fire."

Dominic closed his eyes as fingers caressed his hair. He could have happily remained that way all day, but soon they would need to sleep. First, he had to bring Jacob up to speed on business. There was also the matter of a certain phone call. Dominic decided to start with that. "I'm going to meet with him in two weeks."

"At the club?"

"Yes," Dominic answered. The couple agreed long ago that Vincenzo would never step foot inside their home.

Jacob slid down in the bed. Dominic placed his head on the vampire's chest, listening to the stillness of his dead heart.

"Dominic?"

"Yes?"

"I know we can't stop him from meeting Xan, but I'd prefer to keep their contact to a minimum."

Nodding, Dominic grabbed Jacob's hand and held it close, his pale fingers sliding over brown skin. "To be honest, I would feel better if that applied to you as well. It's difficult being tactful when all I want to do is hurt him for insulting you."

"Why do you think I hang around? I love it when you fight for me." Jacob's mischievous grin gradually faded. "Do I need to worry?"

"No."

Dominic failed to add that he was already worried enough for the both of them. With any luck, Vincenzo would show up long enough to relieve Dominic of a hefty sum of money—something he would feel he was owed in addition to the monthly gifts he already received—and then go away for another fifty years or more. But he couldn't shake the feeling that the visit was going to end badly. Things *always* tended to end badly when it came to the ancient vampire. Dominic knew that better than anyone for reasons that no one, not even his lover or his brother, would ever know.

Jacob pushed him onto his back. "After all these years, don't you think I know when you're not telling me everything?" he asked. "Why must you carry the weight of the world on your shoulders?"

Dominic touched Jacob's cheek. "So you don't have to."

"If you're trying to get laid, I'll have you know that you're going about it the right way."

"Trying? I thought it was a foregone conclusion."

"Ah, so it is."

Jacob turned out the lights. They had the rest of the morning to talk. First, Dominic wanted to do things to Jacob that would make him scream, starting with the tongue thing he loved ever so much.

EVEN THOUGH HE HAD done a piss-poor job of inflating the air bed, Michael slept better than he had in weeks. And longer, too, according to the clock on the wall behind the television that read 7:09 p.m. Almost eleven hours.

He sat up and saw that he was alone; Xan must have let the dog out sometime during the day. He stood and stretched, using one hand to hold on to his borrowed shorts to keep them from falling any lower than they were already. Then he shuffled over to the fridge. Minutes later, he was heading up the basement steps with a mug of warm blood.

"Good evening," Michael said as he entered the living room.

"Hey." Xan paused his game—*GoldenEye 007*, of course—and smiled at him from the floor where he and the dog were sitting. "How'd you sleep?"

Michael was too distracted to speak right away because he noticed that Xan's arms were covered in tattoos. He hadn't figured the young man to be the type who would have any tattoos at all, let alone so many of them. It was a pleasant discovery.

"Like a rock, apparently. I didn't even hear you take her out of the basement."

Xan scratched the mutt's back, and she pawed at him to encourage more of the same. "I took her outside," he said. "And then I gave her a bath."

"I could have done that."

"I didn't mind at all. Oh, I also got your clothes. They're in the dryer right now."

Michael took a seat on the sofa. "I really can't thank you enough for all of this, Xan."

"You thanked me. That's enough." Xan tossed a second controller at him. "Let's see what you've got."

"I haven't played in years," Michael reminded him, staring uncertainly at the controller.

As Xan switched the game into multiplayer mode, Michael slid down to the floor and tried to familiarize himself with the controller buttons.

"Ready?" Xan asked.

"Not really."

"Tough shit."

They started playing, which more or less amounted to Michael's character running around in circles while constantly getting shot. But the more he played, the more he started to remember the ins and outs of the game, and it wasn't long before he was holding his own against the far superior gamer.

"I know you said you were only going to stay for one day," Xan began, never taking his eyes off the TV screen. "But... how do you feel about sticking around for a little while longer?"

Almost a full minute passed before Michael was able to answer. "If you insist."

"I do."

"Okay. Shit, I'm dead again."

As Michael revived his character yet again, he hoped that Xan wouldn't pick that moment to look his way. It was going to be a while before he was able to stop smiling.

CHAPTER 7

XAN LOVED HIS FATHERS equally, but he was also smart enough to know which parent to call when he needed to say something that would not go over well. Therefore, Dominic was the one he spoke to when he announced that he would be taking the next week off from work. The vampire wasn't thrilled by the news, or the additional revelation that Xan was going to miss next Friday's dinner, but he agreed not to give his son a hard time when the young man offered to host dinner the following Friday. Dominic also promised to try to prevent Jacob from randomly popping in to visit. Knowing Jacob, it wouldn't be easy.

With that out of the way, Xan spent the next seven days getting to know his new friend. They played video games and read comics and watched movies. While Xan hadn't wanted to presume, he was excited when Michael revealed that he was fluent in Japanese and helped him improve on what little he knew of the language himself. When Michael expressed his love of apple-flavored sake, Xan went out and bought some (along with food and treats for the dog), and they drank copious amounts of it while discussing *Star Wars* and *Star Trek* and other sci-fi classics. It was the most fun that Xan ever had with another man without lube.

On Saturday evening, eight days after the night they met, Xan emerged from his bedroom to find Michael sitting in front of the laptop. "Are you looking up porn?"

"I'm looking up me. I just wanted to see if my dad reported me missing yet. It doesn't look like he did."

"But you've been gone for a month now. Why wouldn't he have called the police?"

"Because he cares more about saving face than saving me."

Xan sat down beside him. "Why do you say that?"

"I'm going to need a lot of sake to tell that story."

"You can't get drunk."

"No, but I can try."

Without thinking, Xan placed his hand on Michael's thigh. He felt bad about all the times he had gone on about his own parents now that he knew about Michael's strained relationship with his father. Since he didn't know what to say to make it all better, he decided to change the subject. "Are you sure you don't want to come with me to the club? You can have a few drinks, watch vampires hump each other, fun stuff like that."

"As entertaining as that sounds, I'll pass. Besides, I can't wait to meet your friend."

It was Michael's idea for Becky to come over while Xan went back to work. When asked about his motives, he admitted that he was concerned Xan wouldn't trust him to be alone in the house. Even though Xan assured him that nothing could have been further from the truth, Michael still insisted.

"You may live to regret those words," Xan cautioned. "Becky is... well... you'll see for yourself. And don't say I didn't warn you."

MICHAEL DIDN'T MEAN to stare, but he had never seen anything like it. At least not up close and personal, right in his face.

"Go on, have a good look," Becky offered, wrapping an arm around him and sticking out her chest. "Aren't they fabulous?"

"Will you cut it out?" Xan pulled her away from the paralyzed vampire. "Do you have to be so inappropriate?"

"I'm only inappropriate because I care."

Rolling his eyes, Xan turned to Michael. "Last chance."

Concluding that Becky was harmless overall, Michael replied, "We'll be fine. I think."

Xan looked at his best friend. "As for you, please be nice."

"I'm British," Becky replied haughtily. "It is impossible for me not to be nice."

"You're an asshole to me all the time!"

"That's different."

Never having had any close friends of his own, Michael was fascinated by the way they carried on, trading barbs but so clearly dear to each other. It must have been nice to have that sort of friendship with someone. He never had that for himself, as he was reminded by the lack of personal emails inquiring about his absence. None of his classmates or fellow dorm dwellers seemed to care that he was gone.

"Whatever. I'm leaving. I won't be too late."

Xan paused as if he wanted to say something more but settled for a smile. Michael was too busy returning it to see the way that Becky was watching them.

"And Becky, you have to go out with Ginger," Xan informed her. "I promised her that you would. Don't ask why."

"Wait, what?"

"Bye!" Xan shouted, escaping without explanation.

"That cheeky shit. As for you..." Becky nudged Michael on the arm. "I'm guessing girl parts aren't your thing?"

"Sorry. I'm pretty attached to boy parts."

"Well, do you at least like tea?"

"IF IT ISN'T OUR LONG lost son," Jacob observed when Xan poked his head through the office door. "We weren't expecting to see you until later tonight."

Xan stepped into the room. "I know, but I just thought I'd stop by and see my wonderful, glorious, and magnificent fathers before going to work," he said a little too innocently.

"Were you reading a thesaurus before you got here? What did you do or what do you need?"

"Now, Jacob, I'm sure that Alexander didn't come here and compliment us just because he wants something." Dominic smiled slyly at his son. "Isn't that correct?"

Xan held up his hands in a show of defeat. "All right, I do need something. But it's not that big of a deal." Seeing his parents' skepticism, he decided to come clean. "Fine, it's kind of a very big deal, but it's not for me. Not really."

"This is going to be good," Jacob predicted.

And he was right.

"You want us to *what?*"

They had moved into the kitchen after Dominic demanded that Xan eat something. There were only two human beings in the world he cared about, and he always made sure that they were both well-fed. "This is a strange request, Alexander," he remarked as he gave him a sandwich spilling with cheeses and cured meats before sitting down next to Jacob. "Even for you."

"I know." Xan twirled a platinum band around his index finger. "Just hear me out."

"I heard just fine," Jacob said. "I'm just trying to wrap my head around it. You're saying that you picked up some vampire, took him home, and asked him to live with you. And now you want us to give him a job?"

"He had nowhere else to go." Xan looked down at the sandwich to avoid Jacob's gaze. "And I didn't pick him up," he added stubbornly. "We haven't done anything. It wasn't about sex."

"Was this the young gentleman from last Friday?" Dominic asked. "The one with the dog?"

"Yeah."

"You know who he's talking about?" Jacob demanded to know. "Why didn't you tell me?"

"Because I was... keeping you occupied."

"Gross," Xan mumbled.

Dominic continued, "Secondly, I had no reason to suspect that it was anything more than a one-time social connection, and I know you don't care to hear about things like that."

"Give me some credit," Xan started. "I've been around long enough to know bullshit when I see it. This isn't some elaborate scheme to hurt me or to hurt you guys through me. Michael was turned against his will. He didn't go into specifics, but I think his maker did some really bad things to him even after that."

This news struck a chord with Jacob. He knew more about that particular subject than most.

"He didn't ask me to come here," Xan continued. "He doesn't even know that I'm doing this. Becky's with him right now. If you don't trust my judgment, then talk to her. See what she has to say about him." He clicked his nails against the glossy black surface of the kitchen table. "You raised me to be a good person and to do the right thing. That's what I'm trying to do. He has no home and no way to take care of himself. If he had some sort of stability, like a job, it would be a start."

"I'd like to know more about this maker of his, but your actions are highly commendable, Alexander."

"Thank you, Domi."

Both Xan and Dominic looked to Jacob, waiting for his answer.

"Bring him over tomorrow night," he decided. "If you want us to consider employing him, he'll have to have some sort of interview first."

"... Okay." Xan was shocked that Jacob hadn't put up more of a fight. "Thanks, Dad. This means a lot to me."

"You're welcome. Eat your sandwich."

Xan did as he was instructed. He chose not to comment on the way that Dominic placed a soothing hand on Jacob's thigh, a silent gesture of praise for remaining civil when his first instinct was the exact opposite.

After he finished eating, Jacob and Dominic walked him to the door.

"I'll stop by the office later and say hi."

Dominic plucked a crumb from his son's shirt. "Or you could try working an entire shift without interruption for a change."

"I work very hard at my job," Xan insisted. "I'm constantly bending over for people."

"You mean bending over backwards," Jacob suggested.

"No, he doesn't," Dominic said.

"Thanks again for giving Michael a chance. Well, a chance at a chance. I think you're going to like him. He's..." Xan stopped for a moment, a smile slowly blooming as he reflected fondly on his houseguest. "He's really nice."

He jogged down the driveway, then waved before getting into his car and taking off, unaware of his parents' identical expressions of astonishment and their burgeoning suspicion that hell was about to freeze over.

"HOW HAVE YOU BEEN ADAPTING to the change?" Becky laughed. "Sorry, that sounds menopausal. How have you been adapting to becoming a vampire?"

As the dog snoozed on the floor by his feet, Michael sipped his tea. He had been so busy worrying about staying alive and—infinitely more gratifying—getting to know Xan that he had yet to stop and think about the drastic change he had undergone. "It's... I don't know how to explain it. I still feel like myself, only... more. Does that make any sense?"

"That makes perfect sense," Becky responded. "Xan told me that this was not a voluntary endeavor."

"No, it wasn't."

"I'm very sorry to hear that. No one should ever be turned without consent."

"Apparently, no one mentioned that to *him*." Michael raised a hand to his chest. "I can feel him... in here. Is that normal?"

"Yes, it is. You'll get used to it. Have you had a chance to explore your new abilities?"

"Not too much," Michael started, his toes playfully grabbing at the mongrel's tail. "I know that I'm stronger. That would have come in handy back in high school. And the healing thing is nice, although I'd prefer not to get hurt in the first place. What else is there? Can I turn into a bat or something? That would be cool."

Becky giggled. "Nothing like that, I'm afraid, though you will be able to fly. It takes a while for some of us, but it will happen. There's also your furry friend here."

Michael glimpsed at the sleeping dog. "What about her? She's just some stray."

"Is she? Some vampires have a special kinship with animals. I think this one is going to serve you well." Becky bent over and rubbed the mutt's back. "Mind control is another thing. I don't imagine that is something you're capable of doing yet, being so young and all, but it's only a matter of time."

So that was how Steven had been able to stop him from struggling before killing him. Michael remembered the helplessness he had felt when his body stopped resisting. It was like an invisible hand had held him down while

Steven tore into his neck and drained him. Now he understood why the vampire had resorted to using corpse blood afterwards to restrain him.

"Mind control only works on humans," he said to himself. "I wasn't human anymore."

"What?"

"Nothing. Why would we even be able to do something like that? To make it easier to hurt people?"

Becky placed her cup of tea on one of Xan's many unpacked boxes. "I can tell you're a sweet bloke, Michael, but you have to understand that this is what we are. Before I met Dominic and Jacob, I did what I needed to do to survive. And yes, that sometimes meant hurting people. I hope you're never forced to make that sort of choice."

What Becky didn't know was that Michael had already been faced with that choice. While he had decided not to kill the dog, it was going to be a long time before he stopped feeling guilty about almost doing it.

"It's not all gloom and doom," Becky promised him. "You now have a front row seat to history in the making. You will get to experience what future generations will only learn about in textbooks. If textbooks even exist in the future."

"I'll also get to see people die."

"There is that," the vampire replied. "That's why I never got too close to humans. Not until Xan came along."

"Why didn't he...?" Michael stopped talking. He had no right to question Xan's life choices.

"Why didn't he choose to be turned?" Becky tucked a curl behind her ear. "If you could go back, would you choose it?"

Michael was stumped. If Steven hadn't attacked him, what would have become of him? As much as he had fantasized about standing up to his father, he knew the sad truth was that he would have continued doing exactly what Hideaki wanted him to do. Chemical Engineering degree, well-paying job, submissive Japanese wife, overachieving children... all of the things he never wanted. But was drinking blood and being restricted to the darkness for the rest of time really a better alternative?

"I don't know."

Becky nodded. "Not such an easy decision, is it? Xan has his reasons for remaining human."

"You would want him to turn?"

"He means the world to me. I'd turn him myself if I could." Becky let out a long breath. "But if he never changes his mind then I'll make the most of the years we have left."

Michael suddenly discovered that he was very much opposed to thinking about Xan in finite terms.

"You like him, don't you?" Becky asked.

"What?" Michael was appalled that she had been able to see right through him. "I've only known him for a week."

Becky placed a sympathetic hand on his back. "When it comes to Xan, sometimes that's all it takes."

XAN'S MIND WAS NOT on work. For once, it had nothing to do with sex.

He busied himself doing what he was being paid to do for a change and resisted checking in with Becky to confirm that everything was going well back at his house. After their earlier conversation, Xan just wanted to know that Michael was okay.

"What's wrong with you?" Ginger asked over the industrial tune that was playing in the background. "You haven't taken a 'break' once tonight."

"You complain when I'm not working. Are you going to complain now that I am?"

"I'm just making sure that you're not sick or anything because you're freaking me out."

Xan gave her a middle finger just in time for Paul to see.

"Is that for me?" he asked.

"Hey." Xan removed some empty glasses from the bar top and grabbed a white towel. "Look, I'm sorry about last week. Something came up at the last minute."

"I noticed. He was cute."

"It wasn't like that," Xan said as he wiped down the bar. "He was in trouble and I was just trying to be helpful."

"You didn't fuck him?"

"No."

"Did you want to?"

The murmuring of the crowd caught Xan's attention. Of course Dominic and Jacob were the reason for the disruption. As the owners of the Rising Sun and essentially vampire royalty, it was only natural—if mildly embarrassing for Xan—that they caused so much commotion whenever they arrived.

Paul looked over his shoulder as they moved through the masses. "They've been here every night this week. What's going on?"

"I don't know." Business ran so smoothly that the couple rarely came to the club more than three times in a given week. Xan assumed that their increased appearances had something to do with the shortage he discovered in Elliot's notes last Friday.

He smirked as Dominic prevented Jacob from heading over to the bar, thus sparing the young man even further embarrassment. Jacob was obviously miffed but followed his lover into the elevator, much to Xan's relief.

"How about a drink?" he asked Paul.

"Sure."

"Make that two. On me."

"You got it." Xan saw that the vampire who sat down beside Paul had a brown left eye and a blue right eye. How neat. "What'll it be?"

"HELLO AGAIN," PAUL said after Xan stepped away to fix their drinks. "Did you ever find what you were looking for?"

Steven observed the human as he joked around with the cute redhead.

"No. But I'm getting closer."

JACOB KICKED REPEATEDLY at the bottom of Elliot's desk like a bored school student. "I was just going to get a drink. I know how *not* to humiliate my kid."

"This from the one who tried to choke someone last month in a dazzling display of customer service," Elliot pointed out while diligently scrolling through old camera footage.

"I didn't try to choke him," Jacob said. "I just threatened to do it because he had his hand down Xan's pants."

"Against Xan's will?" Elliot asked, pushing up his glasses.

"That's irrelevant."

"My apologies for bringing up facts."

"Give up, Elliot." Dominic emerged from the vault with two huge brown satchels stuffed full of cash. "Jacob doesn't take too kindly to reason."

"You'd think he would know this by now." Seeing Dominic's haul, Jacob asked, "How much?"

The vampire set the satchels down on top of the desk. "Enough for a rainy day. Several of them. Vincenzo can help himself to the rest of it if he chooses. We still have plenty of money in the offshore accounts."

Elliot glanced up from the monitor. "That won't appease him."

"No, but it won't hurt."

Tuning them out, Jacob resumed reading over Elliot's distribution proposal. Their already more than generous donations to Tomah Hospital and Consolidated Clinical Laboratories would increase by twenty percent. Most of that would come from their homeless shelter, the Dawson House, which was where they acquired most of their overall stock. In return, Elliot suggested a larger discount on the anticoagulants they needed to keep the blood in a suitable state for drinking. All in all, it didn't seem like too much to ask. Anything more might have resulted in a need to bump up the price of the blood they sold privately. This was something they refused to do for fear of driving vampires to violence against humans. No amount of profit was worth that risk.

"We need to reevaluate the gay blood thing. We shouldn't have to miss out because of donation restrictions. What do you guys think?" When neither Dominic nor Elliot answered him, Jacob looked at the monitor and saw a face he knew. "Is that who I think it is?"

"I'm afraid so," Elliot said.

He rewound the footage and played it again, leaving no doubt of the identity of the one on the screen.

"Shit," Jacob muttered.

"Indeed," Dominic agreed.

They had discovered the blood thief. It was someone whom they never would have guessed.

LATER THAT MORNING, Xan sat on the basement floor next to the air bed he had reinflated since Michael's first attempt left much to be desired. The dog was lying beside him on her back, her legs flailing as he scratched the belly that was growing plump thanks to regular meals.

"She needs a name," he said. "We can't just call her 'girl.'"

"She seems to like it."

Michael sat down beside Xan and joined in on the scratching. Xan tried to imagine something that would distract him from the way that Michael's knee rested against his. He thought back to a couple of hours ago when he was leaving the club and happened upon Brian getting a blowjob in his car. The officer had even been kind enough to invite Xan to join them.

Gripping the edge of his shirt with his non-scratching hand, he nonchalantly tugged it down so that it pooled in his crotch for a camouflaging effect. Visualizing threesomes was definitely distracting but not in the way he intended.

"I talked to my dads yesterday." If anything was guaranteed to kill an erection before it started, it was talking about his parents. "I asked them if they would find work for you. They said that they want to meet you tonight."

Xan raised his head and found Michael studying him, but he wasn't yet sure if it was a good thing or a bad thing.

"And you can keep staying here," he continued. "I own the house so money's not an issue, but if you really want to pay me somehow you can...I don't know... take out the trash or empty the dishwasher or something. If you want. But you don't have to. Say something so I'll shut up."

Xan feared that the vampire was mad at him for taking such unsolicited initiative. He was about to apologize when a hand covered his, the weight of it pressing his palm against the dog's stomach. Digits traced over his skin and down along his fingers until they interlocked. Xan couldn't remember the last time he'd held someone's hand in a non-familial way, or if he'd ever done it at all, and as Michael's thumb stroked the inside of his wrist in a lazy, circular motion, he was amazed at how something that simple could feel so incredibly enjoyable.

Michael spoke up after some time, his voice thick with emotion. "Thank you."

The dog was not nearly as moved since the scratching stopped, and she flipped over and stood up, prying their hands apart in the process. Then she stepped onto the bed and lowered her head onto her paws, staring at Xan and Michael in wide-eyed disappointment.

"Someone's becoming spoiled," Xan said, rising to his feet. "I should get to bed anyway." He didn't want to leave, and judging by the look on Michael's face, he wasn't the only one who felt that way. "Sleep well."

"You too."

Xan left the basement. After double-checking that the front door was locked, he walked through the living room and kitchen, flipping off lights as he went. When he reached his bedroom, he crawled into bed and closed his eyes against the slivers of daylight that peeked in through the curtains. He tried not to think about the way that he could still feel Michael's touch on his skin or the reaction it inspired, both physical and emotional.

Last night, Paul had asked him a question. Did he want to fuck Michael? Oh, yes. Without a doubt.

But now Xan was starting to suspect that he wanted something more than that.

FAMILY MATTERS

CHAPTER 8

"IT JUST DOESN'T MAKE any sense," Jacob said as he slid out of the passenger side of Dominic's black BMW on a windy Sunday night. "There has to be a reason."

Dominic peered at him over the roof of the car. "Someone we trusted stole from us, Jacob. The reason doesn't matter."

Jacob agreed... up to a point. Until finding out the identity of the blood thief, he had been just as adamant as Dominic that the perpetrator paid dearly for taking what was theirs. Now that he knew who it was, he was having a hard time getting into the same spirit of vengeance. He had hoped that the culprit was someone they didn't know who had somehow managed to find a way to slip past the club's security and surveillance. It would have been so much simpler dealing with a stranger. Knowing what he knew now, it wasn't going to be easy to do what might have to be done.

When they reached the front door of a white bungalow, Jacob rang the doorbell. He could tell by the sound of shuffling about that the occupant wasn't the type who handled unannounced arrivals very well.

"Dominic, promise me you won't do anything until we know the whole story."

"I promise."

Jacob felt better having gotten Dominic's word. Anyone who had the misfortune of being on the receiving end of that foreboding stare was right to worry about their continued existence. He lifted his hand to ring again when the door was slowly opened by the one whose well-being depended on whatever unfolded over the next few minutes.

"You know why we're here," he said, lowering his arm.

Ginger faced her employers, her light green eyes filled with fear. "Yeah, I do." She moved aside. "Come in."

MICHAEL TUCKED IN HIS shirt and frowned. Then he pulled it out and frowned some more. Then he started all over again. After the fourth rotation, Xan called him on it.

"What are you doing?"

"I want to look nice," Michael explained as he tucked in his shirt for the fifth time and started pacing around the living room. "I don't want your parents to think that I look like crap."

"They're just making sure that you're not a lunatic. They're not going to care how you look."

"*I* care how I look." Michael stopped moving. "Damn it," he groaned, untucking his shirt again.

Xan got up, much to the chagrin of the mutt that had been using his thigh as a pillow since the start of Michael's fashion crisis. "I'm sure I have something else that'll do."

"You've already done more than enough for me."

"Good grief, Michael. I'm offering you a shirt, not a kidney. Now come on."

Knowing that it was an argument he would never win, Michael followed Xan down the hallway and into his bedroom. Xan had given him a brief tour of the house the evening after bringing him home, but this was the first time that Michael had actually been inside of the room. Aside from the boxes that had yet to be unpacked, it was tidy for a man's bedroom—or his perception of one, thanks to the guys in his old dorm. He followed Xan over to the closet and waited for him to go through his selection of shirts until he settled on a few for the vampire's consideration.

"These are tight on me so they should fit you just fine." Xan presented Michael with his choices, each of them bearing the name of a famous designer on the label. "I'm not saying that you're scrawny or anything like that."

"I prefer *svelte*." Michael inspected the shirts and tried to imagine how he would look in each of them. The black and white one was nice but flashy. The green one was way too preppy. The brown one was brown. He decided on the red plaid button-down since it was more hipster than lumberjack. If that didn't make him look halfway decent, nothing would.

Michael took off his shirt and tried on the other one. When he caught Xan staring at him, he wondered if he should have stepped into the bathroom to change. He hardly knew what to think about anything after last night's spur of the moment hand-holding, and he didn't want to take the chance that he was reading way too much into what might have been nothing more than general politeness in the human's actions.

"Well?" he asked after buttoning up.

Xan nodded. "I like it."

"Thanks." Michael turned his head, needing to look anywhere other than directly at that gorgeous face. "Now if I could just do something about this," he said, tugging at his hair. "It has a mind of its own."

"I've seen worse. You'll see when you meet my dad. Jacob-Dad, not Dominic-Dad."

"Do you call them that?"

"Jacob is Dad. Dominic is Dominic. When I was little, I used to call him... something else."

Michael started to ask what that something else was but then Xan's hand was slowly running over his hair, pushing back the locks that had fallen into his face, and he suddenly forgot how to speak. He froze as fingers gently weaved through black strands and almost jumped right out of his skin when they trailed across his cheek.

The vampire risked a glance at Xan. He didn't dare say or do anything that would put an end to what was happening. Right now, Michael couldn't have cared less about clothes or meeting Dominic and Jacob or whether or not Steven was after him or how he was going to make it on his own. All he cared about was the human gazing down at him like he was the only thing in the world that mattered.

"I'm sorry." Xan's voice was barely above a whisper. "It's just that I've wanted to do that since we met."

Then he kissed him.

"And that."

Michael could feel him hovering, their faces inches apart and their bodies achingly close. He kept his eyes closed and focused on the lingering sensation of the warm lips that had pressed briefly but eagerly against his. How he kept from jumping on Xan right then and there, he would never know.

"We should get going," Xan said, stepping back. "If we don't leave right now, I can't promise that we'll get around to leaving at all."

"Yeah," Michael agreed shakily.

They headed out to the garage. After Michael turned down an invitation to ride on the motorcycle (because the last thing he needed was his crotch anywhere near Xan's ass before facing his parents), they got into his car and took off.

"Are you nervous?" Xan asked.

Michael looked out of the window while thinking about their kiss, his eyes taking in all of the sights of a city coming to life under a blanket of dark sky, as well as the reflection of his own smile.

"Not at all."

IN SPITE OF A WELL-crafted reputation to the contrary, Dominic was not a ruthless vampire. Yes, there were occasions throughout the years that called for him to react violently to a situation, as was sometimes the case given the nature of his profession, but he preferred peaceful resolutions to conflict whenever possible. When it came to breaking his trust—something he did not give to just anyone—a peaceful resolution was not always feasible.

He had expected Ginger to give a long-winded justification of why she needed the blood. Instead, she looked blankly at him and Jacob and admitted her wrongdoing. There were no tears or requests for mercy, just a startlingly candid confession.

That was how Dominic knew she wasn't telling them everything.

"What are you hiding, Ginger?"

"What do you mean?"

"You're neglecting to mention something. Whatever it is, it can't be important enough to risk your life."

The redhead fell silent while weighing her options. Eventually, she walked over to a closed door. "It *is* that important." Ginger opened the door and beckoned. "Come on out."

Dominic didn't know who or what was going to emerge from the room. The last thing he expected to see was a child. Then another. And one more. Three children total.

Vampire children.

"Oh, my God," Jacob whispered.

Having lived for 530 years, there wasn't much that Dominic hadn't seen over the centuries. Still, seeing the three undead little ones—two girls and a boy and none of them older than the physical age of twelve—stunned him greatly. There were unwritten rules among their kind, passed down through the ages. One of the most important of all was that children were *never* to be turned. To inflict that sort of fate onto someone who had barely begun to live was unforgivable.

"It wasn't me," Ginger immediately insisted, putting the accusation to rest before it could surface. She ushered the small vampires over to the couch where they watched Dominic and Jacob with curious eyes. "This is Hannah, Joseph, and Rosamelia."

"We call her Rosie." Joseph clapped a hand over his mouth, appalled at having revealed such top secret information.

Ginger ruffled his hair. "Children, this is Dominic and Jacob. Can you say hello to them?"

Hannah and Joseph complied while Rosie offered a shy wave. She seemed particularly interested in Dominic for reasons he did not know.

"How in the world did this happen?" Jacob asked.

Ginger kneeled down so that she was at eye level with the children. "Go back in the bedroom and wait for me."

"Are we in trouble?" Hannah, the oldest of the trio, asked.

"No, honey. You didn't do anything wrong."

Hannah returned to the bedroom with Joseph in tow. Rosie, on the other hand, came up to Dominic and tapped him lightly on the thigh. "Mr. Dominic?"

"Yes?"

"I like your hair."

Maintaining a calm appearance was difficult in the face of so much cuteness. "Thank you."

Dominic thought that would be the end of it. It wasn't.

"Can I braid it?"

"Rosie, no." Ginger tried to steer the girl toward the bedroom.

"Rosie, yes!" Jacob lifted Rosie onto the couch between him and Dominic. "Now you go ahead and make Mr. Dominic pretty while I talk to Ginger, okay?"

"Jacob..." Dominic was not happy.

"Okay!" Rosie was immensely happy.

Jacob disappeared into the kitchen with Ginger, leaving Dominic captive to the tiny, amateur stylist.

"Finished!" Rosie showed him the result of her efforts, a long black braid that was rather well done. "Do you like it?"

Dominic was reminded of the times when a young Xan would play with his hair, though he had never mastered the art of braiding like Rosie. "I like it very much. You may braid the rest if you want."

"Really?" The young vampire's face brightened. "You're nice, Mr. Dominic."

Dominic turned slightly in his seat, giving her full access to the rest of his hair. "Don't tell anyone."

XAN TRIED NOT TO LAUGH when he introduced Michael to Luca, but the vampire's stupefied expression was too amusing. It wasn't every day that most people met someone almost three times their size.

"Where are they?" he asked.

"Taking care of some business," Luca informed him. "They'll be back soon."

Well, that was disappointing. If Xan had known that Dominic and Jacob weren't even going to be there, he would have waited longer to leave, which would have meant more time alone with Michael to do... whatever things might have come about as a result of their kiss. Things he wanted to explore later in full detail.

"Do you boys want a drink?"

"No, thank you," Michael answered.

"I'm good," Xan replied.

"I'll be in the kitchen if you need me." Luca excused himself, but not before giving Xan a goofy eyebrow wiggle of approval.

"This is a really nice house," Michael said. "You grew up here?"

"We moved here when I was fourteen. Before that we lived on the other side of Harborview. It was a smaller house but equally pretentious." Xan took him by the arm. "Come on, I'll show you around."

After going through all of the rooms on the first floor, Xan led him upstairs. He saved his old bedroom for last. When he heard a loud gasp upon entering the room, he knew that he had done the right thing.

"Get out!" Michael exclaimed when he saw the dresser where a number of Transformers were gathered. "I can't believe you have these."

"The rest are down in the basement," Xan said. "The actual basement, not where my parents sleep. These are just the ones that aren't boxed. I'll move them to my house once I have a place to put all of them."

"You have boxed G1 Transformers?"

"Yeah."

"Which ones?"

"All of them. I'll show them to you later if you want."

Michael steadied himself against the dresser. "I think I'm going to faint."

Xan joined Michael at the dresser, peeking over his shoulder at the figures. "Who's your favorite?"

He expected Michael to say Optimus Prime since that seemed like the most popular choice. But when the vampire leveled a finger at the red and white fighter with the Autobot emblem, he wanted to kiss him all over again, this time for far nerdier reasons.

"I like Jetfire. He's pretty badass."

"Yes, he is."

Xan rested his chin on top of Michael's head, breathing in citrus-scented shampoo. He wrapped his arms around the vampire's waist and pulled him back into his arms, partly to ensure that he remained upright in his awe over being in the same house as such an esteemed collection, and partly because it felt like the right thing to do. Normally, this would have led to a lot of naked fumbling, and with his old bed just a few feet away, the temptation to move things in that direction was strong. However, holding him like this was even better. Xan rarely had the opportunity to do affectionate things *before* having sex with someone, and it was something he did more out of a sense of obligation than anything else. But with Michael, there was no calculation or underlying motive.

He sensed that Michael was about to speak and wondered what the vampire would say. Perhaps it would be some profound observation of their tender moment.

"Soundwave is cool, too. For a Decepticon."

Or perhaps not. Xan grinned into Michael's hair. It wasn't the profound observation he had hoped for, but it was perfect in its own way. Any remaining doubts he had about his feelings for a vampire he just met were completely swept away.

"THEY WERE LOCKED IN a basement with no blood or protection from the sun. According to Hannah, Joseph got burned pretty badly before they understood how much the light could hurt them. They spent days huddled together in the shadows until they finally realized that they were strong enough—and *small* enough—to break through the window and escape."

As Ginger continued telling the story of how a gruesome trail of animal carcasses led to the discovery of three hungry and scared little vampires one year ago, Jacob slumped against the counter, trying to take it all in.

"Who turned them?"

"They wouldn't tell me. I think they were afraid that I would try to give them back. After a while, I stopped asking."

Jacob sighed and pinched the bridge of his nose. Transitioning from living to dead was hard enough for an adult, and it took years for some vampires to adjust. The pain of death, the agony of rigor mortis, and the overpowering thirst for blood... those were things that no child should ever have to go through. Jacob didn't know what kind of monster would do that to three random children of three different races for seemingly no reason, but if he ever found out, they were going to suffer tremendously. "Why didn't you tell us?"

"Because I didn't know what you would do. There are vampires out there who would have killed them without hesitation for what they are. I couldn't take the chance that you or Dominic felt the same way."

"So instead you stole from us."

"Whoever did this to them is still out there, Jacob. I didn't want to draw attention to myself by buying way more blood than one vampire would ever need. You guys know where every drop of blood in this city goes. The club overage was the only way I could get some without getting caught, and it worked until now."

"And you were just going to accept whatever punishment you received?" Jacob asked. "What if Dominic had..." Rethinking his words, he tried again. "What if something had happened to you?"

"They survived for almost two years before I found them. They would have been okay. That's all that matters to me. Kill me if you have to, but please don't hurt them."

"Oh, shut up. No one is going to kill you." Jacob brought out his phone. After a few swipes of the finger, he held it to his ear. "Hey, Tuck. It's Jacob. Listen, I need you to do something for me..."

BY THE TIME JACOB AND Ginger returned to the living room, Dominic's hair was done in dozens of braids. The vampire looked at his partner and his employee and warned, "Not one word."

Ginger kept her mouth shut, although it wasn't easy. Jacob also kept quiet about Dominic's new hairdo, but that didn't stop him from using his phone to snap a few pictures for future bribing and teasing.

"Do you like it?" Rosie asked them.

"It's very pretty." Jacob held up his hands when Dominic shot him a death glare. "She asked."

"Rosie, honey." Ginger paused to get herself under control before Dominic was tempted to kill her for other reasons. "Go wait for me with Hannah and Joseph. I'll be there in a minute."

"Okay." The little girl tugged on Dominic's sleeve. "Mr. Dominic, will you come play with me again?"

"We'll see," Dominic answered, knowing full well that he would. "Now run along."

He was caught off guard by the suddenness and strength of the child's embrace. After she left, Dominic regarded the two vampires. His attempt at seriousness was negated by his very pretty hair. "Well?"

"From now on, Tuck is going to give Ginger as much blood as she needs to keep the little ones fed," Jacob explained. "The shelter's doing well so we can spare it. Ginger has also offered to pay us back for what she took from the club stock."

"Assuming I'm not fired," Ginger added.

After a quick look at Jacob to confirm that the decision was for the best, he addressed Ginger's concern. "I suppose you can't pay your debt if you aren't employed," he conceded. "Besides, Alexander can barely do his own work, let alone pick up the slack for your absence."

"Speaking of Xan, we need to get going," Jacob said. "I'm sure he's at the house by now. I'll fill you in on the rest in the car."

Ginger accompanied them to the door. "I'm really sorry about this. I wasn't trying to screw you guys over. I was just trying to take care of my kids."

Jacob placed a hand on her shoulder. "I think we know a thing or two about that. But the next time you need something, no matter what it is, *tell us.*"

They left the house and got back into the car. This time, Jacob drove so that Dominic could undo what Rosie had done. He listened carefully as Jacob relayed the story of the three young vampires and how Ginger had found them.

"Who would do such a thing to a child?" he asked as he finished with one braid and started on another.

"Maybe your new admirer can give you the details."

With everything Dominic had going on already, the last thing he needed was one more thing to do. And even if he was somehow able to find out the identity of the vampire who turned Rosie and the others, it wouldn't change anything for them. They were trapped in their youth, and nothing but death would ever free them. Ginger had been right to worry about what Dominic and Jacob would have done. Had they never experienced parenthood for themselves, their reaction to the children might have confirmed her worst fear. A brutal response but ultimately a courtesy, a release from the imprisonment of their fate.

"Maybe." Dominic noticed that Jacob was smiling. "What?"

"I was just thinking about how Xan used to play with your hair."

"I thought of that as well."

"You were so cute back there with Rosie."

"Don't call me cute."

"Precious?"

"Jacob."

"*Adorable.*"

Dominic gave up. "Don't tell anyone."

"I won't," Jacob promised.

"Thank you."

When they got home, Jacob kept his word and refrained from telling Luca and Xan about Dominic's accidental playdate. Too bad he didn't promise not to show them the pictures he took.

WHEN IT BECAME OBVIOUS that neither Michael nor the human, Xan, were going to show up at the club anytime soon, Steven took Paul up on his offer for company. After a week of watching and waiting, he had become highly annoyed with having to chase down what was rightfully his. Their brief, over-the-clothes romp in Paul's car the week before was messy fun, but tonight he needed a good hard fuck to alleviate some of his stress.

After arriving at Paul's place, Steven removed his shoes and accepted the drink that was poured for him. He wasn't in the mood to be social, but he would tolerate it for as long as he could.

"I noticed the way that you were looking at Xan last night," Paul said, sitting down beside him. "Are you interested in him?"

Interested in Xan? That was laughable. Steven preferred that his human companions weren't quite so willing. And even if he had been interested, hurting the son of the two most powerful vampires around wasn't a good way to stay alive. Given his love for torture, Steven wanted to stay away from Dominic and Jacob as long as he could. "No, but he's preventing me from taking back what's mine."

"This 'thing' you lost wouldn't happen to be that cute vampire he left with last Friday, would it?"

"That's the one."

"You turned him."

"I did."

"Was he your first?"

"Not my first but definitely my favorite." The more Steven thought about Michael, the more irritated he became. It was one thing to tire of his toys and discard them when he saw fit. That this particular toy took it upon himself to escape aggravated Steven to no end. He had plans for their reunion. Sharp, *painful* plans.

And if Xan got in the way of those plans, Steven knew better than to physically hurt him. But if the human happened to hurt *himself* because of some unseen influence...

He finished his drink and set the glass aside. Then he turned to face Paul, one brown eye and one blue eye trained intently on him. "I'd like to fuck you now."

Paul did not object. Steven followed him into the bedroom and roughly pushed him onto the bed while, at that very moment, tales of his abuse were being shared with the two vampires he had hoped to avoid.

LATER, PAUL STEPPED out of the shower and wrapped a towel around his waist. He would dry off momentarily, but first he had a call to make.

He sat down on the bed, pushing back the sheets that had come loose while Steven had his way with him. While he wasn't normally the bottoming kind, the soreness from being fucked was already gone, and he felt no discomfort at all. One of the many perks of being a vampire.

Sweeping back wet black locks, Paul grabbed his phone and found the number he wanted to call. Just when he thought that he was going to have to leave a message, the sensual voice he loved so much spoke into his ear.

"Hello, Paolo."
"Hello, Vincenzo."

FAMILY MATTERS

CHAPTER 9

"WILL YOU SETTLE DOWN?" Luca regarded the fidgety young man sitting across from him at the kitchen table with a mixture of amusement and concern. "They're just getting to know him. His life isn't in danger."

Xan raised a brow. "Have you *met* my dad?"

"I highly doubt that his life is in danger," Luca amended. "Relax. Michael wasn't even this nervous, and he's the one who has every reason to be."

Xan wanted to believe that he had something to do with that lack of nervousness, courtesy of their earlier bonding over shirts and Transformers. "What do you think of him?" he asked his former guardian.

"He seems like a nice boy," Luca replied.

"He is."

"And he's cute."

Xan smiled. "He *is.*"

He kept on smiling as Luca moved over to the counter to top off his coffee. When the big man sat down again, Xan divulged something that he had only come to terms with himself a few hours ago.

"I like him, Luca."

"I can tell."

"You don't think that's weird?"

Luca frowned at him over his cup. "Why would that be weird?" he inquired before taking a sip.

"Because I'm not the 'bring a boy home' kind of guy." Xan smirked. "At least not to meet my parents."

"There's a first time for everything. If seeing this boy, or dating him, or whatever you kids call it makes you happy, then Godspeed."

"What about you? Are you seeing anyone these days?"

"Not lately. Not wanting to have sex isn't exactly a selling point."

"Have you ever thought about, you know, interest specific dating sites or something like that?"

"You mean lack of interest specific, don't you?" Luca grinned and took another sip of coffee. "I have, but it's not something I feel the need to rush into. Being single suits me just fine right now."

For one who loved sex so much, Xan couldn't fathom Luca's lack of desire for it. His asexuality was rarely a topic of conversation, but since he brought it up, Xan decided to ask about something that had bothered him for years.

"Are you ever... disgusted by me?"

"What do you mean?"

"Because... you know..."

When Luca realized what Xan was implying, he crossed over to the other side of the table with a speed that belied his size and wrapped a meaty arm around Xan's neck. "Of course not, silly boy. I don't give a damn what you do with your dick."

Xan struggled to breathe as knuckles grazed his fauxhawk. "Thanks, Luca," he managed.

After a while, and thankfully before Xan started to fear for his consciousness, Luca planted a kiss on top of his head and let him go. "Are you hungry?"

"I could eat. It wouldn't really feel like a visit unless food was being shoved in my face."

"Dominic and I are Italians. It's what we do." Luca went over to the refrigerator and began rooting around inside of it. "How about some prosciutto and provolone?"

"Sure."

Xan felt like a kid again, waiting eagerly at the kitchen table while his beast of a babysitter made him a sandwich, although a prosciutto and provolone panini was a far cry from his childhood diet of peanut butter and jelly sandwiches sans crust.

They discussed a number of things as Luca busied himself at the stove, like drunken closet adventures (because Xan refused to let him live that down) and the Old Man's travels. Luca had phoned him regularly since he departed to see the world, and they even had a bet to see how long it would take for Xan to destroy his former home.

"Jerks," Xan mumbled when told about that.

Despite stuffing his face, he was still concerned about Michael and whatever was taking place behind the closed door of his parents' office. He hadn't yet heard any screams or shouts or general chaos so that was a good sign. And Jacob was usually on his best—or at least *better*—behavior when Dominic was around. Maybe he was getting all worked up over nothing.

Then Dominic came out of the office with his phone to his ear, visibly troubled.

Dominic was never visibly *anything*.

SOON THERE WOULD BE no place where Steven could hide from the couple that was now determined to find him. Michael thought that Xan had been exaggerating about the magnitude of his fathers' authority. After telling them about Steven, he now suspected that Xan had understated it.

"Should I be worried?" he asked Jacob after Dominic left the office.

"Not anymore."

The vampire's words were kind, but Michael could feel the anger coming off of him like heat from a fire. "I'm sorry. I know that all of this was Xan's idea, but I don't want to cause any trouble."

"You're not the one causing it." Jacob rounded the desk and leaned against the front of it, regarding the young vampire. "If this Steven is attacking innocent humans... well, you can understand why we would have a problem with that."

Michael nodded. While it appeared that Xan was safe from harm, he was still a human being. As long as vampires like Steven existed, his well-being would never be fully guaranteed.

"It's a horrible thing, having your life stolen from you," Jacob continued. "I'm guessing Xan told you we have that in common."

"Yeah, he did."

"If I may offer some advice on the matter, accept it and move forward. You don't want to let that sort of thing eat away at you."

"Do you—never mind." Michael closed his mouth in a hurry.

"Do I what? Let it eat away at me?"

"It's none of my business."

Jacob waved his hand at that and took a seat in the empty chair next to Michael. "The world was a different place when I was turned. For all I knew, it was never going to change. I would have rather died than spend the rest of existence as someone's property. I *tried* to die." He looked at the ring on his finger. "But then Dominic found me and... here we are."

Michael had a strong feeling that this was something few others knew. "You didn't have to tell me that."

"I know." Jacob smiled. "What are your plans for the future? You have a whole lot of it ahead of you."

"I'm still getting used to everything. Sometimes certain things hit me out of the blue, like how I'll never eat again or see a sunrise." Michael paused, blinking into space as the reality of his condition struck him all over again. "I'm never going to see a sunrise again. Not the real thing, anyway. If I'd known what was going to happen to me, I would have paid more attention to them."

"I've always preferred the darkness myself so I can't say that I miss sunrises or daytime in general. But sometimes I do miss food. There are so many things I never had the opportunity to try." Jacob crossed his legs. "One of our shelter employees misses food so much that he chews gum. I've never tried it myself, but it seems to work for him."

"A vampire who chews gum," Michael mused.

"Weird, huh?"

"It's definitely different. As far as future plans go... one thing I need to do is see my father."

"You don't sound very excited about that."

"We've never been close. I could vanish into thin air for all he cares as long as it doesn't shame him in some way."

"What about your mother?"

"She died right after I was born. My father never remarried."

"I'm sorry," Jacob said. "Speaking as a father myself, you might be wrong about yours not caring. Then again, speaking as a son, you might be right." He chuckled wryly. "But that's a story for another time. Now tell me, Michael, do you know how to mix drinks?"

AFTER HEARING XAN'S account of the vampire with the mismatched eyes and confirming his identity with Ginger, who had also served him, Dominic called Elliot to have him review the camera footage from the past week. Although he hid it well, as he did most things, he was livid at the thought of this Steven having been anywhere near his son.

"I know you just returned to work, but I want you to stay home until this is resolved," Dominic informed Xan. "I don't suppose I can talk you into staying here?"

"And stick Michael with the two of you? No way." Xan cast a concerned look in the direction of the office. "Will you go back in there and make sure that Dad isn't being Dad?"

"I'm sure they're fine," Dominic insisted. "I'm far more worried about you and Michael being alone in that house with no way to fend for yourselves. I don't think you understand how fortunate you are that this vampire chose not to come after Michael at any point over the past week." He folded his arms on the tabletop as Luca handed him a glass of Chivas Regal. "Since I correctly presumed that you would not tolerate having your parents protect you, I have already arranged for someone else to guard you for the rest of the night."

"Who?" Xan wanted to know. "Oh, no. It's not Becky, is it? She'll drive me crazy."

"It's not Rebecca."

"Then who is it?"

Right on cue, Demetrio stormed into the kitchen. "Who's fucking with my nephew and why haven't we killed him yet?"

Dominic could only roll his eyes.

Demetrio ruffled Xan's hair and sat down next to him. "Who threatened you?"

"No one threatened *me*," Xan explained. "It's my friend. The one being threatened, I mean."

"Your friend?" Demetrio perked up. "Is he a friend or *a friend*?"

That was Dominic's breaking point. "Demetrio!"

"Would you like a drink, Demetrio?" Luca asked suddenly, attempting to defuse a potentially hazardous situation.

"Sure."

"Anything in particular?"

"Surprise me, beefcake."

Dominic was annoyed at having to rely on his twin, but since Demetrio was the only other vampire in the family who equaled him in strength, he didn't have much of a choice. "I know I shouldn't have to stress the importance of this situation to you, but since it's you..."

"You don't have anything to worry about, little brother. When it comes to looking out for this kid, I'm all business." Demetrio proceeded to prove this by giving Xan a noogie.

"Not again," Xan groaned.

Dominic sipped his drink and pushed his jealousy aside, as he often did whenever he saw his brother and son interacting so cheerfully. He never wanted to think that Xan had ever wished for him to be more expressive, but during times like these, it was hard to tell.

"What's going on in here?" Jacob asked as he entered the kitchen with Michael. When he spotted Demetrio lovingly assaulting Xan, he glanced at Dominic. "What did I miss?"

Instead of answering his lover, Dominic finished his drink and helped himself to the one that Luca made for Demetrio. He could think of nothing to say about his brother right now that wouldn't trigger an argument.

Upon noticing Michael, Demetrio released his nephew. "Is this the friend? He's cute."

"Um, yeah, that's Michael," Xan said, attempting to discourage the vampire's ogling. "Michael, this is my uncle, Demetrio."

Dominic could tell that the boy was trying to understand how someone with the exact same face behaved so differently. It was a reaction he recognized all too well.

As Demetrio boldly invaded Michael's personal space and started asking him a thousand questions, Xan tried to come between them and turn Demetrio's attention elsewhere. While that was happening, Jacob sat down in the seat vacated by his son.

"Why is your brother in our kitchen nagging that poor kid?"

"I'll explain it later," Dominic answered wearily. "For now, just enjoy the show."

And what a show it was, with Demetrio now giving Michael all the details about castrated singing vampires he wanted to have sex with.

"Another drink, Dominic?" Luca offered.

"Yes, please... On second thought, just bring me the bottle."

AFTER ANOTHER UNSATISFACTORY night—aside from getting laid—Steven was in a foul mood. He had been tempted to throw caution to the wind and look for Xan's house; with his blood running through Michael's veins, he was confident that he would have had no trouble finding it. But because he was cruel and not crazy, he decided instead to lure an unsuspecting human down to the basement and take out his frustrations the fun way.

Steven ignored the doorbell. The last thing he felt like doing was entertaining his ass-kissing cronies. What started as a union formed out of a mutual appreciation for violence and misadventure had soured over the years. He only tolerated them now because they were so adept at dealing with whatever was left over from his "dates," which spared him the trouble of getting his own hands bloody after the fact. When the gentle chimes turned into a barrage of loud knocks, he had no choice but to answer the door. The houses in his neighborhood were spread out, but he couldn't chance calling attention to his home with a body in the basement.

"Goddamn it." He got up and prepared to deal with his uninvited guests. "I'm not in the fucking mood, assholes," he growled as he opened the door.

"That's too bad," Paul said.

"What the hell?" Steven blinked at the vampire he had fucked earlier that night. "What are you doing here? How did you even know where to find me?"

Paul came inside without waiting to be asked. "There's no time to go into that right now. I need you to come with me. My master wants to see you."

"What? Why would I do that?"

"Because every vampire in Erie County will be looking for you very soon, if they aren't already," Paul told him. "Michael told Dominic and Jacob what you did to him. They also found out that you've been to their club, the very same club where their human son works. It's no wonder they're in such a hurry to find you."

"But I don't want anything to do with their whore of a son."

"That doesn't matter. They're not the kind of guys who take chances when it comes to Xan. Plus they now know that you're very much into torturing, killing, and turning humans. I can't imagine that went over well with them." Paul inhaled deeply, smelling blood and death in the air. "I take it you didn't feel like turning this one?"

"Shut up." Agitated, Steven ran his fingers through his dark blond hair. "Who is this master you mentioned?"

"Vincenzo Castigliane."

"Bullshit," Steven whispered, which was just about all he could do after hearing that name.

If Dominic and Jacob were vampire royalty, then Vincenzo Castigliane was a god. Steven didn't keep up with the goings-on of his kind, but even he had heard stories about the vampire. He had no real reason to believe that Paul was lying; only a fool with a death wish would fabricate that sort of association. If he truly was being summoned by one of the oldest and most powerful vampires in the world, then that could not end well for him. Not at all. Not ever.

For the first time in his life, Steven was genuinely afraid. "What does he want with me?"

"He wants to save you." Paul wiped a smear of dried blood from Steven's chin. "If you want to live to see another night, I strongly suggest that you let him."

CHAPTER 10

AS DEMETRIO PLAYED video games in the spare bedroom, Xan and Michael sat in the living room and watched Sigourney Weaver destroy a bunch of aliens with extreme prejudice.

"Who would win in a fight between Ellen Ripley and Sarah Connor?" Michael asked.

"Aw, man." Xan took a swig of his Brooklyn Lager. "Tough question."

"You have to pick one."

Xan propped his foot on the edge of the sofa and sat back, his shoulder and arm resting against Michael. "It depends on which movies you're talking about."

"*Aliens* and *Terminator 2*."

"You're killing me."

"I know. Now choose."

"I guess if you held a gun to my head, I'd go with Ripley."

"Why?"

"Because she didn't need Arnold's help."

"Good point."

Xan took another drink and almost choked when he felt a finger tracing along the black tribal design etched onto his forearm.

"Sorry," Michael said, withdrawing his hand. "I just really like your tattoos."

"It's fine. You can touch me whenever you want." Realizing how that sounded, Xan quickly corrected himself. "I meant *them*. You can touch *them* whenever you want. But since they're on me, I guess you would be touching me anyway, so... yeah. I swear I'm usually better at this."

"If you're saying that your rambling is my fault, I'm flattered."

They smiled awkwardly at each other. Xan wanted to kiss him so badly that he couldn't stand it any longer. Sure, his uncle was in the next room, but what were the odds that he would interrupt them at that exact moment?

Pretty high, as it turned out.

"I can make my character run over pedestrians and screw hookers in this game!" Demetrio loudly proclaimed as he entered the living room. "What a world we live in."

Xan wanted to be annoyed, but the look of glee on the vampire's face did not allow it. "Knock yourself out, Uncle Demetrio. Just don't forget that you're here to protect us."

"I can join you right there on the sofa if you're so worried about my ability to keep you safe."

"Go play."

"That's what I thought." Demetrio returned to his game, leaving Xan and Michael to their movie.

"If he and Dominic weren't twins, I would never believe that they were related," Michael said.

"I hear that a lot." Using his toes, Xan stroked the leg of the dog that slept at his feet. He hadn't yet decided if she had sensed that Demetrio was harmless or was just the worst guard dog ever. "So Dominic and Dad were cool with you? No threats of violence or waving stakes around or anything like that?"

"No. Dominic was kind of hard to read, but I don't think he hated me."

"That's just how he is. Once you get to know him, he's... well, he's *still* hard to read. But underneath it all, he's really nice. He just doesn't want anyone to know."

"Is there a reason why they don't use last names?"

"Besides the fact that everyone knows who they are without them?" Xan finished his beer and placed the bottle on the floor. "Dominic took his maker's name, Castigliane, around the time he was turned, then some shit happened between them so he dropped it. I don't know what the shit was, exactly, but it was bad enough for him to never even want to *say* the name. If it wasn't for my uncle, I would have probably never known it at all. And the only surname my dad was ever given was from the family that owned him. Can't really blame him for not wanting to keep it."

"Where did your last name come from?"

Xan scrunched up his face. He had hoped Michael would never ask about that. "Dad was a fan of a popular game show host from the eighties."

"I feel like I should know who you're talking about," Michael said as he tapped the side of his beer bottle. "Dawson... game show host... it sounds familiar."

Xan tried to think of something that would jog the vampire's memory. "*Running Man*."

Michael's face lit up. "Oh, yeah! You were named after *him*?"

"Yep. Alexander Richard Dawson. You can go ahead and laugh now."

"I'm not laughing," Michael insisted while laughing. "I'm sorry. Honestly though, that's not so bad."

"You're the only person who knows that outside of my family."

"Thank you for telling me."

"It's not a big deal."

Except it *was* a big deal. Xan had never opened himself up to another guy like this before, let alone someone he recently met. Out of all the other opportunities he'd had in the past to have more than just sex with someone, he never once felt the desire to do so until now. Whatever the reason, Michael was the one. Maybe not *the* one, but he was definitely someone special enough to rise above the sea of other men who had vied for Xan's heart along with his body.

They continued watching the movie, drinking beer, and commenting on the grossness of slimy aliens. When the sun was less than an hour from rising, Demetrio informed them that Steven still had not been found. While the general search was being called off until sundown, Dominic enlisted the aid of a few human police officers, including Brian Goodridge, to use the advantage of daylight to check into a few leads he had gathered during the night.

"And I'm going home," Demetrio concluded. "Unless we're having a slumber party?"

"Goodbye, Uncle Demetrio."

"Bye, kids. *Have fun*."

Xan locked the door after he left, then turned around to face Michael. They were finally alone. And they couldn't wait any longer.

They met each other halfway, their lips colliding in an enthusiastic kiss. Xan moaned as Michael's tongue slid into his mouth and again when something hard slid against his thigh. He couldn't remember the last time he was so undone over a kiss, and he pulled away, not because he wanted to, but because of the very real possibility of ruining his shorts.

"I've been dying to do that all night," he whispered in the vampire's ear. "I would invite you to my room if the sun wasn't coming up."

"There's always my place, if you don't mind an air bed."

Xan was so turned on that he wouldn't have cared if all they had at their disposal was a concrete slab. "Works for me."

"WELL?" JACOB ASKED after Dominic finished speaking with Demetrio.

"Alexander is fine," Dominic responded. "Michael is fine. And my brother is an imbecile, but also fine."

Jacob let his head fall back against the headboard and tried to relax, a tall order when he felt so helpless now that the night was coming to an end. Perhaps Brian or the other human cops would find Steven's house, if Michael's description of the area where he had been held was accurate. But with so much time having already passed, Jacob was worried that Steven had somehow evaded them. To think that bastard had been right there, at their club, under their noses, *talking to their son...*

Dominic turned off the lights and curled his body around Jacob's. "I must admit that I wasn't expecting you to get along so well with Michael."

"He's a nice kid who ended up in a shitty situation. I can't hate him for that."

"And if a romantic relationship develops between him and Alexander?"

"I can't say that I will ever be completely comfortable with the idea of Xan being with a vampire," Jacob started, frowning into the darkness. "But he thought enough about this one to introduce him to us so I don't want to be a jerk about it."

"You just said that Michael was nice."

"He *is* nice. But he's still a vampire."

"So are we."

"We're also Xan's parents," Jacob argued. "I would stake myself before I hurt him. So would you."

Dominic nodded against his leg. "Try to get some rest," he said as he tugged on Jacob's pajama top. "Officer Goodridge will call if there is anything to report before tonight."

"Brian Goodridge. Now there's a nice, *human* guy. I wouldn't mind at all if Xan wanted to go out with him."

"You wouldn't feel the same way if you witnessed some of their very public parking lot performances."

"I swear to God, we'd have about fifty grandchildren by now if he liked women."

"At least."

"Oh well." Jacob let Dominic drag him down in the bed. "Like I always say, whatever makes him happy."

AND RIGHT NOW, XAN was *extremely* happy.

After stripping off Michael's shirt and pushing him down on the air bed, he spent a few blissfully drawn-out minutes delighting in the soft skin under his fingers. He paid extra special attention to Michael's tattoo, tracing along the dragon's colorful design and loving the way it caused the body beneath him to shudder.

"Why did you decide to get a dragon?" he asked.

"I wanted to piss off my dad."

"Did it?"

"I never showed him." Michael hissed when Xan's fingers closed on his nipple. "But that was only part of the reason. It's actually something I drew years ago."

"You draw?"

"I used to."

"Will you draw something for me?"

Michael's hands ran along Xan's shoulders, following the maze of tattoos down to a sculpted chest and then over his stomach. He grabbed him by the hips and pushed up, rubbing against him. "What do you want?"

"A raven."

"Poe?"

"It's my favorite animal. But also that."

"I'll do it, but it won't be good. I'm out of practice."

Xan looked at Michael and found him staring back in a way that made him ache inside and out. "I'm sure it'll be fine."

He bent forward and kissed him, his pierced tongue exploring every inch of Michael's mouth. Xan then moved down the vampire's lean body, his lips and tongue and teeth teasing the skin in his path as Michael groaned and clutched his shoulders. With unsteady hands, the young man pulled off Michael's shorts and tossed them aside. After taking a minute to memorize his perfect, naked body, Xan took him into his mouth, inch after inch sliding along his tongue until he could take in no more.

"God, Xan," Michael whimpered, pulling on Xan's hair. "*Fuck.*"

Xan did his best to keep up with Michael's frantic thrusts between his lips. He glanced up and saw the vampire's head thrown back, his eyes closed, and his back arched. He heard the cries of pleasure that grew stronger with each passing second. Then, finally, he felt Michael's cock throb against his tongue, spurting into his mouth, filling it.

Michael let go of Xan's hair and fell back against the bed, shaking all over. With his own state of need at a fever pitch, Xan sat up on his knees and pushed his shorts down as far as they would go. He spat into his hand, wrapped it around his cock, and started stroking.

After so much agonizing buildup, Xan was already close. When Michael favored him with a lustful gaze and parted his legs ever so slightly, *inviting* the young man to make a mess of him, he lost it. With one last push into his slick fist and a throat-rending cry, Xan came all over Michael's chest and stomach. He then flopped down beside the vampire, trembling and gasping for air.

"That was..." Michael tried to think of the right word to describe the experience. All he could come up with was, "*Damn.*"

"Yeah. Very damn."

Xan wanted to kiss him again, but he doubted that Michael would care for the taste. Michael proved him wrong by kissing him just as thoroughly as he did earlier.

"You can stay if you want," he offered afterwards, bashfully looking away. "I know this can't be as comfortable as your bed, but I just thought I'd throw it out there."

"Okay, I'll stay."

Xan felt that peculiar ache again when Michael smiled at him. Only this time, without the hindrance of a hard-on, it was different. Purer.

They went into the bathroom to clean up, and then let the dog into the basement. After that, they resumed their discussion about badass fictional females:

"I hear what you're saying, Xan, but Sarah Connor held her own against a T-1000."

"Ripley bitch-slapped a Queen, Michael. *A Queen.*"

"Who would win in a fight between a T-1000 and a Xenomorph Queen?"

And a new debate was born.

It raged on until they fell asleep in each other's arms with a mutt lodged between them.

STEVEN HAD NO IDEA where he was. One of the conditions of going with Paul was that he had to be blindfolded. It made perfect sense that a vampire like Vincenzo would take measures to keep his exact location under wraps, but Steven still found it worrisome. He was alive, though. That was the only thing he cared about.

From what he could gather after Paul drove him in a roundabout way to their destination, he was on an underground level of a large building of some sort. A hotel, he imagined. The room he was in had no furniture other than a single chair. This was not promising.

Steven checked his watch. It was just after ten in the morning. For about the hundredth time since Paul left him, he was tempted to try the door and see what was beyond it or if it was even unlocked at all. But his fear once again trumped all else and he opted to remain put. As he thought about all the ways he planned to make Michael pay for his current dilemma, the door opened and Paul walked in, followed by two fierce-looking and heavily armed vampires dressed in black combat fatigues.

"I'm sorry for the delay. Are you okay?"

"I'm fine." Steven stared anxiously at the guards standing by the open door. "What the fuck is going on?"

"A very good question, though crudely worded." The voice that responded was deep, husky, and *terrifying*.

Consumed with panic, Steven looked to the floor, catching only a glimpse of a black suit when Vincenzo Castigliane stepped into the doorway. But even though he couldn't see the vampire, he could *feel* him, his aura exuding a power thousands of years in the making. The very atmosphere in the room seemed to thicken upon his arrival. Steven had never felt anything like it.

"You have captured the attention of my firstborn," Vincenzo began. "This is not good for you."

"No," Steven nervously agreed.

"My Domenico is reluctant to accept that some vampires want to embrace their true nature. He has been blinded by years of profiting from the domestication of our kind."

Steven froze as a pair of black Oxfords came into his view.

"Some call you a monster, but I disagree," Vincenzo continued. "You are simply doing what you were born to do."

Another step. Then another. Each one closing the gap between them. Steven kept his focus on the floor, rejecting what his peripheral vision attempted to reveal. "Are you..." He swallowed hard and tried again, willing his voice not to falter. "Are you going to kill me?"

"I have plans for you, Steven Middleton. Death is not one of them."

Vincenzo reached out to him. Steven noticed a very old ring on his right middle finger.

"Show me your face, child," the vampire demanded. "And I will show you mine."

Steven allowed the fingers under his chin to lift up his head. He looked Vincenzo in the eyes for the first time.

And then he screamed.

FAMILY MATTERS

CHAPTER 11

"IT FEELS WEIRD TO DRINK blood at the kitchen table." Michael swirled the warm liquid inside the mug cradled in his hands. "Or at any table for that matter. I guess I'll get used to it."

"It's no weirder than eating breakfast at sundown," Xan said as he searched his bowl for any chocolate-flavored flakes that might have escaped him. "You'll fit right in with everyone else on Friday."

"What's happening on Friday?"

Xan scooped up one last flake. "Family dinner. We usually have it at my parents' house, but I said I'd have it here since I blew off last Friday. Which reminds me, I need to finish unpacking by then. Damn it."

"Do you want me around for that?"

"Why wouldn't I?"

"I don't want you to feel like you have to include me because I'm staying here. I don't mind hanging out in the basement. Your old vampire friend left some pretty good books down there."

"If you don't want to join us, that's up to you."

"I want to," Michael admitted.

"And I want you to. Problem solved." Xan ate the remaining flake and verified that it was the last one short of pouring himself another bowl of cereal—something he had not yet ruled out. His face grew warm as he remembered everything they did to each other that morning, which was not a good idea if he wanted to leave the table without any telltale protrusions. "We need to figure this out," he said, pushing the bowl aside and grabbing a glass of orange juice.

"Figure what out?"

"You and me and whatever this is between us. This is the first time I've ever eaten breakfast with someone I was naked with the night before. Or the day before. Or... the same day. You know what I mean. Anyway, I'm not all that sure about what happens next."

"Normally you just fuck them and leave?"

"Or they fuck me and leave, yeah." Xan took a sip of juice to hide his amusement. The vampire was obviously envisioning something that he would get to experience for himself soon enough. "With you, it's different."

"Why?"

"I like you."

"Why?"

"I can be myself with you. I'm myself with other guys to a point, but it's not like I can lure them in with deep, meaningful conversations about video games and Terminators and stuff."

"So you like me because you don't have to hide the fact that you're a huge nerd."

"I'm not a nerd," Xan replied indignantly. "I'm a geek... with some nerd tendencies."

Michael snorted into his mug. "My mistake."

"I don't know where we go from here. You're already living here so it sort of feels like we've skipped a few steps in the process."

"Would it be easier if I left?"

"I don't want you to leave. I'm just not sure how it's supposed to work *because* you're living here. Some couples are together for years before they take that leap."

"... Are we a couple?"

Xan thought about it for a moment. "I don't know. Do you want to be a couple?"

"Do you?"

"I asked you first."

"Shit."

They shared a nervous laugh over the exchange, which, at least for Xan, felt like something straight out of middle school.

"I've only had two boyfriends in twenty-three years," Michael said. "And I never lived with either of them."

"That's still two more than I've ever had so you're the expert."

"Well…" Michael set down his mug. "Why don't we just take it night by night and see what happens?"

"Are we still going to get naked with each other?"

"As often as possible."

"Sounds like a plan." Xan flinched as his canine guest decided to use his foot as a chew toy. "Have you come up with a name for her yet?"

"How about D-O-G?"

"How about no? Just say the first female name that pops into your head."

"Xan, wait—"

"One, two, three, go!"

"Agnes!"

Xan wrinkled his nose. "*That* was the first name that came to you?"

Now it was Michael's turn to be indignant. "Yeah, so what?"

"That's an old lady name." Xan looked at the dog for confirmation. She raised her head briefly as if to let them know that she didn't give two shits what they called her as long as they kept her supplied with food and scratches. "How about Aggie?" he suggested, scratching her back.

"That's like the sound someone makes when they're hacking up something."

"Like Agnes is so much better?"

"Aggie it is."

HAVE STEVEN. MEET MIDNIGHT at the Rising Sun.

After reading the text message for the fourth time and hoping that it had changed since the first three times he read it, Dominic tossed his phone on top of the bed and stepped inside the basement's walk-in closet in search of a different shirt. Once again, he cursed the technology that allowed Vincenzo to contact him so easily.

"I know that someone must have informed him we were looking for Steven. What I don't know is how he managed to locate him so quickly." After selecting a white dress shirt similar to the one he had on, he exited the closet. "You knew nothing about this?"

Demetrio rarely had a chance to see where his brother went to ground, and he paused to appreciate a grainy photo of Dominic and Jacob that was taken in the late 1800s—the first picture they had ever taken together. "No. Even if I did, you know damn well I can't keep a secret from you. Last I knew, he was going to remain in Texas until he saw you next week."

"Why was he in Texas to begin with?"

"Because everything is bigger there? How the hell should I know?" Demetrio sat down on the bed. "Maybe if you stopped shutting him out, you would have a better idea about what he was up to. God knows you're the only one he's ever allowed to have full access."

"I broke that link for a very good reason. I certainly have no desire to feel his presence now."

"Yet you care so much about making a good impression that you're changing your shirt for what looks like the exact same shirt."

"This one has French cuffs. You would know that if your wardrobe didn't consist primarily of blue jeans and T-shirts." Dominic started unbuttoning his shirt. "I don't appreciate being undermined. I intend to let him know that."

He waited for the protest to begin. Demetrio always jumped blindly to Vincenzo's defense, and there was no reason for Dominic to believe that this time would be any different. While he was correct, it was the soft-spoken delivery of the vampire's protest that took him by surprise.

"It's been so long since the last time we were all together, just the three of us." Demetrio stared at his younger twin, his green eyes pleading. "Can you stop hating him for ten minutes so we can be a family again? Is that too much to ask?"

"Demetrio…"

"Please, Nico?"

"I hate when you call me that."

"No, you don't."

Sighing in defeat, Dominic sat down next to his brother. He had spent so many years being wrapped up in his hatred that he sometimes forgot just how much Vincenzo meant to Demetrio. Never having known their own father, it was understandable that he had become so attached to their maker. Dominic had once felt that very same attachment before certain events took place.

"You'll just sit there and pout until I give in, won't you?"

"Give me ten minutes. Then I'll make myself scarce, and he can have you all to himself. Just the way he wants."

"Don't say that."

"I made my peace with it a long time ago." The vampire toed the thick black carpet. "That's the real reason I'm his 'favorite,' to fill the void left by your absence. You were the first one he saw, the first one he turned, and the *only* one he ever loved. Me? I'm just a back-up plan."

Dominic wanted to deny everything that Demetrio said, but all of it was true. If Demetrio was willing to live with that and somehow remain his annoyingly chipper self, then the least Dominic could do in return was honor his request, difficult though it would be.

"Ten minutes," he said.

"Pretty please."

"Fine."

"Thank you."

"Shut up."

"I mean it."

"What part of 'shut up' did you fail to comprehend?"

"I love you, my little Nico," Demetrio said, pinching Dominic's cheek for emphasis.

Dominic elbowed his sibling in the ribs to make him stop. "The feeling is mutual. Now get out."

XAN WAS INSTRUCTED to remain home until Dominic met with Vincenzo to confirm Steven's capture. The young man had hoped for a night of gory movies and bare skin but was denied both when Jacob and Becky showed up at his door. He supposed he couldn't be too mad about that since Jacob was now in the kitchen with Michael discussing the job he and Dominic had chosen for him. But as for the other one...

"Okay, Xanadu. Tell me *everything*."

"I don't know what you're talking about."

"Liar!" Becky punched Xan on the arm, almost causing him to spill his beer. "I can tell you had an orgasm this morning."

"I have an orgasm almost every morning," Xan informed her. "That doesn't always mean someone else was involved."

"Was someone else involved this morning?"

"Well, technically..."

Jacob's head eased through the kitchen door. "We can hear you, you know. Inside voices, please."

"This *is* my inside voice," Becky loudly insisted.

"Sorry, Dad." After Jacob returned to the kitchen, Xan flicked Becky in the chest. "Thanks a lot. Get your tits off me."

Becky moved back to her side of the sofa. "We'll finish this later."

"The hell we will. Did you get in touch with Ginger yet?"

"I'm not sure if I want to after what Jacob told me."

"What did he tell you?"

"... I'm going to make some tea. Want some? No? Okay!"

Becky jumped up and ran into the kitchen, leaving Xan to wonder why. Just as he decided to go find out, Jacob came into the living room and joined him on the sofa.

"I've been dismissed," he said. "As soon as I hear from Dominic, we'll get out of your hair so you can do whatever it was you were going to do that I'm not going to think about."

"We've got all night to do *that*."

"Hush." Jacob jerked his head toward the kitchen. "You know she's going to interrogate the hell out of him."

"I know," Xan replied. "Hey, what's this about Ginger? Becky said you told her something then she ran away."

"Oh, that. I didn't tell her anything specific." Jacob helped himself to his son's beer. "There was a situation that needed to be addressed. Dominic and I addressed it."

Club business, Xan concluded. There was no other reason that he would have received such a vague response. But Ginger was his friend so it was only natural for him to be concerned. "Is everything okay?"

"Right as rain. If you want details, it might be best if you talked to her."

"I'll do that tomorrow, assuming everything goes well tonight."

Jacob nodded. "After we know for sure that Vincenzo was telling the truth about Steven, you and Michael can return to the club."

Xan turned to his father with eyebrows raised. "Me and Michael? He'll be working with me?"

"You're going to train him to be a bartender. We'll start him off with that and see how it goes."

"I thought for sure that you were going to keep us separated," Xan said as he took back his beer.

"It would have been pointless seeing as how he lives here. Please don't make me regret this, Xan."

"He's not going to hurt me, Dad. Any biting that takes place will be consensual."

Jacob raised his arms to make room for the mutt that decided his lap would be a fine place to rest. "Are we doing this? Because I can talk *all night long* about how Dominic likes to—"

"Never mind. You win." Xan didn't think that he would ever stop shuddering.

"Ha!" Jacob glanced down at the dog and back at Xan. "Aggie? Really?"

"It was either that or Agnes."

"You poor dog." After giving the pup a sympathetic hug, Jacob trailed his fingers along his son's ear. "Would you look at that?" he said, showing him a neatly folded fifty dollar bill. "I guess inflation really *is* a bitch."

Xan laughed as he took the money, his heart swelling with love for his overprotective oddball of a father. "Now that's more like it."

"JACOB HATES ME NOW."

Becky reached across the table and squeezed Michael's hand. "No, he doesn't. Well, maybe a little. If it makes you feel any better, he hates every vampire who fucks his son."

"I haven't fu—I haven't done that."

"Yet," Becky muttered into her tea.

Michael looked away in embarrassment. "Stop."

"Sorry, love," Becky said, sounding anything but. "For the record, *I* know that you would never hurt Xan."

"Well, can you make sure Jacob knows so he won't kill me?"

Becky waved her hand. "Don't be daft. Jacob would never kill you for hurting Xan."

"He wouldn't?"

"Absolutely not. He would just spend the next thousand years making you wish that he had." Becky offered him an empty cup and a friendly smile. "Care for some tea?"

ONE MINUTE BEFORE MIDNIGHT, Dominic and Demetrio waited for Elliot to escort Vincenzo to the club office.

"Are you ready for this?" Demetrio asked.

"Not at all."

The door opened. For the first time in almost fifty years, Dominic was face-to-face with his "father."

In contrast to skin so pale that Dominic looked tan in comparison, everything else about Vincenzo was dark. His hair, his eyes, his neatly trimmed beard, his clothes. His very being. To the untrained eye, he was just a handsome and well-dressed man who appeared to be in his mid-to-late forties. In truth, he was the third oldest vampire in existence, one of the most ancient of ancients.

Demetrio broke the tension by crossing the room and sweeping Vincenzo into a crushing hug. "It's good to see you, Father."

"You as well, Demetrio." Vincenzo signaled to one of the two guards who had accompanied him. "I have a gift for you."

The guard handed Demetrio a bottle of grappa.

"*Now* it's a party," he said, holding the bottle to his chest. "Did you make it yourself?"

"You have to ask?" Vincenzo patted the vampire's shoulder. "I thought it would be nice if we shared some before you drink all of it yourself."

"I'll get you some glasses," Elliot offered, using the opportunity to escape the office. Dominic wished he could join him.

Vincenzo turned to his firstborn. "Domenico."

"Vincenzo."

The older vampire waited. Remembering his promise, Dominic advanced. His body tensed as Vincenzo wrapped his arms around him and kissed him right at the corner of his mouth, a gesture far too intimate for Dominic's comfort.

"I've missed you," he whispered, his beard grazing Dominic's skin.

Dominic tried to reject the sudden rush of memories that overcame him, some of them good, most of them bad, all of them unwanted. "Steven isn't with you," he managed as he extracted himself from the vampire's arms. "You said that you had him. Where is he?"

Vincenzo stroked Dominic's cheek. "If I didn't know better, I would think you were implying that I lied just to see you before our scheduled meeting."

Icy fingers slid along Dominic's jaw, and it took every ounce of willpower he possessed not to slap Vincenzo's hand away. "*Are* you lying?"

"Domenico!" a frustrated Demetrio yelled.

"It's all right, Demetrio," Vincenzo insisted, never taking his eyes off Dominic. With his free hand he motioned to the second guard, who handed Dominic a small, nondescript bag.

Dominic reached inside. His fingers closed around something hard and cold and cylindrical. A jar, perhaps. "What is this?"

"Proof," Vincenzo answered. "Go on. See for yourself if I'm telling the truth."

Dominic pulled the mystery item out of the bag. It was indeed a jar filled with clear liquid. And something else.

"Is that what I think it is?" Demetrio examined the jar. "Holy shit, it is."

Resting at the bottom of the jar were two eyes. One was brown and one was blue.

"Do you believe me now?" Vincenzo asked.

Dominic stared at the lurid offering. He had never once taken pleasure in hurting others. When death was the only solution, he always tried to ensure that it was as quick and painless as possible.

He strongly suspected that whatever happened to Steven was neither quick nor painless.

"I believe you."

"Very good." With that resolved, Vincenzo clapped his hands together. "Now let's have that drink."

CHAPTER 12

HAD STEVEN CARED ABOUT how being a vampire worked, he might have been more interested in what was happening beneath the bandages that covered his eye sockets. He never gave much thought as to why he and those like him thrived when their bodies should have withered away. But since he wasn't concerned with the impossibility of his existence, only the power that it granted him, he was free to focus on his anger.

The smell of his scorched flesh, bound in silver, filled the room. As much as the chains hurt, they were a welcome change from what he had encountered hours earlier. He would never forget being carved open from chest to groin or the way his innards slithered through Vincenzo's fingers or the sedate, almost tender look on his hideous face before he relieved Steven of his ability to see.

"He said he wasn't going to hurt me."

"He said he wasn't going to *kill* you," Paul corrected. "I didn't know that this was going to happen. If I did, I would have warned you... a luxury you never gave your own victims, from what I understand. Unfortunately, he is often unpredictable when he feels that his precious Dominic has been inconvenienced in any way."

The sarcasm in Paul's voice did not mask his agitation. "You're jealous," Steven said.

"What if I am? Would that please you?"

"Right now? Yeah, it would."

Steven sensed Paul kneeling down before him, carefully so as not to come in contact with the chains, and he waited for whatever punishment would be inflicted for his comments. Instead of responding with violence, Paul rested his elbows on Steven's knees and folded his arms. His position would have been inviting if not for the circumstances.

"Be nice to me, Steven." Paul caressed the vampire's thigh. "You might find that things will work more to your advantage if you and I become friends. *Good* friends."

"Yeah? How so?"

"It's rather simple, really. You want Michael... and I want Xan."

"Why?" Steven inquired, trying to ignore the tantalizing sensation of Paul's fingers.

"Why do you get off on torturing humans?" Paul countered. "We like what we like, even if the reason doesn't make sense to anyone else." His index finger traced a path up Steven's thigh as he continued. "You need to understand that you've been given an extraordinary gift. Vincenzo chose you. Millions of vampires would give anything for such an opportunity."

"An opportunity for what? To be mutilated?"

"To be favored by one of the first vampires to walk the Earth. You've seen his true face yet you're still alive. There aren't many who can say that."

Steven didn't want to get involved with Vincenzo and didn't care about being "favored" if being deprived of body parts was the price he would pay for upsetting him. But he also had a strong desire to live, and if he wanted to continue doing so, he had little choice but to see where this new path would lead.

"Did he ever do anything like this to you?"

"He did something far more painful," Paul answered wistfully. "He broke my heart. Personally, I'd prefer to have my eyes gouged out."

"Tell him that next time he's in a pissy mood so he'll leave me the fuck alone."

The sound of Paul's laughter had an unexpectedly soothing effect on Steven's mood... as did the hand that grabbed his cock when the laughter died down.

"What are you doing?"

"Being nice to you," Paul replied with a squeeze. He moved between Steven's knees, lowered his head, and started being even nicer.

Steven groaned as he arched up, the pleasure from Paul's mouth blending perfectly with the burn of the restraints. He still wasn't feeling confident about being Vincenzo's brand new lackey, but making nice with Paul didn't seem like such a bad idea.

"DO YOU LIKE THE ACCENT?" Vincenzo asked as he settled into the chair next to Dominic's. "I sound like a proper American now."

Recalling the effort it took to lose his own Italian accent, Dominic nodded. "You do, but the name still gives you away."

Vincenzo reached into his left jacket pocket and pulled out a business card. "My new human associates won't have a clue," he said, handing it over.

"Vincent Castle." Dominic studied the card. "Why are you suddenly dealing with humans directly?"

"It only seems sudden to you because you never keep in touch with me. If you must know, I've been expanding my interests."

"Expanding?" Dominic didn't like the sound of that. Then again, he didn't like the sound of anything that came out of Vincenzo's mouth.

"Times have changed, Domenico. The blood trade will not always be as lucrative as it is now." Vincenzo nodded at the bag on top of Dominic's desk. "Vampires like our friend, Steven, are increasing in number. The time has come to look for other methods of generating revenue."

"You have enough money to last a hundred lifetimes," Dominic pointed out.

"What about the hundred lifetimes after that?" Vincenzo countered. "I haven't survived this long by not being prepared." He took a gold cigarette case out of his right jacket pocket. "May I?"

Dominic would have given just about anything to be Demetrio, who was somewhere upstairs chugging grappa, terrorizing Elliot, and dancing badly. He met his maker's challenging gaze. If Vincenzo had done his homework, or had it done for him, then he knew that smoking was prohibited at the Rising Sun. This was nothing more than a test. Would Dominic break his own fiercely enforced rule or stand his ground?

In the end, Dominic chose peace. At least that was what he told himself since the alternative was unthinkable. The bond between them was broken, and there were certainly no lingering remnants of devotion compelling him to obey. None whatsoever.

Never mind how an ashtray just happened to end up in the desk drawer.

"Thank you."

"Who told you about Steven? How did you know where to find him?"

Vincenzo lit up. "Right to the point, I see. I was hoping that we could spend some time catching up."

"What would you like to know that you haven't already found out by spying on me?"

"What kind of father would I be if I didn't look after you?" Vincenzo's smile was both charming and malicious. "How have you been, Domenico? And how is the slave?"

"Do *not* call him that again," Dominic warned.

"Have it your way," Vincenzo said with a sigh. "How is *Jacob*?"

"He's doing very well. He sends his love."

"You'll forgive me if I doubt that." Tapping a length of ash into the ashtray, Vincenzo continued, "And my... well, my grandson, I should say. When will I get to meet him? I've heard many things about him."

Dominic knew that he would never fully escape Vincenzo's watchful eyes. Realistically, he also knew that the vampire would have learned as much as he could about Xan. That didn't mean he had to like it. "Have you?"

"Yes. He and my protégé recently became acquainted. In the bathroom."

He was talking about the attractive vampire Xan was with before taking Michael home. Upon realizing this, Dominic's hands gripped the arms of his chair before they found their way around Vincenzo's neck instead. "You sent someone here for that?"

"I sent him here to observe. Nothing more." Vincenzo stubbed out his cigarette. "I'm sure I don't need to tell you that your son was the one who initiated the encounter."

Dominic took Elliot's bottle of Cutty Sark from the bottom desk drawer and poured himself a glass. "Your protégé," he began. "You didn't turn him yourself? I imagined that I would have dozens of 'brothers' and 'sisters' by now."

He winced as fingers seized his wrist with enough pressure to crack the bones beneath. The glass in his hand fell with a heavy thump, splashing liquid over the rim and across the desk.

"I wandered the world for over two thousand years before I found someone worthy of my blood." Vincenzo's expression was calm but his eyes blazed with anger, and his voice now held a hint of his old accent. "I do not share my blood lightly, Domenico. Never suggest that I do. It is a grave insult to my affection for you."

Dominic snatched his arm away from the vampire's hold and regarded his broken wrist, which was already starting to mend. He felt a grim satisfaction in having pushed Vincenzo to the point of dropping his gentlemanly façade. "It didn't take nearly as long as I thought it would for you to show your true self."

Standing up, Vincenzo produced a handkerchief from his pants pocket. "I've tolerated your abandonment," he started, wiping the spilled liquid from the desktop. "I've tolerated your relationship with that mulatto abomination. But my tolerance only goes so far." When he was finished, he shoved the handkerchief back into his pocket and leaned over Dominic's chair, his fingers lazily twirling a section of long black hair. "I love you, Domenico. More than anything in this world. But *do not test my patience*."

Dominic stared at him, unflinching. "Is that what happened with Giovanni? Was I testing your patience then?"

He waited for additional censure for mentioning a name that had not been spoken between them in centuries. But instead of lashing out further, Vincenzo simply shook his head and sat down again. Another victory of sorts for Dominic, though not nearly as satisfying as the first.

"Steven belongs to me now," Vincenzo stated coolly, his American accent back. "Call off your search and in return, I give you my word that no harm will come to the vampire you wish to protect."

"What are you going to do with him?"

"That doesn't concern you."

"It concerns me if it is happening in my city," Dominic told him as he bent his healed wrist.

"Your city? Oh, my darling Domenico." Vincenzo lit another cigarette. "We will need to reevaluate what you think is yours and what may soon be mine."

"XAN?"

"Yeah?"

"I'm about to come."

"That's the point." Xan smiled at the vampire on his lap, his lube-slick hand never missing a stroke on Michael's cock.

Michael brought his arms around Xan's neck. "I don't want to do it all over you, dork."

"That's the best part."

Xan stroked even faster and was soon rewarded with a loud cry and wet torso. He planted kisses along Michael's neck and chest while waiting for him to recover, paying no mind to the nails that dug into his skin. After a while, he carefully guided Michael onto his back and wiped off his hand on the towel beneath them.

"That was amazing," Michael said, out of breath.

"Yeah, it was," Xan agreed. He turned onto his side and curled his arm under his head. "I'm glad that my first time was with you."

"Your first time?" Michael's skepticism was obvious. "In this house?"

"In this bed."

"Close enough."

Xan watched him, smirking. "You're cute when you come."

Michael cringed. "Shut up."

"You are!"

After some lighthearted nudging, whereupon they each discovered that the other was ticklish, Xan used his phone to check the time.

"How long do I have?" Michael asked.

"About twenty minutes." Xan tossed the phone aside and wrapped himself around Michael, dragging his tongue along the vampire's tattoo. "I don't want you to go."

"I'm sure you also don't want me melting into your bed," Michael said while tweaking the young man's nipple. "You could join me in the basement."

Xan slipped his hand between Michael's legs. "I had every intention of it."

"Pervert."

"Need I remind you where your fingers were ten minutes ago?"

"I never said I wasn't." Michael swatted Xan's hand away and got out of the bed. "I'm going to take a shower."

"Just wait until we go down to the basement. I need one, too."

"I don't want the dog to see me naked."

"And *I'm* the dork," Xan said as he took a good long look at Michael's backside. He used the towel to wipe himself off and debated joining him in the shower—strictly for cleansing purposes—when his phone vibrated, signaling an incoming text message.

Broke your bum yet? Love you.

After Xan texted Becky back (*Fuck off. Love you, too.*), he sat up and inspected the bed for any signs of damage. The towel did its job, sparing him the trouble of washing the comforter. He put on his shorts and decided to let Aggie out one last time before they retired for the day.

He grabbed a couple of bottles of water from the fridge while waiting for her to do her thing, which, as far as he could see, involved a lot of sniffing around and very little peeing. By the time he let her back inside, Michael had finished showering and joined him in the kitchen.

"Ready?"

"Ready." Xan took Michael's hand and followed him down the stairs. "I think you need a real bed."

"Really?" The vampire fell down on the air bed and stretched out invitingly. "This works for me."

"Well..." Xan was going to say something about his poor back and the joys of firm mattresses, but after one look at Michael, none of that seemed to matter. "Okay," was all he could manage.

"Get down here," Michael ordered him.

"I was going to take a shower, too," Xan reminded him.

"Why bother? I'm just going to get you dirty all over again." Michael pulled him down to the bed, stripped him naked, and proved to be a vampire of his word.

Afterwards, Xan finally got around to showering.

And after that, he and Michael stayed up well into the morning debating which *Final Fantasy* was the best and being generally ridiculous together.

Even later, as Xan caught sight of Michael's sleeping face one last time before closing his own eyes for good, he realized that all the sex with all the guys in the world would never come anywhere close to making him as happy as he was right now.

JACOB KNEW FROM EXPERIENCE that his partner often needed time to himself after seeing Vincenzo. Therefore, he had said nothing when he first smelled the cigarette smoke on Dominic. He remained quiet when the vampire drank the morning away in silent contemplation. But when noon rolled around and Dominic still showed no signs of going to bed, Jacob had enough.

He crossed the space between the bed and the sitting area where Dominic sat and stared at nothing. "Tell me," he said, sitting down and taking him by the hand.

Jacob listened as Dominic told the story of his night, nodding and scowling where appropriate. He was temporarily distracted by an urge to break something upon hearing about Xan's bathroom escapade but kept his agitation in check long enough to finish hearing Dominic out.

"At least we don't have to worry about seeing his face for another fifty years," he said when Dominic finished speaking.

"He's not leaving."

"What? What do you mean he's not leaving?"

Jacob didn't notice that he was crushing Dominic's hand until the vampire pointed it out.

"I don't need any more broken bones today," Dominic added as he carefully rescued his hand from Jacob's death grip.

"What are you talking about? What broken bones?"

"Never mind."

"Dominic—"

"He told me that he might stay," Dominic interrupted. "If he does, we're going to lose control over everything."

"That's not going to happen," Jacob replied, shaking his head. "That *can't* happen. Why would he do this?"

"Money. Spite. It's Tuesday. Take your pick."

"We've worked too hard to build a life here *without him*. He can't just come in and take it away. We can't let him do this."

"What choice do we have? I told you what he did to Steven. I won't risk something like that happening to you or Alexander or anyone we care about." Dominic sighed harshly. "I don't know what to do, Jacob."

Hearing such defeated words come from Dominic's mouth was the last straw. Maybe he didn't know what to do, but Jacob sure as hell did.

After so many years of living under Vincenzo's shadow, he had always known that it would come to this sooner or later.

The time had come for him to confront Vincenzo. Alone.

CHAPTER 13

DOMINIC AWOKE THAT evening to an empty bed. It didn't happen often, but it wasn't unusual. He took advantage of the rare occasion by stretching his long limbs across the length of the mattress, something he could never do when Jacob was with him or else the vampire would complain that he was hogging all the space (while overlooking his own tendency to do the same thing). During times like these, Dominic could understand why Jacob had hounded him so long to get a bed. He missed the snugness of their old coffin and all the coffins that came before it, but he had to admit that the bed was a cozy break from tradition.

He closed his eyes, longing to find a few more minutes of peace, but with so much on his mind, no such luck. Reluctantly, he got out of bed and switched on the lights. After he showered and dressed, he noticed his phone was missing. Knowing that he had taken it to bed with him—as he normally did in case Xan or Elliot called—he presumed that Jacob had taken it upstairs so he wouldn't be disturbed after having been up so late into the day.

As he exited the basement, he was filled with uneasiness. Jacob wasn't there. Again, this wasn't out of the ordinary, but with everything that was happening Dominic found it difficult to chalk his lover's absence up to coincidence.

He went into the kitchen and spotted Luca sitting at the table with a newspaper and a cup of coffee. "Good evening, Luca."

Luca raised his head from the paper. "Hey, Dominic. Do you want some blood?"

"I'll get it. Have you eaten anything?"

"I did a little while ago, thanks."

Dominic went to the refrigerator and grabbed a bag of blood. "Where's Jacob?" he asked, trying to sound nonchalant.

"He said he had to go to the club. He didn't say why."

"Just the club?"

"As far as I know. Is something wrong?"

Luca didn't have a vampire's intuition, but after twenty-two years of friendship he was keen enough to know when something was off. "I'm not sure," Dominic responded, seeing no reason to lie to him. "I don't suppose you've seen my phone anywhere?"

"I saw it on your desk earlier when I gave Xan's mail to Jacob."

The vampire finished heating a glass of blood and headed for the door. "Thank you, Luca," he said, patting him on the back as he passed.

"No problem. Do you need me to stick around?"

Dominic paused at the kitchen door and smiled at the big man. Xan would not be the only human he would mourn someday. "No, thank you. Go home. Enjoy your night."

He went into the office and saw his phone on the desk just as Luca had said. After taking a seat, he attempted to call Jacob. The call went straight to voicemail. He tried again. And again, voicemail. Dominic's bad feeling intensified.

"What are you doing, Jacob?" he asked the empty room.

Dominic drained half the glass and set it down beside a stack of mail bearing Xan's name. After a moment of consideration, he dialed Elliot's number. "Hello, Elliot. Is Jacob there by any chance?"

"You just missed him. He stopped in and asked me to keep an eye on Michael tonight, with the Vincenzo situation and all."

That sounded like something Jacob would have done, although he could have just as easily done it over the phone. "How long ago did he leave?" Dominic asked.

"About thirty minutes ago. Is something going on that I should know about?"

Dominic toyed with the edge of a brown envelope. It was addressed to Xan and had no company name printed with the return address. He suspected that it was porn-related. "No. If that changes, I'll let you know. Thank you, Elliot."

He ended the call and put the phone down. Thirty minutes was plenty of time for Jacob to return home. It was possible that he went to Xan's house, but Dominic didn't dare risk troubling the young man if Jacob wasn't there. He decided to enlist Becky's aid and reached for the phone to call her. That was when he noticed that the call log displayed a call made just after 7 p.m. while he was still asleep.

A call to Vincenzo.

Dominic remembered the last time that someone he loved was alone with Vincenzo.

"Damn it."

Leave it to Jacob to do something astoundingly reckless to protect his family. Dominic snatched up the phone and dialed Vincenzo's number. When Vincenzo answered, his fears were confirmed.

"Let me guess. You're looking for your partner."

OVER THEIR MANY YEARS together, Jacob could only think of two or three times when Dominic had ever been genuinely upset with him. Sure, they had minor disagreements here and there, differences of opinion that came with most relationships, but full-blown arguments were almost nonexistent. That would not be the case tonight. He had done something astoundingly reckless, as he often did when it came to protecting his family, and Dominic wasn't going to let his actions slide without rebuke. Jacob hated making Dominic angry, but after hearing about his meeting with Vincenzo, confrontation was the only option.

"I'm hurt by your accusation, Domenico," Vincenzo said as he paced around the hotel suite. "I would never dream of doing that... Well, there is no need for that kind of language."

If Dominic was using profanity then he was far more upset than Jacob anticipated.

"I will tell him," Vincenzo continued. "Yes... All right... Goodbye." After the call ended, he sat down on a seat opposite Jacob. "Domenico would like you to return home immediately after you leave here." With a callous smile, he added, "He isn't very pleased with you right now."

Jacob forced his own smile. "I'm sure we'll be fine. Our relationship is hardly in jeopardy because of this."

"I'm glad to hear that, Jacob." Vincenzo lit a cigarette and noticed his questioning look. "What is it?"

"I'm not used to hearing you say my name."

The vampire took a long drag and exhaled at the ceiling. "You're my guest. It would be rude of me to disrespect you."

"To my face?" Jacob offered sarcastically.

"I can't very well have you telling Domenico that I was mean to you. He sounded distressed enough." Vincenzo's dark eyes grew even darker. "I don't like to see him distressed."

Jacob refused to let him stoke his guilt. "Then why are you here? Nothing distresses him more than you."

"I'm here because my children are here. Is that so wrong?"

"Your children," Jacob scoffed. "You barely acknowledge one and lust after the other. How fatherly of you."

Vincenzo finished his cigarette and lit another one before speaking again. "You're very bold to talk to me this way. I've killed others for far less offenses."

"You're not going to kill me."

"How do you know I won't?"

"Because you love Dominic more than you hate me."

Vincenzo offered a slight nod, acknowledging the truth of Jacob's words. "What would you have me do? Leave and never come back? I'm sure nothing would make you happier."

"You're right, but this isn't about me," Jacob said. "You want half of the club? Fine. You want a percentage of the shelter, too? Okay. I don't care. Whatever it takes to get you out of Harborview." He took a moment to work himself up to what he needed to say next. "Please."

"Please? That couldn't have been easy for you."

"It didn't feel good."

Vincenzo pointed at Jacob's hand, his eyes locked on the gold signet ring that he had given a young man named Domenico Bellini back in 1503. "He once told me that ring was the most precious thing he owned. Seeing you wear it is difficult for me."

Jacob looked at his ring and then glanced at the matching ring on Vincenzo's finger. He didn't dare reveal that the only reason it had ever come into his possession in the first place was because he knew that Dominic would have regretted disposing of it. He doubted the news would go over well, especially coming from him. "Would you like it back?"

"The significance is lost," Vincenzo replied dismissively. "I was just reminiscing." He stubbed out his cigarette and stood up. "I will consider your request. For Domenico."

Jacob blinked at the vampire. "Just like that?"

"Were you expecting more resistance?"

"Much more."

"I am willing to be reasonable when it comes to Domenico."

It took considerable effort for Jacob to accept Vincenzo's hand. "I'm glad we agree that his happiness is the most important thing."

"Everything I do is for Domenico's sake. Remember that." Without letting go of Jacob, Vincenzo continued, "You were right. My love for Domenico prevents me from harming you in any way."

His smile was almost disarming enough to pass for sane... until he spoke again.

"But should the day ever come when his love for you fades, know that the first thing I'm going to do is tear you apart."

Jacob yanked his hand loose. "Thank you for the warning."

"My pleasure. Shall I have Paolo see you out?"

"No." Jacob had barely managed to stop himself from attacking the vampire when he escorted him to Vincenzo's suite. He wasn't sure that he could be so forgiving a second time.

"Goodbye then."

"Goodbye."

Jacob walked quickly toward the exit. The blood-curdling wrath behind Vincenzo's smile had shaken him to his core, and he wanted to get far away from it, as fast as he could.

"I DOUBT HE'LL EVER care much for me," Paul said after Jacob left.

"I'll never know what Domenico sees in him. He deserves far better than some filthy half-breed." Now that Vincenzo was free from the burden of politeness, he took no measures to hide his anger and disgust. "I've decided not to wait," he announced suddenly. "I'm going to do it tonight."

"... I see."

Vincenzo stared at the younger vampire, his anger slowly dissipating. "You still disapprove?"

"It isn't my place to question you."

"Yet you do, without saying the words." Vincenzo beckoned him over to the sofa. After Paul sat down, he put his arm around him. "My sweet Paolo. Don't you see that you will also benefit from this?"

"But—"

"Enough." Vincenzo's voice was calm but firm. "Has Steven healed yet?"

"Y-Yes," Paul stammered as fingers caressed his face.

"Good. Bring him to me."

AFTER TALKING TO VINCENZO, Dominic walked the length of the foyer, back and forth, over and over. He couldn't sit, he couldn't drink, he couldn't do anything except wait and worry. It was 1647 all over again, the year that his love for a man drove his resentful maker to do unspeakable things. A part of Dominic's heart was still broken, would *always* be broken by the memory of Giovanni's ghastly assault. If anything like that ever happened to Jacob...

He was at the door the second he heard the knob turn. Jacob was barely in the house before being swept into a possessive hug.

"Dominic?"

Dominic could tell by his lover's tone that this was not the reaction he expected. He pulled back, his face full of concern. "Jacob, you can't do that again. *Promise me* you won't do that again."

"I promise." Jacob pressed a palm to his lover's cheek. "I'm sorry."

"It's done," Dominic said with a long sigh. "Now I need blood. And you need to tell me everything he said."

He led Jacob into the kitchen, his apprehension fading with every step. Jacob was home now. Everything was going to be all right.

BECAUSE IT WAS A WEEKNIGHT, business at the club was slow enough for Xan to take his time going over the details of bartending which, for reasons Michael could not ascertain, included loitering in the office and making Elliot's life a living hell. When they returned to the bar, Xan gave him a thick book with a picture of a mixed drink on the cover.

"I thought my days of homework were over," Michael said, staring at it distastefully.

"You won't have to make most of what's in there, but it doesn't hurt to know them all."

"Do *you* know them all?" Michael opened *The Complete Book of Mixed Drinks* to a random page. "How do you make a Velvet Hammer?"

"Very carefully."

"Smartass. Will there be a test?"

"Yes, and I'll make it worth your while if you pass," Xan purred, sliding a finger down the vampire's arm.

Ginger stopped wiping down the bar top and glared at the two of them over her shoulder. "Get a damn room."

"We don't need a room," Xan informed her. "We have a house."

"Sorry, Ginger." Michael didn't want to piss off his co-worker on the very first night.

"Sorry, Mom," Xan added, ducking just in time to avoid the towel that was thrown at him. After learning about her three vampire children, it was a nickname he couldn't resist.

"Go take out the trash, and try not to take half an hour this time," the redhead challenged.

Xan didn't think Michael would care to hear the reason he had sometimes taken so long to return from the dumpster, mainly because it involved sex with others. While Xan had been up-front with him about the extent of his workplace activities prior to meeting him—something Michael would have eventually found out for himself now that he was employed at the club—he didn't want to draw too much attention to it. "I won't," he promised, gathering up the trash bag and tying it off at the top. "Don't believe a thing she says about me while I'm gone," he said to Michael. "Even if it's true."

"Okay," an amused Michael responded.

Xan took the bag out back. As he turned the corner that led to the dumpster, he ran into Brian. "What are you doing back here?"

"Just having a look," the officer said, lowering his flashlight. "I wanted to make sure no one slipped by me while I was occupied."

"Occupied, huh? Anyone I know?"

"You practically recommended him. I forgot his name, but he's got brown hair and blue eyes."

"You've just described half the guys I've ever had sex with."

Brian laughed and lifted the dumpster lid for him. "You and that Michael kid, huh? Everyone's talking about it."

"Are they?"

"Yeah. Is it serious?"

"I wouldn't call it serious yet," Xan said as he tossed the trash into the dumpster. "But it's something."

Brian lowered the lid and regarded him with interest. "Does this mean you're off the market now?" he asked.

Xan smiled as he thought about the vampire waiting for him back at the bar. "Yeah, I think it does."

"Well, shit. If I'd known our last time together was going to be the last time, I would have fucked you extra hard."

"You *did* fuck me extra hard. I could barely walk for a couple of days after." Xan tried not to dwell on how good the cop smelled or the way that nothing but pure heat emanated from his rock-solid body. "I should get back inside. Ginger's timing me."

Xan headed back with more reluctance than he cared to admit. He liked Michael, liked him very much, but that didn't mean his attraction to other guys was going to disappear overnight.

As he turned the corner, he noticed someone standing between him and the door. Upon closer examination, and with dawning horror that made his blood run cold, he saw who it was. Xan opened his mouth to yell for Brian—

"Don't."

—and found that he couldn't speak. He couldn't move. He couldn't do anything at all.

Steven stepped out from the shadows. His mismatched eyes were bloodshot and filled with murderous delight. "Thanks for saving me the trouble of waiting all night."

"Xan? What's going on?"

Xan's eyes widened when he heard Brian's voice coming from behind him. He tried to turn his head to no avail; it was like his entire body was trapped in a vise. Throughout a lifetime spent around the undead, none of them had ever used mind control on him. Now he was experiencing firsthand what a terrible and awesome power it was.

"I'm not supposed to hurt you," Steven said to Xan as he eyed the policeman. "But no one said anything about him." He smacked Xan's cheek hard enough to leave a mark. "Stay right there. You're not going to want to see this."

MICHAEL WAS HOLDING a bottle of vodka (the brand name, Xan, did not escape his notice) and lamenting the club's lack of sake when the sudden awareness of his maker's sinister presence hit him like a line drive to the chest. The bottle slipped from his fingers and crashed to the floor, spraying his feet with glass and liquid. He fell against the counter, eyes wide and chest heaving.

"That's coming out of your paycheck, newbie—Michael? What's wrong?"

"Steven," Michael whispered. "Steven's out there."

Then came the chilling realization that Xan was still out there, too.

"Oh my God."

Ignoring Ginger's cries of warning, Michael bolted into the back room and burst through the door leading outside. He was almost knocked flat by guards racing past him and in turn almost ran into Elliot, who was holding Xan's cop friend in his arms. The man's body was a mangled ruin. Michael could still hear a heartbeat, but it wouldn't last for much longer, not without a vampire's intervention.

"I was so worried about watching you that I didn't see what was happening here until it was too late." Elliot's glasses were gone, along with his usual composure. He looked at Ginger, who was standing behind Michael and paler than usual when she saw what had happened to Brian. "Shut everything down," he told her. "And get him somewhere safe. *Hurry.*"

Ginger nodded. "Michael, come with me."

In the time it took her to reach for Michael's arm, he was gone. He ran around the building in a panic, weaving through the armed vampires and searching every inch of the property for any sign of Xan. The fear he had felt the night Steven killed him was *nothing* compared to this.

"Xan?" he called out over the muffled and steady thump of bass. *"Xan!"*

But there was no answer.

Xan Dawson was nowhere to be found.

FAMILY MATTERS

CHAPTER 14

XAN FELT THAT THE BLINDFOLD wasn't necessary. Even if he knew where he was, there was no way he could have outrun a vampire. The fact that he wasn't even tied in any way to the bed on which he sat was proof enough that he wasn't deemed a threat.

He cautiously flexed his fingers, verifying that his body was free to move on its own. Steven's invasive hold on his mind was gone, as well as Steven himself. His face was the last thing Xan saw before the world went dark around him, but after being taken from the Rising Sun to an undisclosed location at the stomach-churning speed that all vampires possessed, he was shoved into the waiting grasp of another who had yet to speak. It was this new, unknown being who had led him here, wherever here happened to be. The only thing he knew for sure from being led down a flight of stairs was that it was a basement of some sort.

Xan could feel the vampire standing over him, and he flinched when a hand came down on his shoulder. The gentle strokes along his arm did little to soothe him. He thought about mentioning his fathers' names to strike fear in the heart of his captor, but Dominic and Jacob were probably the reason he was in this predicament in the first place. Still, he needed to make some sort of plea for his life.

"Listen, I don't know what you plan to do to me, but—"

A finger pressed against his lips, silencing him. Xan caught a whiff of cologne. It smelled unsettlingly familiar. Hands reached behind him and untied the knot in the folded cloth that obscured his vision. After the blindfold was removed, Xan opened his eyes. When he saw a face he knew, he let out a short, dejected laugh and cursed himself for not making the connection sooner.

"He bought you a drink," Xan recalled. "I thought he was just hitting on you. I should have known."

"This isn't what you think," Paul insisted.

"Is this why you came to the club? Why you sucked my dick?"

"No! I wasn't there because of you. And this... this wasn't my idea. I need you to know that."

"Why should I believe you?"

Paul didn't answer him. Instead, he backed away from the young man. Now angry as well as frightened, Xan jumped to his feet. He was halfway to Paul when another vampire walked into the room.

Xan turned sheet-white, as if the blood in his body was recoiling from the sight of him. The anger that had propelled him to go after Paul was gone, replaced by stark terror.

"Hello, Alexander," the vampire said as he stepped toward him. "Or do you prefer to be called Xan?"

The vampire's smile scared Xan more than anything he had experienced so far that night. He didn't know how much longer his legs would hold him up. "I-I don't care," he managed after finding his voice.

"Alexander then. I'm so happy to finally meet you." The vampire stopped in front of him. "My name is Vincenzo Castigliane. Do you know who I am?"

Xan knew, all right. But that didn't make him feel any better. "You're Dominic's maker."

Vincenzo's smile broadened. "Good boy. I do wish we had more time to talk, but I suspect that Domenico and the slave will be here sooner than I'd planned."

Even in the face of possible death, Xan wasn't about to let anyone talk about his father in a negative way. "Don't call him that."

If Paul's slack-jawed astonishment over his boldness was any indication, what happened next wasn't going to be pleasant.

But Vincenzo only grinned. "I see that you've inherited Domenico's stubbornness," he said with a touch of pride. "I like you, Alexander. I hope you and I will become good friends."

The statement offered Xan a glimmer of hope. "You're not going to kill me?"

"I am," Vincenzo replied casually. "But death will only be the beginning."

THE LAMONTE HOTEL WAS located in the heart of downtown Harborview between an old-fashioned theater which was one of the last of its kind in the area and a baseball field that served as home to the city's minor league team. Decades ago, Dominic persuaded the owners to convert the basement level into light-free lodging for visiting associates. As a result, the hotel thrived through a struggling economy where so many others failed, including the one that would eventually become the Dawson House. The level could only be accessed from the lobby with a four-digit elevator code that was changed on a daily basis... or by ripping the steel door leading below off its hinges and slaughtering every vampire guard in sight. Dominic and Jacob chose the latter.

Having been there only hours before, Jacob led the way as they raced down the steps and tore through the hallway leading to Vincenzo's suite. Upon reaching it, he kicked in the door and charged inside with Dominic right behind him.

"Xan!" he screamed, scanning the room for their son.

"Quit yelling." Steven stopped perusing the contents of a bookshelf and smiled at them. A new pair of eyes replaced the ones removed by Vincenzo, and the whites were now blood-red. "As you can see, he's not here."

An enraged Jacob flew across the room. He pinned Steven against the wall, his fangs bared and his nails sinking into the delicate flesh of the vampire's neck. *"Where is my son?"*

Even if Steven had wanted to answer, the hand around his throat prevented him from speaking. His chest hitched repeatedly as he struggled against Jacob's superior strength. The couple gradually realized that the vampire wasn't choking. He was laughing.

"Bastard," Jacob growled, squeezing harder.

"Jacob, we're running out of time." Dominic pried the vampire's hand loose. Blood flowed from the finger-sized holes in Steven's neck. "Vincenzo knew we would come here first. This is just a diversion." Green eyes turned on Steven. "And for some reason, he wants this one alive."

"That's right, you can't kill me," Steven rasped, the wounds on his neck already starting to heal. "Nice to meet you, by the way."

Jacob tried to choke him again, but Dominic held him back. He spun on his partner, ready to give him hell. Then he saw the look on Dominic's face. Steven wasn't the only one smiling.

When Dominic ripped out those newly formed eyes, Steven *was* the only one screaming.

"You're still alive, as requested," Dominic said coldly as the vampire writhed in agony on the floor next to his detached orbs. "Let's go, Jacob."

The desk clerk waved cheerily as they left, as if blood-soaked vampires strolled through the lobby in the middle of the night all the time. She was in for a nasty surprise when Dominic's influence wore off, but she wouldn't remember the two vampires responsible for the carnage.

Jacob reconsidered their decision to call off the guards, even though he had agreed with Dominic that it was better and, in all likelihood, *safer* for Xan that they didn't go around breaking down doors with an army in tow. "I'm calling Demetrio again," he said once they were outside. "Of all the goddamn nights for him not to answer."

"You don't need to bother."

Jacob saw that Dominic was looking past him. He turned around and found Demetrio waiting for them. "Where the hell were you?"

"Getting laid," Demetrio responded. "You can bitch me out later. I know where they are."

The brothers exchanged glances. It was evident that Demetrio put some of the blame for their situation on Dominic's self-inflicted inability to sense Vincenzo. Had he never severed their connection, he would have known where to go instead of acting on an assumption, logical though it was.

"Wait a minute." Jacob remembered the distraught messages he left for the vampire back at the house. "I didn't tell you where we were going. How did you know to come here?"

Demetrio gestured at his twin. "He's my little brother. I'll always know where to find him. Now come on, we have to go."

ALL OF XAN'S LIFE, the question of his fate had loomed over his head. Would he become a vampire like his fathers or live out his days as a human, however few or many remained? He knew what Dominic and Jacob wanted for him, although they never came out and said it. The only thing they ever stressed was that the choice was his and his alone.

Clearly, Vincenzo did not agree.

"Alexander." The vampire advanced on the young man who had retreated to a corner of the room from which there was no escape. "I don't understand why you wouldn't want this."

"Because I just don't!" Xan inched away from Vincenzo, his back pressed against the wall. He looked beseechingly at Paul, who was still rooted in place with his head down. There would be no help from him.

"I'm giving you eternity. And with my blood, you're going to become one of the strongest vampires on Earth. Others would gladly die for this gift."

"Then they can have it. I don't want it."

"I could have forced you to submit to me at any point during this conversation," Vincenzo told him. "Don't resist me, Alexander. Doing so would be very unwise."

Xan tried to slow his breathing. At the rate he was going, he would pass out at any moment. "What does it matter?" he asked, his voice wavering. "I'm dead anyway."

"There are worse things than dying. Ask your friend, Michael." The vampire gave him a look that attempted to pass for pity. "It will all be over soon."

Xan's legs lost the fight, and he slid down to the floor with a tortured moan. He squeezed his eyes shut, causing a single tear to roll down his cheek. He didn't want to die. Even the promise of resurrection didn't change that.

Please God, he thought, unable to speak the words. *Not like this.*

Seconds passed before Xan realized that nothing happened. He opened his eyes. For the second time that night, he saw Paul where he least expected to find him.

The vampire's arms were locked around Vincenzo, preventing him from moving forward. Every muscle strained to keep the older vampire from attacking.

Vincenzo's face had transformed into the stuff of nightmares. His eyes were completely black and every single tooth in his snarling mouth had grown long and jagged. When Xan thought about those needle-sharp teeth ripping into his throat, he screamed. At some point during all the screaming, he also vomited.

"Release me, Paolo," Vincenzo said, his voice low and guttural.

"In all the years I've followed you, I've never asked you for anything." Paul pressed his cheek against Vincenzo's beard. "Please don't do this. If you care about me at all, let him go."

"This has nothing to do with you. I will not be swayed because his cock was in your mouth."

Paul was suddenly flung to the far side of the room. He hit the wall opposite Xan hard enough to put a crack in it and crashed down to the floor in a broken heap.

Black eyes narrowed at Xan. "Stand up."

The vise was back, only this time it was tighter than ever. Xan was pulled to his feet by an unseen force. He was so distracted by the certainty that his head was about to explode that he didn't immediately register the door to the basement being kicked in or the repeated screaming of his name. When Vincenzo spun around to face the intruders, Xan finally noticed Dominic, Jacob, and Demetrio. They surrounded Vincenzo, ready to strike from all angles.

"I don't want to hurt any of you," Vincenzo said. "Well, maybe you, Jacob."

"You can hurt me all you want. Just leave Xan alone."

"A tempting offer, but I must refuse."

"Father, please," Demetrio pleaded. "What can you gain by killing him?"

"Turning," Paul croaked from the floor, his face bloody and his limbs contorted. "He's going to turn him."

The three vampires looked from him to Vincenzo. Understandably, it was Jacob who took the news hardest of all.

"If you touch my son, I'll kill you," he warned.

"You will *try*," Vincenzo corrected. "And you will fail."

"Why are you doing this?" Demetrio asked.

Pitch-black eyes settled on Dominic. "Ask your brother."

"Dominic?" Jacob looked at his lover. "What is he talking about?"

Dominic's posture straightened and his fangs disappeared. He blinked at his maker, his face a mixture of disbelief and sorrow. "Do you think that this will make up for what you did to Giovanni?"

With Vincenzo's back to him, Xan couldn't see when the vampire's features reverted to normal, but he felt it when the pressure in his head faded away. His body was once again free to move on its own—not that he dared with Vincenzo blocking his path to freedom.

"Not tonight," Vincenzo responded. "Not for a hundred years. Or even a thousand. But one night, when you're still able to see your son's face long after he should have passed, you will thank me. And... perhaps... forgive me."

Jacob was not moved. "So this is all some fucked up plan for atonement?"

"I told you that everything I do is for Domenico's sake," Vincenzo reminded him.

"Whatever Xan decides to do with his life is his choice. You have no right to take that away from him."

"Your choice was taken away. Do you regret it? Or are you happier as a vampire than you ever were as a human?"

Jacob went silent at that. While Demetrio tried his hand at reasoning with his father, Xan's eyes passed over the faces of his parents. Unlike Jacob, who was still focused on Vincenzo, Dominic was staring intently at him, trying to get his attention. Once he had it, he raised his right arm and twisted his wrist slightly before tucking a lock of hair behind his ear. It looked like one smooth and continuous motion from start to finish, but Xan understood what he was being told to do. He had forgotten all about it, just like Dominic once predicted he would. Granted, his life had been in danger—and still was as far as he could tell—so he wasn't thinking clearly. Now that he was, he could see a tiny sliver of light at the end of the tunnel. With a little skill and a lot of luck, he would make it out of this alive. But he had to act fast.

He nodded at Dominic and then looked at Vincenzo's back. The suit jacket provided an extra layer of clothing that might have been problematic, but he didn't trust himself to go for the visible portion of Vincenzo's neck without missing. He flexed his wrist, releasing the stake from the spring-loaded sheath under his sleeve. For one heart-stopping second, he thought it was going to slip through his fingers and hit the floor, damning them all. But no, it was in his hand, secured in a tightly closed fist.

One chance was all he was going to get.

BARELY TWO MINUTES had passed since their arrival, but it felt like hours to Dominic. Too much time had already been wasted. If Vincenzo turned around now and saw what was waiting for him in Xan's hand, it would all be over. It was time for a different type of diversion.

"Vincenzo," he said, interrupting Jacob's curse-filled threats.

"What is it, Domenico?" Vincenzo asked tiredly. "Nothing you say or do is going to change the outcome."

"There is one thing I can do." Dominic started toward him.

"Is that so?" Vincenzo asked, unconvinced.

"Yes. And you told me many times that I did it very well." Dominic cupped the vampire's cheek and stared deeply into his eyes. "You know that I would do anything for Alexander. *Anything*. Let him go and you can have me instead. I'll give you my body in exchange for his life."

Vincenzo trembled visibly in response to his touch. "What are you doing?"

"I'd really like to know the answer to that myself," Jacob said, cocking his head.

Dominic leaned forward and touched his forehead to Vincenzo's, their lips a hair's breadth apart. Out of the corner of his eye, he saw Xan raise his arm. Vincenzo's eyes started to close in expectation of Dominic's kiss... and then flew open when nearly twelve inches of silver penetrated his upper back.

He roared and clawed at the stake. With lightning speed, Dominic reached for Xan and shoved him at Jacob and Demetrio. He snatched the stake from Vincenzo's back and forced him down to the floor, holding it to the vampire's chest and ignoring the sizzle and stench of his own rapidly melting flesh. He could hear Jacob asking Xan over and over if he was okay, but he didn't dare see for himself while he had Vincenzo right where he wanted.

"Jacob, take Alexander upstairs."

"I'm not leaving you down here."

"Nothing is going to happen to me."

"You don't know that!"

"I do," Demetrio said in a tone that was alarmingly uncharacteristic. "Go on. Domenico and I need to sort some things out with our dear old dad."

FAMILY MATTERS

CHAPTER 15

WHILE DOMINIC AND DEMETRIO confronted Vincenzo in the basement, Xan and Jacob waited for them in the living room. Any other night, Xan would have been embarrassed that Jacob was being so parental in front of someone else, but now he welcomed the vampire's repeated queries about his welfare and the one-armed embrace that bordered on a headlock. He had a newfound appreciation for his father's actions that he might have never known if not for his near-death experience.

"Whose house is this?" He looked around the living room as much as Jacob's hold would allow. Now that he was feeling himself again, he wondered about the place in which he almost met his end.

"Steven's, if I had to guess." Jacob furrowed his brow at the now fully healed vampire standing on the other side of the room. "Am I right?"

"Yes," Paul answered, avoiding Jacob's glare.

"Is this where he...?" Xan couldn't bring himself to say the rest.

"Killed Michael," Paul finished for him. "And others." He neglected to mention the human whose corpse had been disposed of just that morning.

Xan felt sick to his stomach all over again. "Jesus."

"I don't understand," Jacob said. "How was Vincenzo able to find this place so fast when our own people didn't know exactly where it was?"

"I assisted him with obtaining that information," Paul explained.

"How?"

"I was in a position to gain access to Steven's identification."

"I can imagine what kind of position that was," Xan muttered. "Was fucking him part of your job?"

"No, that was consolation," Paul replied flatly.

There was plenty that Xan wanted to say about that but not with Jacob right there. "Why would you work for a vampire like Vincenzo?" he asked instead.

"It's a long story."

"Fast forward to the ending."

"He saved my life."

"What a fucking angel," Jacob grumbled. "Stop talking now before I hurt you."

"Stop it, Dad." Xan was glad that Paul had the common sense to heed Jacob's warning. A proper thank-you was in order, he supposed, and he would say it at a later time, if given the chance. For now, he just wanted to get the hell out of there.

Whatever was happening downstairs, he prayed it wouldn't take much longer.

VINCENZO WAS FAR MORE worried about the state of Dominic's hand than the stake that was pointed at his heart. "If you hold that thing much longer, you're not going to have a hand left to use it."

"How do we know that you're not going to do anything to us?" Demetrio asked.

"Because I would have done it already. Now let me up, Domenico. I want a cigarette."

For one brief moment, Dominic considered plunging the stake into Vincenzo's chest and being rid of him once and for all. It would have been the only way to guarantee that something like this never happened again. The thought was so tempting that his grip on the stake tightened in anticipation.

But he couldn't. Now that Xan was out of harm's way, Dominic found that he didn't have it in him to do it. Vincenzo's blood still coursed through his veins and would not allow him to harm his maker.

He dropped the stake with a grunt and backed away from the vampire. Most of the skin and muscles of his hand had melted down to the bone, but the damage was already being reversed. "If you ever do anything like that again, I *will* kill you."

"I wish your devotion to family extended to me." Vincenzo stood up and pulled out his cigarette case. He lit one and regarded his children, specifically Demetrio. "You've never defied me before."

"You've never given me a reason until now," Demetrio said, his voice filled with anger and disappointment. "Father, what did you do to Giovanni? What was so bad that you thought killing Xan was going to make up for it?"

Vincenzo looked at Dominic. "He doesn't know?"

"I never told him."

"Why not?"

"Because he loves you. I didn't want to deprive him of that."

"I'm supposed to be the one taking care of you," Demetrio said.

"And you do, in your own half-witted way."

"That's pretty much the only way I know."

"I'm well aware of that." Dominic smiled at his twin. "Give us a minute, please."

Demetrio gave Vincenzo a distrustful look. "Are you sure?"

"I'll be all right," Dominic promised him. "Tell Jacob I won't be long."

Demetrio wasn't persuaded that all would go well, but he exited the basement as requested, leaving Dominic and Vincenzo alone.

"He's going to hate me," Vincenzo said, dragging on his cigarette.

"Do you even care?"

"Yes. I love Demetrio... though my feelings for you may have overshadowed that."

"He thinks that you would hate him if he didn't have my face."

"He shares a bond with you that can never be broken. I don't hate him. I *envy* him." Lacking an ashtray, the vampire flicked ash onto the floor. "It's been a long time since I've seen you smile. I imagine you do a lot of that when I'm not around."

"It's been known to happen every now and then."

Vincenzo took a handkerchief out of his pocket. He folded it in half and used it to pick up the stake at his feet. "I must be slipping in my old age," he said, staring at it. "I honestly believed that you were going to kiss me."

"I was going to, if it came to that. I had to do something. Alexander was anxious about stabbing you in the back."

"Would you have offered yourself to me if he didn't have the stake?"

"As I said, I would do anything for Alexander."

"I see."

Dominic blinked at Vincenzo. "Am I insulting your affection again?"

"No. You're being a father." Vincenzo handed the stake to Dominic. "I hope he changes his mind one day, Domenico."

"So do I."

The older vampire stepped on the butt of one cigarette and lit another. "Dare I ask what you've done to Steven?"

"He's alive," Dominic said. "Although it might be a day or two before he can see again."

Vincenzo chuckled. "I taught you well, as much as you might hate to admit it. What about everyone else?"

"You're going to have a mess to clean up when you get back to the hotel."

"For goodness sake, Domenico."

"*You took my son.* I would have killed everyone in this city to find him."

"Fair enough." Vincenzo stroked his beard, thinking. "I suppose this is where we discuss the terms of my departure."

"... You're leaving?"

"Isn't that what you want?"

"Yes."

"Then so be it." Vincenzo reached out and touched Dominic's face, his fingers sweeping across the vampire's lips. "You see? I can be selfless. Don't tell anyone."

Dominic turned his head and grinned bitterly. Until that moment, he had conveniently forgotten the origin of one of his own semi-frequent sayings. "No one would believe me."

"This is true," Vincenzo agreed.

"Who told you that we were looking for Steven?"

"I'm not going to tell you. However, that individual understands that there will be consequences if you ever find out on your own." Vincenzo finished the second cigarette and dropped it next to the first. "In addition to your regular tributes, I'll settle for forty percent ownership of the Rising Sun. You and I both know it would not exist without me."

"Thirty," Dominic countered.

"Thirty-five and I'll leave the vault alone," Vincenzo offered. "I imagine you have enough money stored in there to sustain you for years."

Decades, actually, but damned if Dominic was going to tell him that. "Done. Anything else?"

"Your ring. I understand that it has no meaning to you anymore, but I would rather see it in the trash than on his finger. I suspect you would have thrown it away a long time ago if not for giving it to him instead."

"What about the shelter?"

"It's yours. For the time being."

"I appreciate that."

Vincenzo tapped another cigarette against the case. "If this is going to be *your* city, as you have claimed so often over the years, then you need to be certain that you are working with vampires who aren't going to cave under the pressure of an outside influence. The ease with which some of your associates were willing to abandon you at my request was rather alarming."

Dominic knew that no vampire in their right mind would have sided with him over Vincenzo. Still, reminders would need to be given. Harshly, if necessary. But that was a concern for another time. Right now, he just wanted to take his family home. "I'll deal with it."

"See that you do. Send Paolo down here on your way out. I have some apologizing to do."

Dominic begrudgingly offered Vincenzo his hand. The vampire kissed it and held it to his cheek before letting go.

"You'll see me again." Vincenzo's promise felt more like a warning.

"I know." Dominic was halfway up the steps when Vincenzo called out his name. "What is it?" he asked, bracing himself.

"As you know, I make it a point to stay informed about potential allies and enemies. A while back, I learned that one of the Tokyo clans was under new leadership. A woman."

Dominic had no idea where Vincenzo was headed with this story. If hearing him out for another minute or two guaranteed that he could leave without further incident, then he would suffer through it. "A rarity," he said.

"Yes. Rarer still was her youth. It takes a vampire centuries to rise to any significant amount of power, but she did it in an unusually short period of time. That's not the interesting part." Vincenzo lit his cigarette and dragged hard on it. "The interesting part, if my sources were to be believed, was that she had a husband before she was turned. A husband... and a baby."

"A baby..."

"There were plenty of rumors about what happened to them. Some say she killed them both after she was turned. Others say they are alive and well somewhere in Japan. But a few speculated that the husband changed his name and moved to the States with the baby. The only thing I know for certain is that this child would be in his early twenties today." Vincenzo stared pointedly at Dominic. "Does that sound like anyone you might know?"

Dominic shook his head. "That's... that's just a coincidence."

"One that you would do well to investigate," the vampire said as he exhaled a puff of smoke. "I've been told that she is relentless. She would have to be to come into power so quickly. Should the day ever come when she finds her son, I have a feeling that she'll stop at nothing to reclaim him."

MICHAEL STRETCHED OUT his legs, his eyes unfocused on the wall in front of him. Xan's old bed wasn't as spacious as the one in his new house, but until Michael saw for himself that the young man was all right instead of hearing the news secondhand from Becky, it was the only place he wanted to be.

"Michael?" Becky called out from the hallway. "I'm coming in." Without waiting for a reply, she came in and sat down on the bed. After a minute, she pointed at a place on the floor. "I remember when Xan used to sit right there in this awful bean bag chair and read those backwards comic books of his, whatever they're called, for hours at a time."

Michael smiled at the thought of Xan losing himself in the latest volume of *Bleach* or *Naruto*. "Manga."

"That's it. I never did get the hang of reading them myself. The pictures were pretty, though. All the female characters were well-endowed."

"Yeah, they usually are."

"You know this isn't your fault, don't you?"

"Sure as hell feels like it."

"Vincenzo wanted Xan. He would have found a way to get to him even if Steven hadn't been a part of the equation."

"But Xan's friend…" Michael's voice trailed off as the image of Brian's mauled body surfaced in his mind. "That was all Steven's doing. And Steven's only a part of this because of me."

"Brian is going to be fine. Elliot will see to that."

That was all well and good but Michael still felt responsible to some degree. This was one of the things he had feared most after escaping Steven's clutches. He knew what it was like to be the victim of his brutality and was sickened at the knowledge that it had happened to someone else.

"Right then. I'm going back downstairs to keep Ginger company." Becky rose and smoothed out her lavender dress. "Can I count this as a date?"

"If so, it's not a very good one."

"She doesn't like tea, and she's never heard of *Doctor Who*. It'll never work."

"Never," Michael pretended to agree.

Becky swatted his thigh and kissed him on top of the head. "Are you going to be all right?"

"Yeah. Thanks, Becky."

"Anytime."

After she left, he resumed staring into space, feeling somewhat better than before. But it wasn't until he heard the front door open an hour later that he truly felt at ease.

Michael jumped out of the bed and went into the hallway. He forced himself to walk slowly instead of giving in to his urge to run down to the living room and shove everyone out of the way to get to Xan. He descended the stairs and saw Xan sandwiched between Becky and Ginger and griping about being crushed by boobies. In his excitement, Michael didn't notice the curious look that Dominic gave him; his full attention was focused on the blue eyes that stared back at him.

Xan's expression was a combination of joy and relief, and upon seeing it, something in Michael's heart gave way. Irrevocably. In that moment, the truth of his feelings was suddenly and resoundingly clear.

I'm in love with him.

WITH GREAT EFFORT, Xan freed himself from a prison of limbs and breasts and went over to the staircase where Michael stood. He wasn't sure if the vampire's hesitation was because he felt some measure of guilt over what had happened or because his fathers were nearby. The cause didn't matter. What mattered was taking Michael into his arms and holding him tightly and ignoring the undignified cheers of two vampire ladies and one very delighted uncle.

Jacob steered the trio toward the kitchen. "Come on, fangirls."

"I'm not a girl," Demetrio said.

"Sometimes I wonder about that."

As soon as they were gone—with Demetrio defending his manhood every step of the way—Xan kissed Michael and hugged him again. "You smell like vodka," he murmured into his neck.

"You smell like puke," Michael replied.

"Oh, yeah. Sorry. It's been a rough night." Xan held Michael's hand to his cheek, pressing against its coolness. On the way home, he had thought of all the things he wanted to say upon seeing Michael again, but now all he wanted was to touch him, to feel that he was really there.

He lost track of how long they stayed that way. It was long enough for Becky to return to see if they were having sex on the stairs. She sounded disappointed that they weren't.

"We need to have a talk about your obsession with man-on-man action," Xan said to her as he led Michael into the kitchen.

Once there, the couple helped themselves to a drink and joined the others at the table. Dominic, Jacob, and Demetrio filled the girls in on their end of things (though Xan noticed that they neglected to mention Giovanni), and Becky relayed the details of a second call from Elliot, reiterating that Brian was going to make a full recovery. Xan was glad to hear that after what happened behind the club.

"You were at Steven's house." Michael looked at Xan. "I'm so sorry. If I had only told you about him from the beginning—"

"Then this still would have happened to me," Xan said. "You have no reason to be sorry."

"Xan's right. Don't you dare blame yourself for any of this." Jacob walked over to the refrigerator, nudging the young vampire's chin upward as he passed him by. "Anyone hungry?"

Everyone said yes, and as Jacob heated blood for all the vampires and made a poor excuse for a sandwich for Xan, he announced that everyone would be staying for the day due to the early hour.

"Slumber party!" Demetrio cried happily.

"I should try to get home to the kids," Ginger said. "I think I have enough time to make it."

"It's too close to sunrise and you can't fly," Dominic countered. "Call them and explain that you'll be here for the day so they're not worried."

While Ginger stepped out of the room to do that, Jacob served everyone else. "We have plenty of blankets and pillows to go around."

"You also have a really big bed," Demetrio added.

"Don't even think about it," Dominic warned him.

As Becky simultaneously encouraged and refereed an argument between the brothers about sleeping arrangements—one that almost turned into all-out war when Demetrio smugly suggested a Jacob sandwich—Xan glanced at Michael and shrugged. "Welcome to the family."

WITH ABOUT TWENTY MINUTES to spare before the sun breached the horizon, Dominic sat down at his desk and prepared to tell his lover and his brother a tale that was long overdue. After Vincenzo called on him to reveal the reason behind his actions, it was something he could no longer avoid.

Before he began, Xan appeared in the office doorway. Having just showered, he was now wearing a set of Dominic's green silk pajamas, and his blond hair framed his face in damp segments. "I just wanted to let you know that Luca went to my house to let the dog out and grab some clothes for me and Michael."

"Thank you," Dominic said. "We'll be down shortly."

Demetrio waited until Xan closed the door to speak. "He seems to be taking it all in stride."

"I'm not so sure that it's hit him yet," Jacob responded.

Dominic nodded. "Right now, he has all of us to distract him."

"He's a tough kid," Demetrio insisted. "He'll be fine."

Dominic's jaw tightened when the two vampires looked expectantly at him. With no further delays and daylight rapidly approaching, he tried to think of the best way to begin. "You both know most of the story already," he started. "I was in love with a human, we were very happy for a time, and then he died."

"Did Vincenzo kill him?" Jacob asked.

"No, that can't be right," Demetrio said. "Domenico, you told me that Giovanni died of an illness."

"He did. I neglected to tell you that it wasn't a human illness." In his mind, Dominic saw the aged and decrepit body of a once beautiful man. He saw rumpled white hair that held no trace of its former blackness, brown eyes filled with madness, and lips pulled back in a silent scream. His hands, on his thighs and out of view, curled into fists. "We were together for twelve years before it happened. Twelve years. I was still young enough for that to feel like a long time. Vincenzo summoned me one night. He was looking to benefit financially from the revolt in Naples, and I thought that he was going to ask for my help since Demetrio was off somewhere wooing castrati."

His brother smiled weakly but did not interrupt. Dominic wished that he had because he didn't want to go on. But he did.

"He started asking about Giovanni. He wanted to know how things were between us and whether or not I was happy. I didn't believe that he genuinely cared, but I had hoped that his interest meant that the romantic portion of our relationship was finally put to rest. After I left him, I went to Giovanni's house and woke him up so we could spend some time together before sunrise. Then I went home. That night I returned to his house..."

Here Dominic paused and stared at the desktop, his eyebrows drawn together as images from that night raced through his mind and tore at his heart.

"I could smell the blood before I even opened the door. I knocked and called out his name, but there was no answer. I went inside... and found him on the floor... naked... bleeding... and insane."

Demetrio unleashed a string of profanities in his native Italian. Jacob looked ill.

"Vincenzo raped him," Dominic said through clenched teeth. "Tortured him. Destroyed his body and his mind. All because of me."

"Dominic—"

"Don't say that it's not my fault," the vampire told Jacob. "Giovanni's only crime was being loved by me. Now do you understand why I reacted the way I did when you ran off to confront Vincenzo?"

"I do," Jacob answered.

"I healed Giovanni's body, but his mind was out of my reach," Dominic continued. "I wasn't strong enough to bring him back. He was just... gone. I asked Vincenzo to fix him, *begged* him, but he refused. He said I should be thankful that he allowed me the time we had together. I would have killed him then if I could."

"Me too, if I'd known," Demetrio whispered.

"Most of Giovanni's family was lost to the plague. I was the only one he had. I brought him to my house and took care of him. I thought that he might get better as time passed, that he might recognize me and say my name, or say *anything*, but he never did. All I could hope for until the day he died was that he couldn't remember what Vincenzo did to him."

"You should have told me," Demetrio said. "I would have come home sooner. I would have helped you."

"I didn't want to involve you."

"I'm your brother, Domenico."

"All the more reason." Dominic stood up. He had said all that he wanted to say on the subject. "We need to go downstairs now."

He went to the door. Before he could open it, Demetrio grabbed his shoulder and turned him around.

"All these years I gave you so much shit for the way you treated Father. I'm sorry."

"You didn't know."

"Well, I know now. And I'm never going to forgive him."

Demetrio stormed out of the office. The couple followed him through the house toward the open basement door. As cries of merriment floated up from below, a pair of arms wrapped around Dominic from behind.

"Thank you for telling us," Jacob murmured into his back. "I know it wasn't an easy thing to do."

"No, but it needed to be done." Dominic turned around and kissed him until Demetrio, having reached the bottom of the stairs and back to his usual self for the sake of the others, loudly demanded that they stop making out.

"Gross!" Xan yelled.

The lovers broke apart and went down to the basement. Once there, they found Xan, Michael, Becky, and Ginger sitting on their bed and engaged in a fierce game of Monopoly.

"Looks like none of us are getting the bed today," Demetrio said.

Dominic glowered at him. "You were never getting the bed."

"Let's not start that again." Jacob tossed a pillow and blanket to Demetrio. "You can take the couch. Dominic and I will sleep on the floor."

"We haven't done that in a while," Dominic said.

"No, we haven't," Jacob agreed as he spread another blanket on the floor. "Although from what I remember, there was never much sleeping involved. But it sure beat trying to do it in a coffin."

Xan scowled at his parents. "Haven't I suffered enough tonight?"

"You think that's bad?" Becky asked. "Just think about *all the sex* they've had right here on this bed."

While Xan swore that his brain was now permanently broken beyond repair, a highly amused Dominic kicked off his shoes and took a spot on the floor next to Jacob. The conversation turned back to the game, and Xan made it known that being the only human in the room automatically entitled him to Boardwalk. He also stated that having to take bathroom breaks gave him the right to extra funds.

"Back me up here, Dominic," Xan pleaded.

"I haven't urinated since the 16th century. You're on your own."

The young ones played through the morning until they passed out at various angles across the bed with fake money and little plastic houses stuck to their skin. Dominic covered them with a blanket and turned off all the lights before returning to the floor. He curled up beside Jacob and smiled when the vampire gave him a quick kiss on the nose.

The heartache of reliving the past had receded. His family was safe. Everything, for now, was as it should be.

CHAPTER 16

ON WEDNESDAY MORNING, the Lamonte Hotel was evacuated and closed for an "unexpected renovation." On Wednesday night, its one remaining guest roamed the hallway of the basement level and inspected the damage caused by two outraged fathers.

Vincenzo ran his finger along the blood-splattered wall. "I'll need new escorts."

"They'll be here within the hour," Paul replied, walking behind him.

They stepped into Vincenzo's suite and took a seat, ignoring the moans that came from the bedroom. Steven had been rightfully infuriated by the loss of his eyes yet again, but now he knew better than to direct that fury at Vincenzo, even if it was unintentional. Paul wondered how long it would take for the vampire's tongue to grow back.

"Why are you taking him with you?" he asked, hoping he didn't sound as envious as he felt. "Why is he so important?"

"Steven has the potential to become a valuable asset to me. *If* I can tame him."

"Valuable asset." Paul winced at the sting of rejection. "Unlike me? Is that why you're leaving me behind?"

"I'm leaving you behind because you're the only one I can trust to act on my behalf. You're the only one I can trust at all." Vincenzo rested his cigarette in an ashtray and took Paul's hand. "You have a kind soul, Paolo. That kindness is wasted on me, but I have always been touched by your attempts to appeal to my nonexistent better half."

"You could have killed Jacob a thousand different ways over the years without letting Dominic find out you were responsible," Paul said while playing with the ring that meant so much to the older vampire. "And you could have turned Xan last night. You had plenty of time to do it despite my interference."

"You're suggesting that I hesitated on purpose?"

"I'm suggesting that your better half isn't as nonexistent as you claim."

"Let's keep that between us. I have a reputation to protect." Vincenzo reached for his cigarette and started outlining his plans for Paul. Although the vampire would not be there in the flesh, he fully intended to continue making his presence felt. If Dominic wanted control of Harborview, he was going to have to prove that he deserved it. If he failed, Vincenzo would take the city for himself. "And while you're doing all of that, you can continue pursuing my grandson," he concluded.

"I don't have much of a chance with him anymore."

"Nonsense. No one in their right mind would turn you down."

"You turned me down."

"You see? I'm crazy."

Paul leaned his head against Vincenzo's. As the minutes passed and their time together drew to an end, he reconsidered the love he thought no longer existed and wondered when he would see Vincenzo again.

WITH ELLIOT STILL CARING for Brian and a looming uncertainty about Xan's emotional recovery from last night's events, Dominic and Jacob decided that the Rising Sun would remain closed until Friday. Their invitation to Xan and Michael to stay an extra night was predictably but politely declined, but they took what solace they could in their son's promise to call them immediately should the need arise.

"Demetrio was right," Dominic said after giving the matter some thought. "Alexander will get past this."

"He will," Jacob acknowledged. "But what would we do if we didn't worry about him all the time?"

Dominic glanced at his watch. His time was almost up. "At least he's not alone. I feel better knowing that Michael is with him."

"Do you think Vincenzo was telling the truth about that vampire in Japan?" Jacob asked, remembering what Dominic had told him earlier.

"He has nothing to gain by lying about it."

"That's never stopped him before."

"We shall see."

"Mr. Dominic!" Rosie ran over to the couple, her cherubic face spilling with eagerness. "Are you ready?"

"Yes," Dominic told her. "Please proceed."

The child climbed onto the sofa and started removing the hair rollers that covered his head. Across the room, Hannah and Joseph busied themselves with the pile of toys that Dominic and Jacob purchased for them before arriving, having offered to babysit for Ginger while she and Becky went on a date that wasn't prompted by an abduction.

Jacob aimed his phone in Dominic's direction. "We should do this more often."

"Jacob, if you take a picture of me like this..."

"Then what? You'll cut me off?"

"Cut off what?" Rosie asked.

"Nothing," Dominic said since Jacob was too busy laughing to respond.

When the last roller was removed, Rosie held up a mirror. Dominic had no words to describe how he felt about the wavy layers of hair that surrounded his face. Jacob did.

"You look like you belong in a hair band."

Rosie stared at Jacob with large eyes. "Is that a bad thing?"

"Not at all, sweetheart." Jacob swept the child onto his lap and nuzzled the top of her head. "Halloween is coming up soon. I bet if you ask nicely, Mr. Dominic will dress up like an 80s rocker and take you and Joseph and Hannah trick-or-treating."

"I hate you so much right now," Dominic whispered to Jacob as the ecstatic child squealed with joy.

Jacob kissed the sullen vampire on the cheek and took his picture before he could complain any further. "I love you, too."

And little Rosie, who loved them both, only wanted to know one thing. "What's an 80s rocker?"

MICHAEL HELD UP A FIGURE of a classic comic book hero. "Does Superman go with Batman?"

"He did in some of my younger fantasies," Xan replied with a leer. "Yes, with Batman, please."

The vampire carefully placed Superman in his new spot and stepped back to get an overall view of his progress. Xan owned an ungodly number of figures and toys, and the two of them had spent most of the night unpacking and arranging them on new shelves. It was hard work, but the end result was every geek's wet dream.

When they finished in the spare bedroom, they went to work emptying the remaining boxes in Xan's bedroom. This was far easier since most of it was bedding that could be shoved into the closet. Then they moved into the living room to tackle the boxes of books, spending just as much time thumbing through and discussing them as they did putting them away. After another half hour devoted to breaking down all of the boxes and placing them in the garage, they collapsed on the living room sofa. It was one in the morning.

"I'm starving," Xan said.

Michael nodded. "Me too."

Aggie thumped her tail on the floor to remind them that dogs also liked to eat.

They trudged into the kitchen where Xan warmed a cup of blood for Michael and grabbed a couple of slices of leftover pizza for himself and the dog. Michael was pleased to see Xan being his usual self as he gave a detailed explanation of Darth Maul's awesomeness, but the vampire still couldn't help but worry that all was not as right as it seemed.

"Hey, Xan," Michael began after he finished his speech. "Can I ask you something?"

Xan looked up from the floor where Aggie was gnawing on a pizza crust. "Are you going to ask me if I'm okay?"

"Will you be mad if I do?"

"No."

"Are you okay?"

"Yes. I mean, I don't know. Maybe I'll have some post-traumatic shit later on, but right now, yeah, I'm okay." Xan stretched his legs under the table until his foot found Michael's. "This whole thing has given me a lot to think about. Stuff I need to deal with. Stuff I *should* have dealt with a while ago."

"Do you want to talk about it?" Michael asked.

"No, but thanks. I still need to... make sure."

Although none of Xan's words seemed to be directed at him, Michael was concerned nevertheless. What if, in a new appreciation for life, he decided that he no longer wanted anything to do with him? The idea of losing their situation or arrangement or whatever it was filled Michael with dread. He didn't want to believe such a thing might happen, and based on Xan's behavior since their reunion, it wouldn't. But what if it did?

His fears worsened later that morning when Xan announced that he wasn't ready to go to bed yet. Michael, having no choice, went to the basement alone. Although their situation or arrangement or whatever it was didn't require them to sleep together daily, they had done so since it began, and the bed was cold and empty without the warmth of the tattooed body he had grown accustomed to holding.

When the basement door opened that afternoon, Michael almost wept with relief. Xan barely had time to pull the blanket over him before the vampire wrapped his arms around him and held him tightly.

"I fell asleep on the sofa. Sorry."

For all those hours Michael spent working himself into an emotional frenzy, Xan was passed out upstairs. He felt like a fool, but he was a reassured fool all the same. "That's what happens when you think too hard."

"You need to stop hanging out with Becky."

They laughed and kissed and cuddled, and for the next few hours, all was right with the world.

The next night Michael helped Xan remove all the food with little to no nutritional value from the kitchen. "You're as bad as someone hiding porn from their parents," he said as he shoved packages of microwave popcorn and ramen noodles into a garbage bag.

Xan pulled a handful of Snickers candy bars from the cupboard, opened one for himself, and tossed the rest into Michael's bag. "My parents wouldn't care about porn," he said while chomping away. "They *do* care about what I eat. Healthy foods, blah, blah, blah."

Michael could see where Dominic and Jacob were coming from. They wanted their son to live a long time. So did Michael. A diet rich in salt and sugar, while delicious, was not the way to go about it. Maybe Dominic would be willing to give him a few pointers on cooking since Xan was content to live on junk food for the rest of his life.

They finished removing the offensive items from the kitchen, leaving the refrigerator and cupboards pitifully bare. The garbage bag went into the garage next to the broken down boxes. With no firm plans for the rest of the night, Michael assumed that they would play video games or watch movies or both. Xan had something else in mind.

"I need you to come with me somewhere."

"Okay." Michael watched Xan's face for a clue but found nothing out of the ordinary. "Where?"

"You'll see."

Very little was said during the drive. To stave off his growing nervousness, Michael concentrated on the music (Queen, excellent choice) and the view out of the passenger side window. Fifteen minutes after leaving the house, they were driving down a street in an area of Harborview that had seen better days. Xan pulled into the parking lot of the shelter that was named after him, the Dawson House.

"You wanted to show me a homeless shelter?"

"I'm just leaving the car here. It's not far, where we're going."

They got out and started walking. Two blocks up the street, they crossed over. Xan stopped when they reached a short alley between a computer repair store and a thrift shop.

"What is this place?" Michael asked though he had already guessed the answer.

"This is where they found me." Xan pointed down the empty alley. "The dumpster's gone now, but this is it."

Michael walked down the narrow path. He tried to picture a dumpster in his mind, one that was filled with trash and a tiny baby. The very thought filled him with sadness.

"Dad and Dominic were checking out the shelter that night—this was before they opened it. There used to be an adult store a couple of blocks away.

That's where they were going when they heard me." Xan came up behind him. "I'm alive because my parents are perverts. How messed up is that?"

"Did they ever look for who put you there?"

"As far as they were ever able to find out, no one reported a baby missing around the time I was born. They offered to try again when I was younger, after they told me the whole story, but by then there was no way of knowing who it was. It could've been the woman who had me, or it could've been someone else. Whoever did it wanted me dead. And they didn't even have the balls to kill me outright." Xan stared at the empty spot where his life truly began. "I told them that it didn't matter to me. I know who my parents are. They're the only parents I'll ever want."

"You're very lucky, Xan. I hope you know that."

"I know. I wanted to show you this place because it's important to me. And *you're* important to me. And I just wanted to..." Xan bit his lip as he struggled with what he wanted to say next. "This went so much easier in my head."

"Take your time," Michael said.

Xan tried again. "It's one thing to know that life is short. It's another thing to have death staring you right in the face, ready to bite a chunk out of your throat. Even though Vincenzo was going to turn me, the thought of dying... it was..."

Michael nodded. "I know."

"This kind of thing makes you do a lot of reevaluating," Xan went on. "That's what I've been doing the past couple of nights. One of the things I've decided is that I want to give this an honest try, you and me. I've never had a boyfriend before, and I don't know if I'll fuck it up or not, but this is something I really want. If you want it, too. If you don't, I'll under—"

The rest of his sentence was cut off by a kiss. Michael pushed Xan against the brick wall of the thrift store, his fingers weaving through spiked hair and his heart overjoyed.

"Was that a yes or were you just randomly making out with me?" Xan asked after they parted, his hands on Michael's waist, holding him close.

"Of course it's a yes. Did you think I'd turn you down?"

Xan's flushed face was noticeable even in the poorly-lit alley. "I wasn't sure. You have no idea how much you throw me off my game."

"I'm not apologizing for that."

"Good. Let's go home."

They walked back to the car, hand in hand. Xan offered to give Michael a tour of the shelter another time, preferably on a night when a vampire named Tuck was working. Michael realized that this was the same vampire Jacob told him about, the one with the habit of chewing gum. He looked forward to meeting him.

When they got home, after having miraculously managed to keep their hands off each other in the car, they headed straight for Xan's bedroom. The door had barely shut before they were on each other, leaving a trail of hurriedly shed clothing from the wall to the bed. Michael clawed at Xan's hair and back as they slid against each other, kissing and licking and ever so gently biting all the skin he could reach. And later, when Xan straddled him and worked his way down for the very first time, slick and hot and tight around him, Michael thought that he would explode from the sensation.

"*Oh.*" His fingers dug into Xan's hips and his toes curled into the comforter. "Don't move. Don't speak. Don't even breathe."

"Don't blink?" Xan asked, dragging his nails along the vampire's chest.

Michael grinned at the *Doctor Who* reference. "You really *are* a geek."

He pulled Xan down for a long, drawn-out kiss. After that, Xan finally moved. He kept on moving until they both cried out and Michael felt like he had died all over again. Only this time in the best possible way.

XAN WAS PROUD OF MICHAEL for holding his own during dinner that Friday. The vampire even managed to get under Becky's skin with some well-timed zingers, and that alone made Xan's night. He was especially moved when he went into the kitchen for an after-dinner beer and found Dominic schooling Michael on different types of pasta. No one, human or vampire, would ever match his father's culinary expertise, but Xan was looking forward to Michael's attempts.

The only blot on an otherwise perfect family gathering was Dominic's announcement that Paul would be sticking around. It was especially vexing because of a decision Xan recently made that he had yet to tell his fathers.

Later on, he pulled Luca aside and asked if he would assist with moving the coffin out of the basement to make room for a bed. When he confirmed the man's suspicion that it was to be a bed for two, it resulted in a congratulatory chokehold that left him wheezing.

After Luca went home and Demetrio left to meet whomever had texted him repeatedly during dinner (which led to the usual brotherly bickering with Dominic), everyone else piled into Jacob's Audi and went to the club. This was at his insistence since they were all going to the same destination anyway. Xan couldn't resist poking fun at Becky for breaking her usual Friday night tea routine just to see Ginger, and the two friends exchanged verbal jabs until Jacob threatened to turn the car around.

The Rising Sun was packed as usual for a Friday night. As Michael and Becky went to the bar, Xan followed his parents down to the office to ask Elliot how Brian was doing since he wasn't at his car. The last thing he expected to find when he walked into the room was the two of them kissing and groping each other against Elliot's desk.

"*Wow*," Xan exclaimed, his eyes and mouth open wide.

Elliot pushed Brian away, his glasses comically askew. "I was just... I mean we were just... we were going over..."

"Each other?" Xan suggested. His lips curled fiendishly at Brian, who was sporting a very obvious erection. "It's nice to see that you're *up*. And about."

"Uh, yeah, you too," Brian mumbled. "We'll catch up later."

Xan chuckled as the flustered cop slinked past Dominic and Jacob. "You're damn right we will," he called after him. "I'm going to want details. Length, girth, taste—"

"Xan!" Jacob cried.

"Get to work," Dominic said.

"Okay, okay." Xan looked at Elliot. "Later, Ellie."

"What are the chances that you will never mention this again?" the mortified vampire asked, sinking down in his chair.

"Slim to none. Mainly none."

Xan walked out of the office and straight into Paul. The vampire raised his hand to Xan's chest to prevent a collision. He kept it there until Xan carefully pushed it away.

"I assume you've heard that I'll be staying in Harborview for a while."

"Yeah." Xan took a step back. Being too close to Paul still had an effect on him. "Is that your punishment for trying to help me?"

"It's business," the vampire responded, though he didn't seem too persuaded by his own explanation. "I'm glad to see that you're doing all right. Anyone else might have lost it after... all of that."

"I never had a chance to thank you that night," Xan began, avoiding Paul's eyes. "If you hadn't tried to stop Vincenzo, my dads would've gotten there too late. So... thank you."

"You're welcome. Oh, I have something for you." Paul reached into his jacket pocket and brought out a cell phone and a wallet. "For Michael, actually. I found them in a box when I was cleaning up at Steven's house. I checked the I.D. in the wallet and assumed the phone went with it."

"You could have given these to him yourself," Xan pointed out as he accepted the items.

"I know."

"We're together now, just so you know. As in... *together*."

Paul didn't hide his disappointment but still managed to smile. "Congratulations."

"Do you mean that?"

"Yes. I'm perfectly capable of wishing you well even though I still want to fuck you."

Upon hearing that, Xan almost dropped the phone and wallet. "Don't say that."

"Why does it bother you? The feeling is no longer mutual, right?" Paul's smile grew wider. "I'll see you later."

He entered the office, leaving Xan to stare dumbly at the closed door. It took a moment, but Xan gathered his wits and headed upstairs. As soon as he saw Michael, a wave of affection washed over him, and all at once he forgot about Paul and the question that he hadn't been able to answer.

THE FOLLOWING NIGHT, Xan and Michael paid Dominic and Jacob a visit. As was often the case when Xan came over, he was ushered into the

kitchen and seated at the table so that Dominic could feed him. Michael and Luca remained in the living room.

Jacob looked at the helmet that Xan placed on the table and nodded approvingly. "I'm glad to see that you're finally taking precautions on that death trap."

"It was the only way I could get Michael to ride with me."

Jacob was impressed. "Good for him."

Dominic passed him a sandwich and a glass of water and sat down beside Jacob. "You should be grateful that we care so much about keeping your skull intact."

"I am." Xan picked a couple of slices of salami from the sandwich and shoved them into his mouth. "It's annoying, but I get it."

They made small talk while he ate, most of which centered on the newest addition to the Rising Sun's staff. Elliot hadn't been pleased about Paul's sudden and non-negotiable employment but agreed to do his part if it meant Vincenzo would stay away.

"What about you, Alexander?" Dominic asked. "How will this affect you?"

Xan suspected that his father's real concern was whether or not he would be able to keep his hands off Paul. "It is what it is. Actually, that kind of brings me to what I needed to talk about."

"What is it?" Jacob asked.

Xan downed half the glass of water and stifled a burp. He pushed the glass and plate aside. "I'd like a promotion, please."

Dominic inclined his head. "A promotion?"

"Yeah. I want to do something besides bartending. Something different."

His parents exchanged glances before turning their attention back to him.

"Something like what?" Jacob wanted to know.

"I could help with the club or with the shelter. Or I could be a liaison. I'm sure some of your human partners would like not having to wait until the middle of the night to do business with you. Whatever you need me to do." Xan saw Dominic open his mouth and sensed an objection coming. "I know you never wanted me to get involved with what you do," he said, cutting him off. "You want to keep me safe, and I love you guys for that. I really do. But it's time for me to stop coasting through life. It's time for me to grow up."

He heaved a sigh and waited for their response. Dominic and Jacob looked at each other again. After a minute that felt like an eternity, Xan was given an answer.

"All right," Dominic said.

Xan was so certain of a denial that he was about to argue. Then he realized there was no need. "Really?"

"You were expecting us to say no?" Jacob asked.

"Well, yeah."

"Working for us was never our first career choice for you," Dominic admitted. "But it isn't our choice to make. If this is what you want, then we won't try to stop you."

"You understand that this means absolutely no more slacking off," Jacob added. "No more taking days off at a time. No more fucking around."

"Literally," Dominic added.

Jacob continued, "If you want more responsibility, we expect you to take it seriously."

Xan nodded emphatically. "I know. I will."

"We'll need some time to decide what we're going to do with you," Dominic said. "In the meantime, I suggest you make sure that Michael is properly trained to take over your position."

"Okay. Thank you so much."

An anguished cry came from the living room. They went to investigate and found Michael and Luca kneeling on opposite ends of the coffee table. Michael was holding his wrist and pouting while Luca's arms were raised triumphantly.

"What the hell are you two doing?" Xan asked.

"He thought he could beat me at arm wrestling," Luca answered. "I tried to warn him."

Michael was mystified. "How did you do that? You *are* human, right?"

"Luca is special," Jacob informed him, clapping a hand on the muscular man's shoulder. "He's been known to give some vampires a run for their money."

Xan added to this by telling Michael about the time when Luca wrecked the face of a vampire who hadn't been able to take no for an answer. He had taken Xan to see *The A-Team* for his eighteenth birthday while Dominic and Jacob readied the house for the party they were having later that night. Xan had politely declined the vampire's many advances in the lobby and parking lot, not because he wasn't interested but because he was in a hurry to get home and find out if Dominic was going to give him his old BMW. The vampire was unable to take a hint and made the mistake of grabbing him by the arm. Luca stepped between them and the vampire made an even bigger mistake of baring his fangs. In response, Luca bared his fist. The vampire's shattered nose was worth the two broken fingers it had cost him.

"It wasn't that big a deal," Luca insisted.

"You destroyed some vampire's face to protect me. That's a *huge* deal."

"I would have had a crush on him, too, if he did that for me," Jacob remarked.

Xan's face reddened. "What? I didn't have a crush on him!" After seeing the expressions of disbelief throughout the room, he sat down and covered his face with his hands. "How did you know?"

"You weren't very subtle about it," Dominic said.

"Not at all," Jacob added.

"You really weren't," Luca piped in. "Okay, we've embarrassed you enough."

"Have we?" Jacob tapped Michael's shoulder. "Would you like to see pictures of Xan as a baby?"

"Oh no," Xan groaned.

"Sure," Michael replied with far more enthusiasm than Xan thought necessary.

And that was how they came to spend the next hour going through stacks of photo albums while Xan tried unsuccessfully to disappear through the floor. Despite his embarrassment, he was thrilled to see everyone getting along so well. It meant a lot to him that they were all treating Michael so kindly, even if it was at his expense.

He fetched his helmet and announced that they had to leave before Jacob could whip out the home movies. "You'll have plenty of chances to humiliate me later. Pace yourself."

They said their goodbyes and closed the door. As they headed toward the motorcycle, Xan could feel Michael trying to hold in his laughter. "Go on. Let it out."

So Michael did. He laughed so much that Xan was starting to regret telling him to do it. "I love your family," he said after quieting down.

Xan smiled fondly. "Yeah, they're okay." When they reached the bike, he asked, "Have you decided what you're going to do about your dad?"

After charging Michael's recovered phone, the vampire discovered that his father had attempted to call him multiple times. He didn't leave any messages, but Michael took it as a sign that perhaps the man *did* care about what had happened to him. "I'm going to see him. Not yet but soon. Once I decide how to tell him that I'm a vampire. And gay."

"Which one will he take harder?"

"I have no idea."

"Whatever happens, we'll get through it." Xan got on the bike and scooted forward to give Michael room to join him. When the vampire reminded him to put his helmet on, like he would forget, Xan snorted. "Keep that up and I'm going to start calling you Jacob Junior."

"Really?" Michael wrapped his arms around him. "Think about that for a second."

Xan did. "Never mind."

As the bike roared into life, Michael tightened his grip on Xan and kissed him on the shoulder. They took off for the Rising Sun, weaving through traffic without a care, with a full moon high above them and a promising future ahead.

JACOB SMILED WHEN A blanket was placed over his shoulders. He had been so worried about remembering one to sit on that he forgot to bring a second. "My hero," he cooed as Dominic sat down beside him.

"One of us needs to think about regulating your body temperature."

"You could have warmed me up without the blanket."

"The last time we did that out here, someone called the police."

Jacob remembered that night well. Like tonight, they had been watching the moon and listening to the waves. One thing led to another and before Jacob knew it, he was lying flat on his back and screaming at the sky. The flashing lights of squad cars came shortly after that. "That was hilarious."

They chatted for a while about silly things like Jacob's long ago dream of opening an adult store for the sole purpose of getting free flavored lube and not-so-silly things such as Demetrio's anger over Vincenzo's actions. The vampire had refused to say goodbye to him and changed the subject whenever Dominic tried to talk to him about it.

"Having a father was always important to him," Dominic said. "I hate that I took that away from him."

"I'm sure that having you is more important to him. Besides, Vincenzo's obsession with you is the reason for all of this. If Demetrio never speaks to him again, he only has himself to blame." A gust of chilling wind came in from the lake. Jacob put his arm around Dominic, sharing the blanket with him. "You know that I probably would have gotten all of us killed if you had kissed him."

Dominic's body quivered with suppressed laughter. "I know. I do love your possessive side."

"Thanks." Jacob gave him a lopsided grin. "Quick thinking, though. I'll give you that much."

They snuggled beneath the blanket and listened to the night sounds. Had it been May or June instead of the first week of October, Jacob would have suggested a short, naked dip in the lake. He was willing to settle for a long, naked soak in the tub later.

"Michael will be good for Alexander," Dominic commented, interrupting his visions of bath time.

Jacob nodded. "I can't believe I'm saying this, but I hope it works out for them."

"I don't imagine it will be easy."

"Most relationships take work. Ours did, in the beginning." Jacob drew circles in the sand. "I don't know how you put up with me back then."

"You were hurt. After what James did to you, you had every reason not to trust me or any other vampire."

"I didn't trust humans either," Jacob pointed out. "Not after *that* night. I was just a hot mess all around."

"You were. But you were also worth the wait." Dominic presented the vampire with a black velvet ring box. "I should have done this sooner. I'm sorry that I didn't."

Jacob wiped off his hand and took the box. Even though he knew what to expect, he still gasped when he opened it and saw the thick gold band that seemed to glow under the light of the moon. It was the perfect replacement for the ring that was now hidden away at the back of the safe in their office.

"I love it." He took it out and held it in his palm.

Dominic picked it up and slid it onto Jacob's left ring finger. "I hoped you would."

It didn't take long for Jacob's kiss of gratitude to turn into something more. Dominic broke away with a sigh, one hand caressing the vampire's scarred back. "I should check in with Elliot," he said, moaning as Jacob lightly bit him on the neck. "And one of us should go to the shelter. We're heading into the busiest time of the year."

"Or we could stay home and have sex and do the rest of that stuff tomorrow night," Jacob suggested.

"I like that option."

"Race you to the house."

"That's very immature, Jacob."

"I know. Ready, set, go!"

They tossed the blanket aside and started up the pathway leading back to the house. Dominic took to the air and beat Jacob easily. Jacob responded by calling him a cheater.

"I'll make it up to you," Dominic promised while pulling his scowling lover through the door.

He led Jacob down to the basement and pushed him onto the bed. Shortly before dawn, a hoarse and trembling Jacob finally forgave him.

After a long, leisurely bath, they returned to bed. Jacob stared into the darkness and played with the strands of Dominic's hair that had fallen across his chest.

Vincenzo was still out there, now with a maniac under his wing. Someone had turned Ginger's kids and possibly others. On top of all of that, thanks to Vincenzo, was now the additional task of reestablishing authority over any vampire or human who might object to their rule. For every obstacle they had encountered the past two weeks, there was another one waiting to take its place. Things were peaceful right now, but how long was it going to last?

With a firm shake of the head, Jacob pushed the negative thoughts out of his mind. All of that worrying was ruining his afterglow. He and Dominic would face whatever challenges awaited them the same way as all of the other challenges they faced over the past 210 years.

They would face them *together*.

"Jacob?"

"Yes?"

"Are you braiding my hair?"

Jacob sneakily loosened the braid that he had started. "No. Now go to sleep."

BONUS CHAPTER 2.5

FUCK CHEMICAL ENGINEERING.

Michael closed his textbook and placed it on top of all the other textbooks that were stacked neatly on the upper right corner of his desk. He had a sudden urge to knock them all down to the floor, but he knew that such an act of defiance was meaningless. Aside from being the sole witness to his rare outburst of anger, he would also get stuck with the mess, which would only make him angrier. So instead, he sat back in his chair and stared blindly at his laptop where a flurry of screensaving bubbles danced over a blank document upon which he would churn out some eloquently written bullshit. The agitation would pass, same as it had since the day he first began his collegiate endeavor six years ago at the age of seventeen. Same as it had his entire overachieving life.

It was during times like these when Michael hated his father. If given the choice, he would have pursued an education in something far less boring and practical. Something like art, for instance. He loved to draw and used to be pretty good at it. Unfortunately, Hideaki Fukuhara had greater plans for his only child. Michael's dreams meant nothing compared to his father's honor, and there was no honor to be found in what Hideaki dismissed as frivolous sketches. He couldn't recall ever having a discussion with the man that wasn't about some aspect of his schooling, and for as long as he could remember he had felt like a trophy instead of a person, the ultimate representation of his father's ego. Along with upholding Hideaki's pride, there was also the matter of carrying on his name. Hints were already being dropped about settling down and making babies, preferably boy babies. Michael despised the idea of marrying some random woman just because daddy said so. Being gay didn't help.

When he was younger, he was perfectly willing to give up his boyhood hobbies for Hideaki's acceptance. Gone were the sketchbooks and video games and manga, sacrificed for a whiff of parental approval. Now that he was older and less than a year away from devoting the rest of his life to all the things he did not desire, Michael realized that he wanted more. He wanted to be free. Sometimes he thought about dropping everything and running far away to a place where he could start over again, but just like his aspirations of old, it was never going to happen, at least not without some drastic intervention. Maybe not even then. Hating his father was easy but defying him was unimaginable. Therefore, Michael took what satisfaction he could from his small acts of rebellion. Okay, getting the tattoo wasn't such a small act. He would try to refrain from doing anything that extreme tonight.

Screw the report. It wasn't due for two more weeks so waiting an extra day to begin wasn't going to hurt. Michael closed his laptop without shutting it down—the most daring thing he'd done all day—and pushed his feet into his favorite pair of black boots. There was a bar a few blocks away from Mercymore College that seemed to be a popular gathering spot for most of the guys in his dorm. Michael wasn't a heavy drinker himself but to hell with it, he would be tonight.

He grabbed his wallet and phone and stepped out of his room, where he was almost knocked over by a couple of boys who were roughhousing in the hallway. At least they were kind enough to stop groping each other long enough to say hello. Michael walked out of the building and into the crisp air of the night. He wished that he had a driver's license or a friend with a car, but since he had neither, walking would have to do. Fifteen minutes and some jaywalking later, he entered Opella's Pub and took a seat at the bar where he was approached by a female bartender he recognized from campus.

"Hey there, cutie," she said, smiling sweetly. "What'll it be?"

Michael highly doubted that the place served what he really wanted. Although he didn't drink nearly as much as everyone else in his dorm—if the near nightly sounds of partying were to be believed—years of occasionally sneaking into Hideaki's stash had caused him to develop a taste for flavored sake, apple in particular. For tonight, beer would have to do. "I'll take a Yuengling, please."

"You got it." She winked and walked away, and how she did that while wearing what appeared to be the world's tightest jeans was a mystery to Michael.

"She likes you."

Michael almost didn't hear the guy's comment because of the song blaring from the speaker beside him, an older tune from a band that had something to do with deaf leopards. "What makes you say that?" he asked, leaning across the empty stool between them to hear him better.

"She's never called me cute."

Well, he *was* cute, that was for sure. He didn't look much older than eighteen, let alone the minimum age of twenty-one that was required for entrance into the bar. His blond hair was dark, bordering on a lighter shade of brown, and his eyes were two different colors, the left one brown and the right one blue. It was the first time that Michael had ever seen a case of heterochromia in person.

"Maybe I'm not as cute as I think I am." The young man slid over to the empty stool and stared at Michael with those fascinating eyes. "What do *you* think?"

Was this guy flirting with him? Michael didn't think that he would inquire about his attractiveness without some secret and possibly (hopefully) sexual agenda.

He decided to answer honestly. "I think you're very good-looking."

"Thanks. You're pretty hot yourself."

Michael barely noticed when the bartender brought him his drink. He was far too mesmerized by his present company to pay much attention to anyone or anything else around him. The stranger pulled out his wallet before it occurred to Michael that he still needed to pay and gave her a twenty to cover the Yuengling plus another drink for himself.

"I'm Steven," he said as he extended his hand.

"Michael."

"Very nice to meet you, Michael."

Steven's hand was cool to the touch. Michael wondered how it would feel on other parts of his body. "Do you mind if I ask you something?"

"You want to know how old I am."

"Yeah," Michael admitted.

Steven smiled knowingly. "I'm not jailbait, if that's what you're worried about. Not that I'm clarifying under the assumption that you want to fuck me. Unless you want to fuck me."

Michael almost choked on his beer. And even more potentially embarrassing than hacking up a lung in public was the erection forming between his legs.

"Are you okay?" Steven asked, his eyes filled with amusement.

"Yeah. I just wasn't expecting that." Michael took a drink without choking this time and definitely didn't imagine the suggestive look he got when he wrapped his lips around the top of the bottle.

"I'm sorry if I made you uncomfortable. I've never had much of a filter."

"You didn't make me uncomfortable," Michael insisted. "And filters suck."

Steven tapped his glass to Michael's bottle. "They sure do."

After three more rounds, he asked if Michael wanted to come over to his place.

"I promise not to bite," he added.

If only that was the truth.

Was a one-night stand with a stranger as extreme as a tattoo? By Michael's mildly inebriated logic, a one-night stand was just that—one night—unlike his tattoo, which was forever. Either way, he was a little too drunk and way too horny to care about specifics. He hadn't had sex in two years, and this sure beat the hell out of returning to his room and masturbating to gay porn for the rest of the night.

"Okay."

After finishing his drink, he followed Steven out of the bar... and right into the worst mistake of his life.

FIRST CAME THE DARKNESS. Then came the pain.

Michael was aware of both as he emerged from the murky depths of unconsciousness. The darkness was easy to figure out; he was blindfolded. It was the perfect accompaniment to whatever was being used to gag his mouth. The pain was harder to pinpoint. He hurt *everywhere*. Most of it seemed to be located in his head, leading him to briefly speculate that he had a hangover. But he hadn't been that drunk. Now that the fog in his mind was clearing, he remembered that he'd only had three, no, four beers. Enough to make him tipsy but not nearly enough to incapacitate him.

Then it hit him, the memory of what happened after he got into Steven's car. Just as Michael was fastening his seat belt and looking forward to a long night of fucking (but not too long because he had class the next morning), Steven punched him in the face with surprising ferocity, causing the back of his head to slam into the passenger side window. The last thing Michael heard before losing awareness was laughter, and the last thing he saw was a set of sharp fangs.

Hold on. Fangs? That was impossible. Not to mention insane. But that didn't matter because Michael had far more important things to worry about than his declining sanity. Now that he was wide awake, the darkness and pain were joined by a crippling sense of fear. As much as he had wanted to escape the demands of his father, getting himself murdered was certainly *not* the way he wanted to do it.

He tried to move, but the chains that held him to the bed prevented it. There was something slippery beneath him, and when he determined it was some kind of plastic or tarp that was probably meant to keep anything from staining the bedding underneath, his heart began to pound.

"You need to calm down before you give yourself a heart attack."

Michael shuddered when he heard Steven's voice. There was no malice in his tone, but that did nothing to take the edge off Michael's panic. He cringed when those same cold fingers he fantasized about earlier caressed his face and slid under the blindfold, pulling it up and over his head. Michael squinted until his eyes adjusted to the light. When he was able to open them completely, he saw his attacker hovering over him with a disturbingly serene expression.

"I was only going to kill you, but then you had to be so damn adorable," Steven continued, sitting down beside him. He ran his hand along Michael's arm, stopping to fiddle with the metal cuff around his wrist. "I decided to keep you. I haven't wanted to keep someone in years. You should take that as a compliment."

Michael's eyes widened when Steven climbed on top of him. He started thrashing wildly, trying desperately to buck him off. Even if he couldn't do anything about dying, he wasn't about to let this madman have his way with him. Not without a fight.

"Be still, Michael."

To Michael's shock and horror, his body complied. He no longer had any control over his muscles. It was a sensation he would come to know well over the next few weeks.

Steven nuzzled the young man's cheek. "I am going to savor *every drop* of you."

Then he smiled. The fangs Michael thought he imagined were very real. And very painful.

THE TARP WASN'T INTENDED for blood, though there had been plenty of it. It was for the vomit, piss, and shit that forcefully exited Michael's newly deceased body, and hadn't that just been fantastically disgusting. Steven had taken off his clothes and washed him without complaint, which was only right since he was the one responsible for the mess in the first place. Days after his demise and an agonizing bout of rigor mortis that had him screaming for hours, Michael was still secured to the bed, his now naked body continuing to grapple with the transition from human to vampire.

"You're past the worst part," Steven said. He lifted Michael's head and held a glass to his lips. "Drink."

Michael was so hungry that he didn't even try to resist. There was a strange feeling of pressure in his gums as his eye teeth elongated in reaction to the smell of the blood. He gulped down the dark liquid, appalled by his actions but unable to stop. When Steven pulled the glass away from him, he whimpered and craned his neck for more.

"That's enough for now." Steven set the glass aside. "Are you feeling better?"

"Fuck you," Michael whispered.

He let his head fall back against the bed and glared at the vampire. Three days ago, the idea of dying scared him more than anything. Now that he was dead, what was left for him to fear? There was nothing else that Steven could do to make him suffer more than he had already.

Then Steven pulled a knife out of his pocket and proved him wrong. He smiled the entire time.

After Michael's body healed, Steven did it again. And again.

By the end of the second week, death was starting to look good.

TONIGHT WAS THE NIGHT. Steven had announced that he was stepping out. In response, Michael flipped him the bird. That was twenty minutes ago, which was all the time it took for his broken finger to heal. He didn't know if he was strong enough to do what he needed to do. His body was weak from hunger and the corpse blood that Steven used to immobilize him while he... did things. All Michael knew was that he had to try.

If the cuffs around his wrists and ankles had been even the slightest bit thicker or made with silver, he would have been screwed. It took everything he had, twisting his body in ways it was never meant to bend, but he eventually managed to break the chains that connected the cuffs, as well as the larger ones that bound him to the bed. He cracked the bones in his left wrist and right ankle and also broke a couple of ribs from the effort, but he could already feel them mending.

Michael sat up for the first time in weeks and glanced around. His clothes were folded neatly on a table across the room and his boots were on the floor. He stood up slowly, half expecting his legs to succumb to atrophy. To his amazement, he was able to move just fine. Michael grabbed his clothes and quickly got dressed, then snatched up his boots. He didn't know where his wallet and phone were, nor did he have time to hunt for them.

He ran up the steps leading out of the basement. It was only when he reached for the door that he considered the possibility of being locked in. Thankfully, he wasn't. He walked out of the room and down a long hallway until he reached a plainly decorated living room. It looked like the kind of place where an older person might live, which made some sense as Steven had revealed to him that he was fifty-four. Michael would never forget that because it was the same night they had played an excessively gruesome game of autopsy.

He spotted a set of keys on a coffee table next to a remote and a mug that was caked with dried blood. They weren't the kind made for doors. He wasn't sure if they would be useful but he wanted to be far away before he gave them a try.

The house wasn't exactly in the middle of nowhere, but the nearest neighbor was at least a half-mile away. That would explain why his many screams had gone unnoticed. Michael started running, his bare feet smacking against the road. He had no idea where he was or where he was going. Returning to Mercymore in his present state was out of the question, as was going to his father's house. Maybe someday, but not today. Still, he had successfully escaped the lair of a lunatic. That was a good start.

He kept to the side roads as a precaution. The farther he ran, the more familiar his surroundings became. He was somewhere in Crusherville, a small town just outside of Harborview, about half an hour from the college.

After verifying that there were no cars around, Michael sat down on a bus stop bench. He tried the keys and was able to remove the cuffs from his wrists and ankles. His good start was getting better. With that out of the way, he put on his boots and pondered his next move. While doing so, he heard the patter of approaching feet, too soft and nimble to belong to a human.

The stray stopped and sniffed at the cuffs he had thrown on the ground. Concluding that they were not edible, she stared at Michael as if to accuse him of trickery.

"Hey, don't look at me like that," he said. "If it makes you feel any better, I'm hungry, too."

The dog stepped closer to Michael and rested her chin on his knee. He could hear her heartbeat, and on the heels of that came a thought so atrocious that he pushed it out of his mind before it could fully form.

He wasn't *that* hungry.

Michael got up. He needed to find somewhere to hide for a while.

As he started walking again, he saw a convenience store about a mile up the road. That was as good a place as any.

191

BONUS CHAPTER 4.5

AFTER PARTING WAYS with Xan in the bathroom, Paolo Marinelli, known by the dreadfully boring but necessary alias of Paul Marin, returned to the bar and ordered a drink. Seeing as how just about everything else on Xan's body was pierced or tattooed, Paul had been surprised (and slightly disappointed) that his cock wasn't. It was a nice, uncut cock, but still just a cock. Over the past few months of discreet observation, Paul had grown increasingly fascinated by all of Xan's jewelry and ink, two things that seemed more fitting for a burly biker than a spoiled rich kid. Perhaps he chose to mark his body as an act of rebellion or to establish his individuality, though Paul could think of nothing more individual than being a lone human in a world of bloodthirsty beings. Whatever the reason, the vampire intended to find out later, after Xan was done with work and they were able to pick up where they left off.

For now, Paul resigned himself to drinking and trying to go soft. He wasn't normally into humans, sexually or socially, but this one... this one was different. In spite of their limited verbal interaction so far, Paul could tell that there was more to Xan than his obvious willingness to bed anything with a dick. There was something deeper there, lurking just beneath the seductiveness, and Paul wanted to know what it was.

He saw nothing of immediate interest behind the bar—the redhead who had interrupted them was cute but not his type—so instead he waited for Xan to return from seeing his father, since Dominic was the *real* reason that he was even there in the first place. When Vincenzo first instructed Paul to report any sightings of the vampire, he warned him that Dominic's presence would be limited at best, as the accountant-looking vampire was the one who kept things going while he was "cavorting with that slave." Paul was under no obligation to do anything other than watch, but if given the chance, he supposed it wouldn't hurt to press Xan for information about Dominic's actions.

As he sipped his drink, a berry-flavored liqueur that went a long way toward eliminating the taste of the young man from his mouth, he contemplated the mission that brought him to Harborview in the first place. He had no idea yet what Vincenzo planned to do, but he had a feeling that it involved staying in the city for a while. Paul had no opinion on that one way or the other because his place was by Vincenzo's side, wherever that might be.

As for what Vincenzo was going to do to Xan... Paul had *very strong* opinions about that.

By the time he finished his drink, he changed his mind about waiting. The music was starting to get on his nerves, plus if he went down to the lower level, perhaps he would catch a closer glimpse of Dominic. Paul was intrigued by his master's most prized possession. Although his own feelings for Vincenzo had diminished years ago, leaving only a fierce sense of loyalty in place of the love that would never be returned, he wanted to know more about the vampire who had so foolishly denied the affection of one who rarely gave it. What was it about Dominic that made him so special? Whatever it was, it didn't seem to apply to his twin brother, whom Paul suspected Vincenzo tolerated primarily because of their resemblance.

"Are you leaving?"

Paul regarded the human who had managed to sneak up on him while he was lost in thought. "I was going downstairs."

"To find me?" Xan asked.

"Maybe." While not exactly the truth, it wouldn't hurt for him to believe that.

"Well, I'm back now, so have a seat. Besides, you're too young to hang out with all those old fogeys."

"You're an expert at guessing vampire ages?" Paul sat back down and leaned against the bar top, resting his chin on his palm. "How old do you think I am?"

Xan studied him for a moment. "You can't be over a hundred," he guessed.

"I'm flattered," Paul replied. "Add fifty to that. It still makes me pretty young compared to the vampires down there, but I'm hardly a baby."

"I guess not."

"Do you have anything against fucking older men?"

"Not when they look like you."

Paul clenched his teeth as fingers wandered over his chest. So much for going soft. "You should probably get back to work," he said.

"Yeah, he should," the redhead behind the bar angrily agreed.

Xan chuckled and shrugged. "Fine." He slowly traced the outline of Paul's left nipple and gave it a pinch for good measure. "Sit tight. I'll bring you another drink."

Paul shifted around on the stool until he found a way of sitting that wasn't too uncomfortable. He graciously accepted the drink Xan mixed for him and hid his smile behind the glass as the redhead reprimanded him for avoiding his duties. Poor girl. Xan didn't come across like the kind of person who had much of a work ethic. Paul couldn't imagine how frustrating it must have been to work with someone like that, especially when that someone was the owners' son.

After being lectured, Xan went back to work, taking an order from two vampires on the other end of the bar. Paul wasn't sure if they were a couple or not. If they were, then the younger one—who was awfully cute in a disheveled sort of way—didn't appear to be too thrilled about it. As a matter of fact, he looked downright repulsed. Paul couldn't blame him; he had seen the older vampire making the rounds before, trying and failing repeatedly to charm his way down everyone's pants. He had once attempted to chat up Paul before a murderous glare sent him scrambling for cover.

Paul let his mind and eyes wander elsewhere, namely to the dance floor where two vampires were grinding on each other so hard that it was a miracle they didn't burst into flames from the friction. When the older vampire passed through his line of sight, visibly disgruntled and very much alone, Paul turned back to the bar.

He saw Xan speaking to the young vampire, and his lust took a temporary backseat to his curiosity. What were they discussing that caused such a look of concern on the vampire's face? Why did the older vampire take off so suddenly? He debated asking when Xan brought him another drink but decided not to when he sensed a change in the human's demeanor. While

Xan was still being his flirtatious self, Paul could tell that he was distracted. But why?

He spotted the young vampire staring their way. It didn't take a genius to guess where that downward gaze was focused. Not that Paul could blame the kid; Xan had a great ass.

"He looks ready for another," the vampire suggested, nodding toward Xan's audience of one.

Xan turned his head. The kid looked away so fast that it was a wonder he didn't give himself whiplash.

"Yeah, I should get back over there. Are you good?"

"I am. Thank you."

Paul sipped on his drink as Xan served the vampire another glass of blood and poured himself a shot. Whatever they were talking about was serious enough for Xan to ignore the other patrons who were waiting to be served.

... And serious enough for him to follow the vampire out of the club.

"Well, this is interesting," Paul muttered into his glass.

Perhaps the vampire forgot something. Paul had no clue what that something could have been since he had arrived at the bar with nothing but a pervert attached to his hip. Another possibility, one that was far more displeasing, was that Xan sought to continue their conversation somewhere more private.

But no, that couldn't be right. After what happened in the bathroom, there was no way that Xan would just up and take off without him.

Paul continued drinking, confident that Xan would be back shortly.

One hour later, he accepted defeat.

In addition to being disappointed, Paul was still quite aroused thanks to Xan. When a good-looking, *young*-looking vampire sat down beside him, he realized that the night might not be a total bust after all.

The stranger glanced his way. His left eye was brown and his right eye was blue. "How are you?" he asked.

"Other than being ditched, I'm good." Paul scooted closer to him, unaware that he would soon be witness to the brutal extraction of those captivating eyes. "What about you? What brings you out tonight?"

"Me? Oh, I'm just... looking for something I lost."

BONUS CHAPTER 7.5

TUCKER FRANKLIN COULDN'T see the lining of his coffin as he was presently encased in the life-preserving darkness it provided, but he could imagine it clearly, pristine and white and annoyingly virginal. One of these days, he wanted to have it replaced with a far more tolerable color like blue or green or purple. Until then he would just deal with it. As long as the coffin served its purpose and kept him from becoming a steaming pile of ashes and glop, he supposed it shouldn't matter that the interior made him feel like he was trapped in the center of a satiny cloud.

He laced his fingers across his chest and twiddled his thumbs. Being in an airtight space, he couldn't even express his boredom with a sigh. Waking up before sundown was such a pain in the ass. If he hadn't preferred to spend most of his money on clothes, he would have bought a house with a basement so that he could black out the windows and piss around at his leisure on the occasions when he didn't sleep until nightfall. There were only so many ways to pass the time while cramped in such a tight space; he was sick to death of playing cell phone games in the dark, and masturbating in a coffin was awkward and messy. With no other options, he decided to let his mind wander instead.

It was Sunday evening and would be a cool one if the forecast kept its word. Tonight was also the one night of the week that he had to work, although doing something that came naturally and getting paid a ton of money for it hardly seemed like a job. A few hours once a week and some softly spoken words, those were the only things required of him. Piece of cake.

As he often did during those precious few hours before he was scheduled to be at the Dawson House, Tuck thought of his employer and, for his part at least, friend. He had such an insatiable crush on Jacob, five years and counting, and the rare Sunday nights when the vampire stopped by the homeless shelter made Tuck downright giddy. On the inside, of course. Had their respective journeys played out differently, Tuck might have let his feelings be known. But what Dominic and Jacob had was nothing short of impenetrable, and that was never going to change. He also had a sneaking suspicion that he reminded Jacob of Xan, with their similar hair and eye colors, Tuck's being a few shades darker. They were even close to the same height. Even if Jacob was available, Tuck doubted that he would be into fucking someone who looked like his son. Therefore, he was content to bear his feelings in silence and keep his schoolboy infatuation to himself.

After spending the next hour fantasizing about things that would never be, Tuck raised the lid of his coffin and stepped out onto the floor. He crossed the bedroom and entered a closet that was almost just as big. Moving past the more expensive attire, he settled on blue jeans and a white T-shirt, shaking his head at his own hypocrisy in choosing to wear the very same color he hated so much. There was no point in getting decked out for work. He was able to connect with the people much easier when he didn't look like some rich yuppie.

Tuck showered and dressed, then heated up some blood. He headed into the living room to fast forward through the football games that had recorded on the DVR while he slept. The Steelers were doing okay so far this season and the Browns... well, they tried. Like many in Harborview, a city that was a little over an hour's drive to both Pittsburgh and Cleveland, he loved both teams equally and refused to pick one over the other. When he finished his liquid meal, he popped a stick of spearmint gum into his mouth. The one thing that Tuck missed most about being human was food; his late wife, rest her soul, had accused him many times of nearly eating them out of house and home. Although chewing gum wasn't the same by a long shot, going through the motions had a pacifying effect on him.

After he was done with football—both teams won—he locked up the condo and left for the shelter. Since the forecast turned out to be accurate, he drove to his destination with the windows down, the chilly autumn air filling his Lexus along with the sound of Thin Lizzy. Upon arriving at the shelter, Tuck parked in the back. Any attempts to downplay his true net worth were pointless if he was spotted driving a luxury vehicle. Using a swipe card, he entered the building through a door not accessible to the public and made his way down a flight of stairs that led to the underground collection area.

The Dawson House was well-known for being a place where no one in need was ever turned away, something that was especially appreciated during the bitter winter months when conditions were more hazardous than usual for the homeless. Privately funded by Dominic and Jacob, the shelter provided food and lodging every single day of the year and received nothing in return from the humans who sought refuge there... as far as those humans knew. Which was where Tuck came in.

"Hello, Tucker."

"Hello, Ruth."

Tuck smiled at the vampire as she catalogued numerous bags of blood spread out over a counter and separated by type. She moved speedily and efficiently as they needed to be placed into storage until they could be tested, and Tuck decided not to bother her further until she was finished. While he waited, he contemplated the differences in their physical appearances. Ruth looked older, her black hair laced with streaks of white, but Tuck was ten years her senior at sixty-seven, frozen in the same body he had back in 1973 when he was twenty-six. It was weird for him, knowing that he was her elder when he didn't look or act anything like it. Surely Ruth felt the same way, but he could never bring himself to ask.

"How'd we do?" he asked after the last bag was put away.

"The numbers aren't as good as last time," she said, her grey eyes moving over the clipboard in her hands. "We'll have a much better turnout when the temperature starts to dip." She tossed the clipboard onto the counter and held out a box of cigarettes. "Want one?"

"Sure." Tuck wasn't a smoker, but since many of the people who resided there had the habit, he decided it wouldn't hurt if they smelled it on him.

Ruth lit two cigarettes and handed one to Tuck in exchange for throwing out his gum. "Mr. Crawford has aspirations of leaving again. You know what you need to do."

Tuck took a deep drag and exhaled. "Yeah," he replied with a nod, even though he didn't necessarily agree. Wiping memories of donations was one thing, and it was vital to do so if they were going to maintain a steady influx of blood. One of the keys to their livelihood was that people had no idea the price they truly paid for staying at the shelter. But preventing someone from leaving was different. The Dawson House wasn't a prison, and while most people voluntarily chose to stay, Tuck wasn't comfortable with the thought of keeping anyone there against their will.

"It's for his own good," Ruth said, understanding his concern. "Better for him to stay here than wander the streets where he might end up feeding a vampire the hard way."

She was right. What they did there at the shelter kept humans safe by keeping vampires fed through means other than hunting and killing. Sure, there was the business side of it, and blood trafficking was no different than any other trafficking in most respects. But unlike guns or drugs, the blood they collected *saved* lives. Tuck wanted to believe that Jacob and Dominic cared about that end of things on top of making money. Even if they didn't, he did.

He finished his smoke and went to work on another piece of gum, then stepped into the long hallway where two dozen rooms branched off, twelve to a side and with a human waiting in each one. The donation schedule was staggered, with one vampire assigned a day of the week and a certain number of humans. This way, they were able to collect blood discreetly and raise no red flags among outsiders. Tuck knocked on the first door to his left and went inside the room where good old Mr. Crawford was shoving a chocolate chip cookie into his mouth and chasing it with a cup of orange juice.

"Tuck!" he cried happily, spraying crumbs every which way.

"Hey, Mr. Crawford." Tuck closed the door and rolled a stool next to the donor chair where the old man sat. "How are you doing?" he asked as he took a seat.

"Not too bad." Mr. Crawford smiled at Tuck, exposing uneven rows of teeth that had seen far better days. "I hope they don't find anything in my blood. I didn't know what rubbers were back in my day."

Tuck had heard this story before, many times. There was no point in revealing to him that his blood was clean because he would only forget again.

"I'm sure it'll be fine," he reassured him as he casually ran a hand over his nose. Judging from his sense of smell, Mr. Crawford had apparently elected not to make frequent use of the shelter's free soap and water. "Ruth tells me that you're thinking about leaving us."

"Yeah, I like it here, but it's about time I hit the road and see what I can find."

Tuck was pretty sure that the only thing the elderly vagrant wanted to find was alcohol. "You should stay. You're safer here."

As he spoke, he gave the old man a mental push, just enough to reach the part of his brain that would bend him to Tuck's will. Some vampires were able to do this better than others; according to Ruth, Tuck was one of the best she had ever seen. Like the emergence of his fangs or his ability to fly, he had no idea how it worked. It just came naturally.

Mr. Crawford's eyelids fluttered briefly. A frown passed over his wrinkled face but didn't last for more than a few seconds. "I should stay," he said slowly, like he was waking from a dream. "I'm safer here."

"Yes, you are. Where else are you going to get a warm bed and three squares every day for free?" Tuck pushed again, a little harder. The thing about altering or completely erasing memories this way was that it didn't last forever. What he did here tonight had to stick for eight weeks, until it was time for this group to donate again. The entire operation would be jeopardized if one of them suddenly remembered giving a whole lot of blood over a long period of time.

"You're right. I got it real good here, don't I?"

Tuck was given another aesthetically-challenged smile. He considered pushing the man into brushing his teeth more often—and taking a damn shower—but chose not to press his luck. Human minds were far too fragile things. One wrong push would leave him a drooling lump for the rest of his life.

He stayed for a while and talked with Mr. Crawford. By the time their conversation ended, the man had no memory whatsoever of giving blood in spite of the bandage on his arm. Tuck wished him well as one of the shelter employees escorted him back to his room, and then he spent the next few hours repeating the process with all the others.

When his work was done, he helped Ruth set up for Monday's collection. It wasn't a part of his job, but it was the polite thing to do. After locking up for the night, Tuck walked her to her car and even opened the door for her. No matter how young he looked, he was from a time when that was the sort of thing you did for a lady.

"Do you want to get a drink?" he offered as she got in.

"I always say no," she responded, lighting a cigarette. "When are you going to learn?"

"Never."

Ruth made a shooing motion with her hand. "Go on, do whatever it is you kids do on the weekends."

"Did you just call me a kid? I'm older than you."

"Goodnight, Tucker."

"Goodnight." He grinned as he closed the door and waited until she left before getting into his own vehicle. It was a shame that mind control didn't work on vampires. He wanted to know what secrets were buried under that strictly business exterior.

When Tuck got home, he changed into clothing that was far more his style: a black and obscenely snug single-breasted Armani suit that had cost him approximately one week's four-figure pay. The Rising Sun wouldn't be nearly as crowded on a Sunday night as it usually was, but that didn't mean that he wasn't going to look his best.

After a much-needed application of mousse and a fresh stick of gum, Tuck was ready to go. He was almost to the door when his phone began to ring. Assuming it was one of his exes or Ruth, Tuck grabbed his phone and checked the display. He almost swallowed his gum when he saw the name. That would not have ended well.

He had to swipe at the screen twice to answer the call. Once he got it right, he brought the phone to his ear, his eyes closing in anticipation of hearing the voice he would imagine later when he shot off into his own hand. Or someone else's, if the night went well. "Hello?"

"Hey, Tuck. It's Jacob. Listen, I need you to do something for me..."

FAMILY MATTERS

BONUS CHAPTER 15.5

BRIAN OPENED HIS EYES and blinked at a ceiling he didn't recognize. The bed was also unfamiliar. His mattress was so cushiony that a person could get lost in it for days. This one was way too firm. It wasn't the first time he had come to in a stranger's bed, but it *was* the first time he couldn't remember the night before. He was exhausted but didn't feel the usual aches that accompanied a night full of fucking. There was, strangely enough, a maddening itch along his torso.

He lifted his arm to scratch at his stomach and discovered that his midsection was bandaged. "What the hell?" he croaked, tugging at it.

"I wouldn't do that if I were you." Elliot was sitting near the stairs, his legs crossed and a book draped over his thigh.

"Elliot?" Brian rasped. "Why am I in your basement? Did we have sex?"

The vampire's incredulous look and subsequent laughter told him all he needed to know.

Wait—had he ever heard Elliot laugh before? Brian didn't think that the vampire was even capable of possessing a sense of humor.

"You don't remember anything about last night?" Elliot asked, pushing up his glasses.

Brian frowned. He remembered inviting a cute little thing into the squad car and the blowjob that followed. After that, he remembered getting out of the car and walking behind the club. Xan had been there, taking out the trash. They had talked about his new vampire friend and then—

He sat up when he remembered the rest. "Where's Xan?"

"He's fine." Elliot set the book down and came over to the bed. "And so are you, but you need to get some more rest. Your body went through quite an ordeal."

Relieved that his friend was safe, Brian allowed Elliot to push him back down and check his bandages. There were things he *didn't* want to remember about last night, like being sliced open and the surreal and sickening sensation of his insides spilling out. He should be dead right now.

"You gave me your blood," he said thoughtfully.

"I did," Elliot replied.

"Why?"

"Why wouldn't I?"

Brian recalled the night that Elliot hired him. Initially, he hadn't known what to make of the bland, business-only vampire in the Buddy Holly glasses. "You warned me about the risk I was taking. I always assumed that if something happened to me, you'd just get rid of my body and find someone else to take my place."

Elliot drew back, offended. "If I'm not mistaken, I also told you that we're not all monsters."

"Yeah, you did. I'm glad I was wrong."

Their eyes met. For how long, Brian couldn't say. Eventually, Elliot averted his gaze and straightened up, then pushed up his glasses again.

"I don't have any food," he said regretfully. "I'll order something if you're hungry."

"I'm too tired to eat. Do you have anything to drink besides blood?"

"I have water and coffee."

Brian waited for him to finish listing the choices. There were no more. "No booze?"

"Not here. I only drink at the club. And even then, not very much."

"That's odd."

"Is it?"

"It is. I'll take some water, please."

Elliot grabbed a bottle of water from a refrigerator on the other side of the basement. He gave it to Brian and returned to his seat. After filling him in on what he knew of Xan's rescue, he became quiet and fidgeted with the edge of his book. Brian tilted his head to read the title. It was *War and Peace*.

"Why don't you drink very much?" he asked when the silence became too great.

"I've never had an overwhelming urge to do it."

Brian almost inquired about what other things Elliot never had overwhelming urges to do, but posing those types of questions to the boss who just saved his life didn't seem like the best idea. "Not even when you were human?"

"No. And it seems even more pointless to me now since we're not affected by alcohol anyway."

"It's a good thing most vampires don't feel that way or you'd be out of a job." Brian finished his water and placed the bottle on the floor. He folded his arms over his stomach and tried not to squirm. "How long am I going to itch like this?"

"It should lessen as the day goes by. Vampire blood usually works quickly, but given the extent of your wounds, it's taking longer."

Brian rubbed at the bandages until he caught Elliot's look of disapproval. "I broke my arm when I was fifteen," he began, gripping the blanket that covered him to distract his hands. "I was at the park and wanted to show off for my brother's best friend by walking across the monkey bars. It worked pretty well until I slipped off and busted my ass."

"Ouch," Elliot said, cringing.

"Fuck yeah, ouch. I broke my arm and had to wear a cast for a month. Talk about itching."

"That must have been awful."

"It was. I unfastened one of those old wire hangers and shoved it down in there. Ended up scratching the hell out of my arm, but at least it didn't itch after that."

"I never had any broken bones when I was a boy," Elliot told him. "Or scratches or bruises. I wasn't the active type."

"What did you do for fun?"

"I read." The vampire touched the book on his lap. "A lot."

"I should've done more of that myself. But breaking my arm got me my first French kiss so I can't really complain."

"Your brother's friend?"

Brian smiled proudly. "Yep."

"But you were only fifteen."

"So?" The officer narrowed his eyes at Elliot. "How old were you when you kissed someone for the first time?"

The vampire shifted in his seat. "I—I was a late bloomer."

"How late?"

"I was twenty."

Brian was tempted to call bullshit but could think of no reason that anyone would lie about that. Besides, reading people was a skill he had acquired over his years as a cop. Elliot was telling the truth. "Damn. How old were you when you lost your virginity?"

"That's none of your business."

"You're right." Brian smirked. "It's none of my business if you're still a virgin."

Elliot took the bait as Brian suspected he would. "I've had sex," he said defensively. "Once."

"One time?"

"One person. Multiple times."

Brian thought it was positively criminal that someone that hot wasn't getting laid on a regular basis. "Why only one person? Are you waiting for Mr. Right?"

"No."

"Mrs.?"

"I'm not waiting for anyone." Elliot nervously drummed his fingers against the cover of his book. "I've never been good at being social outside of work. From what I understand, that is usually a prerequisite for intercourse."

"You're talking to me."

"You're in my house. I can't ignore you."

"Well, thank you for not ignoring me."

Their eyes met again and remained that way until Elliot cleared his throat and turned away. "You should get some more sleep," he said, studying his feet.

"I can go upstairs," the policeman offered. "I assume you have a bedroom up there."

"I turned it into a library when I moved in."

"A couch?"

"I have a couch, but I don't trust you not to scratch yourself."

"I probably would." Brian slid over and patted the empty area beside him. "There you go."

Elliot looked at the bed as though it might bite him. "I'm fine where I am," he insisted.

"You can't sleep in a chair, Elliot. Get over here."

"Don't tell me what to do. I'm your supervisor."

"Yeah, but we're off the clock. Come on."

Reluctantly, Elliot turned out the lights and walked over to the bed. He took off his shoes and climbed in, keeping so close to the edge that he seemed in danger of falling out.

Brian heard the soft click of glasses being placed on the nightstand. He decided to ask about the one thing that had piqued his interest from the very start since he wasn't sure if he would ever have another chance. "Why do you wear glasses? I can't imagine that you actually need them."

He thought that he had finally crossed a line when Elliot didn't say anything at first. As he started to apologize, the vampire spoke.

"I was terribly nearsighted when I was human. I wore glasses all my life, even as a child. After I was turned and my vision had improved, I was... sad. In a way."

"Why?"

Elliot went silent again. After some time, he continued, "I was sad because the old me was dead. I don't regret my choice, but I wasn't expecting to mourn my human life as much as I did. I don't know if all vampires feel that way when they're first turned or if it was just me. So, to answer your question, I wear glasses because it's my way of remembering who I used to be." He took a deep breath. "And there you have it. Why do you ask? Did you think that I was just being a hipster?"

"Kind of, yeah."

Brian didn't have to see Elliot to know that he was smiling. He felt a sudden urge to reach out and caress his face, so he did. The vampire jerked back so violently that Brian was certain he was about to topple right out of the bed.

"I'm sorry," he said, bringing his arm back to his side. "I shouldn't have done that."

"No, I just... I mean... it's fine," Elliot replied cautiously. "You almost poked me in the eye."

The statement gave Brian hope. "Are you saying that I can touch you as long as I don't stick my finger in your eye?"

"Why would you want to do that?"

"Stick my finger in your eye?"

Elliot chuckled softly. "Why would you want to touch me?" he clarified.

Since Elliot had shared with him, Brian felt it only fair to return the favor. "I've wanted to touch you since the night I met you."

There was a sharp intake of breath from Elliot's side of the bed. "You wanted... but... you and Xan... that same night..."

Brian pieced together what Elliot was trying to say. "Yes, we had sex," he admitted. "That night and many other nights."

"I know. It was hard not to notice all the times your squad car was rocking."

"You watched us?"

"I was checking the cameras," Elliot said, bristling at the accusation. "It's part of my job. Speaking of which, I don't recall ever telling you that having sex in your car was a part of yours."

Brian laughed until his stomach ached along with the itch. This sounded more like the Elliot he knew. "Am I fired?"

"No."

"Can I touch you?"

"... I wouldn't object if you did."

Brian stroked Elliot's cheek, this time taking care to avoid his eye. His fingers eased over silky skin and down Elliot's chest and stomach, pausing when they reached the cool metal of a buckle. After unbuckling and unbuttoning Elliot's pants, he carefully lowered the zipper down over his erection. He had no idea which one of them moaned the loudest when he reached inside and took it into his hand.

It barely took a full minute. Brian wished that he could see Elliot's face; one of his favorite things in the world was a countenance contorted in the ecstasy of an orgasm, and he imagined that Elliot's was exquisite. He wiped his hand off on the vampire's shirt since it would need to be changed anyway. Then he leaned back and waited for him to come to his senses, which took longer than the act itself.

"That feels so much better with someone else's hand," Elliot whispered, still shaking. "Shall I do the same thing for you?"

Brian's cock twitched at the offer, but he wanted more than a quick handjob in the dark. "Next time."

"Next time? You're being presumptuous, aren't you?"

"Yes." Brian was elated by the vampire's carefree laughter. He moved back to his side of the bed as Elliot got up and changed his shirt. After he got back into bed, Brian asked, "Why did you let me do that?"

"You said that you've wanted me since the night we met."

"Yeah."

"Did it ever occur to you that I wanted you, too?" Without waiting for an answer, Elliot rolled over, his back to the cop. "Goodnight, Brian."

"Goodnight, Elliot."

Brian turned onto his side, facing the opposite direction. He had a feeling that the next few days were going to be an unforgettable experience.

He closed his eyes. Sleep wouldn't find him easily as his erection had yet to wither, but at least it took his mind off all that goddamn itching.

TUCK AND CHUCK

Author's Note: Flash fiction. Picks up where Bonus Chapter 7.5 leaves off,
but from another vampire's POV.

IT WASN'T THE KIND of club that Charles "Chuck" Rayborn would have normally frequented back when he was living in Texas. There was no blinding glow of neon or country music or gaggles of good ol' boys gathered out front swapping tall tales and, occasionally, bodily fluids. But since he was no longer living and Texas was a distant memory, it would have to do.

He got out of his truck with a sigh and started across the parking lot toward the rundown building that appeared to be crawling with weirdos, most of whom were dressed in black, right down to their lipstick and fingernails—the women *and* the men. Apparently these were his people now, a thought so discouraging that Chuck briefly considered getting back into his truck and hightailing it out of there. In just under an hour, he could have been back home relaxing in his recliner and scrolling through bad movies or infomercials or whatever else happened to be on the television that night. He had plenty of blood and booze and cigarettes to keep him occupied. What more did a vampire like him need?

The answer was simple: sex. Chuck needed sex. And lots of it. He hadn't been laid in four months now and the urge to stick his dick somewhere warm and tight was strong enough to keep him moving forward in spite of his reservations. He could only find so much satisfaction from Internet porn and his right hand, and it was with great reluctance that he finally broke down and decided to check out the most popular vampire nightspot for miles.

Hell, it was the only vampire nightspot for miles as far as he knew. The Rising Sun. Har, har. The place was his only option if he wanted to find someone he wouldn't be tempted to bleed dry after fucking. And from the looks of things, he would just have to be willing to overlook a little guyliner to achieve his objective.

On his way to the entrance, he noticed a human cop sitting in a parked car off to his right. Maybe he was good for keeping other humans away, but Chuck highly doubted that he would be worth much of a damn if something were to happen that required serious muscle. Speaking of serious muscle, the two vampires who were guarding the doors looked menacing as hell. While Chuck came close to matching them in height, they trumped him at least two times over in width. They were pretty attractive though, and if he were the bottoming kind, he wouldn't have minded being stuck between them. They gave him a brief once-over as he strolled past them, at which point Chuck concluded that his attire was acceptable, or at the very least not worth raising a fuss about. With his plaid, Western-style shirt, dark denim jeans, and square-toed cowboy boots, which weren't exactly common in such a Yankee town, he hadn't been sure what to expect.

The interior of the club looked like something out of that one movie, the one where that cute vampire chick did a whole lot of shooting and not nearly enough biting. The air was surprisingly clean; the rumors he had heard about the owners keeping the place smoke-free for their human kid must have been true. As someone who enjoyed cigarettes just as much as alcohol, Chuck was somewhat disappointed. There was a strange tune in the air, one that sounded like it came right out of a bad dream. Industrial music, they called it. Personally, he preferred to call it crap.

He could feel the weight of dozens of stares as he made his way to the bar, although he wasn't sure if it was because they were into him or because he missed the memo that he was expected to dress like that Marilyn Manson fellow to blend in. A provocative female vampire wearing next to nothing brushed against him as he weaved through the crowd. Sexy though she was, she was missing the one thing that he craved the most. Shame, because she really was a looker.

"Excuse me, Ma'am," he drawled with a courteous nod before moving on.

Chuck took a seat at the bar and ordered a beer from a cute bartender with a lip ring. He occasionally wished that he had pierced something before being turned. Then again, he was turned during a time when only women were pierced and never anywhere except for their ears.

When the vampire returned with a bottle that displayed a name he couldn't pronounce, he hoped for the best and took a long swig. It wasn't great, but it would do the trick. For what it had cost, Chuck suspected that he was paying more for the brand than the taste. After choking down the first one, he ordered another, which went down a little easier. By the time he got to the fourth one, he decided that it wasn't all that bad.

"You strike me as more of a Budweiser kind of guy."

Chuck turned toward the owner of the voice and found a blond-haired, blue-eyed vampire watching him curiously. He was one of the handful of folks in the place who weren't dressed like they were in some S&M porno, and as a result, he had Chuck's immediate attention.

And that was when he noticed something peculiar.

"Are you chewing gum?"

The vampire grinned. "Yeah."

In a building full of oddities, Chuck found that to be one of the oddest things of all. "Why?"

"It's a long story."

"You miss eating food?"

"Apparently not that long of a story."

So he was fuckable *and* interesting. Suddenly things were looking up for Chuck. "You were saying that I look like a Bud man. Is it because of the way I'm dressed?"

"Not just that. But mostly that." The stranger smirked while looking him over. "Let me guess. You left your Stetson at home?"

"Shows how much you know. I left it in my truck."

The vampire's laugh rang out over the music. "I should have known better," he said, extending his hand. "Tucker. Most people call me Tuck."

"I'm Chuck," an amused Chuck replied as he shook his hand. "Nice to meet you."

"Your name is Chuck. Are you serious?"

"Yes, Sir."

"Tuck and Chuck, huh? How fortuitous." Tuck took a sip of his beer. "So, Chuck, what brings you out tonight? No offense, but this doesn't really seem like your kind of place."

"None taken, because it really isn't," Chuck admitted. "But I was in the mood for some company."

"Beer-drinking company or naked company?" Tuck inquired.

A sinful smile spread on Chuck's face. "Naked, beer-drinking company."

"Is that so?" Tuck leaned in close to Chuck, boldly meeting his suggestive gaze. "Maybe I can help you with that," he offered.

"Just like that? I could be some cold-blooded killer."

"Aren't we all?" Tuck finished his drink and stood up. "Your place or mine?"

TO PROTECT AND
SERVE

Copyright 2015 by C.L. Ingro
Author's Note: Flash fiction. Officer Brian learns about his new job from his
new boss before meeting the sexually generous son of the club's owners.

2012

"I TRUST YOU UNDERSTAND the significant risk that comes with this
position."

Brian Goodridge stared at the vampire in the Buddy Holly glasses and
willed himself not to laugh. Significant risk? Talk about the understatement
of the century. Going to war was a significant risk. Playing Russian roulette
was a significant risk. Intentionally surrounding oneself with bloodthirsty
beings on a near nightly basis? That was practically suicide.

However, suicide or not, there was no way in hell that he was about to
turn down a six figure salary.

"Yes, I understand," he responded dutifully.

The vampire, Elliot, looked up from the single sheet of paper that
highlighted all of Brian's qualifications. Although Brian hadn't been a police
officer for long compared to his other brothers in blue, he had already proven
himself to be quite capable when it came to the job. When the owners of
the club reached out to his superiors to fill the spot that had been recently
vacated by a gentleman who decided that he would rather become a vampire
than guard them, Brian's name topped the list of all possible candidates.
Being a single man with no immediate familial attachments had tipped the

scale in his favor. If he happened to succumb to any "significant risk," it would be far easier to cover up.

"The job is a simple one, really," Elliot said as he rested his arms on top of the desk where he sat. "Although this particular area sees very little in the way of human traffic, we do get the occasional straggler. Usually homeless. You are responsible for keeping them out. If it turns out that they have nowhere else to go, you should direct them to the farm—excuse me, the shelter. The important thing is that they do not linger on the property. To allow them to do so would be... a very bad idea."

To say the least. Brian was all too aware of the looks he'd received when he followed Elliot to his office. While he usually didn't mind being ogled, the vampires had looked at him like he was nothing more than a piece of meat to be devoured. Literally.

"Although you will technically be off-duty, we prefer that you use your squad car," Elliot continued. "Most humans tend to be deterred by the sight of that alone. You are free to wear civilian attire as long as you are properly armed. You will also be provided with weapons more suitable for non-human threats, though that will be more for your own protection than anything else. No one expects you to intervene should a conflict arise between two vampires. We have additional security for that, gentlemen who are far more capable of dealing with that sort of situation. Now then, do you have any questions for me?"

"Do you think that I will ever need to use these non-human weapons?" Brian wasn't a fool. Yes, he knew the job was potentially hazardous, but he also expected Elliot to be straightforward about what he should expect.

Elliot removed his glasses—did he even need them anyway?—and contemplated the man in front of him. Brian couldn't help but notice that he was much better looking without them.

"Despite what most stories say about us, we are not monsters, Officer Goodridge." Elliot paused for a moment, his lips curving in a humorless smile. "Well, maybe some of us are. But I don't think that you will find any here at the club. Dominic and Jacob have worked very hard to provide vampires with their basic needs so that they won't resort to... other measures. While humans are not allowed here, I would like to think that they would be safe if they were ever permitted to—"

"Ellie!"

Brian turned around to see the cause of the interruption and found a young man standing in the doorway. With his too-tight black shirt, long legs encased in tight blue denim, endless earrings, and spiky blond hair, he looked like he would have been right at home in a punk rock band. Brian had never met him before but immediately knew who he was all the same.

This was Xan, the human son of Dominic and Jacob. Brian had heard a number of things about him, namely that he was extremely fond of sex.

"Oh, sorry. I thought you were alone." Xan entered the office without waiting for an invitation, his blue eyes studying Brian intently.

"Always a pleasure to disappoint you," Elliot mumbled, putting his glasses back on. "What do you want now, Xan?"

"The same thing I always want. You, naked and spread out on top of your desk. Except for the glasses. Keep those on."

Brian had to admit that he wasn't exactly opposed to that idea himself.

Elliot glared at the human. "Don't hold your breath."

"You don't know what you're missing."

"And yet I've somehow managed to survive."

Xan chuckled and turned his attention to Brian, not even bothering to hide the way he looked the officer up and down. "Xan Dawson," he said, offering his hand. "Bartender, son of the owners, and love of Elliot's life."

"Brian Goodridge." Brian shook his hand and tried not to show just how much he was affected by the thumb that slowly and teasingly grazed the top of his hand. If the gleam in Xan's eyes was any indication, his efforts were useless.

"Officer Goodridge will be handling the human end of security from now on," Elliot explained.

"Then I feel safer already," Xan purred.

The vampire shook his head. "Get back to work, Xan. And Officer Goodridge, I think we're done here, unless you have any other questions. You will start tomorrow evening."

"I'm good," Brian replied.

"Are you?" Xan asked. He let go of Brian's hand and took a step back. "Come on, I'll walk you out. Bye, Ellie."

"Are you ever going to stop calling me that?"

"Are you ever going to stop asking me to stop calling you that?"

Brian thanked the frustrated vampire and rose from his seat. He followed Xan out of the office, his eyes trailing down to the young man's backside. Those tight jeans left nothing to the imagination and right now, Brian was imagining plenty.

"It doesn't bother you, working in a place like this?" he asked as they weaved their way through the crowd that swayed to the sensual beat of the music.

"I've been around vampires all my life," Xan told him. "So it's not really something I worry about. Plus, you know, my dads and all."

Brian was hardly in a position to judge Xan's decision to work at the club, considering he was about to do the same. And if the rumors of Dominic and Jacob's overprotectiveness were true, then only a fool would ever try to hurt Xan in any way.

He was so busy trying to keep up with Xan—and still staring at his ass—that he didn't realize he had been led astray until they reached the back room. "What are we doing here?"

"I just wanted to show you where the bathroom was." Xan stepped into a small room located between a supply closet and what Brian presumed to be an electrical room. "Just in case you ever need it. For things."

The meaning was crystal clear. Brian watched the other man fold his arms and lean invitingly against the doorway. Although his cock was already starting to respond to the offer, he still had enough common sense to hesitate.

"I... I really should probably go." He swallowed hard, his mouth suddenly dry. "Like you said, you're the son of the owners."

"My parents are almost never here," Xan reassured him. "They don't need to be because Elliot runs this place like clockwork. By the way, don't ever tell him that I gave him a genuine compliment. It'll ruin my rep."

Brian smiled. Maybe it was the erection talking, but for having only known this guy for five minutes, he was already starting to like him. "Mum's the word."

Xan lowered his arms, his hand conveniently sliding over the substantial swell in his jeans before resting against his thigh. "So... are you coming?"

Weighing his options, Brian stared at Xan. To think that he could have that tall, lean body bent over the sink in a matter of minutes.

It really was a bad idea to start his new job by fucking the bosses' kid.

But oh, how good that bad idea would feel.

"I don't know," he murmured, inching toward Xan until he was right up on him, close enough to feel the heat and desire coming off of him. "That depends on you."

With a devilish grin, Xan grabbed Brian by the shirt and pulled him into the bathroom.

"Believe me, you won't be disappointed," he promised as he closed and locked the door behind them.

LAST LOOK

Author's Note: Flash fiction. Jacob pays one last visit to the family member he'll never know.

1982

JACOB SENSED DOMINIC moving swiftly around the many pecan trees that decorated the backside of the property, the sound of his arrival blending in with the noise from the leaves that rustled and swayed in the mild breeze. Instead of looking at his lover, he kept his eyes trained on the house in front of him, carefully committing every door and window and brick to memory. After tonight, he would never see it again.

"Are you trying to sneak up on me?" he asked when Dominic appeared by his side.

"That would be impossible." The vampire leaned against a tree opposite of Jacob, his pale skin looking even more so under the moonlight that filtered down through the branches over his head. "I was debating whether or not to join you because I thought you might want to be alone."

Jacob smiled. There was that sweetness that few others knew about. "It's fine," he said. "I always appreciate it when you stalk with me."

They watched the house in silence, listening to the faraway sounds of conversation and laughter within. After a few minutes, the back door opened. Jacob tensed as a young woman stepped outside and lit a cigarette, even though he knew from experience that there was no chance of being spotted given their distance from the porch.

She was in her twenties now, twenty-three if Jacob's calculations were correct. Like Jacob, she had a haphazard brown mess on top of her head, except that hers ran over her shoulders and down the length of her back. She was beautiful in a natural way, her face bearing no ounce of makeup whatsoever. As far as Jacob could tell from his observations over the decades, such flawlessness was a common trait among the women in his mother's family.

"I have everything I could possibly ever want. Forever." Jacob finally looked at Dominic. "So why am I so jealous of a girl I don't even know?" he asked, verbally acknowledging for the first time something he had felt for years.

Dominic was not shocked by the question. He knew Jacob better than anyone. "Because the woman who gave birth to you murdered your father and sold you into slavery to protect her lies," he replied. "That girl is the descendant of the brother you never knew. The son with the socially acceptable complexion who was given everything that should have gone to you first, including that whore's love."

Although his voice was calm as always, Jacob could feel Dominic's anger just beneath the surface. And he was right. Jacob had always wondered just how much his mother must have doted on her other children while keeping the existence of her firstborn a secret. For all he had gained after breaking the shackles of his enslavement, for all the happiness and joy he had experienced throughout his time with Dominic, there was still so much hurt over the fact that his own mother had sold him off like an unwanted possession. The pain wasn't quite as strong as it was during his human years, but it was still there, lodged in his heart like a thorn that could never be removed and reminding him that the one person who should have loved him most couldn't have cared less whether he lived or died.

In spite of that horrible truth, Jacob understood that this girl was not to blame. Neither she nor the ones who came before her were responsible for the sins of the woman who started it all.

"I wonder what she's like," he said as he resumed his watch. "I'd like to think that she's a nice person. She looks like a nice person."

"You could have introduced yourself," Dominic pointed out.

"What would I have said? 'Hi, my name's Jacob and I'm your great-great-great-great half-black vampire uncle?'"

Smirking, Dominic said, "I was thinking something a little more subtle than that."

Jacob shook his head. "No, it's better this way. The last thing I need is to get close to a human, even if she is family." He glanced at Dominic, who was nodding slowly and perhaps, Jacob suspected, contemplating the human he rarely ever talked about.

The girl extinguished her cigarette and tossed it into a trashcan before disappearing inside the house. Jacob had a ridiculous urge to wave goodbye, even though she was already gone.

"Dominic. Tell me."

"I thought you didn't want to know."

When Dominic had used his vast resources to acquire the girl's address, same as he had the locations of many of Jacob's other relatives in the past, Jacob hadn't wanted to know her name. He didn't want it etched into his memory for the rest of time, a permanent reminder of the family he never had. But now he discovered that he wanted to have that emotional souvenir after all, especially since he knew that this was the last time he would ever seek out this or any other family member.

"I changed my mind," he said. "Tell me her name."

"Alexandra."

"Alexandra." Jacob thought about it for a moment. "I like that name," he concluded.

"So do I," Dominic agreed, holding out his hand. "Are you ready?"

Jacob closed his hand around Dominic's. "Yeah. Let's go home. What little while longer we can call it that."

They took the long way back, avoiding all signs of human life as they strolled hand in hand. Tonight they would finish packing up their things, and tomorrow night they would take a red-eye back to their primary home up north in Pennsylvania. Only this time for good. Instead of bouncing back and forth between states, they were going to focus all of their business efforts in one place. Among other things, they would finally be able to open that club they'd been talking about for years. Plus it would be nice to be close to Demetrio and Becky on a more permanent basis. As annoying as they were,

Jacob also considered them family. Family that transcended blood, but family all the same.

He squeezed Dominic's hand as they walked, thinking back to what he had said earlier about having everything he could ever want. And he really did. Jacob couldn't think of anything that would make his life any more perfect than it was already.

Except for one thing. But there was no way that it was ever going to happen.

Besides, how crazy would that be, two vampires raising a kid?

AN UNEXPECTED ADDITION

Author's Note: A Harborview Immortals extra. Jacob and Dominic are about to discover the one thing that they've been missing in their long lives: fatherhood.

1992

"I THINK WE SHOULD OPEN a sex shop."

Jacob rolled onto his right side and propped himself up on an elbow, grinning when he spotted green eyes peering skeptically at him through a curtain of black hair. After almost two hundred years together, he would have thought that Dominic was used to his random topics of post-coital conversation. At least this time he wasn't asking about the gastrointestinal nightmare that occurred when a vampire ingested solid food, something he had always been morbidly curious about. After hearing a disgustingly detailed account of what happened to undigested food in an undead body, he decided it was best to limit all future queries to the topic of sex.

"A sex shop." Dominic frowned as he contemplated the idea. "Like a brothel?"

"No, not a brothel." Sometimes Jacob had to remind himself that despite his partner's youthful appearance, he was actually quite old (508 years old this year, to be exact) and, like some vampires his age who were slow to adapt to the ever-changing world, ignorant of certain things. "Like a shop that sells sex goodies," he explained. "Magazines and movies and toys—"

"Toys?"

"Dildos and vibrators," Jacob clarified. "And lube." He grabbed the bottle of lube that had been carelessly tossed aside earlier when he screamed at Dominic to hurry up and fuck him after what felt like a human lifetime of blissful finger-play. "Did you know that this stuff comes in different flavors? Just like ice cream."

"Why would there need to be different flavors?" Dominic sat upright, his long hair spilling down over his shoulders and chest and tapering to an end just above his navel. He took the lube from Jacob and studied the container. After thinking it over, he figured it out. "Never mind. I can definitely see how that would be advantageous."

"Yep." Jacob smirked. "Do you remember how creative we had to be before lube was invented? I swear I can't look at a bottle of olive oil without getting turned on."

"Stop it."

"It's true!"

Dominic's lips curved upward, his somber countenance melting into a rare smile. "I don't know," he said as he ran his fingers through Jacob's wavy and disheveled brown hair. "A place like that sounds perverted."

"I didn't know you were such a prude."

"You're accusing me of being a prude after what I just did to you?"

"I'm kidding." Jacob moved his head onto his lover's leg. Given all of the ways that Dominic had pleasured him over the past two hours—including that earth-shattering thing he did with his tongue that almost resulted in a broken neck due to Jacob's frantic jerking about—he could verify that Dominic was not shy when it came to sex. Far from it.

Jacob froze when the vampire's fingers slid through the chaos of his locks and down to his back. He tried not to cringe as they started moving over his scars, those ghastly souvenirs of a time when the barbarity of bigoted men destroyed the fragment of happiness he had found in such an otherwise bleak existence. While it was an improvement over the days when he wouldn't even let Dominic *see* his back, Jacob still found it impossible to be completely at ease whenever Dominic touched them. But he was getting there. Maybe in another decade or two it wouldn't bother him at all.

"Jacob," Dominic said quietly, sensing his discomfort.

"I'm sorry. Old habits." Sitting up, Jacob pushed away the memory of whips and sadistic onlookers. This was not the time to think about the past. Preferably never, but certainly not now. He untangled his legs from the nest of bundled up blankets and shed clothing that comprised their makeshift bed on the basement floor. An actual bed would have been ideal, but since Dominic was fiercely adamant about maintaining vampire traditions, they continued to use a specially made coffin for two during the daytime. No matter how many times Jacob told him that all the cool vampires were now sleeping in beds, he knew that Dominic wasn't going to budge on the issue anytime soon. "Anyway, I brought up the sex shop since you had mentioned starting a new business. Sex sells, Dominic. And if we owned a place like that, we would have free flavored lube until the end of time. It's a win-win situation."

"As tempting as that sounds, I was thinking of something a little more charitable."

"I happen to think that butt plugs are extremely charitable under the right circumstances."

Dominic didn't just smile this time. He laughed. "You're as bad as Demetrio. I see why you get along with him so well."

"Your brother and I do share a certain immaturity," Jacob admitted. "And I've seen him naked. Sort of."

Dominic groaned. "He does love to remind me of that. Don't you start."

"That's what you get for being a twin." Jacob gave him a lighthearted nudge and stood up. "Let's get cleaned up and then you can tell me all about this charitable and tragically sexless business idea."

"Why don't I show you instead?" Dominic's gaze traveled up the length of Jacob's naked body, lingering on the areas that bore the slick evidence of their lovemaking. He was smiling again, but this time there was a hungry, almost predatory quality to it. "Later," he added before grabbing Jacob by the hand and pulling him back down to the floor for another round.

IT WAS A WARM JUNE weeknight so the couple decided to leave their cars at home. They took to the sky instead, steering clear of the many streetlights that would give them away. Although there were a select number of humans who knew about the existence of vampires, namely ones in positions of authority who were richly compensated for a variety of services that benefitted both parties, most of the general public didn't know about them, and Dominic and Jacob preferred to keep it that way.

They moved up and over the few cars that were out and about in the middle of the night, past all of the downtown Harborview stores and medical buildings and restaurants that lined the roads, past one of the city's numerous universities—Mercymore College—and the rows of nearby streets that were filled with off-campus housing. They skirted along the tranquil waters of Lake Erie, then over an adjoining section of million dollar lakefront homes. Dominic had occasionally mentioned purchasing one of those insanely oversized and overpriced houses for the two of them, but Jacob, being low maintenance when it came to shelter, was more than content with the spacious home they shared now.

Within minutes, they reached another cluster of buildings that were significantly shabbier in location and appearance, and they landed on the roof of a recently closed hotel that was in urgent need of renovation. From a block or two away, most likely at one of the city's even more numerous bars, came the sound of loud rock music and even louder profanity. Then police sirens.

"Here we are." Dominic gestured at the building beneath their feet.

"You want to open a hotel?" Jacob asked doubtfully.

"I was thinking more along the lines of lodging for those who have none."

"You mean a homeless shelter?"

"Yes." Dominic walked over to an air conditioning unit and leaned against it. "We would provide a place to stay for those who need it in exchange for donations."

Jacob inclined his head. "I assume you're not talking about monetary donations."

"No, I'm not," Dominic replied. "The shelter would serve as... well, a farm, of sorts. We'll sell a percentage of the donations we receive to our associates and keep the rest for club stock and private distribution. We're doing well enough now, but this way we won't have to rely on outside sources to acquire blood."

"I'm guessing that no one would remember making these donations?"

"We won't alter their memories more than we have to," Dominic promised. "Consider the alternative, Jacob. The homeless have always been easy targets. If we do this, people will be safe. And we will make a lot of money."

"We already have a lot of money." Jacob stared out into the night. The noise had died down and all was quiet for now. He didn't necessarily like the practice of influencing human minds, something he had only ever done himself over the years as a last resort. But Dominic's plan was not a bad one. Quite the opposite, if they could pull it off. "How would we do this?" he wanted to know. "Keeping the club private is one thing, but people are going to notice if a bunch of homeless folks start shacking up here."

"It would have to be a public endeavor. No secret gathering of vampires gyrating on a dance floor this time. I don't imagine it will be too difficult to persuade one of our daytime acquaintances to play the part of philanthropist." Dominic stared at his lover, trying to gauge his reaction. "Do you think it's a bad idea?"

"Not at all." Jacob hesitated, debating the right way to phrase what he wanted to say next so that it was more observation than accusation. "You care about them, don't you? Humans, I mean."

Dominic considered the vampire's statement. "Care is a strong word. I don't hate them. I've never hated them. But I have learned that it is much easier not to be around them."

Jacob knew the reason for that, had known for some time now. Dominic, being just over three full centuries older, had a life long before Jacob was even born, and a human had been a part of that life. The pain of loss was hard enough for a normal lifespan, but when that pain stretched out over the ages... He could understand why Dominic went out of his way to distance himself from people.

"Let's do it," Jacob concluded. He walked over to Dominic and brought his arms around the vampire's neck, twirling and teasing his silky hair. "We'll make some money and save some lives and piss off Vincenzo, which is reason enough for me."

Dominic's brow furrowed at the mention of his maker. "Agitating him does delight me," he acknowledged. "All right. Tomorrow night I will talk to Elliot and start the process."

"Tomorrow? We're not stopping by the club tonight?"

"No." Dominic swept back Jacob's hair, which had become even more tousled than usual from flying. There was affection in his eyes, affection that was just as strong as it was one long ago night when two lost vampires found each other under the very same moon that shone down on them now. "There are other things I would rather do tonight."

Jacob pinned him against the A/C unit and kissed him deeply, his tongue exploring Dominic's mouth while Dominic's hands rubbed and cupped and groped everything they could reach. "Okay," he whispered after they parted, both of them gasping and half-hard. "But we need to stop somewhere first."

"I CAN'T BELIEVE I LET you talk me into this."

Smiling triumphantly, Jacob kicked an empty soda can out of his way with a black loafer as they walked down the sidewalk. "I've talked you into far worse."

Dominic's face was serious as always, but his eyes gleamed with amusement. "And you will continue to do so, I'm sure."

"It's really your fault, when you think about it. This is what happens when you decide to start a business five blocks away from Coxen Things."

"That name..."

"Clever, isn't it?" Jacob's smile widened. "But hey, if you're so offended that you'd rather not try out some flavored lube tonight—"

"We're already close so we might as well stop by," Dominic said with mock resignation.

"What a generous soul you are."

The conversation turned to their existing business, as it often did once they were fully clothed. They opened the Rising Sun a decade ago, soon after they made the move from Georgia to Pennsylvania for good. From the outside, it was merely an old, boarded up textile mill that had fallen victim to a harsh economy. After the sun went down, it became a place where vampires could lose themselves in blood, alcohol, music, and each other, all without interruption from the living. A true den of iniquity, as Jacob frequently called it. And an immensely profitable one at that.

"The Old Man thinks that we should tone things down on the lower level," Dominic said as they crossed an intersection. "Because, as he puts it, not everyone goes there for the sole purpose of humping the nearest available leg."

Jacob nodded. He could imagine their mutual friend, an elderly-looking vampire who was actually close to his own age, saying such a thing in his gruff Irish accent. "He's got a point. How is he doing, anyway? I haven't seen him in a while."

"He's as ornery and foul-mouthed as ever."

"Is he still going on about selling his house and traveling the world?"

"He is, but I highly doubt he'll do it, especially now that Luca is moving back to Harborview."

This was news to Jacob. "So he finally found him. I wasn't sure that he ever would."

Dominic pushed back the hair that had blown in his face during a surprise gust of wind. "We've been asked to find employment for him. Luca, that is."

"What can he do?" Jacob asked.

"I'm not sure. The Old Man says that he is extremely smart for someone so young. And rather imposing as well."

"How old is he?"

"Seventeen."

"Wow, he's still a kid." Jacob pondered for a few paces. "Well, we've always tossed around the idea of having someone watch over the house during the day."

"Someone we *know*," Dominic corrected.

"That's a pretty short list when it comes to humans," Jacob reminded him. "But you're right. As much as we trust the Old Man, we shouldn't automatically assume that—"

He stopped abruptly, his head cocked to one side. A vampire's hearing was remarkably sharp, but he still wanted to be certain of what he thought he just heard.

"Did you hear that?"

There it was again, cutting off Dominic's response. Every muscle in Jacob's body tensed, and the first stirrings of dread formed deep within him. Suddenly, buying lube—flavored or otherwise—was the last thing on his mind.

Somewhere, somewhere close, a baby was crying.

Pinpointing the general location of the noise, Jacob turned toward the street, his brown eyes scanning the dark storefronts on the other side, hoping that one of the buildings had an upstairs apartment that might have been home to a little one who was simply having trouble sleeping. None of them did.

What he did see was a shallow and poorly lit alley tucked between a pawn shop and a title loan business. And in that alley, a dark blue dumpster with a black lid, property of the same company that picked up the couple's garbage on Tuesday nights.

Then came another cry, loud but somewhat muffled. This time there was no mistaking where it came from. Jacob didn't even realize that he had started shaking.

Dominic did. "Jacob, wait—"

But he was already gone, across the street in the blink of an eye. Jacob approached the dumpster, his dread gradually giving way to anger. Reading about this sort of thing or seeing it on the news was nothing compared to the unfolding horror of experiencing it firsthand. He was reminded of his own grim beginnings, having been sold into slavery by his own deceitful mother, and with each step his anger steadily swelled into full-blown rage.

"Jacob, listen to me." Dominic was behind him now, his voice understanding but firm. "This is a terrible thing, but it doesn't concern us. We need to call the authorities immediately and let them handle it."

The vampire paused with one hand on the dumpster lid. Dominic was right, and deep in his heart, Jacob knew it. Human interaction for business was one thing, and they tolerated it out of necessity. Anything more than that, anything *personal*, was unwise. And he could think of nothing else right now that was more personal to him than a child who was abandoned and left to die.

Had it been someone older, Jacob might have been able to force himself to step away, despite his fury. As cruel as it seemed, he knew from Dominic's silent suffering the importance of avoiding any situation in which an attachment to a mortal could be formed. But when the sound of yet another cry hit his ears, this one the loudest and most desperate of all, his emotions took over and he flung open the lid. This time Dominic didn't try to stop him.

Jacob ignored the overwhelming stench of refuse and peered inside the dumpster. What he saw tore at his heart and renewed his resolve to murder those responsible. There, partially concealed by random pieces of trash, beer bottles, and garbage bags full of waste, were two tiny legs and a right arm, all of which were twitching and shivering helplessly. A human baby boy.

"Oh, my God." Jacob started uncovering his nude little body, working carefully in case of broken glass or other sharp objects that could harm him. When he was finished, he reached inside and lifted him out, holding him at arm's length while checking him over for injuries.

"I changed my mind," Dominic said, his voice filled with contempt. "I hate some humans, after all."

Jacob was hardly an expert on babies. Most of the slave infants from his human days—including the ones with suspiciously light brown skin like his own—had been sold right after being born, and he had managed to avoid most children completely after being turned. If he had to guess, this one wasn't fresh out of the womb, but close enough. One week old, or possibly two, and even more possibly premature, if his scrawny form was any indication. Jacob couldn't believe that so much noise had come from such a tiny, fragile thing.

The area that would become his belly button was caked with dried blood and pus, and there was a deep and nasty gash across his left cheek that came to an end dangerously close to his eye, presumably the result of something poking through one of the bags that had been pressed against his head. That was all Jacob could see as far as external injuries, but as for internal damage, it was hard to say. Surely the child was hungry at the very least. He wasn't able to do anything about that yet, but for now, he would do what he could.

Jacob gingerly balanced him in the crook of his left arm and opened his mouth to reveal sharp fangs. As Dominic looked on in concern, he punctured the tip of his right thumb against one of the pointed teeth and held the bleeding digit over the boy's mouth, allowing drops of blood to trickle inside. The baby lurched and sputtered and coughed but eventually swallowed. Shortly after that, the cut on his face and his infected belly both started to heal.

Afterwards, he pulled him close, shielding his cold body against the night air. The baby's chest hitched a few times, and then he exhaled with a small whimper and a shuddering sigh.

And Jacob fell in love.

"Dominic…"

Dominic looked from the child's face to his partner's. "I know," he said softly. "Let's take him home."

FOR A COUPLE OF VAMPIRES who had learned, sometimes begrudgingly, to make use of all the modern conveniences that the world now had to offer, Dominic and Jacob were quickly discovering that diapers were one of the most frustrating modern conveniences of all.

"You need to pull it up in the back," Jacob instructed as Dominic fumbled a diaper around the fidgeting infant. He inspected the package that his lover had purchased from the all night drug store down the street along with a bunch of other baby-related items (much to the confusion of the clerk who usually rang up their lubricant) and then glanced down at the freshly bathed child as he wriggled and writhed on the living room floor. "And then tuck the front part down and pull out the sticky things—"

"I don't see any sticky things," Dominic grunted.

"They're right there on the… oops." Jacob tugged on the front end of the diaper. "It's backwards," he said apologetically. "You'll have to turn it around."

With an exasperated sigh, Dominic took the child by the legs and gently lifted his rump. He pulled out the diaper and turned it around, then placed it into position once again. "I see the sticky things now," he announced. "I think I can figure it out from here."

Once the diaper dilemma was resolved, Jacob slid one of his old white T-shirts over the baby's head and tied it off at the sleeves and bottom so that his arms and legs could move freely. It wasn't much, but it would work for now.

"There we go." He picked up the baby and offered him a bottle of formula, the second one that night. Having no idea how much or how often infants fed, Jacob figured it wouldn't hurt to keep at it every couple of hours or until he fell asleep.

Dominic watched the boy suck away at the bottle. He tentatively reached out and touched the smooth bottom of a miniature foot, which caused the baby's entire leg to jolt in reaction.

"He's ticklish," Jacob observed. "Just like you."

"...You swore you would never speak of that again."

"No, I didn't."

"Well, you should."

Jacob snickered at Dominic's indignation. "I promise not to mention one of your cutest qualities."

"Thank you."

"For the rest of the night," Jacob amended under his breath. He stared at the child in his arms, his expression softening. "This is crazy, isn't it?"

"It is," Dominic agreed, running his hand over a crown of fuzzy yellow hair. "If we were thinking clearly, we wouldn't even be considering this."

"Are you saying that because he's human or because you truly think that he would be better off with Child Protective Services?"

Dominic moved behind Jacob, his long legs stretched out on either side of him. He rested his chin on the vampire's shoulder so that he could have a better view of the feeding. "Both," he admitted. "How in the world are we supposed to take care of him, Jacob? We don't know the first thing about babies."

"Most new parents don't. We'll figure it out as we go along."

"What about when the sun comes up? Do we just keep him locked in the basement with us because we can't go anywhere?"

Jacob had to think about that one. "We'll get one of those nanny-sitters. If this Luca turns out not to be some psycho pedophile, maybe we can hire him for the job."

"What about food? We can't feed him blood."

"Formula and baby food."

"And when he's older?"

The nanny-sitter can cook for him, too. Unless you plan on doing that yourself."

"Not likely," Dominic responded coolly. "Education?"

"Homeschooling."

"Friends?"

"Our friends will be his friends. I bet Becky is going to love him."

"Suppose she gets the urge to bite him?" Dominic asked. "What if we get that urge ourselves? We may not feed on humans anymore, but you know the impulse never disappears completely."

"Were you frequently overcome with the desire to bite the last human being you cared about?"

"Of course not."

"And it won't happen this time, to either of us. We're vampires, Dominic. Not monsters. We don't hurt children." Jacob leaned back and turned his head so that Dominic could nuzzle his neck. "I know this is insane, but I can't help but feel like we were meant to find him. Think about how many things had to fall right into place for us to find that exact dumpster on this exact night. Let's give it a day or two. After that, if you honestly believe that he would be better off with a human family—assuming he even gets adopted by one—then we'll turn him over."

"I never knew you wanted to be a father so badly."

Jacob shrugged. "I had no reason to think it would ever happen so I kept it to myself."

"Is there anything else you haven't told me that I should know?"

"Sometimes I braid your hair while you're asleep."

Dominic had already smiled more that night than he had in weeks. And there he was, doing it again. "What happens when he grows up?" he asked, becoming serious again. "When he grows old? Every single day of a human's life brings them one step closer to an inevitable end. I know how it feels to lose someone. No vampire should have to live with that kind of pain. Especially you."

The baby finished his meal and Jacob set the bottle on the floor. He raised the infant to his shoulder and rubbed his back, something he remembered seeing on television, being the avid watcher that he was (unlike Dominic, whose own television preference began and ended with reruns of *Dark Shadows*). "You're right. I don't know how much it must hurt to lose someone the way you did. But I do know what it's like to be abandoned. Someone literally threw him away like he was garbage, Dominic." He pressed his nose against the baby's skin and breathed him in. It wasn't quite the new baby smell that the mothers on TV raved about but, having done the best he could using the kitchen sink, it was far better than the smell of trash and rotten food. "I want to make it up to him by giving him the best life possible. I know it's not our place to do it, but I want to."

Dominic took the child and mimicked Jacob's burping motions. "So you think this is fate?"

"Yeah, I do." Jacob turned around and faced them. "Getting thrown in a dumpster is a pretty shitty way to start living, but we found him, the same way we found each other." He beamed at the boy, who was cooing steadily into Dominic's neck. "How is that not meant to be?"

The lovers regarded each other. After a minute, Dominic relented. "We'll give it one day."

"One day," Jacob agreed. "Maybe two. Or three."

"All right."

A loud burp caught them both off guard. Jacob was once again amazed that such a small body could produce such a big noise. "The sun will be up soon," he said, glancing at his watch. "We should head down to the basement."

Dominic gave the baby a few pats on the back. "We saved your life, and now you get to sleep in a coffin like the dead. What do you think about that?"

The baby opened his mouth and let Dominic know precisely what he thought. All over his shoulder.

"It's running down my back. I think it's in my hair." Dominic closed his eyes, his face twisted in disgust. "Please do something. Please do something now."

"Calm down," a laughing Jacob told him as he reached for a box of powder-scented wipes. "You think this is bad, just wait until we get to deal with what comes out of the other end."

ONE DAY LED TO TWO, and then, unsurprisingly, two to three. After a week, Dominic and Jacob stopped pretending that contacting Child Protective Services was even an option anymore. They postponed opening the homeless shelter and temporarily left club matters to their trusted associate, Elliot, who was more than capable of running the place without them. They eagerly embraced their new roles as fathers and spent every waking moment bonding with the infant who had thrown their lives into such unexpectedly joyous upheaval.

"We'll need to get him a crib," Dominic said on the seventh night. He paced around the kitchen with the child in his arms and a towel wisely draped over his left shoulder. In place of an old shirt, the baby was now wearing a mint green onesie. It was one of the dozens that the vampire had purchased for him during an awkward nighttime shopping spree at Teensy Totz, the local baby store, where almost every single woman in the place had ogled him in fascination while he shopped. "And I suppose it's time we gave him a name. We can't call him 'the baby' forever."

After hand-washing the last of the bottles, Jacob turned away from the sink and leaned against it. Although he had thought of a name the first night they brought the boy home, he hadn't wanted to suggest anything until he knew for sure that Dominic was equally passionate about keeping him. His mind turned to a young woman living down in Georgia with wavy brown hair like his own, a girl named Alexandra who would never know of the distant half-uncle who had secretly watched over her for a good portion of her life.

There was only one name it could be. One that served as a reminder of the family he was never allowed to know because his father's skin had been the wrong color.

"Alexander."

Their eyes met. Dominic nodded approvingly. "That's a good name."

"He needs a nickname."

"Why? Are four syllables too taxing for you?"

"Very funny." Jacob dried off his hands. "Alex? Al? Um... Xander? What do you think?"

Dominic looked at the small human, who had a lock of his hair clutched in a tiny fist. "Xan."

"Xan," Jacob repeated, testing the sound of the name. "I like it."

They moved into the living room and relaxed on the sofa with a yawning baby on the cushion between them. Seven days later and they still couldn't make heads or tails of Xan's sleep pattern; as far as they could tell, he slept just as much during the day as he did at night.

Jacob watched him for a few minutes and tried to resist playing with his adorable little appendages. How had he come to love someone—especially a human someone—so much in such a short period of time? There wasn't anything in the world he wouldn't do for this child, no sacrifice or risk too great in order to protect him. So this was what fatherhood felt like. Jacob found it both scary and exhilarating.

"He'll need a middle and last name, too," he suddenly remembered. "I'd rather not use either of ours." He glanced at the muted game show where one family was competing against another for money. It was one of his favorite programs, formerly hosted by a handsome and charming man who had a penchant for kissing all of the female guests. Jacob had often fantasized about being on the receiving end of one of those kisses. "I think I got it."

Dominic looked from Jacob to the television and back to Jacob again. "You can't be serious."

Jacob's smile was wicked. "Oh, but I am."

"I'm sure he will be pleased to learn that he was partially named for a man you once wanted to screw," Dominic muttered, pressing a hand to his forehead.

"Not screw, just smooch." Jacob leaned over and kissed Xan on top of the head. "Welcome to the world, Alexander Richard Dawson."

FAMILY MATTERS

OVER THE MONTHS THAT followed, life changed a great deal for the new family. After much debate and an eventual acceptance of what would likely be a futile search effort, Dominic and Jacob chose not to worry themselves with the question of Xan's origin. They would confront the subject again when Xan was old enough to understand what had happened to him, but for now they left it alone and focused instead on being thankful that they had found him at all. One of the unused bedrooms on the first floor was turned into a nursery and Luca Melani, who was luckily neither psycho nor pedophile, began watching over Xan so that the couple could get a full day's rest. Xan had taken an instant shine to the muscular young man and almost never cried when he was around—something his parents noticed with a hint of jealousy. Their dearest friend, Becky, became so infatuated with the child that she was constantly visiting just to spend time with her "little Xanadu." Even Dominic's brother, Demetrio, was slightly less annoying while doting on Xan. Incidentally, that was just about the nicest thing that Dominic had said about him in years.

As time went by, the lovers discovered that they now preferred peaceful nights at home instead of in a factory full of horny vampires and loud music. They still checked in once or twice a week, but Elliot was managing just fine without them. Plans for the new homeless shelter were still on hold, but Jacob already knew what they were going to call it: the Dawson House. Each passing day with Xan was one that they would never have again, and they wanted to spend as much time with him as possible, before he reached the age when he felt that there were better things to do than hang out with his dads.

When news of their human adoptee spread throughout Harborview, some vampires made it known that they didn't care for the couple's decision. To them, humans were only good for food and fucking, and taking one in as family was disgraceful. But after what Jacob did to the poor vampire who had foolishly hinted that Xan would make a good appetizer, no one was stupid enough to say anything else that even remotely resembled a threat. Dominic and Jacob were intimidating enough as vampires. As fathers, they were downright frightening.

Since they didn't know when Xan was actually born, they determined that the night they found him—June 10—was as good a date of birth as any. A few days shy of a year from that night, Jacob brought up the idea of throwing him a birthday party.

"A birthday party?" Dominic asked with a raised brow.

"Yes, Dominic. A birthday party." Jacob smiled sweetly at the toddler staggering around the living room. "I know birthdays don't mean as much when you've had hundreds of them, but this is Xan's first one. It's important."

"I'm not disagreeing... but do we have to invite my brother?"

"Yes," Jacob insisted. "You'll just have to suck it up for one night."

Xan swayed to and fro before plopping down to the floor on his diaper-padded butt. Bright blue eyes blinked questioningly at the two vampires in an effort to understand how such a thing might have happened.

"I suppose I can do that," Dominic relented with a heavy sigh. He looked at Xan. "Do you see the torture I'm willing to go through just for you?"

For reasons known only to himself, Xan considered Dominic's question to be the most hilarious thing ever, and he cackled merrily, showing off his new teeth. There were eight of them now, four up top and four below. A few months ago, when there were only six, he had developed a strangely endearing habit of gnawing on his parents. Hands, arms, feet—whatever body parts he could get to that weren't concealed by clothing. "And I was worried that we were the ones who would do the biting," Dominic had said then, presenting Jacob with a finger that was covered with bite marks and drool.

"He's making the face," he warned now after noticing Xan's troubled scowl. "I do believe it's your turn to change him."

"It's always my turn."

"I've noticed that."

Jacob rolled his eyes and rose from the sofa. "Fine, I'll deal with the poop and you can call your brother."

Dominic reconsidered. "On second thought, I think that I would much rather deal with a loaded diaper."

XAN'S FIRST BIRTHDAY party went off with only one hitch. Halfway through the celebration, an overly enthusiastic Demetrio started telling stories about Dominic as a child, which resulted in Dominic telling off his twin in Italian, which resulted in a heated exchange expressed entirely in bared fangs and a foreign language. Jacob had had no idea what they were saying to each other as he could only make out Demetrio's use of Dominic's given name, Domenico. However, the comically mortified look on Luca's face was hardly a good sign. (When asked later to translate, the teenager flushed and explained that most of the conversation revolved around an invitation to perform an illicit act on a goat and speculation over which sibling would best perform said act.) Everyone had a good time aside from the brotherly squabble, especially the birthday boy, who had no clue what was going on but babbled and cooed through it all.

A few hours before dawn, Demetrio and Becky said their farewells. As Luca and Xan disappeared into the nursery to play with all of the child's new toys, Dominic and Jacob remained in the living room to clean up. When they were finished, they went into the nursery and found Luca and Xan in a chair, both of them fast asleep.

"Should we wake them?" Dominic asked. "Or at least put Alexander to bed?"

Jacob stared at the two of them, noting with fondness the way that Luca was slouched down in the seat and how Xan was sprawled across his massive torso with a strong, protective arm holding him in place. "No. They'll be fine."

Dominic went to the closet and grabbed a multi-colored blanket that Becky had knitted for Xan. He spread it over the sleeping pair as Jacob stepped out of the room.

"Haven't you already taken enough pictures tonight?" he asked when the vampire returned with a camera.

"I want to take as many pictures of him as I can while he's just a baby."

So he did, forever capturing one of the many tender moments of Xan's childhood that would be gone too soon.

They left the room and, after locking up and turning out all the lights, went down to the basement. Jacob switched on a lamp and fell down on the sofa with a thud and a sigh while Dominic went over to the refrigerator where they kept an emergency supply of blood in case they wanted some while the sun was up.

"Are you hungry?" he asked, holding up a bag of A Positive.

"No, thank you."

Dominic returned the blood to the fridge and reached for the bottle of Macallan on the neighboring countertop. "Thirsty?" he offered.

"Yes, please. Don't bother with a glass."

"How refined," Dominic commented sarcastically.

"Hush."

Dominic joined him on the sofa and handed him the bottle. After taking a long drink of the expensive whiskey, Jacob offered it to Dominic, who was hesitant to engage in such an act of considerable crudeness.

"Go on, live a little."

"Strange thing to say to a dead person," Dominic replied as he accepted the bottle. After much inner turmoil, he consented to a sip.

"Way to go, rebel," Jacob said with a wink. He took the bottle back and turned sideways, bringing his legs down across Dominic's thighs. "Don't worry. Your indecency will remain our secret."

"Thank you."

Jacob grinned and took another drink, his free hand squeezing the one that rested on his knee. "One year," he said, his eyes hazed over in reflection. "It went by fast."

"Time tends to do that where humans are concerned."

"Was it the same for you back then?"

"Yes. One day Giovanni and I were both young together. Before I knew it..." Dominic paused, his jaw tightly clenched, and his eyes filled with the pain of a memory untold. Then, with a shake of the head, he continued as if nothing had happened. "Before I knew it, I was still young and he was an old man."

It hurt Jacob to think of the same thing happening to their son. "Xan might choose to be turned," he said hopefully.

"And he might not," Dominic countered. "We need to be prepared for that possibility. Some humans aren't tempted by immortality."

Jacob knew the truth of those words. "I wasn't tempted," he admitted. "But I wasn't given a choice."

"I hate that you were forced into becoming a vampire." Dominic raised Jacob's hand to his lips and kissed it. "But I'm also grateful because it brought us together."

Jacob ran a thumb along Dominic's cheek. He, too, was grateful that his stolen life had led him to this. Everything that he had endured—the abandonment, the slavery, the betrayal, and the scars—seemed ultimately a small price to pay for all the things he now enjoyed. "I love you, Dominic."

"I love you," Dominic said as he leaned into the fingers that were weaving through his hair. "And I have a present for you."

"You do?" Jacob asked, perking up.

Dominic slid from beneath Jacob's legs. He crossed the basement and grabbed a brown paper bag that was hidden inside of the coffin.

Jacob pulled up his legs so Dominic could sit down again. "What is this?" he asked as he accepted the bag.

"Open it and see."

Setting the whiskey aside, Jacob opened the bag and looked inside. What he saw made him laugh.

"Do you like it?" Dominic asked.

Jacob reached into the bag and took out a bottle of strawberry-flavored lube. After looking it over, he gazed slyly at his partner. "I like it. Very much."

"I thought you would."

"How did you decide on strawberry?"

Dominic cleared his throat and took a sudden interest in a random spot on the far wall, facing away from his lover. "I tasted them all," he mumbled.

Jacob tried to imagine a vampire like Dominic walking through Coxen Things, making his way up and down rows of dildos and cock rings and porn (and, of course, those charitable butt plugs). When he pictured him taste-testing dozens of flavors of lube to find one that was to his exact liking, all he could do was laugh some more.

"It isn't that funny," a sullen Dominic insisted.

"Yes, it is." Jacob swept him into a fierce embrace. "You're adorable, you know."

"Don't tell anyone."

Jacob didn't have the heart to tell him that their family and friends already suspected as much. Playful pecks on the cheek turned into a trail of slow, sensual kisses along Dominic's neck. "Shall we use it now?" he murmured into his ear, punctuating the question with a lick and a nibble.

Dominic rocked against the hand that had found its way between his legs. "That depends. Do you think you'll be able to keep your voice down?"

Out of all the struggles that parenthood presented, being quiet while making love was one of the hardest for Jacob. He had gotten better over time, but there were still some occasions when his orgasms got the best of him. Although he didn't fret too much over it now since Xan was still a baby (and Luca was a pro at pretending to be deaf), he knew that he would have to improve before the boy was old enough to know what was going on. Jacob had heard stories about parents who mentally terrorized their kids by being too open about their bedroom activities. He was confident that he would never embarrass his own son in such a shameful way.

"I'll do my best," he assured Dominic, leaning back and pulling the vampire on top of him.

THE STRAWBERRY LUBE was a resounding success. And Jacob did keep quiet. Mostly.

Later, the lovers retired to their coffin. With a satisfied sigh, Jacob pressed his cheek against the cool satin lining and draped an arm over the one that was curled possessively around his chest. "Everything is so perfect," he said dreamily.

Dominic nudged past his hair and kissed him on the shoulder. "I'd like to think so."

"There's only one thing I can think of that would make our lives even more perfect."

"We're not getting a bed."

Jacob chuckled heartily and reached for the coffin lid. "It was worth a shot," he said, pulling it closed.

SCARS FROM THE PAST

Author's Note: A Harborview Immortals extra. Jacob returns to Georgia and finds himself remembering all the heartaches and horrors of a human life that he would much rather forget.

August 2000

JACOB DIDN'T UNDERSTAND why so many of his fellow centuries-old vampires hated airplanes. While it was true that they had lived during a time when the idea of large objects flying high in the sky would have seemed impossible and terrifying, he thought it utterly silly to harbor such dread when they were now perfectly capable of flying high in the sky themselves. At least with a plane, one could reach their destination in a timely manner and without an overabundance of exertion.

He looked out of the window. While his eyes took in the darkness of a clear night sky, his thoughts were on the family he had left behind, and an unexpected snort of laughter escaped him as he reflected on events from earlier that evening. Xan had spent a number of hours following up his usual random acts of endearing silliness with bold and repeated proclamations that he had only been "taking a piss," and it had taken a long and awkward minute to deduce that the eight-year-old had apparently misunderstood the phrase "taking the piss" from their beloved British vampire friend Becky. Dominic's legendary stoic demeanor had no chance against the hilariousness of the situation, and even he had let slip a brief chuckle while Jacob had laughed so hard that he came close to crying.

It had only been an hour since he kissed them both goodbye, but he missed them fiercely and was already counting down the days until he saw them again.

His smile gradually faded as his mind turned to the plane's destination. Returning to Georgia was not something he had planned to do anytime soon—or ever again, if he could help it—and the closer he got, the more those little pinpricks of trepidation in his chest that he hadn't been able to ignore started to feel like outright stabs. Soon, he would be in the presence of the son of his former owner... who also happened to be the man he had once loved... who also happened to be the vampire who had killed and turned him against his will.

The last time Jacob saw James had not ended well, to say the least, and it had taken an astronomical display of Dominic's dark power to finally convince him to stand down and leave Jacob alone. Now he was going back without the safety net of his lover's protection, a fact that understandably worried Dominic. But the James he would soon be facing was no longer the James of old, a tormented soul who had done unspeakable things in response to an act of cruelty he had been forced to commit in order to save the life of the one he loved. Jacob knew that he hadn't been the only victim that awful night. While his physical scars were only skin-deep, James' emotional scars had run right down to the center of his being, corrupting everything that Jacob had loved about him until only madness remained.

Jacob pushed those thoughts aside. There would be more than enough time later to contemplate what was. His mind turned to the other reason, the main reason, he was making the trip. His niece, and Xan's namesake, Alexandra. James would have never even bothered contacting Jacob if not for her and the ordeal she was currently facing with an ex-boyfriend who was about to learn that the wrong kind of persistence would very likely get him killed. Jacob couldn't help but notice that her present situation was much like his own had been, all those years ago. Surely James had noticed it, too. Perhaps that was why he had reached out to him in the first place, out of a desire to avoid bearing witness to history repeating itself in the worst possible way.

He rested his head against the back of the seat as he absentmindedly thumbed the cover of the book on his lap, his newest copy of *Bertram Cope's*

Year, one of his favorites. (The old copy, a highly coveted and often-read original, had been retired to the bookcase where many of the rare first edition books Jacob had collected over the years also ended up.) While he didn't think he would fall asleep, he must have, because the next thing he knew, the plane was landing and the pilot was announcing their arrival over the intercom:

"Welcome to Georgia, Mr. Corbin."

Jacob cringed upon hearing the surname he had vowed never to use again. However, he didn't fault the pilot for using it; the private plane ride was a courtesy extended by James and as far as he knew, Jacob still acknowledged the last name that they shared, a gift from James' father—one given by birth, one given by ownership.

He tucked the book into his black leather duffle bag and headed toward the exit, sparing a friendly nod for the pilot who regarded him with open fascination. It was an expression many humans in the know had in the presence of vampires, although to Jacob, it was the equivalent of being giddy around any apex predator. Slowly, he descended the stairs, and then, at last, he stepped onto the pavement of the private runway.

For the first time in eighteen years, he was in the place he had once considered home.

Two figures approached him from a distance. Even under the cover of night, Jacob knew immediately that the taller of the two was James. Their vampiric bond, while somewhat muted after almost two centuries of separation, was still there, drawing them together. The shorter figure was also a vampire, and Jacob could sense the familiarity in him straight away; James had turned him, too. By choice, Jacob hoped.

The shorter vampire stayed back as James continued his approach, gradually emerging out of the darkness and into the lights of the runway. The tall, tan, and muscular vampire flashed Jacob a hesitant smile, and his thick, jet black hair swayed in the breeze. He still had the bluest eyes that Jacob had ever seen; even when they were children, it was all he could do not to constantly stare directly into them, mesmerized by their beauty.

"Hello, James," he said, now that they were finally face to face.

"Hello, Jacob," James replied in the gentle drawl that hadn't faded over the years. "How was the flight?"

"It was fine. Thank you again for making the arrangements."

"You're welcome." James paused before cautiously continuing. "How is... your Eye-talian?"

Jacob knew that it wasn't an easy thing for James to inquire about Dominic, but his Southern upbringing demanded politeness, even if it caused discomfort. As a slave, he had been continually flabbergasted at a society that saw no wrong in owning people yet expressed pearl-clutching horror over any lack of pleases and thank yous.

"He's doing well."

"I'm surprised he didn't come with you, all things considered."

"I told him that everything would be okay," Jacob said with a reassuring nod. "So he decided to stay home with our son."

James' eyes widened upon hearing that. "You have a son?"

It was just as well that the pilot chose that exact moment to interrupt them by giving Jacob his suitcase. "Thank you very much," he said when he realized that James was too stunned to acknowledge the man.

The pilot took his leave, and the other vampire who had been waiting patiently approached the duo. The sense of familiarity that Jacob had felt when he first saw him intensified, along with a touch of déjà vu. He was certain that he had never seen this vampire before, and yet felt he knew him all the same.

"I'll take that for you," he offered, reaching for Jacob's suitcase.

"Thank you... um..."

They both looked to James, who was still visibly reeling over Jacob's casual admission of fatherhood.

"Oh." The vampire jerked back to reality and remembered his manners. "Pardon me. Jacob, this is my companion, Nathaniel. Nathaniel, this is my... this is Jacob."

Nathaniel smiled kindly. "It's so nice to finally meet you. I've heard a lot about you."

"Good things, I hope," Jacob said, glancing at his former lover.

"Very good things. And not just from James."

Jacob frowned in confusion. "Then who...?"

Now it was Nathaniel's turn to glance at James, who gave him a nod of encouragement. "From my Papa Solomon."

Jacob's lips moved, but it took a few seconds for enough shock to subside for him to form words. "Solomon was your grandfather?"

"Yes, he was," Nathaniel replied proudly.

That long ago night, after Jacob was given the twenty lashes that left his back raw and bloody, a fellow slave named Solomon had carefully carried him to one of the shacks where the rest of the slaves resided. After what had happened, along with James' subsequent disappearance, it was correctly presumed that he was no longer welcome inside the main house. Jacob had spent an entire month face-down on a musty cot while Solomon had tended to his wounds, and he was certain that the man's intervention was the only reason that he hadn't succumbed to infection or been sold off to the bastard who demanded he be punished in the first place for daring to refuse his advances.

There were so many things about Jacob's time as a slave that he didn't care to remember. However, the kindness of Solomon was one of the few things he recalled fondly.

"It's an honor to meet you," Jacob said, still awestruck. "Solomon was one of the best men I've ever had the pleasure of knowing."

"He certainly was," James agreed.

Nathaniel nodded appreciatively. "Thank you, both. I'll be at the car whenever you're ready."

He left them there, wheeling Jacob's suitcase alongside him.

"Are the two of you...?" Jacob asked.

"Of course not," James replied. "I watched him grow up. And in case you were wondering—"

"I was."

"—yes, he wanted to be turned."

"Good."

James sighed and blinked at Jacob, his blue eyes so bright that they seemed to glow. "I'm not the same vampire I was back then."

"I wouldn't be here if I thought you were," Jacob told him. "Now, let's get out of here before a plane lands on us."

AFTER NATHANIEL DROPPED them off and excused himself with a knowing gleam in his eyes to go "run errands," Jacob could only stand there and gape at the house. After parting ways with James back in 1804, he and Dominic had relocated three hundred miles north to an area not far from what would become Atlanta before permanently moving to Harborview, Pennsylvania in 1982. He'd had no intention or reason to believe he would ever come back to this place. Now, there he was.

"I bet you broke a lot of hearts when you did this," he said, marveling at the gorgeous contemporary home that now stood in place of the old plantation house.

James shrugged. "Yeah, well, I don't much give a damn that I did. Besides the old house being a reminder of the past, I wanted to make the entire thing light tight, not just the basement."

"The whole house is lightproof?" Jacob gawked at all of the blacked out windows, impressed.

"'Tis. Every inch of glass is laminated and has multiple layers of light resistance, plus backup blackout shutters. Nathaniel oversaw the whole project from start to finish."

"Did he now?"

James shook his head when he saw Jacob's raised brow. "I watched him grow up," he reminded him.

"And just how long has he been grown up now?"

"I... he... just..." Flustered, James grabbed Jacob's suitcase. "Come on."

Any ill feelings Jacob thought he might have upon entering the house proved to be non-existent. It was so far removed from everything he remembered that it was simply a house. Nothing more.

"Old things are passed away," he murmured as he followed James through the living room and up the stairs.

"Behold, all things are become new," James said, completing the verse. "I guess all those bible lessons we had to suffer finally paid off."

"Better late than never."

"Indeed." James opened a guest bedroom door and gave him the suitcase. "Here you go. Feel free to look around. I'll be downstairs if you need anything."

He paused as if he wanted to say more. Ultimately, he just nodded and walked away, leaving Jacob simultaneously curious as to what he had been planning to say and relieved that he didn't say it, whatever it was.

Once James was out of earshot, Jacob pulled out his phone and called Dominic to let him know he had arrived. He barely had time to go into specifics before Xan confiscated the phone from Dominic and proceeded to inquire about an "Uncle Bob." After picking the child's brain some more, Jacob concluded that he was referring to another bit of British slang ("Bob's your uncle") and made a mental note to thank Becky later for confusing the hell out of his kid by inadvertently leading him to believe he had another uncle besides Dominic's twin brother, Demetrio.

Nathaniel stopped in the hallway just outside of the doorway and raised his hands apologetically when he saw that Jacob was on the phone. Jacob beckoned with his free hand in return, inviting him into the bedroom.

"I'm going to go now, goober. Give Dominic a kiss for me, and give you a kiss for me, too... Oh, shush, that's not gross... Okay, I love you... Bye." Jacob returned the phone to his pocket. "My son," he explained.

"I gathered," Nathaniel replied thoughtfully.

"You're wondering how I have one?"

"It doesn't matter, as long as you have him."

Jacob jolted at the profoundness of the vampire's statement. It felt as though he were face to face with a younger-looking version of his old friend, from the compact body, unblemished brown skin, and soulful brown eyes.

"That sounds like something Solomon would have said," he remarked wistfully. "I know you're not him, but I see so much of him in you. It's surreal." Jacob shook his head. "I'm sorry, I shouldn't put that on you. You are your own person."

Nathaniel smiled. "Thank you for recognizing that. I don't mind the comparison, though."

"What was he like as a grandfather?"

"The same way he was when you knew him, I imagine. Probably more outspoken since James treated him—and everybody—as equals and not property. We weren't free as far as the country was concerned, but we were free here at home."

"I'm sure that didn't go over so well," Jacob guessed as he took a seat on the edge of the large bed in the center of the room.

"It didn't matter," Nathaniel said, sitting down in a chair at a nearby desk. "James inherited everything after his father died, including Papa and the others. There was nothing that anyone could do about it."

Jacob's hands were clasped in his lap and his thumb caressed the gold signet ring that Dominic had given him shortly before nearly delivering on his vow to kill a delirious James if he didn't leave Jacob alone. "I was worried about how things would be after I left. I'm glad to know that everything worked out. At least something good came out of what happened that night... I assume you know the story?"

"Broad strokes," Nathaniel responded. "Papa never wanted to talk about it too much and James never wanted to talk about it at all, but I pieced together what I could from eavesdropping on the others. You were quite the topic of conversation around the house sometimes, long after you were gone."

Jacob tucked an unruly lock of hair behind his ear. "It was a party, a big one full of all kinds of fancy and important people," he started with a long sigh. "I was told to keep to the kitchen. I think my complexion hit a little too close to home for some of the guests. Maybe some of them even knew who my mother was. One of Mast—"

He paused, cutting off the word and hating just how easily he had almost slipped right back into slave-speak.

"One of James' father's friends came into the kitchen and found me. He chased the others out and decided he was going to have his way with me. I pushed him off me and then all hell broke loose." Jacob laughed bitterly. "All because I made the grave mistake of considering myself a person. Silly me."

"You don't have to go on," Nathaniel told him. "I know what happened next."

"Did you know they all cheered with every single lash? My punishment was very entertaining, apparently. I guess it's a good thing they didn't hang me. The show would've been over much quicker."

Jacob blinked away the tears he didn't know he had left over everything that had happened that night.

"But they all died bloody and I'm still here, so the joke is on them," he concluded.

"I'm glad James came back and did what he did to them," Nathaniel said softly, his eyes hazed over in anger. "I know it's wrong, but I am."

"I am, too," Jacob admitted. "I'm not going to pretend to be heartbroken that he killed his father and all the other people who were there that night. I just wish it would've ended with them. Well, I don't wish for it now, but back then..." He studied the other vampire. "I'm glad you were given a choice. That's the way it should always be."

"It didn't feel like a choice, really. I just knew I wanted to be near him forever."

"You're in love with him."

"All my life," Nathaniel said, his expression full of adoration. "But he still thinks of me as the little kid who followed him around everywhere."

"That could change," Jacob pointed out. "You never know."

"I know that the only thing James is capable of loving is his guilt over what he did to you. You moved on, the entire world moved on, but a large part of him is still stuck in 1804. I'm afraid it always will be."

The faint sound of a closing door caught their attention. The vampires looked at the bedroom doorway and then each other.

"James?" Jacob asked.

Nathaniel nodded. "He's going to the tree. He goes there a lot."

Jacob looked at the doorway again. He knew what he needed to do.

So did Nathaniel.

"If you'll excuse me, I'm going to finish preparations for your trip tomorrow," he said as he rose to his feet.

"You're not coming with us?"

"This situation with your niece is too important. I would just get in the way."

Jacob strongly suspected that his refusal to accompany them had absolutely nothing to do with Alexandra, but he opted not to interrogate him further.

After Nathaniel left the bedroom, Jacob made his way down the stairs and through the massive house. It took some searching but he finally found the door that led out back and stepped outside.

He halted, frozen in place, frozen in time, as he laid eyes on the enormous Southern live oak tree that dominated the backyard. Memories of random moments under the tree with James bombarded him, from childhood to adulthood and all the years in between. Sharing a pilfered peach and thinking he had never tasted anything so divine. Discreetly tracing letters on each other's hands before James boldly decided to teach him the alphabet properly. Holding hands, holding each other, their first kiss, their first everything, right up against the tree with bark digging into his back, screaming into one of James' hands and spilling into the other.

With a shaky sigh, Jacob walked over to the tree and stood beside James.

"I couldn't bring myself to get rid of it," James explained. "I hope you don't mind."

Jacob craned his neck, peering up to the top of the huge oak. "This tree represents the little bit of beauty that we found in a fucking ugly world. Never cut it down."

"I figure it's one of the oldest trees in the state," James said. "And one of the biggest."

"I'd like to think we're responsible for that."

"How so?"

Jacob smirked. "As much as we... contributed... to it, it had to have some benefits."

James blinked at Jacob, nonplussed. "I... I don't think that particular type of... contribution... has any effect on plant life."

The vampires stared at each other before laughing, which was the last thing Jacob expected he would do that night.

Equally unexpected was James' laughter. The sound of it was inexplicably pleasing.

"It's nice to hear you laugh again," he said quietly. "It's been too long."

"It has," James concurred just as quietly while lowering his head.

"James—"

"Tell me about your son."

Recognizing the deflection for what it was, Jacob consented to a reply. "His name is Alexander," he began, reaching into his pocket for his wallet. He flipped it open to one of the many pictures he carried of the boy and showed it to James. "Xan for short. He just turned eight a couple of months ago."

"He's a human child?"

"Yes."

James' curiosity was palpable. But Jacob knew that the same learned politeness that prompted the vampire to inquire about Dominic when he couldn't have cared less also prevented him from demanding to know how two vampires ended up parents to a mortal.

"He's precious," James said after realizing that Jacob would not volunteer any additional information. "And I reckon you spoil him rotten."

"A little." Jacob looked up from the picture to see James watching him carefully. And a touch sadly. "You know we'll need to talk about a few things you may not want to talk about before I leave, right? It doesn't have to be a whole thing, but something."

"I know. I was just hoping to put it off because this was going much better than I thought it would."

He had a point. Jacob certainly hadn't anticipated ending up at the tree under and against which he'd had copious amounts of forbidden sex and discussing whether or not the results of all that sex had acted as some sort of weird, growth-enhancing fertilizer. The idea made him chuckle again, and he decided to cut James some much-needed slack.

"Let's just focus on my niece," he said. "We'll head out at sundown tomorrow, deal with that situation, and get back here before dawn. But after that..."

"After that," James conceded. "Thank you, Jacob."

"You're welcome, James."

Jacob reached out and gently touched James' shoulder before returning to the house, feeling strangely optimistic. He went upstairs to the guest bedroom, changed out of his casual suit into even more casual pajamas, and crawled into bed where he talked to Dominic until dawn.

THE NEXT NIGHT, DURING the two hour drive to an area near Brunswick, James filled Jacob in on the details of Alexandra's life that he had missed out on since leaving Georgia. She was forty-one now, which was the only thing Jacob had known for certain. After selling and moving out of her family's house, and then moving to her present location, she opened what would become a rather successful coffeehouse called Alexandra's. While the name wasn't all that original, much of the menu was, and it was one of the many reasons why the place was so renowned.

She never married or had children, but as far as James had been able to ascertain, she also had no pressing desire to do either of those things. It was her reluctance over the former that was at the heart of their journey. Alexandra came from old money. A *lot* of old money. And it seemed that the old boyfriend was doing his damnedest to stick around in order to acquire a share of it.

Now, as they sat at a table and enjoyed a Caffè Americano, some light jazz, and the immensely calming atmosphere of the establishment, James used his head to motion ever so subtly to his left. "That's him, blond hair, appalling goatee, sitting alone at the table by the wall. The one who keeps looking around like he's expecting someone." He took a sip of his drink in an effort to look casual. "He's waiting to see if she'll come out from the back."

Jacob ran a hand through his hair and used the opportunity to look to his right. He spotted the man James described and instantly hated him. "Has he ever put his hands on her?" he wanted to know.

James glowered at the vampire, obviously affronted. "We wouldn't be here if he had because he would be dead."

"I wasn't implying that you would have allowed that to happen. What's his name?"

"Roy Edwards."

"And he comes here every night?"

"My sources say yes," James replied. "He doesn't go to her house anymore since there's an order barring him from the property, so he just sits there in that same spot, waiting to see if she shows her face."

"Does she?"

"After he gives up and leaves right before closing, yes."

That was unacceptable to Jacob. And the more he contemplated it, the angrier he became.

"What are you going to do?" James asked.

Jacob glanced at the man again, his hands tightly gripping the glass coffee mug. "Something I normally don't like doing. But in this case, I'll gladly make an exception."

He maintained his grip on the mug for another five minutes, until the beverage had cooled down. Then he rose to his feet, mug in hand, and casually weaved his way through patrons and tables until he reached Roy's table and suddenly "tripped," spilling his drink all across the tabletop and the man's formerly white shirt.

"Shit!" Roy looked down at his ruined shirt and then up at Jacob. "What the fuck?"

"I am so sorry," Jacob said, feigning remorse.

Roy stood up and glared at Jacob. "You damn well should be, you clumsy mother—"

"Stop talking."

Wide blue eyes stared at Jacob. Roy's lips moved, but no sound came forth.

Jacob acted fast, before the concerned server headed their way could hear him. "You will tell her that everything is fine."

"Oh, my goodness," she drawled when she reached them. "I'll get this cleaned up for y'all right away."

"Everything is fine," Roy told her in a monotone voice.

She looked from Roy to Jacob for confirmation.

"Please don't trouble yourself because I'm a klutz," Jacob said with a disarming smile. "But thank you very much for offering."

He sweetened the deal with a wad of bills pressed into the palm of her hand. She peeked at her hand and gasped; clearly she had been expecting all ones.

"Follow me," he said to Roy after the server left them.

There was no need for Jacob to look over his shoulder to make sure that the human was behind him. His hold on Roy's mind was firm and unrelenting. He was a prisoner in his own body, forced to do whatever Jacob wanted. It was a feeling Jacob remembered all too well, because he had experienced the exact same thing right before James killed him.

He stepped outside into the warm night air. To avoid the bulk of the people who were coming or going or loitering out front, he walked about twenty paces down the sidewalk and casually leaned back against the side of the building. At a glance, they merely looked like two guys shooting the breeze.

"You have questions," Jacob began, locking eyes with Roy. "Unfortunately, I don't have time to give you answers, and it wouldn't matter anyway because you aren't going to remember parts of this conversation. What *does* matter is that Alexandra is my niece, and your behavior will no longer be tolerated. If you ever go near her again, you will die. And if you're wondering how it will happen..." Jacob flashed a deadly, fang-filled smile. "Use your imagination."

Roy moaned worriedly when the vampire pushed off the wall and stood directly in front of him. It was all he was capable of doing to express the sheer terror he must have felt.

"You won't remember me," Jacob continued. "You won't remember what I am. But any time you even *think* about her, you'll remember the fear you feel right now."

He contemplated adding in a bonus, like making Roy piss himself whenever he acted like an asshole, but the reasonable part of his conscience knew he had done enough.

"Now walk away and don't look back."

Jacob watched as he left, his sharp eyes trained on the back of Roy's head until he was just another shadow in the darkness. He wondered whether or not he had sent the bastard scurrying off while his car was still in the parking lot but then decided that he didn't care. With that out of the way, he went back into the coffeehouse.

As he was about to return to his table, deciding to order another Caffè Americano to replace the one he didn't finish, he spotted James glancing pointedly at the counter. Jacob looked in that direction... and saw Alexandra staring directly at him.

Then she started walking toward him.

She was just as naturally beautiful as she was the last time he saw her in 1982. Her hair, even pulled up in a ponytail, was still a lovely brown mess, much like Jacob's. While that was where their physical similarities began and ended, for Jacob, it still felt like he was looking in a mirror in many ways. And it made his heart ache.

"Was that man... was he bothering you?"

Like James, her drawl was gentle. Soothing, even. Jacob imagined that his mother's voice must have sounded similar and he hated her all over again.

But Alexandra wasn't his mother, and for all he knew, she might have had no idea who the woman even was. Jacob didn't think that was likely, though. Many Southern families obsessively tracked their history, some as far back as their arrival from overseas, all while giving no thought whatsoever to their ancestors having destroyed the histories of others.

"Sir?"

"I'm sorry." Jacob shelved his sour feelings as best he could and focused his attention on the only living proof that he had ever existed. "He wasn't bothering me, and he will no longer bother you."

The woman's mouth opened in astonishment. "How did you know?"

"I know what it's like to have an ex-boyfriend who refuses to let go. I guess I recognized the signs."

Alexandra smiled gratefully. "Well then... thank you."

"You're quite welcome."

"Would you like—"

"We're actually about to leave," Jacob interrupted, trying to keep his voice level. "We're not from around here, and we've got a long drive ahead of us."

"If you're ever in the area again, please stop by," Alexandra offered.

Jacob, who had no intention of ever returning again if he could help it, nodded appreciatively. "I'll be sure to do that. Take care of yourself, Alexandra."

He walked away before common courtesy got the better of him and made him introduce himself. James stood up as he approached.

"Let's get out of here," he said, his eyes full of sympathy.

They exited the coffeehouse and returned to James' black Volvo. Neither vampire said anything for the first half of the trip, and Jacob was content to let Steve Perry serenade them all the way back to James' house. But once they hit Highway 82, he decided that he needed to vent, after all.

"How many men like my father do you think were tortured and killed because of women like my mother?" he asked as he leaned back against the headrest and stared blindly out of the passenger window.

"Too many to count," James responded.

"And they just got away with it. Do you think any of them felt guilty about what they did?"

"I don't know, Jacob."

"I hope she did," Jacob said harshly. "I hope she never knew a minute of peace until the day she died."

He peered down at the upturned hand that rested on his thigh and covered it with his own. There was nothing romantic in the gesture; it was an offer and acceptance of solace, and nothing more. Often were the times during their past human lives when James had consoled him in the very same way for the very same reason.

When they finally got back, James escorted Jacob to the guest bedroom door because he was a gentleman through and through. While there were still a few hours left until dawn, Jacob wanted to be alone to process everything he had gone through that night.

"Will you keep watching over her?" he asked.

"For the rest of her life." After a moment, James added, "Why didn't you just tell her who you were?"

"Telling her who I am would've served no purpose except to satisfy my own desire for revenge against a woman long gone. It's not my niece's fault that she is my mother's descendant."

James nodded in understanding. "Are you going to be all right? You're more than welcome to join me and Nathaniel in the parlor."

"Tomorrow night," Jacob promised. "After we've talked."

"Then I'll leave you to it. If you need anything..."

"I'll holler."

James chuckled. "Okay. Sleep tight."

Jacob went into the bedroom and closed the door, then he trudged over to the bed and flopped down on it, face-first. He missed Dominic, he missed Xan, he missed home, and he wanted nothing more than to be away from Georgia, away from his past, and away from all the reminders of who and what he used to be. But first, he needed to rip off the scab of tentative peace that he had forged with James since his arrival and confront the festering wound of their troubled past. It was time for a resolution.

And, with any luck, healing.

THE NEXT NIGHT, AFTER a dinner that consisted of blood and wine, they got the ball rolling by walking past the tree and around the rest of the expansive backyard that comprised most of the property. There was nothing back there now except grass, vibrant in color even in the moonlight, but Jacob could clearly picture the rows of cotton and derelict shacks as they once were, including the one he had lived in until being granted the privilege of moving into the main house at the age of fourteen.

"Why didn't you do anything with all of this?" he asked, gesturing at all the open space. "Build something? Plant something?"

"Because it would've been disrespectful to all the people who lived and died here," James answered dolefully. "I tried my best to do right by all of them."

"I believe you did."

"I tried to do right by you, too."

Jacob's jaw clenched. He had wanted to have this conversation, and now it was happening. His right hand slid into his pants pocket and absentmindedly toyed with a quarter; he always kept one in there to pull out of Xan's ear at any time.

"I felt so goddamn helpless when my father gave me that ultimatum," James continued, refusing to meet Jacob's eyes. "And after... after I..."

"Whipped me," Jacob whispered.

James winced as if he had been struck. "After... that... I had to do something. That's why I tried to make it up North, get some help, and find a way to get you out of Georgia. But then another solution presented itself."

Jacob remained silent. He knew how the story ended.

"I truly thought you would see being a vampire as an opportunity." James turned to face Jacob, finally able to return his gaze. "A chance to be free from racist trash. We could've gone anywhere, we could've done anything. No one could've stopped us."

"James, that's easy to say when you're not the one considered property. I couldn't imagine the idea of slavery not existing because it was all I had ever known. Even in that supposedly magical place called the North, slavery was only just abolished the same year you came back." Jacob paused and ran a hand over his face. " How different would our lives be today if you had only given me time to work up to the idea of being turned instead of forcing it on me?"

"I've asked myself that same question every single day for almost two hundred years," James said regretfully.

"And it's time for you to stop," Jacob replied firmly. "I forgave you a long time ago for turning me. Now you need to forgive yourself." Sensing a rebuttal, he grabbed the vampire by his muscular arms. "*I'm happy*, James. And despite how it happened, I owe that happiness to you. Now you deserve some happiness of your own, and it's closer than you think, if you would just stop making excuses and accept it."

"Jacob, I can't."

"Yes, you can. Why did you even give him the choice to become a vampire if you didn't want to be with him?"

Jacob waited, ready to continue arguing if need be. But instead of arguing, James took a long, deep breath in resignation.

"I... I'll... I'll try."

"See that you do." Jacob smiled warmly. "Now, are you going to invite me to share some of that Macallan I spotted in the parlor, or have you lost all credibility as a Southern gentleman?"

James gasped. "How dare you?"

The vampires grinned at each other and headed back to the house. They entered the parlor where Nathaniel was waiting for them with whiskey glasses.

For the rest of the night, they drank and shared various tales from the past, like the time when a bible-thumping do-gooder was gracious enough to inform James and Jacob that the Lord loved all of his creations, even "lesser ones" like the Negroes.

"She really said that?" a horrified Nathaniel asked.

"She really did," Jacob confirmed. "And so James called her..."

"... a rank bitch," James said before gulping down the rest of his drink. "I thought for sure my father was going to punish me but he didn't. Apparently the woman was hoping to get his attention, romantically. My assessment of her character prevented any chance of that, which was exactly what he wanted."

"Lucky for you," Nathaniel said as he held out his glass for James to fill again.

Their eyes met while James poured. Jacob sipped on his own drink to keep from telling them to kiss already.

When dawn was nearly upon them, Jacob decided to turn in because he wanted a full day's rest for the plane ride home the next night. He glanced back at the parlor where James and Nathaniel remained, sitting on opposite ends of a brown leather sofa and never taking their eyes off each other while conversing. It was adorable.

While there would always be occasions when some unpleasant element of his former life would rear its ugly head, Jacob was thankful that he had been given the opportunity to confront the demons of the past. He was also thankful that he had nudged James in the direction of confronting his own. Someday, the demons would be laid to rest for good. One advantage to immortality, whether voluntarily acquired or forcibly received, was that they would have plenty of time to work on it.

He crawled into bed and reminded himself that at the same time tomorrow, he would be in his own bed with Dominic's arms wrapped around him. Realizing this, he fell asleep with a smile.

THE SAME PILOT WHO had flown Jacob to Georgia now took his suitcase and waited at the private plane to return him to Pennsylvania.

"I asked him to stop calling you by my last name," James said as he handed Jacob his duffle bag. "I figured you weren't too keen on it anymore since it was never your own."

"I appreciate that," Jacob replied to James before turning to Nathaniel, who stood beside him. "Keep an eye on him for me."

"I'll do my best." Nathaniel offered his hand. "I'm so glad we had a chance to meet. I hope we can do this again one day, under less troublesome circumstances."

Jacob shook the vampire's hand. "I hope so."

Nathaniel left him alone with James, who favored him with a melancholy smile.

"You and I both know that you're never coming back to Georgia," James said.

"I'll admit it's not high on my to-do list, but never say never," Jacob replied. "Besides, you've got much better things to do now than worry about my travel plans."

"Well, that is true."

"Don't break him."

"Hush." A frown briefly passed over James' handsome face. "Make sure that Eye-talian takes care of you and your boy."

"He will."

"May I hug you?"

Jacob nodded and found himself pulled into an embrace that was every bit as comforting as it had been ages ago. After allowing himself a few seconds to wallow in the sensations it caused, he stepped back and looked up at his first love, his killer, his maker... his *friend*... with eyes that weren't exactly dry.

"Goodbye, James."

"Goodbye, Jacob."

Jacob got onto the plane and settled into a seat, and any lingering sadness vanished as the anticipation of seeing his family grew stronger. He peered out of the window and saw James and Nathaniel waving at him, and he waved back. Then he pointed at the two of them and gave a thumbs up with an eyebrow wiggle, which caused them both to burst into unheard laughter. It was the best conclusion to the trip that he could have hoped for.

Shortly after, the plane took off. His past was behind him once again. Every minute and mile that passed brought him closer to Harborview.

And his future.

SMALL PACKAGES

Author's Note: A Harborview Immortals extra. Jacob has found the perfect gift for Dominic, one that will change both their lives, and he can't wait to give it to him.

Christmas Eve 2006

THE VIEW OUTSIDE OF the living room window was far more breathtaking than many of the Christmas-themed pictures and paintings that Jacob had ever seen. There was snow as far as the eye could see, about three or four inches of it, blanketing the massive front lawn and driveway. The street beyond was covered as well, though the sound of the plows two blocks over indicated that would not be the case for much longer. Snow fell in large clumps from the bare branches of the sugar maple tree in front of the house across the street. All of the neighbors' houses were festively decorated with numerous strings of bright, blinking lights that cut through the darkness with alternating flashes of red and green. Some of the houses displayed Nativity scenes while others had Santa and his reindeer. The Taylors, who lived two houses down on the other side of the street, had both. It was a combination that amused Jacob to no end—even more so because of the zombie garden gnomes that were acting as stand-ins for two reindeer and one of the Wise Men.

"We should've decorated the outside of the house." He turned his head slightly to the right to acknowledge the vampire who had joined him at the window. "Maybe the neighbors would like us then."

"Do you really care if they like us or not?" Dominic asked.

"No, but it would be nice if they didn't stare at our house like it was a part of some circus freak show."

Dominic leaned forward to peer through the glass, his chin resting on Jacob's shoulder. "We are a gay, interracial couple living in a conservative neighborhood, Jacob. Holiday decorations aren't going to make much of a difference to most of these people. I can only imagine how they would react if they knew that we were vampires." After a moment, he added, "Are those zombies?"

"Yeah," Jacob replied with a grin. "At least we're not the only weirdos on the street."

He closed the curtains and turned around. While the view outside was indeed lovely, it was the view in front of him that pleased him most. A fire burned steadily in the fireplace, filling the room with enough heat to counter such a cold winter night. An enormous Christmas tree sat in the corner, adorned with huge, twinkling balls and stars, blinking lights, endless tinsel, and some of the handmade ornaments that Xan had made over the years that Jacob couldn't bear to part with. Piles upon piles of prettily wrapped presents were under the tree, most of which were reserved for the fourteen-year-old who sat on the floor beside them while eagerly waiting for the clock to strike midnight. Speaking of which...

"Come on, Dad," Xan said over the sound of Bing Crosby's velvety vocals, staring at Jacob with his big blue eyes. "It's almost midnight."

Jacob smiled warmly at the boy, who looked like he was about to burst out of his skin with excitement. "You've waited all year for this. You can wait twenty more minutes."

When Jacob failed to succumb to his charm, Xan turned to his other father. "Domi?"

"Twenty minutes," Dominic repeated. "You'll survive."

"I'm not so sure about that," said Dominic's identical twin, Demetrio, from his chair by the tree. He offered Xan his empty wine glass. "Why don't you get me a refill? That'll take at least a minute. Or two, if you take your time."

Xan groaned and took his uncle's glass. "Can I have a sip?" he asked suddenly, his impatience temporarily forgotten in the hopes of scoring some booze. "Domi lets me have some champagne every New Year's Eve."

Demetrio looked to Dominic, who looked to Jacob for a final answer. "Last I checked, it wasn't New Year's Eve."

"No fair," Xan pouted, though it was plain to see that his heart wasn't truly in it.

Jacob strolled over to the teen and helped him up. "Poor baby," he said as he ruffled Xan's blond hair. "You have the meanest parents in the world."

"I know!" Xan's adorable scowl gradually melted into a smile. "Well, maybe not the meanest, but close."

"Then we'll just have to try harder."

Xan stuck out his tongue and ran into the kitchen before Jacob could swat him on the bottom.

"I can't believe how much he's grown this year," said Becky, the British vampire who was also the family's closest friend. She yanked on the front of her Mrs. Claus outfit, which had slid down her sizable cleavage to dangerously revealing levels. "He's almost as tall as you, Jacob."

Luca Melani, the muscular human who watched over Xan during the day, nodded in agreement. "At the rate he's going, he's going to pass you soon. He might even end up as tall as Dominic."

"Probably." Jacob took a seat on the floor while Dominic joined Luca and Becky on the sofa. He wasn't ready to think about craning his neck to look into his son's eyes or what it meant having to do so. The baby who had taken their hearts captive fourteen years ago was becoming a man. Time was passing by far too quickly. "What does everyone have planned for tomorrow night?" he asked, wanting to steer his thoughts away from the inevitable.

"Sex," Demetrio replied.

Dominic grunted in disgust, as he often did when his brother opened his mouth. "Do you have even the tiniest bit of shame?"

"Not really."

"Perhaps you should try having some."

"And perhaps you should try removing the stick from your ass."

"Stop it, both of you." Jacob tried not to laugh; Luca and Becky were doing enough of that for him. It simply wasn't a family gathering if Dominic and Demetrio weren't snapping at each other. Jacob couldn't begin to understand how two siblings who undoubtedly loved each other bickered so much, but such had always been the case for the twins, who were opposites in every way aside from their identical faces. "What about you, Becky?"

"After I bring the rugrat back—"

"I'm not a rugrat!" Xan claimed as he reentered the living room with a glass of wine for Demetrio.

"—I'm going to spend some time with a few friends," Becky concluded.

"You have friends besides us?" Dominic asked with genuine curiosity.

"If you count personal massagers," Demetrio muttered.

Xan, who had plopped himself down on Jacob's lap after giving Demetrio his wine, blinked at the vampire and wanted to know, "Are massagers for sore muscles and stuff?"

"Only if she's doing it right."

"Demetrio." Dominic glared at his twin, agitated but not surprised.

"Moving on," Jacob spoke up before war erupted. "What about you, Luca?"

"I imagine the Old Man will want to stay in and have a few drinks," the big man replied. "So basically the same thing we do almost every other night of the year."

"The two of you are more than welcome to join us at the shelter," Dominic offered.

"I'll ask him about it."

"Are you lot handing out gifts again this year?" Becky asked.

"We sure are, aren't we?" Jacob looked at Xan, who nodded emphatically. "It went over pretty well last year so we decided to make it a yearly tradition."

They spoke for a little while longer about the Dawson House, which was the homeless shelter that Dominic and Jacob opened thirteen years ago for the public purpose of providing free lodging and food for any who needed it. Privately, the shelter was their primary source for obtaining the blood they sold and traded, though the residents had no recollection of making any donations because their memories were wiped immediately afterwards.

Xan checked the clock above the mantelshelf and informed them all that there were only five minutes left until midnight, just in case they hadn't noticed. Then, after another failed attempt at getting a sip of Merlot from Demetrio, he boldly announced that he was going to drink an entire bottle of the stuff the second he turned twenty-one.

"You do that and you may never want to drink again," Luca warned him.

"But first I'm going to get some tattoos," the boy told everyone. "I can do that when I'm eighteen."

Jacob glanced at Dominic, who merely shrugged. Xan had been going on and on about getting tattoos for the better part of the past year. Jacob had no idea where the fascination came from, and he secretly hoped that Xan would change his mind before he was old enough to permanently mark his body. But if he didn't, then... well... whatever made him happy. That was the only thing that mattered to Jacob.

"And I want to get my ears pierced," Xan continued. "I can do that now if Dad and Domi let me."

"Your ears are already pierced," Jacob pointed out, tugging on the platinum hoops in the teen's ears. "You want more?"

"Yep."

"How many more?"

"Lots more. All the way up. And my tongue. And maybe a nipple."

Jacob sighed. His son was never one to aspire to anything half-assed. "How about we stick with your ears until you're older?" he suggested. "After you're eighteen, you can poke as many holes in your body as you want. Deal?"

"Deal."

Jacob pressed his nose against the back of Xan's neck, inhaling the combined scent of soap and shampoo. He wouldn't get too many more chances like this since the boy would soon reach the age when he felt that sitting on his father's lap was for babies, so he wanted to enjoy it as long as he could. Unfortunately, the chiming of the clock brought the moment to an end far sooner than he would have liked.

"Merry Christmas!" Xan screamed as he scrambled to his feet. He pecked Jacob on the cheek and then made his way to the others, sliding in his socks along the hardwood floor as he quickly dispensed obligatory hugs and kisses to all of his family and friends. With that out of the way, he returned to the floor and dropped to his knees, then looked expectantly at Jacob. "Now?" he asked, practically foaming at the mouth.

"Now," Jacob agreed.

Presents were passed out and plenty of pictures were taken; Jacob had an entire photo album reserved just for the occasion. Everyone unwrapped their gifts and expressed the appropriate shock and gratitude, which made Jacob feel much better about the fortune he and Dominic had spent to find the perfect things for each of their loved ones: diamond earrings and an antique earthenware tea set for Becky, a thick platinum and gold bracelet for Luca, and a stunning stainless steel Rolex for Demetrio that was worth as much as a brand new car. Xan bounced and squealed when he saw the Playstation 3 and accompanying games, then the manga, then the comic books, then the action figures, then the shirts with clever gaming references that Jacob didn't understand, and finally the first generation Transformers that had been damn near impossible to find. Jacob feared the kid wouldn't have a voice left the way he carried on, but it warmed his dead heart all the same to see him so ecstatic.

The floor was now covered with piles of torn wrapping paper and ribbons and bows. Luca offered to clean up, but Dominic stopped him, telling him that he would take care of it himself later. Then he presented Jacob with his gift and sat back, waiting.

Jacob pushed aside his presents from the others and crossed his legs. He slowly unwrapped Dominic's gift, partly because he could never bear to rip up something that someone had taken such time and care to wrap, and partly because he knew it drove Xan—who was a dedicated wrapping-destroyer—crazy. He then opened the plain brown box that held the mystery item and looked inside...

"Oh, my God." Jacob gawked at Dominic.

"What is it?" Becky asked, stretching for a closer look and coming close to spilling out of her top again.

Jacob carefully picked up the first edition of Booker T. Washington's *Up from Slavery*, a book he had always treasured about the life of a man he deeply admired. He opened the cover and gasped loudly when he saw that it was signed. "Oh, my God," he repeated, for lack of any other phrase to express his astonishment. "How on earth did you find this?"

"It took a lot of searching, but I had some help. Isn't that right, Alexander?"

"That's right," Xan happily concurred.

"Thank you." Jacob kissed Xan on the forehead and slid across the floor to where Dominic sat. "And thank you," he said, pulling him down for a kiss.

"How sweet," Demetrio said.

"How gross," Xan mumbled, which earned him a kick from Jacob. "Can we do Domi's present now, Dad?"

"Yes." As Xan dove under the tree to get the last remaining gift, Jacob got up from the floor and placed his new old book on the stand near the right arm of the sofa. "Do you mind swapping places with me, big guy?" he asked Luca, who was sitting next to Dominic.

"I don't mind at all."

Jacob sat down in the spot vacated by Luca, who moved behind the sofa to watch them. He took the small gift from Xan and handed it to Dominic while trying not to appear too anxious. Xan was doing a fair enough job of that for the both of them.

Dominic turned the tiny present over in his hands, admiring the glittery red wrap and gold bow. He looked at Xan and then Jacob, his green eyes narrowed questioningly. "It's small."

"You know what they say. Good things, small packages, so on and so forth."

"Is it a ring?"

"... Sort of."

"Hurry up and open it, Domi," Xan insisted as he wedged himself between his parents.

The vampire did as he was told and studied the little black box resting on the palm of his hand. He removed the lid and pulled out a keyring on which dangled two keys.

House keys.

"What is...?" Dominic didn't need to finish the question. He knew exactly what the keys unlocked, and he stared at Jacob in disbelief. "Jacob, you didn't."

"I most certainly did. You are now the proud owner—well, part owner—of the ridiculously gigantic modern style house at 1974 Shore Harbor Drive, complete with backdoor access to Lake Erie and more rooms than we will ever possibly need."

Jacob waited for the news to sink in. Facial expressions of any sort except complete seriousness were rare for Dominic; the stunned look on his face was well worth the house's hefty seven figure price tag.

Before they brought Xan home to live with them, he had often mentioned moving to the exclusive community located in the heart of Harborview. Although the subject was dropped in order to focus on their new son, Jacob had always suspected that Dominic never surrendered his dream. When they found out that one of the houses was up for sale—which didn't happen often—the couple arranged for a late night walk-through. Dominic hadn't said much as they roamed all 5000 square feet of the immaculate dwelling. However, Jacob could tell how much he wanted the place, even though he didn't say the words. What choice did he have but to buy it for him?

"I thought you didn't want that house," Dominic said.

"I never said I didn't want it." Jacob touched his arm. "I don't care where we live, Dominic. To me, home is wherever you are. You love the house, and I love you. So as far as I'm concerned, it's home."

Dominic yanked him into a kiss, much to the horror of the teenager trapped between them. After they parted, he looked around the living room at the knowing gazes of the others. "Did all of you know about this?"

"Yes, we knew," Becky admitted while Demetrio and Luca nodded.

"I couldn't have pulled it off without them," Jacob added. "Especially Luca, who was my daytime accomplice. You'd be surprised how bitchy real estate agents can be when you call them at one in the morning."

Dominic chuckled. "I can't believe you did this. Thank you, Jacob."

"You're welcome. Merry Christmas."

"Are you guys going to make out again?" Xan asked. "If so, I'm out of here."

The couple did him one better by seizing him in a firm embrace from which there was no escape. Xan scowled as his cheeks were peppered with kisses—another rarity for Dominic, whose affection was normally much more subdued—but he soon gave up the fight and resigned himself to being a hostage to his parents' adoration.

Later, after Dominic and Xan picked up all the paper and Jacob refilled everyone's wine (and non-alcoholic eggnog for Xan), the group sat and talked and enjoyed the music and each other. Luca sang along with Bing, his smooth, baritone voice a delight to the ears. Xan was particularly entranced by his singing, which further fueled Jacob's suspicion that the boy was harboring a massive crush on his guardian.

Just before 2 a.m., they called it a night. Luca and Demetrio left first; Demetrio and Dominic even managed to stop insulting each other long enough to hug and exchange a few words of endearment in their native Italian language.

"Make sure he gets some sleep," Jacob instructed Becky while Xan went to his bedroom to grab a change of clothes. "I know he doesn't like to do too much of that when he's with you, but I don't want him dozing off at the shelter tomorrow night."

"And no junk food," Dominic piped in. "No matter how much you try to convince us that potato chips are a vegetable."

"They're called crisps," Becky corrected, rolling her eyes. She spotted Xan entering the room with a heavy black coat in one hand and an overstuffed Star Wars backpack in the other. "Ready to go, Xanadu?"

"Yep." Xan handed her the backpack so he could put on his coat and gloves. "Crisps is a silly word."

"Yes, it is," Jacob agreed.

Becky lightly smacked Xan on the back of the head before covering it with the dark grey cap she had knitted for him two winters ago. "To hell with both of you," she said, slinging the backpack over her shoulder.

Jacob snickered as he stepped toward his son. He ran his hand along the young man's ear and pulled it away to reveal a quarter pinched between his fingers. "Have fun, goober," he said, dropping the coin onto Xan's gloved palm.

"I will." Xan kissed both parents on the cheek and followed Becky to the door. "Goodnight!" he exclaimed with an enthusiastic wave.

Jacob and Dominic waved until they were gone. After they left, Dominic locked the door and turned off Bing mid-croon. Now the house was silent save for the crackling of the dying fire.

"Well, that's that." Jacob sank down on the sofa with a deep sigh. "I hope everyone had a good time."

"I think they did," Dominic responded, sitting down beside him. He took Jacob by the hand, weaving their fingers together. "I still can't believe you bought me a house."

"Don't go expecting one every year."

"I think I can make do with just the one."

Jacob regarded their joined hands as Dominic fiddled with the ring he had given him long ago. "Xan is gone and Luca has the day off. We have the house to ourselves until sundown tomorrow... Whatever will we do?"

"I presume you have some suggestions."

"Only one. But it might take a few tries."

The gleam in Dominic's eyes promised all manner of forbidden pleasures. "Let's find out."

He pulled Jacob into a long, lingering kiss, his tongue gently exploring the depths of Jacob's mouth. Jacob shivered as cool fingers trailed along his skin, over his cheeks and neck, and down his chest and stomach, stopping just as they reached his belt.

"Tease," he panted after they broke apart. He bucked his hips, hoping that Dominic would take the hint and keep going.

"I'm not teasing you. I just thought that you might like to continue this in our bed." Dominic grabbed a handful of sinuous brown hair and pulled Jacob's head back. "Or should I have my way with you right here on the sofa?" he murmured, dragging his tongue along his partner's neck.

Jacob hissed when he felt fangs running over his sensitive skin. He had no idea why he found the threat of teeth so tantalizing since it was a vampire's bite that ended his human life, but the sensation never failed to shoot straight to his crotch and make him hard as a rock. And this time was no different.

"Well?" Dominic asked.

"... I'm trying to decide."

Knowing how long that might take, Dominic stood up. "Come on," he said, extending his hand. "The things I want to do to you require much more space than the sofa provides." After helping Jacob to his feet, he looked down, smirking at what he saw. "Are you going to be able to walk down to the basement with that?"

Jacob looked down as well. He wasn't the only one dealing with a sudden growth. "I could ask you the same thing."

They put out the fire and shut off all the lights, and then, after taking one last moment to admire the eerie gorgeousness of the Christmas tree that lit up the dark room, they went down to the basement. Jacob tried to pounce, with no intention of wasting any more time, but Dominic guided him to the bed and told him to sit down.

"What are you doing?" Jacob inquired when Dominic kneeled down and untied his shoes.

"Isn't it obvious?"

"You're not going to do anything weird to my feet, are you? Not that I wouldn't be into it, but I'm just wondering."

Dominic smiled as he peeled off Jacob's socks and tossed them on top of the shoes he had set aside. "I'll keep that in mind."

Jacob was about to offer a witty retort about his lover's apparent willingness to incorporate feet into their lovemaking when Dominic's head came to rest on his left knee. He shifted to get a better look at his face, which was partially concealed by his long black hair. "What's wrong?"

"I was just thinking."

"About what?"

Dominic went quiet for a spell, his fingers tracing a path around Jacob's ankles. "I was just thinking that I don't know what I would do without you."

Jacob was overcome by a surge of love—pure, unrestrained, and infinite. There wasn't a single thing that he didn't love about Dominic, but if he had to pick the one thing he loved most of all, it was this, the infrequent occasions when the reserved vampire laid bare the truth of his heart.

"Well..." He tried to keep his voice even. "I'm not going anywhere so you don't have to worry about that. You're stuck with me forever. I know that's just a figure of speech to most people, but for me, it's actually true."

Dominic raised his head, and Jacob swept his hair back, tucking it behind his ears to reveal the elegant face that had captivated him for the past 202 years. He would never understand what possessed Dominic to take an interest in a half-breed runaway slave with a scarred body and a broken heart in the first place, but he was thankful all the same.

They kissed again, light pecks and nibbles that soon grew deeper. Dominic, now recovered from his brief bout of emotional turmoil, got up and pulled off Jacob's shirt. Jacob shuddered as the cool air of the underground room hit his exposed skin, but then Dominic pushed him onto his back and unfastened his pants, and he grew warm rather quickly.

After stripping Jacob naked, Dominic climbed on top of him. Jacob reached for his shirt, wanting him to be equally naked, but he was denied the opportunity when Dominic pinned his wrists against the bed. He started to complain, but let out a sharp yelp instead when teeth clamped down on his neck, not puncturing but hurting just enough to feel good.

Dominic slid down Jacob's body, kissing and licking and biting everything along the way. Jacob tried to move his hips, longing to soothe the ache of his erection by grinding against Dominic, but the other vampire held him to the bed, limiting his movements.

"Damn it, Dominic," he growled, trying and failing to free his limbs from his much older and stronger lover.

"Patience," Dominic cooed.

Jacob felt lips curve upward against his hip. Dominic eased up just enough to position himself between Jacob's legs and licked a slow, deliberate trail along his cock, from base to tip.

"Tell me again how you're not a tease," Jacob whispered shakily.

Dominic proceeded to prove that he wasn't by taking him completely into his mouth and sucking him hard and fast. Jacob writhed beneath him, all but consumed by desire, his cock twitching and swelling between Dominic's lips. But just as things were getting good, Dominic pulled away. He let go of Jacob's wrists and hooked his arms beneath the vampire's thighs, lifting his lower half off the bed. Then he parted Jacob's legs and dipped his head. And from there, things got even better.

Jacob cried out the names of all the deities he could think of as Dominic's tongue licked and prodded him everywhere and in every way. His hands, now free to move about, grasped the hair that was fanned out across his abdomen. He widened his legs even more, giving Dominic better access to his most intimate area. The things that Dominic could do with his tongue always drove him to ruin, and tonight was no exception.

"Dominic, please," he begged when he could take no more.

Dominic glanced up from between his legs. "Please what?"

For one who didn't use profanity very often, he seemed to take a great deal of satisfaction in hearing it during sex. Had Jacob been any less aroused than he was now, he might have refused to answer right away, prolonging the game. But Dominic had known exactly what he was doing in whipping him into a frenzy first; being coy was the last thing on Jacob's mind.

"Fuck me," he said, rubbing himself against Dominic's face for good measure. He thought that he could have gotten off just from doing that, and he had to force himself to be still because the mental image of spurting all over Dominic's face was almost his undoing.

Dominic lowered him and got out of the bed. He made a slow show of taking off his clothes, revealing a lean and flawless body that was as perfect as any Italian sculpture. Jacob swallowed hard as he stared at Dominic's thick, full cock, and he wanted it inside of him in the worst way. He took the lube from the nightstand drawer and handed it over, then leaned back with legs open wide.

But Dominic had other plans. "Turn over."

After a split second of hesitation, Jacob complied. Even after all these years, he wasn't completely comfortable with having his scarred back on full display, but he was far too turned on to care as much as he usually did.

Dominic crawled back into the bed and guided Jacob to his knees. Jacob closed his eyes when fingers lovingly traced over the twenty reminders of the time when he lost what little faith he had in the human race. Fortunately, he wasn't given a chance to fully reflect on the tragedy of that night because those same fingers, now slick with lube, worked their way inside of him, stretching him open.

He rocked back, fucking himself on Dominic's fingers. His cock twitched again, moisture pooling at the tip, and it briefly occurred to him that they hadn't gotten a towel for the bed as their intense couplings sometimes had a way of getting messy. Too late to worry about it now.

Dominic removed his fingers and grabbed him by the hips. He rubbed his cock against Jacob's ass before pushing forward, penetrating him gingerly, allowing him to feel every inch until he was all the way inside. A noise escaped Jacob, one that was part moan and part whimper, and he rode out the initial discomfort until his body adjusted. Dominic brought his arms down beside Jacob's, their fingers intertwining and his upper body draping across the vampire's back. He burrowed his face in the crook of Jacob's neck and waited for him to signal that he was ready. When he did, Dominic began, each thrust slow and deep and right to the hilt. The bed creaked and the headboard banged against the wall, but both of those sounds were drowned out by Jacob's cries, which grew increasingly louder the longer Dominic fucked him.

He reached between his legs and grabbed his neglected cock, matching Dominic stroke for thrust. His balls tightened in anticipation of release and a feeling of warmth spread throughout his entire body, heating up his cold blood and making him feel alive again. Sensing his closeness, Dominic wrapped his arms around Jacob's stomach and hauled him upright. He started ramming up into him, skin slapping against skin, bodies colliding, and the change in angle and pace was enough to tip Jacob over the edge. With an empty house and no reason to hold back, he threw back his head and roared at the ceiling as he came all over the bed. He was still pumping his cock when Dominic froze behind him, grunting into his neck, fingernails digging into his skin and leaving scratches that were already healing.

When Jacob felt that he could move, he lifted an unsteady hand and clumsily cupped Dominic's cheek. He managed to turn his head just enough for their lips to meet and he kissed him, tasting wine, tasting himself.

"We forgot to get a towel," Dominic said afterwards, looking over Jacob's shoulder at his contribution to the comforter.

"Yeah, I thought about that, but I was occupied."

Jacob's smile turned into a cringe when Dominic pulled out of him. He fell down to the bed, and Dominic took a spot beside him, on his side with an arm curled under his head. His hair was everywhere, and his skin wasn't quite as pale as it usually was; Jacob knew that he was extremely biased, but even so, he was convinced that there wasn't a more beautiful sight in the world than his Dominic in such a relaxed and carefree state. And nude. That always helped.

He winced as he accidentally rolled over into the mess of his own making. "Ew."

"Stop wallowing in it," Dominic said, amused by his reaction.

"I'm not wallowing in it," Jacob insisted. "Besides, I'm already gooey on one side, may as well be gooey on the other."

Dominic shook his head. "What am I going to do with you?"

"You just did it. And I suspect you'll do it again before the night is over."

"I will. Unless you object."

Jacob inclined his head. "I haven't objected once in two hundred years. I'm not about to do it now."

He pulled Dominic toward him and nuzzled his cheek. Dominic curled an arm around him, holding him close. They remained that way until the heat generated by their lovemaking dissipated, leaving their naked bodies chilled.

"Get cleaned up," Dominic said, sitting up. "I'll take care of the bed."

"It's the least you could do since it was your idea to fuck me from behind."

Using his vampire speed, Jacob was out of the bed and at the bathroom door before Dominic could grab him. And because he hardly ever acted like the 227-year-old being that he was, he stuck out his tongue for added effect. Xan would have been proud of him. (And then subsequently scandalized by the circumstances.)

"I'll make sure you put that to good use later," Dominic said.

"I bet you will."

Jacob stepped into the bathroom and closed the door, grinning from ear to ear. However, he felt a pang of sadness when he realized that moments like these, in this house, were now numbered and would soon be no more. He hadn't been lying when he told Dominic that he didn't care where they lived, and he certainly didn't regret purchasing the house on Shore Harbor for his partner. But when he thought about all of the milestones that they had experienced—including the night they brought a human baby home and decided that they didn't want to live without him—he acknowledged that there was far more to their house than a bunch of walls and a roof. And he was going to miss it.

"Jacob?" Dominic called out from the other side of the door.

"I'm coming!"

"That won't be the last time you say those words tonight."

Jacob snorted and started the shower. When the water was warm enough for his liking, he hopped in and washed up quickly. There was no need to be too thorough since he was going to have to take another one later. By the time he finished and dried off, he was already thinking ahead to the next round, and he walked out of the bathroom naked and ready... but not before grabbing a towel.

FAMILY MATTERS: A HALLOWEEN INTERLUDE
Harborview Immortals #1.5

Author's Note: Xan and Michael go to Dominic and Jacob's house for the weekly family gathering. After everyone else leaves, they decide to stick around for tiramisu, Transformers, and some rather enjoyable quality time. This short story takes place a few weeks after the end of *Family Matters*.

XAN PAUSED WHEN HE reached the entrance to his parents' house and realized that he had lost Michael somewhere between the car and the front door. He turned around, peering toward the end of the driveway where he had parked. There was Michael, barely recognizable under the dim light of a clouded over moon, quickly tip-toeing up the path with bare feet and cursing with each and every step on the cold concrete.

"I told you to wear some damn shoes," he said, chuckling at the vampire's misfortune.

"L doesn't wear shoes," Michael replied when he caught up with him. "What's the point of dressing up for Halloween if I'm not going to be true to the character? If I'm wearing shoes then I'm just some guy with messy hair and eyeliner."

"Perfectionist."

"Says the one who had to go to three different stores to find the right red tie for his Light Yagami costume."

"Don't make me write down your name," Xan jokingly warned, waving a black journal in Michael's face.

"I'm already dead." Michael sealed his reminder with a kiss. "Let's go, my feet are fucking freezing."

Xan started to open the door, but Becky beat him to it. She was wearing the skimpiest, clingiest witch costume known to man, complete with a black pointed hat and broom.

"Happy Halloween!" she cried as she swept the couple into her arms.

Michael squirmed uncomfortably against the large breasts that were pressed against him—her standard greeting. "Happy Halloween, Becky."

"Nice outfit." Xan pried himself from her grip and stepped into the house. "Where's the rest of it?"

"Up your bum," the feisty Brit answered, moving aside so that Michael could enter. She took a minute to check out his white long-sleeved shirt and baggy blue jeans, and then contemplated Xan's brown suit jacket, white dress shirt, and red tie. "Who are you supposed to be?" she asked, running her fingers along golden blond hair that, for once, wasn't spiked all to hell.

"I'm Light," Xan told her.

"And I'm L," Michael added.

Becky blinked at them, oblivious.

"*Death Note*," they clarified in unison.

"If you say so," Becky replied with a dismissive shrug. "Come on, everyone's here."

They made their way through the foyer, with Xan barely managing to avoid being assaulted with a broom after commenting to Michael that Becky lacked the coolness to recognize the characters from one of his favorite manga. The trio walked through the living room and into the dining room, where the first thing Xan and Michael saw was a table loaded with food; Dominic had once again outdone himself for the Friday meal by preparing more than Xan and Luca could dream of eating in one sitting. He was at the table with Jacob and Luca, all of them drinking wine and waiting for their arrival.

"It's about time," Jacob said, though the sternness of his voice was lessened by the smile on his face. He was dressed as a pirate for the occasion, which explained why a hook sat in the middle of the table like some strange centerpiece.

"What took you so long?" asked Dominic. As the result of a promise that was made to a vampire child of irresistible cuteness, he was decked out in 80s rocker fashion with wildly teased hair adorned with a red bandana, a black fishnet shirt, a faded denim vest, and—Xan noticed with amused horror—a pair of skin-tight zebra print pants.

"We got cornered by kids as we were leaving the house," Xan explained. "I had to run back inside and raid the cabinets for something to give them."

"Microwave popcorn," Michael said, shaking his head and taking a seat next to Frankenstein's monster, aka Luca.

"Hey, at least it's a vegetable. Sort of." Xan sat down next to his uncle, who didn't appear to be wearing a costume of any kind. "It's Halloween, Uncle Demetrio. Why didn't you dress up?"

"I did," Demetrio insisted. He turned in his seat and pointed at his bright red T-shirt, which said...

"Slut." All Xan could do was laugh. "All right, then."

"Shameful," Dominic muttered, regarding his twin distastefully.

"You mean shameless," Jacob countered.

"I could go both ways," Demetrio said with a wicked grin. "Actually, I *do* go both ways."

Becky raised her wine glass high in the air. "I'll drink to that."

"Was there ever a time when Demetrio's sex life wasn't a topic of dinner conversation?" Luca inquired as he got the ball rolling by piling Italian sausages on his plate.

Jacob stood up and made his way around the table, topping off everyone's wine and pouring blood for the vampires in attendance. "I don't think so. At least it can never be said that our conversations are boring."

"Inappropriate, but never boring," Dominic conceded.

Demetrio beamed at his brother. "Thanks, Domenico. Maybe you're not as much of a prude as I thought."

"Whereas you are every bit the whore I've always suspected."

While Dominic and Demetrio continued trading insults—another Friday family tradition—Xan dug into a dish of baked ziti and glanced across the table at his boyfriend. Boyfriend... the word still felt new to him, almost alien. As did the relationship itself, which was something that Xan would have never believed possible a month ago. But for someone who had never imagined being tied down to one person until recently, Xan was still as happy as he was the night he and Michael made their arrangement official. And to think that all it had taken for him to open his mind and heart to the possibility was being abducted and nearly murdered by Dominic's maker.

After the blood and food were consumed (Xan and Luca hadn't put much of a dent in Dominic's spread, but they gave it their best shot), the group retired to the living room to relax and converse before dispersing for the night. They talked about the fickle Harborview weather and speculated whether or not they would see the season's first snow by the end of the following week as predicted by the so-called experts. When Dominic made mention of Michael's lack of footwear, his green eyes narrowed in parental disapproval, Xan gave them all a rundown of the *Death Note* series (or "the one with the Shinigami with an apple fetish" as Jacob remembered it). Luca announced that the Old Man was flying into Harborview for the weekend and promised to bring him to the Rising Sun if he was feeling up to the challenge of a crowd.

"But you know he's a moody old shit so don't hold your breath," he concluded.

"What about you, Demetrio?" Becky asked between sips of wine. "What are you getting into tonight?"

"A nice, tight hole, if all goes well."

"Good grief," Jacob mumbled.

They spoke of other things, like the imminent arrival of Demetrio's favorite immortal castrato, Niccolo Alessandrini, and the apparent and wholly unexpected relationship between Elliot and Brian—another vampire/human union that might have never happened at all if not for Vincenzo's deadly meddling. Although Xan was nothing but supportive of the new couple, he had to admit that he was curious about what went on between them behind closed doors, aside from what he and his parents had walked in on not too long ago at the club. Brian was now privy to things that Xan had always wondered himself about the solemn vampire, lucky bastard.

Sometime later, Dominic checked his watch and motioned to Jacob. "We need to leave."

"Thank you again for taking Ginger's kids trick-or-treating," Becky said. "We haven't had much of a chance to spend some quality time alone."

"Aw, someone's horny," Xan said with mock sympathy.

This time, the broom didn't miss its target.

"You can thank Jacob," Dominic told her. "This was his brilliant idea."

"Don't say that like you're not looking forward to it," Jacob replied as he slid his left hand into the cuff of his fake hook.

"What are you going to do with all the candy the kids get?" Michael asked. "It's not like they can eat it."

"I'll eat it," Xan offered.

"We're giving it to the children at the shelter," Jacob said.

"Damn."

Everyone else got up and said their goodbyes. For Xan and Becky, this meant an exchange of playful smacks and pinches that only ceased when Jacob threatened to ground them both.

"Dad, we don't live here," Xan pointed out.

"Like that would stop him." Luca pulled the young man into his usual lung-crushing embrace. "See you later."

Xan hugged the big man back, taking care not to lose an eye to the bolt that was glued to his neck. "Tell the Old Man hello for me."

Jacob, who was across the room and doing his damnedest to keep two vampire twins from killing each other, raised an eyebrow at his son. "What was that?"

"Mr. O'Malley," Xan corrected with an eye roll.

Having decided not to murder his brother for now, Dominic approached Xan and Michael. "You don't have to be at the club for a few more hours. Are you going back to your house?"

Xan shook his head. "I'm going to stay and have some tiramisu since you went through the trouble of making it, and I've digested enough to force some down—"

"Don't eat it all!" Luca piped in while putting on his coat.

"—and then I'm going to pack up the rest of my Transformers now that I've got the space for all of them. Is that okay?"

"Of course. Just lock the door when you leave."

"Will do. Thanks for dinner, Domi."

"You're welcome, Alexander. Drive carefully."

"I always do."

"No, you don't. Speaking of driving carefully..." Dominic studied Michael, who had recently decided that the time had come for him to learn how to drive himself. "How have your lessons been going?"

"If we were living in a Grand Theft Auto game, I'd fit right in," Michael responded with a self-deprecating grin.

Dominic frowned briefly. "I don't understand the reference, but I presume it isn't good."

"He's not that bad," Xan spoke up. "He just needs more practice."

"Well, good luck with it." The vampire flashed a rare, heartfelt smile. "Goodnight, boys."

Xan and Michael waited until everyone was gone before heading into the kitchen. The tiramisu was retrieved from the fridge, and Xan helped himself to an enormous serving. They sat down at the table and Xan proceeded to devour the decadent Italian dessert, much to the delight *and* protest of his already full stomach.

"So..." Michael began, a smile slowly forming. "Domi?"

Xan cringed. "I'm surprised that didn't slip out sooner in front of you."

"That's what you called him when you were a kid?"

"Yep. Daddy and Domi. I outgrew the one, but apparently I'm still working on the other." Xan took another bite of tiramisu and moaned in ecstasy. "My God, this is one of the best things in life."

"It looks good," Michael observed wistfully.

"It's better than good." Xan saw the look of longing on his lover's face and felt a pang of guilt for the way he was practically orgasming over the dessert. Unlike the others, who had gone ages without solid food, Michael had only been a vampire for a couple of months and knew exactly what he was missing. "I wish you could have some."

"Me too."

"Do you miss it?"

"Food? Hell yeah, I miss it. But it's not a bad trade-off, the way things ended up."

Michael wiped a splotch of cream from the corner of Xan's mouth with his index finger. Xan parted his lips and took the slender digit into his mouth, sucking on it gently but eagerly. Their eyes met, and Xan soon forgot about the tiramisu and the Transformers and the fact that they were sitting in his parents' kitchen. He rolled his pierced tongue around Michael's finger, causing the vampire to gasp loudly in response.

"Jesus, Xan." Michael pulled away with a shudder. "Finish eating."

There was something else that Xan would have much rather had in his mouth besides tiramisu. Although he could think of no logical reason why he shouldn't just yank Michael up on the table and take advantage of him, he decided to be a good boy and finish his dessert.

When he was done, he cleared the table and washed his plate and fork, then double-checked to make sure that the kitchen was as spotless as he found it. Dominic had always been somewhat laid back (compared to Jacob) about Xan's former and ever so numerous sexual adventures, but *God forbid* the young man left the kitchen in disarray. They exited the kitchen and went down to the non-bedroom portion of the house's massive basement so that Xan could grab a plastic container and bubble wrap for the precious cargo he would be transporting.

"I still can't believe that Dominic makes his own sauce," Michael said as he stared in disbelief at the rows upon rows of canning jars that lined one of the walls.

"And pasta, if he has the time."

"Can you even taste the difference?"

"Homemade pasta is definitely better. But I try to downplay it because he already puts so much effort into cooking for me. Honestly, I'd be fine with just ordering a pizza as long as the family is together, but it's important to him to make everything himself."

"I wish..." Michael hesitated and then reconsidered. "Never mind. If my dad had ever cooked dinner for me, I probably would have accused him of trying to poison me."

Xan thought about pressing forward with the subject of Michael's father. Although the vampire had yet to visit or speak to him, he had taken a vital first step at reestablishing communication via text message to let the man know that he was all right. (Actually, Michael had almost texted that he was still alive, but Xan reminded him that wasn't exactly true.) Xan had no idea if Hideaki Fukuhara received or replied to his son's text as Michael turned off the phone right after pressing "Send" and hadn't bothered checking it since, most likely to spare himself any potential grief in the event that he didn't receive a response. For those reasons, Xan decided to let the topic rest. When Michael was ready to deal with his father, he would be there for him. No matter what.

So instead, he handed Michael a roll of bubble wrap and picked up a large clear plastic container. They left the basement and made their way up the stairs. When they got to Xan's old bedroom, they went to work wrapping and packing his rare first generation Transformers while discussing the pros and cons of the most recent live action movie that had come out shortly after Xan's birthday earlier that year, *Transformers: Age of Extinction*. Michael liked it. Xan thought it was so-so.

After every last Autobot and Decepticon was wrapped and packed away, Xan placed the lid on the container and snapped it shut. With a heavy sigh, he looked around the bedroom, his blue eyes taking in the vast empty space that had been his own special corner of the world for eight years.

"I know this is going to sound stupid, but now that I'm taking the last of my toys, this doesn't feel like my room anymore. It's just... a room."

Michael came up beside him and snaked an arm under his jacket and around his waist. "It'll always be your room," he reassured him. "And I bet Dominic and Jacob feel the same way."

"Thanks." Xan suddenly snapped his fingers. "Oh, I almost forgot!"

He went over to the bed and dropped to his knees, then lifted the comforter and shoved his hand beneath the top mattress.

"What are you doing?" Michael asked.

"Just looking for... found it!" Xan pulled out a tube of lubricant and held it up so that Michael could see. "Emergency lube."

Michael gawked at the young man. Then he laughed. "I guess I shouldn't be surprised."

"No, you shouldn't." Smirking, Xan straightened out the comforter and sat down on the edge of the bed. Recalling their kitchen encounter, an idea began to form. "Come over here."

Understanding what Xan had in mind, Michael shook his head. "Are you crazy? This is your parents' house."

"And they're not home."

"We can't."

Xan inclined his head. "You don't want to?"

"Yeah, I want to," Michael admitted, running a hand over his tousled black hair. "I always want to. But still—"

"Michael, listen." Xan tossed the lube aside and leaned back on the bed. "I've had plenty of company in this room over the years, so this would hardly be the first time. But it would actually mean a lot to me if my last time was with you."

"... Damn, you're good."

"I know," Xan agreed smugly. "I really do mean it, though."

After one last moment of internal debate, Michael gave up. He walked over to Xan and stood between his long, outstretched legs, staring down at him tenderly. A finger lightly traced over Xan's right ear, which was lined with several tiny holes from the hoops he had removed in order to maintain accuracy with his chosen costume. Xan pressed his face against Michael's shirt and breathed in soap and cotton and the woodsy fragrance of his cologne.

"I like your hair like this," Michael observed while toying with a section of Xan's hair.

"You do?"

"Yeah. I mean, I like it the other way, too, but this looks good on you."

Xan raised his head and smiled warmly at Michael. He wasn't sure yet if he loved him; having never known the feeling before in the romantic sense, he didn't know what it was supposed to feel like. But whatever this was, it was enough for him to be put off by the mere thought of being with anyone else. Oh, he still looked at other guys because he wasn't blind. However, he now understood and accepted that there were limitations to his attractions to other men. He could talk to them and flirt with them—Xan wasn't sure that he could ever stop flirting altogether if he tried. But as for having sex with someone besides Michael? No way. Being interested in other men was one thing (and when it came to a certain vampire with supermodel good looks who had gone down on him in the bathroom at the Rising Sun, he was still very interested), but Xan knew in his heart that he was, at least for now, stuck where he was. And he was glad for that.

He grabbed Michael by the shirt and pulled him down into a slow, lingering kiss that was just the right combination of tongues and teeth, but no fangs—Michael probably wasn't ready for that level of freakiness yet. The lovers fell back on the bed, kissing and grabbing and groping each other. They made short, clumsy work of getting naked, leaving a pile of clothes scattered on the floor along the side of the bed. Michael pinned Xan's wrists above his head and kissed him again, deeper this time. Xan curled his legs around the vampire's waist, thrusting his hips and grinding their stiff cocks together.

"Keep that up and we're not going to need lube," Michael murmured into Xan's neck.

He let go of Xan's wrists and worked his way down the human's perfect tattooed torso, his tongue running along a complicated maze of tribal ink. Xan weaved his fingers through Michael's hair, encouraging him, guiding him lower. His mouth was warm (well, warm for a vampire), wet, and extremely eager, and when he finally reached his destination it took all of Xan's willpower not to buck up into his mouth and gag him. Instead, he spread his legs wider and let out a desperate moan when Michael took the hint and sucked him off even harder.

"Fuck yeah," he whispered, rubbing every inch of himself along Michael's tongue. "Just like that."

It wasn't long before familiar heat surged throughout his body, and his balls tightened in warning. With a sharp hiss, he pulled the vampire up by the hair before ruining the moment and Michael's face.

"Give me the lube," Michael demanded.

Xan handed the bottle of lube over and closed his eyes, waiting. He heard the snap of a cap and, shortly afterwards, felt a slick finger pressing gingerly against him. The lube was cold, and his body's first instinct was to tighten up, but he gradually relaxed, allowing Michael to slip one finger in... then two... then, with a little more effort, three.

He reached between his legs and lazily stroked his cock as Michael stretched him open. Xan opened his eyes and glanced downward. Then, in a moment of random silliness, he chuckled at the look on his partner's face. Michael's grave expression reminded him of countless movie scenes in which someone, usually a police officer of some sort, was attempting to defuse a bomb with only seconds to spare.

Michael peeked up at him. "Are you laughing at me?"

"A little bit."

"Why?"

"Because you look like the fate of the world rests on your fingers being in my ass."

Michael snorted in amusement. "Shut up. I'm trying to make you feel good."

"You are. Trust me."

Xan squeezed his cock, resulting in a burst of pre-cum that dribbled down his hand. He let go of his shaft and offered his hand to Michael, who leaned forward and licked his fingers clean. The erotic gesture was almost Xan's undoing. Nothing was funny after that.

"Get up here," he said, his voice low and full of need.

Michael removed his fingers and, after lubing up his cock, positioned himself between Xan's legs. He hooked his arms under Xan's thighs and pressed forward, penetrating him slowly. Steadily. Completely.

Clenching his teeth, Xan rode out the initial discomfort. For all the sex he'd had since losing his virginity to Ryan Douglas five years ago, there was still that touch of pain upon entry. Fortunately, it never lasted too long, and after about a minute, he was ready. Michael began fucking him hard and fast, just the way he liked it. The bed creaked and groaned beneath them, and Xan vaguely wondered how the poor thing had held up over the years given the limits to which he had pushed it.

He winced as Michael's nails sank into the soft skin of his thighs. The vampire's face was contorted in pleasure, and Xan knew that he wasn't going to last much longer. He took his cock in hand and started stroking again, this time with purpose, his eyes locked on Michael, watching him, feeling him. For someone who had only ever topped once before, as Michael had revealed to him after their first time together, he knew exactly what he was doing, and damn, he was doing it well.

"Xan..." Michael's entire body was shaking.

"Do it," Xan commanded breathlessly. "Come."

After one last thrust into the tightness of Xan's body, Michael pulled out and jerked himself to completion, his cock throbbing and spurting, coating the young man's stomach. Xan followed soon after, his hand pumping furiously as he shot his load across his chest. His eyes rolled back and his body trembled. Throughout all of it he was still, barely, coherent enough to wonder if the neighbors had heard him.

Michael fell down on the bed with a grunt. There wasn't a dry spot to be found on Xan's chest for resting his arm so he settled for curling up beside him, seeking out the warmth of his body. "How was that for a last time?"

"Best last time ever." Xan stared at the ceiling, thinking. "You know, there's no reason that we can't do this every Friday after dinner."

"Your parents don't go trick-or-treating every Friday, Xan. We should stop while we're ahead."

Xan pouted. "I guess."

He looked at Michael, who was watching him with open adoration. Although he was still trying to determine the depth of his own feelings, the vampire's feelings for him were quite obvious.

Xan gave him a quick peck on the lips and rolled onto his side, his hand sliding beneath the mattress one more time.

"What are you doing now?"

Michael got his answer when Xan retrieved a towel.

"I'm all about being prepared," Xan said, tossing it to him.

"I can see that. What else do you have under there?"

Xan felt around some more. "Some condoms. And—what the hell?—oh, a cock ring."

"An emergency cock ring... Okay."

"You never know when you'll need one."

They took turns cleaning themselves off with the towel. When they were finished, Xan bundled it up and placed it on the floor, making a mental note to take it home to wash. He turned over and reached for Michael, but the vampire suddenly bolted up and out of the bed with uncanny speed.

"What's the hurry? We still have plenty of time."

"I just heard the front door," Michael whispered, frantically sorting out his clothes from the heap on the floor. "Someone's here."

"What?"

Sure enough, the sound of Jacob's voice floated up from the bottom of the stairs. "Xan?"

"Damn it!" Xan tumbled out of the bed, almost knocking Michael over. "I'll be right there!" he bellowed at the bedroom door that had foolishly been left open, praying that Jacob wouldn't come upstairs.

They got dressed as fast as they could. Xan came close to strangling himself in his mad rush to tighten his tie. Grabbing his jacket, he ran out of the room and down the stairs, where his father was waiting with a knowing smile.

"Hey." He put on his jacket and smoothed back his disheveled hair. "Why are you back so soon?"

"I forgot my eye patch," the vampire explained. "What kind of pirate would I be without it?"

"A pretty crappy one, I guess," Xan responded, laughing nervously.

Brown eyes glanced over Xan's head toward the top of the stairs. "Looks like I'm interrupting."

"That's okay. We just finished."

Jacob's knowing smile widened.

"Um..." Xan felt his cheeks heat up. "I mean... because we were just... uh... packing my Transformers."

"Yeah, I heard. You must have been packing pretty hard to make that much noise."

Putting on his best innocent face, Xan looked his father in the eyes. "I don't know what you're talking about, Dad."

"Your zipper's down."

"Shit."

Xan spun around and zipped up while Jacob went to get his eye patch, laughing the whole way. He was still laughing by the time he returned with his left eye properly covered.

"Carry on," he said, waving with his hook as he left the house.

Xan sat down on the bottom step and slumped against the railing. He supposed that he would always feel a little guilty—and plenty embarrassed—whenever one or both of his parents caught him in the act. Or shortly after it. "You can come out now," he yelled to the vampire who was still hiding in his bedroom.

"Oh, man." Michael descended the stairs and sat down beside Xan. "Your dad is going to murder me in so many ways."

"Nah... Well, at least I don't think he will."

"That's not very comforting."

"What were you going to do if he hadn't left?" Xan wanted to know. "Hide out up there for the rest of the night?"

"Either that or jump out of the window."

Xan snickered at the thought of Michael scrambling through a second story window to escape Jacob's wrath. He wouldn't have been the first vampire to exit his bedroom that way. "If my dads were going to kill you for sleeping with me, they would have done it already, so relax. They like you, Michael. They think you're a keeper."

"They do?"

"Yeah."

"... Do you?"

Xan lowered his head. He noticed that at some point during the conversation, their fingers had intertwined.

"I do," he replied quietly, pulling Michael's hand to his mouth for a kiss.

Was this love? Xan didn't have a clue. But considering the way his heart soared at the sight of Michael's affectionate smile, he thought that maybe, just maybe, he was close to figuring it out.

Eventually, they headed back up the stairs. Side by side. Hand in hand.

Thank you so much for reading this book. For more information about the *Harborview Immortals* series plus other writing projects and random geekery, please visit https://cl-ingro.com. You may also reach me directly at CLIngro.Author@gmail.com.